THE BEAST

BY J. R. WARD

THE BLACK DAGGER BROTHERHOOD SERIES

Dark Lover
Lover Eternal
Lover Awakened
Lover Revealed
Lover Unbound
Lover Enshrined
The Black Dagger Brotherhood: An Insider's Guide
Lover Avenged
Lover Mine
Lover Unleashed
Lover Reborn
Lover at Last
The King
The Shadows

BLACK DAGGER LEGACY

Blood Kiss

NOVELS OF THE FALLEN ANGELS

Covet
Crave
Envy
Rapture
Possession
Immortal

THE BOURBON KINGS

The Bourbon Kings

J.R.WARD

THE
BEAST

A NOVEL OF THE BLACK DAGGER BROTHERHOOD

 New American Library

NEW AMERICAN LIBRARY
Published by New American Library,
an imprint of Penguin Random House LLC
375 Hudson Street, New York, New York 10014

This book is an original publication of New American Library.

First Printing, April 2016

For more information about Penguin Random House, visit penguin.com.

LIBRARY OF CONGRESS CATALOGING-IN-PUBLICATION DATA:
Names: Ward, J. R., 1969– author.
Title: The beast: a novel of the Black Dagger Brotherhood/J. R. Ward.
Description: New York: New American Library, [2016] I Series: Black Dagger Brotherhood; 14 I Identifiers: LCCN 2015050391 (print) I LCCN 2015045714 (ebook) I ISBN 9780698192973 (ebook) I ISBN 9780451475169 (hardcover)
Subjects: LCSH: Vampires—Fiction. I Paranormal romance stories. I BISAC: FICTION/Romance/Paranormal. I FICTION/Romance/General. I GSAFD: Romantic suspense fiction. I Fantasy fiction. I Occult fiction. I Horror fiction.
Classification: LCC PS3623.A73227 (print) I LCC PS3623.A73227 B43 2016 (ebook) I DDC 813/.6—dc23
LC record available at http://lccn.loc.gov/2015050391

INTERNATIONAL EDITION ISBN 978-0-399-58304-9

Printed in the United States of America
10 9 8 7 6 5 4 3 2 1

Penguin
Random
House

DEDICATED TO:
ALL THREE OF YOU.
THAT SAYS IT ALL xxx

ACKNOWLEDGMENTS

With immense gratitude to the readers of the Black Dagger Brotherhood!

Thank you so very much for all the support and guidance: Steven Axelrod, Kara Welsh, and Leslie Gelbman. Thank you also to everyone at New American Library—these books are truly a team effort.

With love to Team Waud—you know who you are. This simply could not happen without you.

None of this would be possible without: my loving husband, who is my adviser and caretaker and visionary; my wonderful mother, who has given me so much love I couldn't possibly ever repay her; my family (both those of blood and those by adoption); and my dearest friends.

Oh, and my WriterDog, Naamah. Congratulations on your promotion!

GLOSSARY OF TERMS AND PROPER NOUNS

ahstrux nohtrum (n.) Private guard with license to kill who is granted his or her position by the King.

ahvenge (v.) Act of mortal retribution, carried out typically by a male loved one.

Black Dagger Brotherhood (pr. n.) Highly trained vampire warriors who protect their species against the Lessening Society. As a result of selective breeding within the race, Brothers possess immense physical and mental strength, as well as rapid healing capabilities. They are not siblings for the most part, and are inducted into the Brotherhood upon nomination by the Brothers. Aggressive, self-reliant, and secretive by nature, they exist apart from civilians, having little contact with members of the other classes except when they need to feed. They are the subjects of legend and objects of reverence within the vampire world. They may be killed only by the most serious of wounds, e.g., a gunshot or stab to the heart, etc.

blood slave (n.) Male or female vampire who has been subjugated to serve the blood needs of another. The practice of keeping blood slaves has recently been outlawed.

the Chosen (n.) Female vampires who have been bred to serve the Scribe Virgin. They are considered members of the aristocracy, though they are spiritually rather than temporally focused. They have little or no interaction with males other than the Primale, but can be mated to Brothers at the Scribe Virgin's direction to propagate their class. Some have the ability to prognosticate. In the past, they were used to meet the blood needs of unmated members of the Brotherhood, and that practice has been reinstated by the Brothers.

chrih (n.) Symbol of honorable death in the Old Language.

cohntehst (n.) Conflict between two males competing for the right to be a female's mate.

Dhunhd (pr. n.) Hell.

doggen (n.) Member of the servant class within the vampire world. *Doggen* have old, conservative traditions about service to their superiors, following a formal code of dress and behavior. They are able to go out during the day, but they age relatively quickly. Life expectancy is approximately five hundred years.

ehros (n.) A Chosen trained in the matter of sexual arts.

exhile dhoble (n.) The evil or cursed twin, the one born second.

the Fade (pr. n.) Nontemporal realm where the dead reunite with their loved ones and pass eternity.

First Family (pr. n.) The King and Queen of the vampires, and any children they may have.

ghardian (n.) Custodian of an individual. There are varying degrees of *ghardians*, with the most powerful being that of a *sehcluded* female.

glymera (n.) The social core of the aristocracy, roughly equivalent to Regency England's *ton*.

hellren (n.) Male vampire who has been mated to a female. Males may take more than one female as mate.

hyslop (n. or v.): Term referring to a lapse in judgment, typically resulting in the compromise of the mechanical operations of a vehicle or otherwise motorized conveyance of some kind. For example, leaving one's keys in one's car as it is parked outside the family home overnight—whereupon said car is stolen.

leahdyre (n.) A person of power and influence.

leelan (adj.) A term of endearment loosely translated as "dearest one."

Lessening Society (pr. n.) Order of slayers convened by the Omega for the purpose of eradicating the vampire species.

lesser (n.) De-souled human who targets vampires for extermination as a member of the Lessening Society. *Lessers* must be stabbed through the chest in order to be killed; otherwise they are ageless. They do not eat or drink and are impotent. Over time, their hair, skin, and irises lose pigmentation until they are blond, blushless, and pale eyed. They smell like baby powder. Inducted into the society by the Omega, they retain a ceramic jar thereafter into which their heart was placed after it was removed.

lewlhen (n.) Gift.

lheage (n.) A term of respect used by a sexual submissive to refer to his or her dominant.

Lhenihan (pr. n.) A mythic beast renowned for its sexual prowess. In modern slang, refers to a male of preternatural size and sexual stamina.

lys (n.) Torture tool used to remove the eyes.

mahmen (n.) Mother. Used both as an identifier and a term of affection.

mhis (n.) The masking of a given physical environment; the creation of a field of illusion.

nalla (n., f.) or *nallum* (n., m.) Beloved.

needing period (n.) Female vampire's time of fertility, generally lasting for two days and accompanied by intense sexual cravings. Occurs approximately five years after a female's transition and then once a decade thereafter. All males respond to some degree if they are around a female in her need. It can be a dangerous time, with conflicts and fights breaking out between competing males, particularly if the female is not mated.

newling (n.) A virgin.

the Omega (pr. n.) Malevolent, mystical figure who has targeted vampires for extinction out of resentment directed toward its sister, the Scribe Virgin. Exists in a nontemporal realm and has extensive powers, though not the power of creation.

phearsom (adj.) Term referring to the potency of a male's sexual organs. Literal translation something close to "worthy of entering a female."

princeps (n.) Highest level of the vampire aristocracy, second only to members of the First Family or the Scribe Virgin's Chosen. Must be born to the title; it may not be conferred.

pyrocant (n.) Refers to a critical weakness in an individual. The weakness can be internal, such as an addiction, or external, such as a lover.

rahlman (n.) Savior.

rythe (n.) Ritual manner of assuaging honor granted by one who has offended another. If accepted, the offended chooses a weapon and strikes the offender, who presents him- or herself without defenses.

the Scribe Virgin (pr. n.) Mystical force who is counselor to the King

as well as the keeper of vampire archives and the dispenser of privileges. Exists in a nontemporal realm and has extensive powers. Capable of a single act of creation, which she expended to bring the vampires into existence.

sehclusion (n.) Status conferred by the King upon a female of the aristocracy as a result of a petition by the female's family. Places the female under the sole direction of her *ghardian*, typically the eldest male in her household. Her *ghardian* then has the legal right to determine all manner of her life, restricting at will any and all interactions she has with the world.

shellan (n.) Female vampire who has been mated to a male. Females generally do not take more than one mate due to the highly territorial nature of bonded males.

symphath (n.) Subspecies within the vampire race characterized by the ability and desire to manipulate emotions in others (for the purposes of an energy exchange), among other traits. Historically, they have been discriminated against and, during certain eras, hunted by vampires. They are near extinction.

the Tomb (pr. n.) Sacred vault of the Black Dagger Brotherhood. Used as a ceremonial site as well as a storage facility for the jars of *lessers*. Ceremonies performed there include inductions, funerals, and disciplinary actions against Brothers. No one may enter except for members of the Brotherhood, the Scribe Virgin, or candidates for induction.

trahyner (n.) Word used between males of mutual respect and affection. Translated loosely as "beloved friend."

transition (n.) Critical moment in a vampire's life when he or she transforms into an adult. Thereafter, he or she must drink the blood of the opposite sex to survive and is unable to withstand sunlight. Occurs generally in the mid-twenties. Some vampires do not survive their transitions, males in particular. Prior to their transitions, vampires are physically weak, sexually unaware and unresponsive, and unable to dematerialize.

vampire (n.) Member of a species separate from that of Homo sapiens. Vampires must drink the blood of the opposite sex to survive. Human blood will keep them alive, though the strength does not last long. Following their transitions, which occur in their mid-twenties, they are unable to go out into sunlight and must feed from the vein regularly. Vampires cannot "convert" humans through a bite or transfer of blood, though they are in rare cases able to breed with the other species. Vampires can dematerialize at will, though they must be able to calm themselves and concentrate to do so and may not carry anything heavy with them. They are able to strip the memories of humans, provided such memories are short-term. Some vampires are able to read minds. Life expectancy is upward of a thousand years, or in some cases, even longer.

wahlker (n.) An individual who has died and returned to the living from the Fade. They are accorded great respect and are revered for their travails.

whard (n.) Equivalent of a godfather or godmother to an individual.

THE BEAST

ONE

BROWNSWICK SCHOOL FOR GIRLS,
CALDWELL, NEW YORK

Ants under the skin.

As Rhage transferred his weight from one shitkicker to the other, he felt like his bloodstream had come to a soft boil and the bubbles were tickling the underside of every fucking square inch of his flesh. And that wasn't the half of it. Random muscle fibers misfired all over his body, the spasms causing fingers to twitch, knees to jerk, shoulders to tighten like he was about to go tennis racket on something.

For the one millionth time since he'd materialized into his position, he peeper-swept the ragged, overgrown meadow up ahead. Back when the Brownswick School for Girls had been a functioning entity, the field in front of him had no doubt been a rolling lawn that had been well mowed in the spring and summer, de-leafed in the autumn, and snow-covered pretty as a children's book in the winter. Now, it was a touch-football field from hell, studded and tangled with gnarled bushes that could do more than just aesthetic damage to a guy's crotchticular region, saplings that were the ugly, misshapen stepchildren of the more mature maples and oaks, and late-October brown long grass that could trip you like a little bitch if you were trying to sprint.

Likewise, the brick buildings, which had sheltered and provided living and instructional spaces to the privileged elite's offspring, were aging badly without regular maintenance: windows broken, doors rotting, off-kilter shutters opening and shutting in the cold wind as if the ghosts couldn't decide whether they wanted to be seen or just heard.

It was the campus from *Dead Poets Society*. Assuming everyone had packed up after the movie had been shot in 1988 and nobody had touched a fucking thing since.

But the facilities were not empty.

As Rhage took a deep inhale, his gag reflex did a couple of push-ups in the back of his throat. So many *lessers* were hiding in the abandoned dormitories and classrooms that it was impossible to isolate individual scents from the sinus-numbing stench of the whole. Christ, it was like putting your face in a chum bucket and inhaling like the world were about to run out of oxygen.

Assuming someone had added baby powder to all the day-old fish heads and goo.

For that sweet finish, don'tcha know.

As his skin went on another shimmy-shimmy, he told his curse to hold its hey-nannies, that hell yeah, it was going to get let off the chain ASAP. He wasn't even going to attempt to hold the damn thing in— not that trying to throw the brakes on it was ever successful, anyway— and whereas giving the beast free rein was not always a good thing, tonight it was going to be an offensive bene. The Black Dagger Brotherhood was facing how many *lessers*? Fifty? A hundred and fifty?

That was a lot to handle, even for them—so yeah, his little . . . present . . . from the Scribe Virgin was going to come in handy.

Talk about your ringer from out of town. Over a century ago, the mother of the race had given him his own personal T.O. system, a behavior modification program that was so onerous, so unpleasant, so overwhelming that it did, in fact, manage to bring him back from the brink of total douche-baggery. Courtesy of the dragon, unless he managed his energy levels properly and moderated his emotions, all hell broke loose.

Literally.

Yup, in the course of the last century, he had become largely successful at making sure the thing didn't eat his nearest and dearest, or get them on the nightly news with a "*Jurassic Park* Is Alive" headline.

But with what he and his brothers were facing right now—and how isolated this campus was? If they were lucky, the great purple-scaled bastard with the chain-saw teeth and the hollow-legged hangry was going to get his Nobu on. Although, again, a *lesser*-only diet was what they were looking for.

No brothers as Hot Pockets, please. And no humans as tapas or dessert, thank you very much.

The latter was more out of discretion than affection. Shit knew those rats without tails never went anywhere without two things: a half dozen of their evolutionarily inferior, nocturnally codependent, fuck-twit buddies, and their goddamn cell phones. Man, YouTube was a total pain in the ass when you wanted to keep your war with the un-dead under wraps. For nearly two thousand years, vampires fighting the Omega's Lessening Society had been no one else's business except for the combatants involved, and the fact that humans couldn't stick to their core competencies of ruining the environment and telling each other what to think and say was only one of the reasons he hated them.

Fucking Internet.

Changing gears so he didn't get loose too soon, Rhage GoPro'd his vision to a male taking cover about twenty feet away from him. Assail, son of Whoever-the-Fuck, was dressed in funeral-cortege black, his Dracula-dark hair requiring no camouflage, his handsome-as-sin face furrowed so tight with murder that you had to respect the guy. Talk about doing a solid—and a one-eighty. The drug dealer had come through for the Brotherhood, making good on his promise to cut busi-ness ties with the Lessening Society by delivering the *Fore-lesser's* head in a box to Wrath's feet.

And also divulging the location of this bolt-hole the slayers had been using as HQ.

Which was how everyone had ended up here, up to their nuts in the overgrowth, waiting for the countdown on their V-synchronized watches to hit 0:00.

This attack wasn't some bullshit, buckshot approach to the enemy. After a number of nights—and days, thanks to Lassiter, a.k.a. 00-a-hole, having done recon during sunshine hours—the attack was prop-erly coordinated, staged, and ready for execution. All of the fighters were here: Z and Phury, Butch and V, Tohr and John Matthew, Qhuinn and Blay, as well as Assail and his two cousins, Fang I and II.

'Cuz who cared what their names were as long as they showed up weaponized with plenty of ammo.

The Brotherhood medical personnel were also on standby in the area, with Manny in his mobile surgical unit about a mile away and Jane and Ehlena in one of the vans at a two-mile radius.

Rhage checked his watch. Six minutes and change.

As his left eye started to do the stanky leg, he cursed. How the fuck was he going to hold his position for that long?

Baring his fangs, he exhaled through his nose, blowing out twin streams of condensed breath that were nothing short of a bull's charging notice.

Christ, he couldn't remember the last time he was this juiced. And he didn't want to think about the why of it. In fact, he'd been avoiding the whole *why* thing for how long?

Well, since he and Mary had hit this strange rough spot and he'd started to feel—

"Rhage."

His name was whispered so softly he wrenched around, because he wasn't sure whether or not his subconscious had decided to start talking to him. Nope. It was Vishous—and given his brother's expression, Rhage would have preferred to be pulling a split-personality on himself. Those diamond eyes were flashing with a bad light. And those tattoos around that temple were so not helping.

The goatee was a neutral—unless you assessed it on style. In which case the fucker was a travesty of Rogaine proportions.

Rhage shook his head. "Shouldn't you get into position—"

"I've seen this night."

Oh, hell, no, Rhage thought. Nope, you are not doing this to me right now, my brother.

Turning away, he muttered, "Spare me the Vincent Price, 'kay? Or are you trying for the guy who does the movie trailer voice-overs—"

"Rhage."

"—'cuz you got a future in that. 'In a world . . . where people need . . . to shut up and do their jobs—'"

"Rhage."

When he didn't look back, V came around and glared up at him, those fucking pale eyes a twin set of nuclear blasts that spelled mushroom cloud forward and backward. "I want you to go home. *Now.*"

Rhage opened his mouth. Clapped it shut. Opened it again—and

had to remind himself to keep his voice down. "Look, it's not a good time for your one-eight-hundred psychic headquarters shit—"

The Brother snapped a hold on his arm and squeezed. *"Go home. I'm not fucking you."*

Cold terror washed through Rhage's veins, bottoming out his body temperature—and yet he shook his head again. "Fuck off, Vishous. *Seriously.*"

He was so not interested in testing out any more of the Scribe Virgin's magic. He wasn't—

"You're going to fucking die tonight."

As Rhage's heart stopped, he stared down into that face that he'd known for so many years, tracing those tattoos, and the tight lips, and the slashing black brows . . . and the radiant intelligence that was usually expressed through a filter of samurai-sword sarcasm.

"Your mother gave me her word," Rhage said. Wait, was he actually talking about him kicking it? "She promised that when I die, Mary can come with me unto the Fade. Your mother said—"

"Fuck my mother. *Go home.*"

Rhage looked away because he had to. It was either that or have his head explode. "I'm not leaving the brothers. Ain't going to happen. You could be wrong, for one thing."

Yeah, and when was the last time that had happened? Eighteen hundreds? Seventeen hundreds?

Never?

He spoke over V. "I'm also not going to run scared from the Fade. I start thinking like that, and I'm finished with a weapon in my hand." He put his palm all up in that goatee so the brother cut the interrupting. "And the third fuck off? If I don't fight tonight, I'm not going to make it through the day locked in the mansion—not without my purple friend coming out for breakfast, lunch, and dinner, you feel me?"

Well, and there was a number four, too. And the fourth rationale . . . was bad, so very bad that he couldn't entertain it for more than the split second required for the piece of shit to come to mind.

"Rhage—"

"Nothing's going to wreck me. I got this—"

"No, you don't!" V hissed.

"Okay, fine," Rhage bit out as he tilted forward on his hips. "So what if I die? Your mother gave my Mary the ultimate grace. If I go

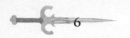

unto the Fade, Mary just meets me there. I don't have to worry about ever being separated from her. She and I will be perfectly fine. Who really fucking cares if I kick it?"

V did some lean-in of his own. "You don't think the Brothers will give a shit? Really? Thanks, asshole."

Rhage checked his watch. Two minutes to go.

Might as well be two thousand years.

"And you trust my mother," V sneered, "with something that important. I never thought you were naive."

"She managed to give me a fucking T. rex alter ego! That's some good fucking credibility."

All at once, a number of birdcalls sounded out around them in the darkness. If you hadn't known better, you'd have assumed it was just a bunch of night owls going *Pitch Perfect*.

Damn it, the pair of them were yelling over here.

"Whatever, V," he whispered. "You're so goddamn smart, worry about your own life."

His last conscious thought, before his brain went *Zero Dark Thirty* and nothing else registered outside of the aggression, was of his Mary.

He pictured the last time they'd been alone.

It was a ritual of his before he engaged with the enemy, a mental talisman that he rubbed for luck, and tonight he saw her as she had stood in front of the mirror in their bedroom, the one that was over the tall bureau where they kept their watches and their keys, her jewelry and his Tootsie Pops, their phones.

She was up on her tiptoes, angled over the top, trying to put a pearl stud into her earlobe and missing the hole. With her head tilted to the side, her deep brown hair flowed over her shoulder and made him want to put his face into the freshly shampooed waves. And that wasn't the half of what impressed him. The clean cut of her jaw caught and held the light from the crystal sconce on the wall, and her cream silk blouse draped over her breasts and was tucked into her tight waist, and her slacks fell to her flats. No makeup on her. No perfume.

But that would be like touching up the *Mona Lisa* or hitting a rosebush with a shot of Febreze.

There were a hundred thousand ways to detail his mate's physical attributes, and not one single sentence, or indeed an entire book, that could come close to describing her presence.

She was the watch on his wrist, the roast beef when he was starving, and the pitcher of lemonade when he was thirsty. She was his chapel and his choir, the mountain range to his wanderlust, the library for his curiosity, and every sunrise or sunset that ever was or would ever be. With one look or the mere syllable of a word, she had the power to transform his mood, giving him flight even as his feet stayed on the ground. With a single touch, she could chain his inner dragon, or make him come even before he got hard. She was all the power in the universe coalesced into a living, breathing thing, the miracle that he had been granted in spite of the fact that he had long been undeserving of anything but his curse.

Mary Madonna Luce was the virgin Vishous had told him was coming for him—and she was more than enough to turn him into a God-fearing vampire.

On that note . . .

Rhage took off without waiting for the Go Now from his team. Rushing headlong across the field, he had both guns up in front of him and premium, high-test gas funneling into his leg muscles. And no, he didn't have to hear the precise curses of frustration as he blew their cover and started the attack too soon.

He was used to the boys being pissed off at him.

And his demons were way harder to deal with than his brothers.

SAFE PLACE, MARY'S OFFICE

As Mary Madonna Luce hung up the phone, she kept her hand on the receiver's smooth grip. Like a lot of the equipment and furnishings at Safe Place, the set was a decade old, a used AT&T leftover from some insurance company or maybe a real estate agent's upgrade. Same with the desk. Her chair. Even the rug under her feet. At the vampire race's only domestic violence shelter and resource for females and their children, every penny that came from the King's generous coffers was spent on the people receiving support, treatment and rehabilitation.

Victims were allowed to come free of charge. And stay in the large, roomy house for however long they needed to.

Staffing, of course, was the largest expense . . . and with news like what had just come through that old phone, Mary was really fricking grateful for Marissa's priorities.

"Fuck you, death," she whispered. "Fuck you so goddamn hard."

The squeak that her chair let out as she leaned back made her wince even though she was used to the complaint.

Looking up at the ceiling, she felt an overwhelming urge to take action, but the first rule of being a therapist was that you had to control your own emotions. Half-cocked and frantic did the patient no good, and contaminating an already stressful situation with drama that was self-infused on the part of the professional was utterly unacceptable.

If there had been time, she would have gone to one of the other social workers to get debriefed, re-centered and perma-composed. Given what was happening, though, all she could spare was a minute's worth of Rhage's patented deep breathing.

No, not the sexual kind.

More his yoga variety that had him inflating his lungs in three separate draws, holding the oxygen, and then releasing it all along with the tension in the muscles.

Or trying to release the tension.

Okay, this was getting her nowhere.

Mary rose to her feet and had to settle for two almost-theres in the composure department: one, she retucked her silk blouse and ran her fingers through her hair, which she was growing out; and two, she Halloween-masked her features, freezing everything into a semblance of concerned, warm, and not freaking out over her own past trauma.

When she stepped into the second-story hall, the scent of melting chocolate and baking sugar, butter and flour announced that Toll House Cookie Night was in full swing—and for an insane moment, she felt like popping open a bunch of windows and letting the cold October air scrub the smells out of the house.

The contrast between all that homey comfort and the hammer she was about to drop seemed disrespectful at best, one more part of the tragedy at worst.

Safe Place's facilities had started out as a three-story, turn-of-the-twentieth-century roof-and-four-walls that had all the grace and distinction of a bread box. What it did have were bedrooms and bathrooms in abundance, a serviceable kitchen, and enough privacy so that the

human world was never going to get tipped off that vampires were using the thing in their midst. And then came the expansion. After Tohr's Wellsie died and he made a gift in her name to the facility, the Wellesandra Annex had been built by vampire craftsmen out back. Now, they had a community room, a second kitchen that was big enough for everyone to eat together in, and four more suites for additional females and their young.

Marissa ran the facility with a compassionate heart and a fantastic logistical head, and with seven counselors, including Mary, they were doing necessary, purposeful work.

That, yes, some times broke your heart in half.

The door to the attic made no sound as Mary opened it because she had WD-40'd the hinges herself a couple of nights before. The stairs, however, chattered the whole time as she ascended, the old wooden planks popping and squeaking even as she made sure her flats didn't land too hard.

It was impossible not to feel like some kind of Grim Reaper.

On the landing above, the yellow light from the old-fashioned brass fixtures in the ceiling brought out the red tones of both the hundred-year-old unpainted wainscoting and the braided runner that led down the narrow hall. At the far end, there was an oval oculus, and peachy illumination from the exterior security light above it bled in and got sliced into quadrants by the divides of its panes.

Of the six suites, five doors were open.

She went to the one that was shut and knocked. When a soft "Hello?" came, she cracked the panels and leaned in.

The little girl sitting on one of the two twin beds was working the tangles out of a doll's head with a brush that was missing a number of bristles. Her long brown hair was pulled back in a ponytail, and her loose dress was handmade of a blue material, well-worn, but with seams that had stayed strong. Her shoes were scuffed, yet tied carefully.

She seemed very small in what was not a very large space.

Abandoned not by choice.

"Bitty?" Mary said.

It was a moment before pale brown eyes lifted. "She's not doing well, is she."

Mary swallowed hard. "No, sweetheart. Your *mahmen* isn't."

"Is it time to go say good-bye to her?"

After a moment, Mary whispered, "Yes, I'm afraid it is."

TWO

"Are you *fucking* kidding me!"

As Hollywood's massive body and stupid frickin' pea-brained head broke rank and took off toward the dorms, Vishous was of half a mind to run after the guy just so he could beat the living shit out of his brother. But nooooooooooo.

You couldn't snatch and grab a bullet after the trigger had been pulled.

Even if you were trying to save the piece of fool lead from its grave.

V whistled into the night, but it wasn't like the rest of the fighters weren't also watching the bastard's backside go bat-out-of-hell rogue.

Members of the Brotherhood and the other males exploded free from behind their covers of trees and outbuildings, falling into wing formation behind Rhage, guns up and daggers ready. Shouts from the enemy announced that the attack was noticed almost immediately, and everyone was only halfway to goal when *lessers* began streaming out of doorways, wasps from the hives.

Cluster-fuck much? Hollow *pops!* sounded as Rhage discharged his weapon all over the place, nailing slayers in the face, his big-bore bullets blowing out the backs of those skulls and dropping the un-

dead into tangles of writhing arms and legs. Which was great—but couldn't possibly last as the slayers sought to close off behind the guy, isolate him, and create a second front line against the rest of the brothers.

Thank you, Mr. Premature Charge and your early-work-release, independent-study project that bent over the plan they'd worked on for nights.

Total chaos took over, although unlike Rhage's bolt, that was expected: Just as you could trust every hand-to-hand combat to eventually end up on the ground, you could guarantee that the best-planned attack would, after a while, spin into the land of goatfucks and goddamn-its. If you were lucky, that inevitability took some time to land on your head, and your enemy sustained crippling losses beforehand.

Not with Hollywood around

Oh, and P.S., when someone tells you you're going die tonight, how about you don't run headlong into a triple digit of your enemy? You fucking asshole.

"I was trying to save you!" V hollered into the fight. Just because he could now that their covers were blown.

Rhage was such a hothead. And knowing this, V should have confronted the idiot back at the mansion, but he'd been too distracted getting his own shit together to plug into the vision. It wasn't until he'd gotten out to the abandoned campus that he'd blinked a couple of times . . . and realized, yes, this was when it happened for Rhage. Tonight. In this field.

Keeping quiet about it would have been like putting a bullet into the guy himself.

Of course, saying something had worked out so fucking well.

"Fuck you, Hollywood!" he yelled. "I'm coming for you!"

'Cuz he was going to get that bitch off this field if it was the last thing he did.

V held his fire until he got within a ten-foot range of his first target—it was either that or run the risk of hitting one of his brothers or another of their fighters. The *lesser* that he bull's-eyed was one with dark hair, dark eyes, and the kind of aggression you'd find in a grizzly bear: lumbering with a lot of spit spools. One bullet into the right eye socket and the bastard was good as lawn on the ground.

There was no stabbing the thing back to the Omega. Vishous jumped over the still-moving, but no longer mobile, piece of meat, and

gunned for his next one. Identifying a blond slayer about fifteen feet to the left, he quick-checked the peripheral to make sure the Brotherhood wasn't getting wagon-wheeled. Then, using his glove-covered trigger finger, he picked off the guy who looked like Rod Stewart, ca. 1980.

On to numbers three to infinity. V hit whatever was safe to take out, making sure that he didn't cross-hair or impair friendly fire while still remaining effective. Some hundred and fifty yards of video game later and he'd reached both cover and danger: the first of the dorms, which they had originally planned to ambush. The damn thing was a hollowed-out shell with plenty of hidey-holes only a fool would assume were empty, and he was careful to monitor his six as he back-flatted down the side of the brick building, ducking under windows, jumping over low bushes.

The cotton-candy/rancid-meat stench of *lessers* leaking everywhere swirled around in the cold gusts, mixing into a war salad with the echoes of gunshots and the shouts of the enemy. Anger in his gut drove him forward and kept him focused at the same time as he tried to drop targets without getting shot himself.

As soon as he got to Rhage, he was going to fat-lip that goddamn beauty queen.

Assuming destiny didn't black-shroud the SOB first.

The good news? With the *Fore-lesser* gone, the Lessening Society's response was no more coordinated than the Brotherhood's attack had been, and the fact that the enemy was poorly armed and pathetically untrained was another bene. There seemed to be a five-to-one slayer-to-gun ratio, and a one-in-ten competent fighter rate—and given the numbers? That might just save their asses.

Left, *pop!* Right, *pop!* Dodge. Drop and roll. Spring up and keep running. Over two downed slayers—thank you, Assail, you crazy sonofabitch—*pop!* right in front of him.

The magic happened about five minutes and fifty thousand years into the fight. Without warning, he separated from his body, peeling free of the flesh that was working so hard and with such accuracy, his spirit floating above the adrenaline that forest-fired his arms and legs, his essence witnessing himself pumping off rounds and pressing forward from a position over his own right shoulder.

It was the zone, and usually something that took him over pretty much as soon as he started fighting. But with Rhage under his skin, up his ass, and fucking his head, the shit was late to the party.

It was because of his above-the-fray perspective that he noticed the catch-22 first.

Sometimes the counter-intuitive, the WTF, the against-the-grain, was as important as all the things you expected to see in a battle.

Like, for example, three figures running laterally across the theater of engagement for the exit. Yeah, sure, it could be *lessers* who'd pissed their pants and were deserting—except for one thing: The Omega's blood in their bodies was one fuck of a GPS locator, and having to tell that kind of boss that you'd pantywaisted out of an engagement like this would guarantee the sort of torture that made Hell look like a couch surf.

Goddamn it, he couldn't let them go. Not when they could end up calling cops and adding another layer of FUBAR to this funhouse.

Assuming they hadn't already done that.

With a curse, Vishous took after the three free-thinkers, demate-rializing out in front of where the trio seemed to be heading. As he re-formed, he knew they were fucking humans even before he saw that the one in the rear was running backward with what was no doubt a cocksucking Apple, iConformist POS front and center and on video record.

He fricking iHated anything with a goddamn Macintosh trade-mark.

V jumped out into the guy's path, which of course J. J. Abrams didn't notice, because, hello, he was too busy getting footage.

Vishous extended his shitkicker, and as the human went into grav-ity shock, the phone airborned and V caught the thing and shoved it into his leather jacket.

Next move was to stomp the guy's sternum and put a gun in his face. Staring down at the holy shit and sputter that was going on, it took all of V's self-control not to slit the guy's throat, then go Jason Voorhees all over the pair who were still on the run. He'd beyond had it with humans. He had real work to do, but noooo, he was once again wiping the asses of these rats without tails so that the rest of them didn't get upset that vampires walked among them.

"D-d-d-d-don't h-h-h-h-hurt me," came the whine. Along with a whiff of urine as the guy pissed himself.

"You are so *fucking* pathetic."

Cursing again, V pulled a mental snatch-and-grab, checking to see if the CPD had been contacted—which was a "no"—before wiping clean the kid's memories of his pot smoking rendezvous with his buddies being interrupted by all hell breaking loose.

"You had a bad trip, you dumb-ass," V muttered. "Bad trip. This is all just a bad fucking trip. Now run the fuck along back to Daddy and Mommy's."

Like the good little preprogrammed toy he now was, the kid was up on his new old-school Converses and tearing off after his friends, a look of total confusion on his flushed face.

Vishous pulled another jump ahead and intercepted Frick and Frack. And what do you know, V's mere presence, materializing out of thin air, was enough to bust through their panic—the pair hard-stopped like they were chained dogs that had run out of steel links, jerking back in their shoes and pinwheeling their matching Buffalo Bills parkas.

"You asshats are always in the wrong place at the wrong time."

Mentally lights-outing them, he patted them down, cleaning their pockets and their short-terms at the same time—then he sent them off on their pussyfooted flee once again, praying that one or the other of them had an undiagnosed heart condition that would suddenly show up under the strain and kill him outright.

Then again, V was a nasty bastard, so there you had it.

No time to waste. He headed back to try to catch Rhage, re-outing his forties and looking for the most efficient way to the sonofabitch. Too bad dematerializing into the thick of things was a no-go, but shit, there were guns pointing in every direction of the compass. At least necessary coverage came quick, first in a series of maple trees and then in the form of a building that had to have been yet another dormitory.

Slamming his back against the cold, hard brick, his ears tuned out the heaving breathing of his lungs. The heaviest discharges from firearms were on the left, up and forward of his position, and he quickly dumped both clips even though he had three bullets remaining in one and two in the other. Fully restocked, he jogged toward the far corner of the building and put his head—

The slayer popped out of the last window he'd ducked under, and without the creak of the sash, V would have gotten drilled. Instinct rather than training had his arm swinging out and around before he was conscious of moving, and his index finger pumped off a pound of lead right into the fucker's face, clouds of black blood exploding out the rear of the skull like ink bottles getting dropped from a great height.

Unfortunately, an autonomic contraction of the slayer's grip on whatever autoloader it had in its hand caused a number of bullets to go flying, and the burning stripe on the outside of V's hip meant he'd been hit at least once. But better there than any other place—

A second slayer came around the corner, and V caught it in the throat with his left-hand gun. That one appeared to be unarmed, nothing of note dropping to the overgrown grass as the thing grabbed for the front of his neck to try to hold in the black gusher.

No time to peel any weapons off either of them—or to stab them back to the Omega.

Up ahead, Rhage was in trouble.

Out in the heart of the campus, in the town square–like area formed by a circle of buildings set some five acres apart, Rhage was center-of-attention with a peanut gallery of at least twenty slayers closing in on him.

"Jesus *Christ*," V muttered.

No time for strategy. Duh. And no one else coming to Hollywood's aid, either. The other brothers and fighters were engaged all around, the attack having dissipated into half a dozen skirmishes that were being fought in different quadrants.

There was nobody to spare in a situation that could have used three to four wingmen.

Instead of one who had a thigh wound and a grudge the size of Canada.

Goddamn it, he was used to always being right, but sometimes it sucked ass.

Vishous surged forward and focused on one side of the melee, picking off slayers as he tried to give his brother a viable escape route. But Rhage . . . fucking Rhage.

He was somehow on it. Even though the math didn't add up to anything but a casket equation, the dumb bastard was a thing of deadly beauty as he slowly circled 'round and 'round, discharging his weapons on a first-come, first-served basis, refueling his autoloader without missing a beat, creating a ring of writhing, half-dead undead bodies like he was the eye of a helter-skelter hurricane.

The only thing that wasn't in control? His handsome-for-the-history-books face was contorted into a monster's snarl, the killing rage within him not even partially leashed. And that would have been al-most acceptable.

If it weren't for the fact that he was supposed to be a professional.

That sort of murderous emotion was an amateur's downfall, the kind of thing that blinded you instead of focused you, weakened you instead of made you invincible.

Vishous worked as fast he as could, spot-on'ing chests, guts, heads, until the stench saturated the open air even with the wind blowing in the opposite direction. But he had to compensate for Rhage's ever-rotating shooting field, staying out of range himself, because shit knew he had no confidence that the brother would differentiate between targets.

And that was the fucking problem when you were half-cocked in battle.

Then it was done.

Kinda.

Even after those twenty or twenty-five *lessers* were down on the ground, Rhage still spun around and continued shooting, a death car-ousel with no more riders left on its demon horses that was too stupid to know where its own off switch was.

"Rhage!" V glanced around as he kept his guns up, but stopped his own discharging. "You fucking idiot! Stop!"

Pop! Pop! Pop-pop!

Hollywood's muzzle kept coughing out flashes of light even though there was nothing to shoot at—except other fighters off in the distance who just happened to be out of range for the moment.

But were not guaranteed to stay that way.

Vishous moved in closer, stepping over the animated corpses on the ground, keeping at Rhage's back as the rotation continued. "Rhage!"

The temptation to shoot the guy in the ass was so strong, his right hand lowered a muzzle to butt-cheek level. But that was just a fantasy. Giving Hollywood a lead injection would only trigger the beast when V himself was within appetizer range.

"Rhage!"

Something must have gotten through to the brother, because the barrage of do-nothing shooting slowed . . . then stopped, leaving Rhage in a panting, sagging neutral.

That was so out in the open, they both might as well have had neon arrows over their heads.

"You're out of here," V barked. "Are you fucking even kidding me with this shit—"

That was when it happened.

One second, he was moving around to get in front of his brother . . . and the next, he saw, out of the corner of his eye, one of the not-dead-enough *lessers* lift an unsteady arm . . . that had a gun attached to the end of it. As the bullet came blasting out of that muzzle, V's brain did the triangulation as fast as the lead slug flew.

It was going into Rhage's chest.

Right into the center of Rhage's chest—because, hello, that was the biggest target outside of one of the fucking dormitory doors on the campus.

"No!" V screamed as he went to jump into the path.

Yeah, 'cuz him dying instead was such a great outcome? Lose/lose, either way.

No blaze of pain as he airborned, no resounding kick of a bullet's entry into his side, his hip, his other thigh.

Because the goddamned thing had already found home.

Rhage let out a grunt and both of his arms punched to the sky, that patented, autonomic compression on the triggers in those hands emptying those clips: *Bang, bang, bang, bang!* up to the sky, up to the heavens, as if Rhage were cursing in pain.

And then the brother went down.

Unlike the Omega's boys, a direct hit like that would knock out any vampire, even a member of the Brotherhood. Nobody walked away from that shit, nobody.

As V screamed again, he hit his own patch of ground and discharged one of his weapons, plowing the slayer with the hole-in-one shot with enough lead to turn the fucker into a bank vault.

Threat neutralized, he scrambled to his brother, crab-walking on his guns and the balls of his shitkickers. For a male who never felt fear, he found himself looking into the gaping maw of pure terror.

"Rhage!" he said. "Jesus fucking Christ— Rhage!"

THREE

avers's new clinic was located across the river, in the center of some four hundred acres of forest that were vacant but for an old farmhouse and three or four new-built kiosks for entry into the subterranean facility. As Mary drove the last stretch of the twenty-minute trip in her Volvo XC70, she kept glancing in the rearview mirror at Bitty. The girl was sitting in the backseat of the station wagon and staring out the darkened window next to her as if the thing were a television and whatever show was on was captivating.

Every time Mary refocused on the road ahead, she cranked down harder on the steering wheel. And the accelerator.

"We're almost there," she said. Yet again.

The meant-to-be-reassuring statement was doing nothing for Bitty, and Mary knew she was just trying to soothe herself. The idea that they might not make it to the bedside in time was a hypothetical burden that she couldn't help trying on for size—and, man, did that crying-shame corset make her feel like she couldn't breathe.

"Here's the turn-off."

Mary hit the blinker and took a right onto a single-laner that was uneven and exactly what all her internal rush-rush didn't need.

Then again, she could have been on a perfectly paved super-highway and her heart still would have been conga-lining it up in her chest.

The vampire race's only healthcare facility was set up to evade both human attention and sunlight's merciless effects, and when you brought someone in, or sought treatment yourself, you were assigned one of several entry points. When the nurse had called with the sad news, Mary had been told to proceed directly to the farmhouse and park there, and that was what she did, pulling in between a pickup truck that was new and a Nissan sedan that was not.

"You ready?" she asked the rearview mirror as she cut the engine.

When there was no response, she got out and went around to Bitty's door. The girl seemed surprised to find they'd arrived, and small hands fumbled to release the seat belt.

"Do you need help?"

"No, thank you."

Bitty was clearly determined to get out of the car on her own, even if it took her a little longer than it might have otherwise. And the delay was maybe intentional. The what-next that was coming after this death was almost too terrible to contemplate. No family. No money. No education.

Mary pointed to a barn behind the house. "We're going over there."

Five minutes later, they were through a number of checkpoints and down an elevator shaft, whereupon they stepped out into a sparkling-clean, well-lit reception and waiting area that smelled exactly like all the ones in human hospitals did: fake lemon, faded perfume, and faintly of someone's dinner.

Pavlov had a point, Mary thought as she approached the front desk. All it took was that combination of antiseptic and stale air in her nose and she was flat on her back in a hospital bed, tubes running in and out of her, the drugs trying to kill off the cancer in her blood making her feel at best like she had the flu, and at worst like she was going to die then and there.

Fun times.

As the uniformed blonde behind the computer screen looked up, Mary said, "Hi, I'm—"

"Go that way," the female said urgently. "To the double doors. I'll release the lock. The nursing station is right ahead of you. They'll take her in directly."

Mary didn't wait to even say thank-you. Grabbing Bitty's hand, she rushed across the buffed, shiny floor and punched through the metal panels as soon as she heard the clunk of the mechanism shift free.

On the far side of the cozy chairs and the well-thumbed magazines of the waiting area, it was all clinical business, people in scrubs and traditional white nursing uniforms striding around with trays and laptops and stethoscopes.

"Over here," someone called out.

The nurse in question had black hair cut short, blue eyes that matched her scrubs, and a face like Paloma Picasso's. "I'll take you to her."

Mary fell in behind Bitty, guiding the girl now by the shoulders as they went down one hallway and then another to what was obviously the ICU section of the place: Normal hospital rooms didn't have glass walls with curtains on the insides. Didn't have this much staff around. Didn't have dashboards with stats flashing behind the nursing station.

As the nurse stopped and opened one of the panels, the beeping of the medical equipment was urgent, all kinds of frantic blips and squeaks suggesting that the computers were worried about whatever was going on with their patient.

The female held the curtain aside. "You can go right in."

When Bitty hesitated, Mary leaned down. "I'm not leaving you."

And again, that was something Mary was saying for herself. The girl had never seemed to particularly care which of Safe Place's staff were or were not around her.

As Bitty remained in place, Mary looked up. There were two nurses checking Annalye's vitals, one on each side of the bed, and Havers was there, too, putting some kind of drug into the IV that ran into a shockingly thin arm.

For a split second, the tableau sank in hard. The figure on the bed had dark hair that had thinned out and skin that was gray and eyes that were closed and a mouth that was lax—and during that first infinite instant as Mary took in the female who was dying, she couldn't decide whether she was seeing her own mother or herself on that bright white pillow.

I can't do this, she thought.

"Come on, Bitty," she said hoarsely. "Let's go hold her hand. She's going to want to know you're here."

As Mary led the girl in, Havers and his staff disappeared into the background, retreating without a fuss as if they knew damn well that there was nothing they could do to stop the inevitable, so Bitty's chance to say her good-bye was the critical path.

Over at the bedside, Mary kept her palm on Bitty's shoulder. "It's okay, you can touch her. Here."

Mary leaned forward and took the soft, cold hand. "Hello, Annalye. Bitty's come to see you."

Glancing at the girl, she nodded encouragement . . . and Bitty frowned.

"Is she dead already?" the girl whispered.

Mary blinked hard. "Ah, no, sweetheart. She's not. And she can hear you."

"How?"

"She just can. Go ahead. Talk to her. I know she'll want to hear your voice."

"Mahmen?" Bitty said.

"Take her hand. It's all right."

As Mary inched back, Bitty reached out . . . and when contact was made, the girl frowned again.

"Mahmen?"

All at once, alarms started to go off with renewed panic, the shrill sounds cutting through the fragile connection between mother and daughter, bringing the medical staff toward the bed in a rush.

"Mahmen!" Bitty grabbed on with both hands. *"Mahmen!* Don't go!"

Mary was forced to pull Bitty out of the way as Havers started barking orders. The girl fought against the hold, but then collapsed as she screamed, her arms stretching toward her mother, her hair tangling.

Mary held on to the small straining body. "Bitty, oh, God . . ."

Havers got up on the bed and began chest compressions as the crash cart was brought over.

"We've got to go," Mary said, pulling Bitty back toward the door. "We'll wait outside—"

"I killed her! I killed her!"

As Vishous skidded up to Rhage, he fell to his knees and went for the brother's leather jacket and shirt, ripping the layers wide, exposing—

"Oh . . . *fuck*."

The bullet had entered to the right of center, exactly where the six-chambered heart of a vampire beat within its cage of bone. And as Rhage gasped for breath and spit blood, V looked around with a whole lot of frantic. Fighting everywhere. Cover nowhere. Time . . . running out—

Butch came running at them, head ducked, body hauling ass and then some as he shot a pair of forties all around himself, pumping rounds off so that the slayers in range had to hit the ground and go fetal to avoid getting plugged with lead. The former cop slid into base feet-first, his weapons still up and kicking, his bulldog legs and torso plowing to a stop in the thick brown grass.

"We gotta move him," that Boston accent announced.

Rhage's mouth opened wide, and the inhale that came next rattled like a box of rocks.

Ordinarily, V's brain was slick as shit, his intelligence so great that it was as much a personal characteristic as a faculty, defining everything about his life. He was the rational one, the logical one, the cynical sonofabitch who was never wrong.

And yet his gray matter promptly crashed.

Years of performing medical assessment and intervention in the field told him that his brother was going to die within a minute or two, assuming that the heart muscle had in fact been torn or pierced and one, or more than one, of the chambers was spilling blood into the chest cavity.

Which would both cut off cardiac function as the peritoneal sac flooded and fatally compromise blood pressure.

It was the kind of catastrophic injury that required immediate surgical intervention—and even assuming you had all the necessary technology and equipment available in a sterile clinical situation, success wasn't on lock.

"V! We gotta move him—"

Bullets sizzled by and they both hit the ground. And with a terrible mental recalculation, V's processing unit came to an untenable conclusion: Rhage's life or theirs.

Fuck! I did this to him, V thought.

If he hadn't told the brother about the vision, Rhage wouldn't have run out early and he would have been more in control during the fight—

Vishous upped his muzzles and dropped three slayers who were closing in, while Butch twisted on the ground and did the same in the opposite direction.

"Rhage, stay with us," V grunted as he popped out the empty clips and refilled the butts of his guns one after the other. "Rhage, you've got to—shit!"

More shooting. And he was hit in the goddamn arm.

As his own blood flowed, he ignored it, his brain reengaging to find a solution that didn't equal Rhage on a funeral fucking pyre. He could call his Jane in, because she couldn't be killed. But she couldn't perform open-heart surgery here, for fuck's sake. What if—

The flash of light was so bright, so sudden, that he wondered who the hell was wasting time stabbing a slayer back to the Omega—

The second blast of illumination had him cranking around and looking down at Rhage. Oh . . . *shit*. Twin shafts of brilliant light streamed out of the brother's eye sockets, lasering up into the sky in parallel streams that could have bull's-eyed the face of the moon.

"Fuuuuuck!"

Total change of plan. The motherfucking theme of the night.

V hauled over to Butch and peeled him off Rhage. "Move it!"

"What are you doing—Holy Mary, mother of God!"

The pair of them broke out in a crouched run, their heads ducked, their legs ripping across the open area as they jumped over writhing *lessers* and varied their course to make themselves more difficult targets. When they reached the closest abandoned classroom building, they one-after-the-othered around the corner and went into auto-cover, V taking the front, Butch on the back.

With his chest pumping, Vishous leaned around. Out in the center of the clearing, the change was torturing Rhage's downed body, his arms and legs contorting as his torso jerked and twisted, the beast emerging from the flesh of the male, the great dragon breaking free from the DNA it was forced to share.

If Rhage hadn't died out there already, this was surely going to kill him.

And yet there was no way of stopping the transformation. The Scribe Virgin had embedded the curse into every single one of Rhage's cells, and when the thing came out, the process was a train that no one could slow down or stop.

Death was going to take care of the problem.

Rhage's death . . . was going to stop all this.

V closed his eyes and screamed inside.

A second later, he popped his lids and thought, No fucking way. No fucking way he was going to let this happen.

"Butch," he barked. "I gotta go."

"What? Where are you—"

That was the last thing Vishous heard as he up and disappeared.

FOUR

No pain.

There was no pain from the gunshot in Rhage's chest. And that was his first clue that shit was critical. Wounds that hurt tended not to be the kind that put you into shock. No sensation? Probably a good indication, along with the fact that he'd been blown off his shitkickers and the hit was right at his breastbone, that he was in mortal danger.

Blink. Try to breathe. Blink.

Blood in his mouth, thick in his throat . . . a rising tide that went against his efforts to get oxygen down to his lungs. Hearing had been reduced to a muffled version of same, as if he'd lain back in a bathtub and the water level had come up over both his ears. Sight was in and out, the night sky above him revealed and obscured as things failed and kick-started again. Breath was getting harder and harder to draw, a gathering weight settling on his chest, first like a duffel bag, then a linebacker . . . now in station wagon territory.

Fast, this was happening very fast.

Mary, he thought. *Mary?*

His brain spit out his *shellan's* name—maybe he was even saying it?—as if his mate could hear him somehow.

Mary!

Panic flooded into his bloodstream and poured right into his rib cage—along with the plasma he was no doubt leaking all over the fuck. His only thought, more than of his death or the battle or even his brothers' safety, was . . . oh, God, let the Scribe Virgin hold up her side of the bargain.

Let him not end up in the Fade alone.

Mary was supposed to be able to leave the earth with him. She was supposed to be allowed to follow him when he went unto the Fade. That was part of the arrangement he'd made with the Scribe Virgin: He kept his curse, his Mary survived her leukemia, and because his mate was infertile from her cancer treatments, she got to stay with him for however long she wanted.

You're going to fucking die tonight.

Just as he heard Vishous's voice in his head, the brother's face shot into his vision, replacing the heavens. V's mouth was moving, that goatee shifting around as he enunciated his words. Rhage tried to bat the male away, but his arms weren't listening to his brain.

Last thing he needed was someone else dying. Although as the son of the Scribe Virgin, V was probably the least likely to worry about something as vanilla as popping his cog. But as Butch, the number three in the troika, arrived on a slide-in and started yapping, too? Now, there was a guy with no Grim Reaper hall pass—

Shooting. Both of them started shooting.

No! Rhage ordered them. *Tell Mary I love her and leave me the fuck here before you get—*

V recoiled as if some kind of lead had found something of his.

And that was when it happened.

The scent of his brother's blood was what did it. The second that copper sting hit Rhage's nose, the beast awoke within its cage of his flesh and began to come out, the change initiating internal earthquakes that snapped his bones and shredded his internal organs and transformed him into something else entirely.

Now there was pain.

As well as the sense that this effort was a waste of fucking time. If he was dying, the dragon was just taking his place at the crap table.

"Tell Mary to come with me," Rhage shouted as he went completely blind. "Tell her . . ."

But he had the sense that his brothers had already taken off, and thank God for it: V's blood was no longer on the air and there was no reply coming back at him.

Even as his life force ebbed, he did his best to go with the flow as the ripping and tearing racked his dying body. Even if he'd had the energy, fighting that tide was wasted effort, and didn't make things any easier. Still, as his mind and soul, his own emotions and consciousness, receded, it was eerie that he didn't know whether it was the death, or the transformation that was backseating him.

As the beast's nervous system took over completely and the sensations of pain disappeared, Rhage retreated into a metaphysical float zone, like who and what he was had been put in a snow globe up on the time continuum's shelf.

Only in this instance, he had the sense he would not be taken back down.

And it was funny. Each and every entity that had consciousness and an awareness of its own mortality inevitably wondered, from time to time, about the when and where, the how and why of its demise. Rhage had been guilty of that morbid drift of thought himself, especially during his pre-Mary period, when he'd been alone with nothing but a catalog of his failures and weaknesses to keep him company during the dense, deserted hours of daylight.

For him, those rambling questions were being unexpectedly answered tonight: "Where" was in the middle of the field of conflict, at an abandoned girls' school; "how" was by bleeding out at the heart, as a result of a gunshot wound; "why" was in the line of duty; "when" was probably in the next ten minutes or so, maybe less.

Given the nature of his work, none of that was a surprise. Okay, maybe the prep-school part, but that was it.

He was going to miss his brothers. Jesus . . . that hurt more than the beast stuff. And he was going to worry about all of them, and the future of Wrath's kingship. Shit, he was going to miss seeing Nalla and L.W. grow up. And Qhuinn's twins being born hopefully alive and well. Would he be able to see them all from the Fade?

Oh, his Mary. His beautiful, precious Mary.

Terror hit him, but it was hard to hold on to the emotion as he felt himself weaken even further. To calm down, he told himself that the Scribe Virgin didn't lie. The Scribe Virgin was all powerful. The Scribe

Virgin had determined the balance needed to save his Mary's life and had given them a great gift to counter-balance the fact that his *shellan* could not have children.

No children, he thought with a pang. He and his Mary would never have children in any form now.

That was so sad.

Strange . . . he hadn't thought he'd wanted them, at least not consciously. But now that it would never happen? He was totally bereft.

At least his Mary would never leave him.

And he had to have faith that when he went to that door to the Fade, and he proceeded through it to whatever was on the other side, she would be able to find him.

Otherwise, this whole death thing would have been unbearable to go through. The idea that he could be dying and would never see his beloved again? Never smell her hair? Know her touch? Speak his truth even though she already knew how much he loved her?

All that was why death was such a tragedy, he thought. It was the great separator, and sometimes it struck without warning, a vicious thief robbing people of emotional currency that would bankrupt them for the rest of their lives. . . .

Shit, what if the Scribe Virgin was wrong? Or had lied? Or wasn't all-powerful?

Abruptly, his panic refueled, and his thoughts began to jam up, getting stuck on the distance that had come between him and his *shellan* lately, distance that he had taken for granted that he had time and space to correct.

Oh, God . . . Mary, he said in his head. *Mary! I love you!*

Shit. He should have talked out the stuff with her, dug down deep to discover where the problem was, mended them back so that they were once more soul-to-soul.

The trouble was, he realized with dread, when your heart finally stopped beating in your chest, everything that you wished you'd said but hadn't, all the missing pieces of yourself that you had yet to give, all the failures you had stuffed under the rug in the guise of life being so very busy . . . that stopped, too. The mid-stride step, never to be completed, was the worst regret anyone could have.

You just maybe didn't learn that until all the things you'd ever wondered about your death actually happened. And yup, those questions you'd wondered about, the how's and why's, where's and when's . . . turned out to be pretty goddamned immaterial when you left the planet.

They had been losing ground, he and Mary.

Lately . . . they had been losing touch with each other.

He didn't want to go out like this—

White light wiped out everything, eating him alive, stealing his consciousness.

The Fade had come for him. And he could only pray that his Mary Madonna would be able to find him on the other side.

He had things he desperately needed to say to her.

Vishous resumed his form in a white marble courtyard that was open to a milky sky so vast and bright that there were no shadows thrown by the fountain in the center or by the tree full of colorful, chirping finches over in the corner.

All of whom went silent as they sensed his mood.

"Mother!" His voice echoed, bouncing between the walls. "Where the fuck are you!"

As he strode forward, the trail of blood that he left in his wake was brilliant red, and when he stopped at the door to the Scribe Virgin's private quarters, drops fell from his elbow and his leg with soft impacts. When he pounded and called her name some more, speckles of the shit hit the white panel like nail polish dropped on a floor.

"Fuck this."

Slamming his shoulder into the thing, he broke into his mother's quarters—only to pull up short. Over on the bedding platform, beneath sheets of white satin, the entity who had created the vampire race, but also bodily borne forth him and his sister, was lying in utter stillness and silence. There was no corporeal form to her, however. Just a three-dimensional pool of light that had once been brilliant as a flash bomb, but was now that of an old-fashioned oil lamp with a clouded shade.

"You have to save him." As Vishous crossed the bare marble floor, he was dimly aware that the room was empty but for the bed. Who cared, though. "Wake the fuck up! Someone who matters is dying and you're going to stop it, goddamn it."

If she had had a body, he would have grabbed her and forced her

to pay attention. There were no arms for him to drag her out of bed with or shoulders to shake.

He was about to yell again when words were spoken throughout the quarters as if they were piped in through Surround Sound.

What shall be will be.

Like that explained everything. Like he was a cocksucker for coming and bothering her. Like he was wasting her time. "Why did you create us if you don't give a shit."

Exactly what are you concerned with. His future, or yours.

"What the hell are you talking about?" Oh, and yeah, he knew you weren't supposed to question her, but fuck that for a laugh. "What's that supposed to mean?"

Is translation truly necessary?

As V locked his jaws, he reminded himself that Rhage was beasting out and dying in that incarnation down on the field: Trading bitch slaps with mommy dearest wasn't the critical path here.

"Just save him, all right. Move him out of the theater of conflict so we can operate on him and I'll leave you to rot in peace."

And that would solve his destiny how.

Okay, now he knew why humans with mother issues went on Lassiter's talk shows. Every time V got around this female, he came down with a case of womb-induced psychosis.

"He'll keep fucking breathing, that's what'll be solved."

Destiny will simply be served by other means.

V pictured Hollywood pulling a bath-mat slip-and-fall that killed him at home. Or a choke job on a turkey leg. Or God only knew what else that could carry a brother off.

"So change it. You're so fucking powerful. Change his destiny right now."

There was a long pause, and he wondered whether or not she'd fallen asleep or some shit—and, man, did he hate her. She was such a goddamn quitter, pulling out of the world, sequestering herself up here as a recluse in a sulk because no one was kissing her ass like she wanted.

Boo-fucking-hoo.

Meanwhile, one of the best fighters in the war, who was an absolute mission-critical part of the King's private guard, was about to go *poof!* off the planet. And V was the last person to want somebody else to wipe his butthurt away, but he had to give saving Rhage his best shot, and who the fuck else had this kind of pull?

"He's important," V snapped. "His life matters."

To you.

"Fuck that, this isn't about me. He matters to the King, the Brotherhood, the war. We lose him? We've got a problem."

Does it not occur to you to be honest.

"You think I'm worried about him and Mary? Fine. I'll throw that shit in, too—'cuz right now, you don't look like you could stand up much less escort a non-entity who you took off the mortal continuum across the divide unto the Fade at a determined time of that female's choosing."

Fuck. Now that he said that out loud, he really had to wonder whether this limp thing on the bedding platform could actually perform on that promise she'd made back in what felt like the old days, even though it was only three years ago.

So much had changed.

Except for the fact that he still hated weakness of any kind. And continued to want to be anywhere but in his mother's presence.

Leave me. You tire me.

"I tire you. Yeah, 'cuz you got so many fucking things to do up here. Jesus Christ."

Fine, fuck her. He'd figure something else out. Some other . . . something.

Shit, what else was there?

Vishous turned away for the door he'd busted open. With each step he took, he expected her to call him back, say something else, put a stinger into his chest that would be almost as lethal as what Rhage had been taken down with. When she didn't, and the door shut directly behind him, nearly catching him in the ass, he thought he should have fucking known.

She didn't even care enough to shit on him.

Back in the courtyard, the blood trail that he'd left on the marble pavers was like the destiny he'd followed in his life, jagged and messy, providing evidence of pain he largely failed to acknowledge. And yeah, he wanted the stain to seep into the stone, like maybe that would get her attention.

On that note, why didn't he just throw himself on the goddamn ground and pull a temper tantrum like he was in the aisles at fucking Target and pissed off over a Tonka toy.

As he stood there, the silence registered as a sound in and of itself.

Which was both illogical and precisely the experience he had as he realized how truly quiet it was up here now. The Chosen were all on Earth, learning about themselves, separating into individuals, turning away from their traditional roles of service to his mother. The race was just the same, existing in modern times where the old cycles of festivals and observances were mostly ignored, and traditions that had once been respected were now at risk of being forgotten.

Good, he thought. He hoped she was lonely and felt disrespected. He wanted her nice and isolated, with even her most faithful turning their backs on her.

He wanted her to hurt.

He wanted her to die.

His eyes went to the birds he had brought her, and the flock cowered from him, shuffling to a set of branches in the back of the white tree, huddling together as if he were going to snap their necks one by one.

Those finches had been an olive branch from a son who had never been truly wanted, but also hadn't behaved all that well. His mother probably hadn't spared them much more than a glance—and what do you know, he had moved beyond that brief flare of conciliatory weakness, too, back to the shores of his enmity. How could he not?

The Scribe Virgin hadn't come to them when Wrath had been almost killed. She hadn't helped the King keep his crown. Beth had nearly died giving birth and had had to give up any future of having more children to survive. F.F.S. Selena, one of the Scribe Virgin's own Chosen, had just died and broken the heart of a goddamn good male—and what was the response? Nada.

And before all that? Wellsie's passing. The raids.

And ahead of that? Qhuinn was shitting his leathers, worried that Layla was going to die birthing his twins. And Rhage was expiring down there in the middle of a fight.

Need he say more?

Twisting his head around, V glared at the door that had been re-shut by her will. He was glad she suffered. And no, he didn't trust her.

As he dematerialized back to the field of combat, he had absolutely no faith at all that she would do right by Rhage and Mary. He had taken a gamble and lost going to his mother, but with her, that was the way it always went.

Miracle. He needed a fucking miracle.

FIVE

The water rushing over Mary's hands was cold, and yet it burned her skin—proving that opposite ends of the thermometer could coexist at the same time.

The ladies' room sink she was standing at was white and porcelain. Its drain was shiny and silver. In front of her, a wall-length mirror reflected three stalls, all of which had their peach-colored doors closed, only one of which was occupied.

"You okay in there?" she said.

The toilet flushed, even though Bitty hadn't used it.

Mary focused on her reflection. Yup. She looked as bad as she felt: Somehow, in the last thirty minutes, black bags had formed under sockets that had sunken in, and her skin was pale as the tile she was standing on.

Somehow? Bull crap. She knew exactly how.

I killed her!

Mary had to close her eyes and pull yet another recompose. When she opened things up again, she tried to remember what she was doing. Oh. Right. There was a little stack of paper towels on a shelf, the kind that interlocked fold-to-fold, and as she went to take one and dripped water all over the others, she thought it was strange that Havers, who

was so precise about his facility, promoted such messiness. Oh . . . got it. The dispenser on the wall by the door was broken, the lower part hanging loose.

Just like me, she thought. Fully stocked with the education and experience to help people, but not doing my job right.

Take her hand. It's okay . . .

I killed her!

"Bitty?" When that came out as nothing but a croak, she cleared her throat. "Bitty."

After she dried her hands, she turned to the stalls. "Bitty, I'm coming in if you don't come out."

The girl opened the middle panel, and for some reason, Mary knew she would never forget the sight of that small hand curling around, gripping and not letting go as she stepped out.

She had been crying in there. Alone. And now that the girl was being forced to show her face, she was attempting to do exactly what Mary herself was desperately shooting for.

Sometimes composure was all you had; dignity your only consolation; the illusion of "all right" your sole source of comfort.

"Here, let me . . ." As Mary's voice dried up, she went back for the paper towels and wet one in the sink she had used. "This will help."

Approaching the girl slowly, she brought the cool, soft cloth to the child's flushed face, pressing it onto the hot, red skin. As she blotted, in her mind she was apologizing to the grown-up Bitty would hopefully become: *I'm sorry I made you do that. No, you didn't kill her. I wish I had let you do it on your own terms and in your own way. I'm sorry. No, you didn't kill her. I'm sorry.*

I'm so sorry.

Mary tilted the girl's chin up. "Bitty—"

"What do they do with her now? Where does she go?"

God, that pale brown stare was steady. "They're going to take her to . . . well, they're going to cremate her."

"What is that?"

"They're going to burn her body into ashes for the passing ceremony."

"Will that hurt her?"

Mary cleared her throat again. "No, honey. She won't feel anything. She's free—she's in the Fade, waiting for you."

The good news was that at least Mary knew that part was true.

Even though she'd been raised Catholic, she had seen the Scribe Virgin for herself, so no, she wasn't feeding the girl false, if compassionate, rhetoric. For vampires, there was in fact a heaven, and they did, really and truly, meet their loved ones there.

Heck, it probably proved the same was true for humans, but as there was less visible magic in that world, eternal salvation was a much harder sell to the average joe.

Wadding the paper towel up, Mary took a step back. "I'd like us to return to Safe Place now, okay? There's nothing more we can do here and it's getting close to dawn."

The last piece was just habit, she supposed. As a pretrans, Bitty could tolerate any amount of light the sun could throw at her. And the real truth was that she just wanted to get the girl away from all the death here.

"Okay?" Mary prompted.

"I don't want to leave her."

In any other circumstance, Mary would have crouched down and waded gently into the waters of what was going to be Bitty's new world. The awful reality was that there was no mother to leave behind anymore, and getting the girl out of this clinical environment where patients were being treated, sometimes in dire situations, was entirely appropriate.

I killed her.

Instead, Mary said, "Okay, we can stay as long as you like."

Bitty nodded and walked over to the door that led out into the corridor. As she stood before the closed panel, her heavily-washed dress seemed on the verge of falling off her thin frame, her ill-fitting black coat like a blanket she had wound around herself, her brown hair feathering from static across the knobby fabric.

"I really wish . . ."

"What?" Mary whispered.

"I wish I could go back to earlier. When I woke up tonight."

"I wish you could, too."

Bitty looked over her shoulder. "Why can't you go back? It's so strange. I mean, I can remember everything about her. It's like . . . it's like my memories are a room I should be able to walk into. Or something."

Mary frowned, thinking that was a way too mature comment for someone her age to make.

But before she could reply, the girl pushed her way out, clearly not interested in a response—and maybe that was a good thing. What the hell did you say to that?

Out in the corridor, Mary wanted to put her hand on that small shoulder, but she held off. The girl was so self-contained, in the way a book would be in the midst of a library, or a doll in a line-up of collectibles, and it was difficult to justify breaching those boundaries.

Especially when, as a therapist, you were already feeling very shaky in your professional shoes.

"Where do we go?" Bitty asked as a pair of nurses ran by them.

Mary glanced around. They were still in the ICU section of the clinic, but some distance away from where Bitty's mom had passed. "We could ask for a room to sit in."

The girl stopped. "We can't really see her again, can we?"

"No."

"Maybe we should go back, I guess."

"Whatever you want."

Five minutes later, they were in the Volvo heading for Safe Place. As Mary took them over the bridge, she once again bobble-headed the rearview mirror, checking on Bitty every fifty yards. In the silence, she found herself back on the apology train in her head . . . for giving bad advice, for putting the girl in the position of suffering even more. But all that gnashing was self-serving, a search for personal absolution that was totally unfair to the patient, especially one that young.

This on-the-job nightmare was something Mary was going to have to come to grips with on her own.

An entrance onto I-87 appeared as soon as they were on the downtown side of the bridge, and the directional signal sounded loud in the interior of the station wagon. Heading north, Mary stayed at the speed limit and got passed by a couple of eighteen-wheelers doing eighty in a sixty-five. From time to time, lights marking merger zones flared overhead in a rhythm that never lasted long, and what little local traffic there was thinned out even more as they continued onward.

When they got home, Mary decided she was going to try to feed the girl something. Bitty hadn't had First Meal, so she had to be starving. Then maybe a movie until dawn, somewhere quiet. The trauma was so fresh, and not just the stuff around losing her mother. What had happened at Havers's had to be bringing up everything that had come before—the domestic abuse, the rescue where Rhage, V and

Butch had killed the father to save Bitty and her mom, the discovery that the mother was newly pregnant, the loss of the baby, the lingering months afterward where Annalye had never fully recovered—

"Ms. Luce?"

"Yes?" Oh, God, please ask me something I can answer decently. "Yes, Bitty?"

"Where are we going?"

Mary glanced at a road sign coming at them. It read, EXIT 19 GLENS FALLS. "I'm sorry? We're going home. We should be there in about fifteen minutes?"

"I thought Safe Place wasn't this far away."

"Wha—?"

Oh, God.

She was heading for the damn mansion.

"Oh, Bitty, I'm sorry." Mary shook her head. "I must have lost track of the exits. I . . ."

What had she been thinking?

Well, she knew the answer to that—all the hypotheticals she'd been running through her head about what they were going to do when they got out of the car were things involving the place where Mary lived with Rhage, the King, the Brothers, the fighters and their mates.

What the *hell* had she been thinking?

Mary got off at exit nineteen, went under the highway, and hopped back on going south. Man, she was just hitting it out of the park to-night, wasn't she.

At least things couldn't get any worse.

Back at the Brownswick School for Girls, Assail, son of Assail, heard the roar even through the sensory overload of battle.

In spite of the chaos of all the gunshots and the cursing and the mad sprints from cover to cover, the thunderous sound that rolled out across the abandoned campus was the kind of thing that got one's at-tention.

As he wrenched around, he kept his finger on the trigger of his autoloader, continuing to discharge bullets straight ahead at a line-up of the undead—

For a split second, he fell off from his shooting.

His brain simply could not process what his eyes were suggesting had magically appeared a mere fifty yards away from him. It was . . . some kind of dragon-like creature, with purple scales, a barbed tail, and a gaping mouth set with T. rex teeth. The prehistoric monster was a good two stories high, long as a tractor trailer, and fast as a crocodile as it went after anything that ran away—

Free fall.

Without warning, his body went flying forward and a searing pain streaked down the front of his calf and sliced across his ankle. Twisting in midair, he landed face up in the tangled grass—and a breath later, the partially wounded slayer who'd gotten him with a knife lurched up onto his chest, that blade arc'd over its shoulder, its lips curled into a snarl as black blood streamed out all over Assail.

Right, fuck this, mate.

Assail grabbed a fistful of still-brown hair, shoved his muzzle into that wide-open maw, and hit the trigger, blowing open the back of the skull, incapacitating the body such that it fell on him as a writhing deadweight. Kicking the animated corpse off, he sprang to his feet.

And found himself directly in the cross hairs of the beast.

His movement up to the vertical was what did it, the dragon's eyes snapping to him and narrowing into slits. Then, with another roar, the killer came at him, pounding over the ground, crushing slayers under its massive hind feet, its front claws curled up and ready to strike.

"Fuck!"

Assail surged forward, no longer worried about where his gun was pointed and absolutely unconcerned about the fact that he was now headed directly into an advancing line of *lessers*. The good news? The beast took care of that little problem. The slayers, likewise, garnered one look at all the hell-hath-no-fury coming at them and scattered like leaves unto the autumn wind.

Naturally, there was naught directly up ahead that provided any cover. By bad luck, his escape route offered nothing but scrub and brush, without any meaningful protection. The nearest building? Two hundred yards away. At least.

With a curse, he ran e'er faster, reaching down into the muscles of his legs, calling for more and more speed.

It was a race the beast was due to win—a victory that was inevitable when a five-foot stride tried to outrun a set of legs that could cover twenty-five in a single bound. With every second, that pounding grew louder and closer until hot blasts of breath hit Assail's back, flushing him in spite of the cold.

Fear struck to his core.

But there was no time to try to harness the panic that flooded his mind. A great roar blasted at him, the force of the sound so great that it spurred him forth, providing a gust of foul-smelling air that ushered him along. Shit, his only chance was—

The bite came after the great roar, those jaws snapping so close to the nape of Assail's neck that he cringed down even though it slowed his gait. Too late to save himself, though. Airborne. He went airborne, plucked from the ground in mid-stride—except why wasn't there more pain?

Surely if the beast had gotten him by the shoulders or the torso, he would have been racked with—no, wait, it had him by the jacket. The thing had him by the leather jacket, not the flesh, a band of constriction cutting across his pecs and lifting him by the armpits, his legs flopping, his gun firing as he made fists of his hands. Below him, the landscape tilted like it was on a seesaw, the bolting *lessers*, the fighting Brothers, the overgrown bushes and trees flipping around him as he was shaken all about.

The fucking thing was going to toss him up and gullet him. This back-and-forth nonsense was just tenderizing a meal.

Goddamn him, he was the vampire equivalent of a chicken wing.

No time. He let his gun go and went for the zipper at his throat. The shaking motion made his tiny target fast as a mouse, slick as a marble, all needle-in-a-haystack for his trembling hands and slippery, sweaty fingertips.

The beast's very hold did more for him.

With those teeth locked in the back of the jacket, the leather couldn't hold his weight, and he broke free, falling from the jaws, the hard ground rushing to greet him. Tucking into a roll so that he didn't break anything, he landed in a heap nonetheless.

Directly on his shoulder.

The crack was something that registered throughout his body and rendered him as useless as a babe unattended, all breath lost, his sight blurring. But there was no time if he wanted to live. Wrenching around, he—

Pop! Pop! Pop! Pop! Pop—BOOM!

His cousins came out of the night, running as if they were being chased when in fact they were not. Ehric had two autoloaders up and discharging . . . and Evale had an elephant gun on his shoulder.

That was the *BOOM!*

Indeed, the weapon was, in fact, an actual elephant gun, an enormous firearm that had been left over from the time of the Raj in India. Evale, the aggressive bastard, had long ago seemed to have bonded with the thing in an unnatural, "my precious" kind of way.

Thank the Fates for unhealthy preoccupations.

Those forty-millimeter bullets did nothing to slow the beast down, pinging off the purple scales as if they were peas cast upon a motor vehicle. But the elephant gun's payload of lead caused a howl of pain and a recoil.

It was Assail's only opportunity for escape.

Closing his eyes, he focused, focused, focused—

No dematerializing. Too much adrenaline on top of too much cocaine with too much pain from his shoulder as a chaser.

And the beast went right back on the attack, refocusing on Assail and giving him the dragon equivalent of a fuck-you in the form of an enormous roar—

The massive shotgun went off a second time, catching the thing in the chest.

"Run!" Ehric bellowed as he reloaded his forties, clips kicking out of the butts of his little guns. "Get up!"

Assail used his good arm to shove himself off the ground, and his legs reengaged with admirable aplomb. Holding his injured limb to his chest, he hauled as hard as he could, the remnants of his jacket flapping, his stomach rolling, his heart pounding.

BOOM!

Anywhere, anywhere—he had to get anywhere the fuck out of range—and fast. Too bad his body wasn't listening. Even as his brain was screaming for speed, all he could do was lurch like a zombie—

Someone caught him from behind, hipping him up off the ground on a snatch-and-drag that quickly turned into an over-the-shoulder fireman carry. As he slammed into place head-down, he vomited from the agony, starbursts lighting his eyes up as his stomach emptied itself with violence. The good news was that he hadn't eaten for twelve to

fifteen hours at that point, so he didn't cream up his cousin's pant leg too badly.

He wanted to help the effort. He wanted to hang on himself. He wanted . . .

Bushes lashed him in the face, and he squinted to protect his eyes. Blood began to flow and it filled his nose. His shoulder got more and more painful. Pressure in his head grew unbearable, making him think of over-inflated tires, bags with too many things in them, water balloons that popped and spilled their contents everywhere.

Thank God for his cousins. They never deserted him.

One must remember to reward them in some manner.

The outbuilding seemed to canter toward them as opposed to the other way around, and from Assail's upside-down vantage point, the thing appeared to be hanging from the earth instead of planted upon it. Brick. Even with the jostling and the darkness and the alternating strides, he could tell the shack was brick.

One could only hope for a sturdy construction.

His cousin broke down the door, and the air inside was musty and damp.

Without warning, Assail was dumped like the trash he was, and he landed on a dusty floor with a bounce that made him retch again. The door slammed shut, and then all he heard was his cousin's heavy breathing. And his own.

And the muffled sounds of the battle.

There was an abrupt flare of orange light.

Through the haze of his pain, Assail frowned—and then recoiled. The face illuminated as a hand-rolled cigarette was lit was not that of either of his cousins.

"How badly are you hurt?" the Black Dagger Brother Vishous asked as he exhaled a most delicious smoke.

" 'Twas you?"

"Do I look like Santa Claus?"

"An unlikely savior you are." Assail grimaced and wiped his mouth upon his jacket sleeve. "And I apologize for your pants."

V looked down at himself. "You got something against black leather?"

"I vomited down the back of them—"

"Shit!"

"Well, one can get them cleaned—"

"No, asshole, it's coming for us." V nodded to a cloudy window. "Damn it."

Indeed, off in the distance, the thundering pounding of the dragon's gait sounded once again, a storm gathering and heading in their direction.

Assail flailed around on the floor, looking for somewhere to hide. A closet. A bathroom. A cellar. Nothing. The interior was empty except for two floor-to-ceiling supports and a decade's worth of rafter decay. Thank the Virgin Scribe that it appeared to be a stout brick and more likely to withstand—

The roof lifted and splintered on a oner, debris raining down, asphalt shingles slapping on the floor as if the shed were heralding its own demise with a round of applause. Fresh night air cleared away the musty smell, but it was hardly a relief given what had precipitated the access.

The beast was not a vegetarian, stipulated. But it also wasn't worried about its fiber intake: the thing spit that old wooden roof out to the side, arched down, and opened up its jaws, releasing a sonic boom of a roar.

There was nowhere to run. The creature was standing over the building, poised to strike at what had become its lunchbox. Nowhere to take cover. No suitable defense to bring to bear.

"Go," Assail said to the Brother as those great reptilian eyes narrowed and the muzzle blew an exhale as hot and fetid as a Dumpster in summer. "Give me your weapon. I'll distract it."

"I'm not leaving you."

"I am not one of your brothers."

"You gave us this location. You gave us the head of the *Fore-lesser*. I'm not fucking leaving you, douche bag."

"Such gallantry. And the compliments. Do stop."

As the beast let out another roar and tossed its head as if it were prepared to toy with them a bit before consuming them, Assail thought of his drug dealing . . . his cocaine addiction . . .

The human female with whom he had fallen in love and had had to let go. Because she couldn't handle his lifestyle, and he was too caught up in it to stop, even for her.

He shook his head at the Brother. "No, I'm not worth saving. Get the fuck out of here."

SIX

Campbell's Chicken & Stars.

As Mary stood over the stove in Safe Place's original kitchen, she stirred the soup 'round and 'round with a stainless-steel spoon, watching the swollen almost-stars of pasta make circuits along with the squares of white meat and wedges of carrots. The pan was the smallest one they had in the house. The broth was yellow, and the sweet smell reminded her of the simple illnesses she'd had as a child . . . colds, flus, strep.

Easier things than cancer.

Or the MS that had taken her mother.

The bowl she poured things into was cream with rings of concentric yellow piping on the lip. She got a fresh spoon out of the drawer and went around the counter to the big, rough-cut table.

"Here," she said to Bitty. "And I'll get you some Saltines."

As if this tragedy were something that you could get over in twenty-four hours if you were just hydrated enough?

Well, at least a simple meal like this wasn't liable to backfire. And as soon as Bitty had eaten it, Mary was going to go find another staff member to attend the girl—and then get some counseling herself.

When she came back from the cupboards with the sleeve of crack-

ers, Bitty was taking a test taste, and Mary sat down across the table so she didn't crowd the girl.

The plastic wrapping refused to cooperate, and Mary split it wide, spilling Saltines and salt grains over the wood. "Damn it."

She ate one herself. And then realized she hadn't had any food in a while and was hungry, too—

"My uncle is going to come for me."

Mary froze in mid-chew. "What did you say?"

"My uncle." Bitty didn't look up, just kept moving her spoon through the steaming soup. "He's going to come for me. He's going to take me home."

Mary resumed the whole mastication thing, but her mouth was like a cement mixer trying to process gravel. "Really?"

"Yes."

With careful hands, Mary gathered up the scattered crackers, stacking them in groups of four. "I didn't know you had an uncle."

"I do."

"Where does he live?"

"Not in Caldwell." Bitty took another spoonful and put it in her mouth. "But he knows how to get here. Everyone knows where Caldwell is."

"Is he your *mahmen's* brother?"

"Yes."

Mary closed her eyes. Annalye had never mentioned any relations. Hadn't disclosed them on paperwork or named a next of kin. And the female had been aware that her condition was deteriorating—so if there had been a brother somewhere, surely she would have told somebody about him and it would have gone into her file.

"Would you like me to try to contact him for you?" Mary asked. "Do you know where he lives?"

"No." Bitty stared down into her soup. "But he will come for me. That is what family does. I read it in that book."

Mary had some vague recollection of a children's book on the different kinds of family: biological, adopted, grandparented, as well as those that resulted from sperm donors, egg donors, IVF. The point was, no matter how they came about or what they looked like, in each instance, everybody was a unit, with a lot of love surrounding them.

"Bitty."

"Yes?"

Mary's phone began to vibrate in the pocket of the coat she still hadn't taken off—and she was tempted to let whoever it was go to voice mail. But with what the Brothers were doing tonight with that huge attack?

As she took her cell out and saw who it was, she thought, oh, God. "Butch? Hello?"

There was interference over the connection. Wind? Voices?

"Hello," she said more loudly.

"—coming to get you."

"What?" She rose from her chair. "What are you saying?"

"Fritz," the Brother shouted. "Coming for you! We need you out here!"

She cursed. "How bad?"

"Out of control."

"Crap," she breathed. "I'll drive out myself. Save time."

There were a series of pops, some cursing, and then distortion like Butch was running. "—text you location. Hurry!"

As the connection got cut off, she looked down at the girl and tried not to sound as panicked as she was. "Bitty, I'm so sorry. I have to go."

Those pale brown eyes lifted to hers. "What's wrong?"

"Nothing. I just . . . I'm going to grab Rhym for you. She'll sit here and maybe you two can have dessert?"

"I'm fine. I'm going to go up and pack so I'm ready for uncle."

Mary shook her head. "Bitty, before you do that, maybe you and I should try to find him first?"

"It's all right. He knows about me."

Steadying breath. For so many reasons. "I'll stop by later and see how you're doing."

"Thank you for the soup."

As the girl resumed eating, she didn't seem to care who was around or not around her—as usual. And it was with a pounding headache that Mary went in fast search of the intake supervisor, who was doing double duty as on-site personnel because one of the other social workers was out on maternity leave. After explaining to Rhym everything that had happened, Mary took off at a run, leaving the house and jumping into the Volvo.

The former Brownswick School for Girls was about a ten-minute drive away. She made it in seven, shooting down back roads, dodging around suburban developments, blowing through orange lights and

stop signs. The station wagon was not built for that kind of workout, the boxy, heavy weight lurching this way and that, but she didn't care. And holy crap, it felt like forever before she got to the outer edges of the neglected campus.

Getting out her phone, she eased off the gas and went into her texts.

Reading aloud, she said, "'Bypass main gates . . . go around—shit!"

Something shot out into the road, the figure moving rag-doll sloppy and tripping directly in front of her car. Slamming on the brakes, she hit the man—no, it was a slayer: The blood that speckled across the windshield was black as ink, and the thing took off once more, even though one of its legs looked broken.

Heart pounding, she swallowed and punched the gas again, afraid there were others behind it, but even more terrified by whatever was happening with Rhage. Rechecking her cell, she followed the directions around to the back side of the school, to a one-laner that took her into the shaggy mess of a landscape.

Just as she wondered where the hell she was supposed to go from there, the question was answered. Off across a meadow, the beast stood out among the abandoned buildings like something out of a SyFy Channel movie. Tall enough to reach the roofs, big enough to dwarf even a dormitory, mean as a tiger teased with a meal, the thing was in full attack mode.

Tearing off the roof of a shed with its teeth.

She didn't bother killing the engine.

Mary threw the Volvo in park and leaped out. In the back of her mind, she was aware that the uneven *bap-bap-bap* in the background was bullets flying, but she wasn't going to worry about that. What she was panicked about?

Whoever the hell was in that building.

As she ran toward the dragon, she put two fingers in her mouth and blew hard.

The whistle was high-pitched, loud as a scream—and made no impression at all as the shingles of the brick structure got spit out to one side.

The roar that followed was something she knew all too well. The beast was ready for his Happy Meal, and that whole rafter-relocation thing was its way of getting into the container.

Mary tripped over something—oh, God, it was a *lesser* that was missing an arm—and kept going, blowing another whistle. And a third—

The beast froze, its flanks pumping in and out, purple scales flashing in the darkness as if the thing were lit from within by an electrical source.

The fourth whistle brought its head around.

Slowing her run, Mary cupped her hands to her mouth. "Come here! Come on, boy!"

Like the beast was just the world's largest dog.

The dragon let out a chuff and then blew through its nostrils, the sound something between a whoopee cushion and a jet engine taking off.

"Come here, you!" she said. "Leave that alone. It's not yours."

The beast looked back at what was now just four brick walls and not much else, and a snarl curled its black lip off jagged teeth that would have given a great white dental insecurity. But like a German shepherd called to heel by its trainer, Rhage's curse turned away from its deconstruction job and bounded over to her.

As the dragon came through the weeds and brambles, its great weight shook the ground so badly, Mary had to put her arms out for balance.

But, impossible though it seemed, the thing was smiling at her, its gruesome face transformed by a joy that she wouldn't have believed if she hadn't seen it every time she was around the monster.

Stretching her hands up, she greeted that great, dropped head with soft words of praise, putting her palm on its circular cheek, letting it breathe in her scent and hear her voice. In her peripheral vision, she saw two people break out of the ruined building—make that one person who was able-bodied and running hard, and another who was up on a strong shoulder, obviously injured.

She didn't dare look directly at them to see who it was. Their best chance was her connection with the curse—and it was strange. As ugly as the thing was, as terrifying and deadly as it could be . . . she felt an abiding love warm her body. Her Rhage was in there somewhere, trapped under the layers of muscle and scales and third-party cognition, but more than that, she adored the beast as well—

The shots came from the right, and on instinct, she shouted and ducked to cover her head.

The dragon took over from there, wheeling toward the shooters at the same time it managed to wrap its tail around Mary and tuck her in against its flank. And then they were on the move. The ride was a rough one, like a mechanical bull suffering from power surges, and she held on to one of the larger barbs for dear life.

Thank God for that bony protrusion. Because what happened next involved a whole lot of "Twist and Shout."

First there were screams. Terrible, nightmare screams that she would have covered her ears to block out—except she didn't dare let go and risk getting thrown free—

Up and over.

A slayer, which was leaking like a sieve, went flying over the beast's back, and black blood hit Mary like bad-stench rain. The thing landed in a broken heap—and the chaser that followed, a second *lesser* that was likewise over-the-shouldered, hit the first like a boulder.

Oh . . . look. No head. Wonder where that—

Something that was vaguely round and had a face on one side and a thatch of blond hair on the other basketballed across the long grass that had been flattened under the dragon's enormous hind feet . . . paws . . . claws . . . whatever.

The beast kept her along for the ride for the rest of the fun and games. Talk about a hearty meal. In its wake, arms and legs, more heads—rarely a torso, because that was probably good eating—littered the ground. Fortunately, nothing looked like a Brother or a fighter, but oh, God, the smell. She was going to have to Neti Pot her sinuses for a month after this.

Just as she was losing track of time, right around the moment that she wasn't sure whether she could hold on for much longer, the beast's momentum slowed and stopped. Its great head swung left and right. Its body pivoted around. More with the searching.

The landscape seemed empty of anything that moved, nothing but static, decaying buildings, trees without leaves, and dark shadows that stayed put wherever she looked. The Brothers had to still be on the campus; no way they would leave without Rhage. But no doubt they were watching the great dragon from behind good cover. And as for the slayers? The balance of the enemy must have either taken off, been incapacitated, or gotten eaten.

The massive attack seemed to be over . . .

Dear Lord, the carnage left behind. How were they going to clean this up? There had to be a hundred *lessers* on the ground writhing, even if they were just in bits and pieces.

Mary patted her palm against the tail's thick base. "Thank you for keeping me safe. You can put me down now."

The beast wasn't as confident as she was and continued to survey the battle scene, the muscles of its shoulders twitching, those huge haunches tensed and ready to jump. Clouds of hot breath steamed out of its nostrils, flaring in the cold night air like part of a magician's show.

"It's all right," she said, stroking those scales.

Funny, she would have thought the things would be rough, but they were smooth and flexible, a fine interlacing of layers that shifted with the dragon's movements and flashed all the colors of a rainbow on top of a purple base.

"Really, it's all right."

After a moment, the beast's barbed hold on her uncoiled, and she stepped off onto the ground. Tugging her coat and her clothes back into place, she glanced around.

Then she put her hands on her hips and stared upward. "Okay, big guy, you did a great job. Thank you. I'm proud of you." As the thing chuffed and lowered its head, she petted the snout. "It's time to go, though. Can you let Rhage come back?"

That great head tossed in the air, the black blood of the *lessers* it had consumed flashing like an oil coating down its throat and chest. Snapping its jaws twice, the teeth and fangs locked with a sound like two SUVs slamming into each other grille-to-grille. The roar that came next was one of protest.

"It's okay," she murmured as she stood at its feet. "I love you."

The beast lowered its muzzle and chuffed out moist air.

And then justlikethat, its body collapsed, a sand castle hit with a wave, a wax figurine heated into a dissolved puddle. In its place, Rhage appeared facedown on the ground, his tremendous tattooed back curving around, his naked legs tucked in as if his stomach bothered him already.

"Rhage," she said as she crouched beside him. "You're back, my love."

When there was no response, not even an I'm-about-to-barf groan, she frowned. "Rhage . . . ?"

As she put her hand on his shoulder, the tattooed image of the dragon in his skin came alive, shifting around so that its head was under her touch.

"Rhage?" she repeated

Why wasn't he moving? Usually he would be disoriented and in pain, but he always turned to her, just as the beast's tattoo did, blindly seeking her voice, her touch, their connection.

"*Rhage.*"

Reaching for his upper arm, she put all her strength into pulling him over flat against the ground.

"Oh . . . God . . . !"

There was red blood on his chest. In the midst of all the black stains from what the beast had consumed, there was a very real, very terrifying, and very expanding fount of red blood in the center of his torso.

"Help!" she screamed at the landscape. *"Help!"*

The Brothers were already coming from every direction, abandoning their covers, sprinting across the battlefield that was strewn with mutilated slayers. And right on their heels, like a beacon from a benevolent god, was Manny's mobile surgical unit—and the RV was heading for them like the good doctor's foot was heavy on the accelerator.

Mary sought Vishous out of the crowd because of his EMT experience. "You need to help him!"

That red stain . . . was right at Rhage's sternum.

And her *hellren* had a strong heart—but it was not impenetrable. *What had happened?*

SEVEN

ishous was the first to get to Rhage as the brother reemerged from the flesh of the dragon—and shit had gone from pre-beast bad to post-curse worse. The guy wasn't moving, wasn't responding even to his *shellan*. His coloring was gray as a granite grave marker, and there was a lot of red blood.

Which was merely the tip of the iceberg. The real issue was how much had to be in that chest cavity.

"Help me!" Mary said as she put her hands over the wound and pushed down like she was trying to stem the leaking. "Help him, oh, God, V—"

The good news was that the surgical unit was hitting its brakes and Jane had come with Manny, having transferred over from her own vehicle. As soon as the surgeons popped the front doors of the RV, both docs hit the ground running with black duffel bags full of medical equipment.

"They're here," V said. Not that the pair could do much of anything.

"Has he been shot? I think he's been shot— Oh, God—"

"I know, come here. Let them look at hi—"

Mary shook her head and fought against being pulled back. "He's dying—"

"Give them some room to work. Come on."

Goddamn it, this was his fault. If he hadn't confronted . . . but what the fuck. The vision had been what it had, and it was this right here and now: Rhage flat on his back naked, his blood everywhere, V holding Mary as she strained and wept.

"Single gunshot wound," V announced. "Probable cardiac bleed with tamponade and pleural effusion."

God, he wished he could cover Mary's ears as he spoke, but like she didn't already know what was up?

The doctors didn't waste a moment, checking vitals as Ehlena jumped out of the back of the RV and brought the stretcher with her.

Vishous caught his mate's eye as Jane listened to Rhage's heart sounds, and when she shook her head, he knew without any further words that everything he was guessing was true.

Shit.

"What are they doing?" Mary babbled against him. "What are they going to do?"

V held the female tighter as she continued to mumble into his shoulder, her head wrenched around toward her mate. "They're going to help him, right? They're going to fix him . . . *right?*"

Jane and Manny began to talk in medical shorthand, and as Vishous caught the gist of the words, he closed his eyes briefly. When he popped his lids again, Manny was on one side of Rhage getting a chest tube in to drain fluids from around the lungs, and Jane was performing pericardiocentesis with a needle that seemed as long as her arm.

Which was a balls-to-the-wall move.

Ordinarily, that procedure was done with ultrasound guidance, but she had no choice except to go in blind through the fifth or sixth intercostal space next to the heart.

If she guessed wrong? Went in too far?

Mary struggled in his arms. "What are they doing—"

"He's arresting," Manny barked.

"Rhage!"

Ehlena was right there with the paddles, but what good was that in the case of a massive exsanguination? Hell, even if the chest tube and that needle did the job, neither was going to fix the trauma to the heart. The only chance of true survival was to put the brother on a bypass machine so Jane could work her magic and repair whatever tear or hole there was in a blood-less and motionless environment.

Abruptly, everything went into slow-mo as Rhage opened his eyes, dragged in a breath . . . and turned his face toward Mary.

His white lips began to move.

Mary shoved against V's hold, and he released her, allowing her to go to him. F.F.S., this could be the female's last chance to communicate with her mate. Make her peace with him. Sort out her arrangements to meet him on the other side.

Vishous frowned as the image of his forsaken mother lying on that bedding platform came back to him.

You'd better fucking make good on that promise, he thought at the heavens. You'd better man up and take care of the two of them.

Mary fell to her knees by Rhage's head and put her ear down to his mouth. The fact that the medical staff backed off was no doubt lost on her, but Vishous knew what that meant and it was nothing good. That heart rate that was being monitored so closely wasn't getting more stable. That blood pressure wasn't getting stronger. That bleeder wasn't fixing itself. And the tube and the needle hadn't gone nearly far enough.

V looked over at Butch, and as the cop stared back across the drama, V thought about how the three of them had formed such a tight bond. The troika, they were called. Tight as ticks, and annoying as shit, in the words of Tohr.

V glanced around. The other Brothers had all circled in close, forming a barrier of protection and worry around Rhage and Mary. None of the fighters had put their weapons away, however, and from time to time, a gunshot rang out as they picked off slayers whose bodies were showing too much animation.

As Mary began to speak with soft desperation, Vishous cursed again as it dawned on him that even though the couple had an endgame that resulted in them being together, the rest of them were going to lose Rhage—and Mary. Goddamn it, it was impossible to imagine the mansion without them.

Shit was not supposed to go down like this.

Strike that, he thought, as he remembered his vision. He didn't *want* it to end like this.

V shifted his eyes to his mate, and as Jane just shook her head, his blood ran cold.

Jesus Christ, *no*.

Abruptly, an image of Rhage at the Pit's Foosball table came to mind. The Brother hadn't been playing at the time; he'd been standing off to the side, chowing down on some kind of bedroll-as-burrito from Taco Bell. He'd been double-fisted eating, actually—with a chimichanga in the other hand. Alternating bites, the SOB had gone on to consume about four thousand calories, what with the mint-chocolate-chip ice cream he'd macked from their fridge and the half a chocolate cake he'd had for dessert before coming over from the main house.

Hey, V, the Brother had said at one point. *You ever going to shave off that ugly bath mat around your piehole? Or are you gonna keep looking like an Affliction reject as a public service for what not to do with a razor?*

So fucking irritating.

And wouldn't he give his remaining nut to have any part of that again. Even if only as a good-bye.

Time was way too finite: no matter how much of it you had with someone you loved, when the end came, it wasn't nearly enough.

"I love you," Mary croaked. *"I love you. . . ."*

As she stroked Rhage's blond hair off his forehead, his skin was so cold and strangely dry. His blood-speckled mouth was moving, but he didn't have enough air in his lungs to speak—and oh, God, they were gray . . . his lips were turning . . .

Mary looked up at Manny. Doc Jane. Ehlena. Then she met the eyes of the Brothers. John Matthew. Blay and Qhuinn.

The last one she stared at was Vishous . . . and she was horrified by the distant light in his eyes.

They had given up. All of them. Nobody was rushing to push her out of the way so they could intubate her mate, or shock his heart back into a rhythm, or crack his rib cage open and do whatever it took to get whatever was wrong back in working order.

Rhage arched with a groan and coughed some more blood up. And as he began to choke, she knew a new definition of terror.

"I'll find you," she told him. "On the other side. Rhage! Do you hear me? I'll find you on the other side!"

The gasping and rattling, the pain on his face, the agony of the group around them . . . everything became so crystal-clear that it hurt her eyes and ears, staining her brain forever. And strangely, she thought of Bitty and her mother and what had happened at the clinic.

Oh, shit, if she left the planet . . . what was going to happen to the girl? Who was going to care as much as she did for the now-orphan?

"Rhage . . ." Mary pulled at his shoulders. "Rhage! No! Wait, stay here—"

Later, she would try to tease out why the synaptic connection got made when it did. She would wonder how she had possibly thought of it all . . . would get into cold sweats about what would have happened next—and what would *not* have happened next—if that bolt of lightning hadn't come out of the blue when it did.

Sometimes the near miss was almost as traumatic as the impact.

But all that came afterward.

In the moment of her beloved's demise, at the very instant that she sensed he had left his body to make the trip to the Fade . . . suddenly, and for no reason that she could think of, she barked, "Roll him onto his side. Do it!"

She started pulling on him herself, but got nowhere—he was too heavy and she couldn't get a good grip on his massive torso.

Looking up, she motioned at the Brothers. "Help me! Fucking help me!"

V and Butch dropped down with her and eased Rhage onto his right side. Arching around her mate, Mary recoiled for a split second. The bright colors of the dragon's tattoo were fading, as if the brilliance of the depiction were a barometer of Rhage's health. Snapping back into focus, she put her hands on the beast's form—and, God, she hated how sluggish the response was.

"Come with me," she said urgently. "I need you to come with me."

This was crazy, she thought as she slowly drew her palms around Rhage's torso—but something drove her on, some kind of will that certainly didn't feel like her own. She wasn't going to argue, though, as the representation of the beast followed her touch—and it was strange: It wasn't until she made her way onto his ribs that she realized what she was doing.

Crazy, she thought again. Completely nuts.

Come on, it wasn't like the dragon had been trained in emergency medicine—much less cardiac surgery.

But she didn't stop.

"Help me," she choked to the beast. "Oh, please . . . figure it out, help him, save him . . . save yourself by saving him. . . ."

She just couldn't let Rhage go. It didn't matter in these last few

moments that there was a cosmic out for the two of them, that because of what the Scribe Virgin had given her, they didn't have to worry about some kind of separation. She was going to try to save him.

Working with her, the Brothers eased Rhage flat on his back again, and Mary's tears dropped onto her mate's bare chest as she transferred her hands over to the deceptively small hole about an inch to the right of his sternum.

God, she felt like the wound should be the size of a grave.

"Just fix it . . . somehow, please . . . *please* . . ."

The tattoo settled where she stopped.

"*Fix it. . . .*"

Time slowed to a crawl, and through watery eyes she stared down at Rhage's chest, waiting for a miracle. As minutes passed and she transitioned to a wretched emotional plane that was more keyed up than full-on panic, much lower than totally depressed, and so vast it was twice the size of the galaxy, she thought back to what Rhage had said about the hours he'd spent at her bedside in that human hospital: knowing she was going to die, unable to affect anything, lost even though he knew the address of where his physical body was.

It was as if gravity had no hold on me, he'd said, *and yet it was crushing me at the same time. And then you would close your eyes, and my heart would stop. All I could think of was that, at some moment in the future, you were going to look like that forever. And the only thing I knew for sure was that I was never going to be the same, and not in a good way . . . because I was going to miss you more than I would ever care about anything else in my life.*

But then the Scribe Virgin had changed all that.

Yet here Mary was . . . fighting to keep him alive.

And the *why*—when she really focused on the question—felt wrong, all wrong, and yet she wasn't going to stop.

At first, the flare of warmth didn't register in the midst of all her emotions. There was too much in the forefront of her mind, and the temperature change was so very subtle. The heat soon became impossible to ignore, however.

Blinking her eyes, she frowned down at her hands.

She didn't dare take her palms away to see what was happening underneath. "Rhage? Rhage . . . are you staying with us?"

The heat quickly became so intense, it radiated up her arms and warmed the air she breathed as she leaned over her mate. And then she felt a thrashing, as if the beast were rolling around—

Without any warning, Rhage threw open his mouth, dragged in a giant inhale, and jerked his torso off the ground, throwing her back on her ass. As her hands went flying, the tattoo was revealed and it was . . .

The depiction of the dragon had lost its contours, its colors having swirled together and yet remaining distinct, like one of those old-fashioned spin-art things she'd done at fairs when she was little.

She could no longer see the bullet wound.

There was a collective gasp, followed by some serious WTF-ing, and then a number of hallelujahs that were uttered with a Boston accent.

"Mary?" Rhage choked out in confusion.

"Rhage!"

Except before she could reach for him, he began to cough in great spasms, his head locking forward, his distended belly clenching, his jaw extending.

"What's wrong with him?" Mary said as she reached forward, even though it wasn't like she could do anything to help. Hell, the medical professionals looked equally confused, and they were the ones with the M.D.s after their names—

Rhage coughed the damn bullet out.

Right into her hand.

With one last, great heave, something came flying from his mouth and she caught the pointed piece of lead on reflex—as Rhage abruptly started breathing in deep, easy draws like nothing had ever been wrong with him.

Turning the thing over on her palm, she started laughing.

She couldn't help it.

Standing the slug between her thumb and forefinger, she held it up for the Brothers and the docs and the fighters—because Rhage was still blind. And then she straddled her mate's outstretched legs and took his face in her hands.

"Mary . . . ?" he said.

"I'm right here." She smoothed his hair back. "And so are you."

Instantly, he calmed even further, a smile pulling at his mouth. "My Mary?"

"Yes . . . I'm right here."

And then, dear Lord, she was crying so hard that she became as blind as he was. But it didn't matter. Somehow the beast had done the job and—

"Mary, I . . ."

"I know, I know." She kissed him. "I love you."

"Me too, but I'm going to throw up."

And with that, he moved her gently out of the line of fire, turned to the side, and vomited all over Vishous's shitkickers.

EIGHT

It was a helluva way to come back from the dead.

As Rhage tossed his cookies all over the place, his brain was nothing but scrambled eggs—

Okay, not a good idea to think of eggs in any form.

Round number two of the abdominal evacs took over his body, contorting him from head to foot, and as he let his guts do the talking, he heard V's dry voice overhead.

"Not my night," the Brother muttered. "So not my night with the barfing."

Huh? Rhage thought, before letting it go. All he really cared about, aside from the fact that he could now breathe and speak again, was his Mary. Sticking his arm out, he went in search of contact with her again—and she grabbed his palm right away, clasping him, holding on, both soothing him and giving him energy.

The instant the connection was made, his confusion started to ebb.

No, that wasn't exactly right. He had no idea how he'd managed to go from standing in front of the door to the Fade, faced with a choice that he was stunned to be confronted by even though he'd been aware that he'd been dying . . . to somehow slamming back into his own body and hearing his Mary's most perfect voice clear as day, without the radio static of fear and pain.

None of that mystery had been cleared up—but he just didn't give a fuck. As long as his Mary was with him? The rest was shit he could—

"Hurt?" he blurted. "Anyone hurt?"

Had the beast—

"Everyone is fine," she told him.

"I'm sorry about being sick." God, the post-party visual blackout was awful—but he'd take it over a dirt nap any night and twice on Sundays as the humans would say. "I'm sorry—"

"Rhage, we need to get you into the RV. And no, I'm not going to leave you—Jane's just going to check your vitals and then we have to get out of here. It's not safe."

Oh, right. They were at the campus, in the battlefield, no doubt sitting ducks—

With an explosion of memory, everything came back to him. The argument with V . . . the bum's rush out into the field . . .

The bullet through his heart.

With his free hand, he slapped against his chest, fumbling around to find a hole, feeling for blood—and finding that though there was a wash of sticky wetness down his torso . . . there was no discernible wound.

Just a strange patch in the center that seemed to glow with the heat of a banked fire.

And that was when the itching started. Beginning with the area over his heart, it shifted around in a solid patch, tracing over his ribs on one side, tickling under his arm, moving to the center of his back.

It was the beast, getting back into position. But why?

Yeah, file that one at the end of a very long line of huh-whats?

"Mary," he said into his blindness. "Mary . . . ?"

"It's all right—let's just get out of here together, and when we're safe, I'll explain everything—or at least tell you what I know."

Over the next hour, his *shellan* made good on that promise—but when did she ever let anyone down? She stayed beside him every inch of the way, from when he was hefted onto a gurney and given a bumpy ride over to Manny's RV . . . from the rough evac off the overgrown campus to the smooth glide of the paved roads to the highway . . . from the stop-and-go of the gate system that protected the Brotherhood's training center . . . to the at-last arrival and processing into his recovery room at the clinic.

The trip exhausted him—then again, he spent most of it throwing up *lesser* parts and choking on their foul-tasting black blood. And it was funny: Usually, he suffered through this aftermath part pissed off and ready for the suffering to be over. Tonight? He was so fucking grateful to be alive he didn't care that he had the world's worst stomach flu/food poisoning/seasickness thing going on.

You're going to fucking die tonight!

Damn it, Vishous was always right. Except Rhage had somehow beaten the prediction and come back from the Fade: For some reason, by some miracle, he was back—and he didn't think it was because the Scribe Virgin had done him a solid. She had already made a lottery-win deposit in his existential account when she'd saved his Mary, and besides, for the past couple of years, the Mother of the Race had been as out of touch as that kooky old relative you'd just as soon have backed off anyway, thank you very much.

So had his brother been wrong? The short answer to that was yup, considering Rhage was currently lying in a hospital bed instead of on some cloud up in the sky.

But why?

"Here," his Mary said. "I've got what you need."

True on so many levels, he thought as he turned his head toward the sound of her voice. When a series of bubbles tickled his nose, he shuddered in relief.

Plop-plop, fizz-fizz, fuck, yeah.

"Thank you," he mumbled—because he was afraid that if he tried to enunciate things too much he was going to start hurling again.

He drank everything that was in the glass and sagged back against the pillow—and then the sound of Mary putting the empty down and the feel of her weight on the mattress made him tear up for some stupid reason.

"I saw the Fade," he said quietly.

"Did you?" She seemed to shudder, the bed transmitting a subtle tremor from where she sat. "It's really scary to hear that. What was it like?"

He frowned. "White. Everything was white, but there was no light source. It was weird."

"I would have found you, you know." She took a deep breath. "If you hadn't come back, I would . . . I don't know how, but I would have found you."

The exhale he released lasted a lifetime for him. "God, I needed to hear that."

"Did you think otherwise?"

"No. Well, except for wondering if it was possible. You must have thought the same or you wouldn't have worked so hard to save me."

There was a quiet moment. "Yes," she whispered. "I did want to save you."

"And I'm glad it worked." Really, he was. Honest. "I, ah . . ."

"You know that I love you so much, Rhage."

"Why does that sound like a confession?" He forced a laugh. "I'm just kidding."

"I really hate death."

Okay, something was up. And not just about him. She sounded strangely . . . defeated, which was not the affect of a female who had dragged her *hellren's* sorry ass back from death's door.

Like, literally.

Rhage fumbled around to find her hands, and when he took hold of them, they trembled. "What else happened tonight? And don't say nothing. I can sense your emotion."

He couldn't smell it, though. There was too much *lesser* in his nose and in his digestive tract. You want to talk about fucking GERD?

"It's not as important as you." She shifted up and kissed him on the mouth. "Nothing is as important as you."

Where are you? he wondered to himself. My Mary . . . where have you gone?

"God, I'm tired," he said into the silence between them.

"Do you want me to leave you so you can sleep?"

"No." Rhage squeezed her hands and felt like he was trying to tether her to him. "Not ever."

In the quiet of the hospital room, Mary found herself studying Rhage's face as if she were trying to re-memorize the features that she knew darn well were indelibly marked in her brain. Then again, she wasn't actually dwelling on all that ungodly beauty. She was looking for some courage inside herself. Or something.

You'd think, given her profession, she'd be better in a moment like this.

Tell him, she thought. Tell him about Bitty and her mother, and the fact that you fucked up on your job and you feel like a failure.

The trouble was, all that confession-oriented blabber seemed so selfish considering he'd died only about an hour ago: It was like running up to someone who'd been in a bad car accident and wanting to explain to them how your night had sucked, too, because you'd gotten a speeding ticket and a flat tire.

"I would have absolutely come and found you somehow." As she repeated the words she'd already spoken, she knew he'd hit the nail on the head—because she did feel like she had something to confess. "Really. I would have."

Great, now *she* was sick to her stomach.

Except God, how could she possibly tell him that she'd fought so hard to save him not because of them and their relationship, or even his Brothers and the tragedy his loss would have been to the whole household, but because of someone else entirely? Even if that someone else and all her problems were an arguably noble cause? Even if that third party was a child newly orphaned in the world?

It just seemed like such a betrayal of the two of them and their life together. When you found true love, when you'd been granted that gift, you didn't make life-and-death decisions based on anybody else's situations or problems. Unless it was your child, of course—and heaven knew that she and Rhage would never, ever have any children.

Okay, ouch. That hurt.

"What hurts?" Rhage asked.

"Sorry. Nothing. I'm sorry—it's just been a long night."

"I know the feeling." He released her hands and stretched his enormous arms wide, the muscles carving out of his skin and throwing sharp shadows. "Come lay down. Let me feel like a male instead of a slab of meat—I wanna hold you."

"You do not have to ask twice."

Stretching out next to him on the bed, she put her head on his chest, right over his sternum, and took a deep breath. As the dark spice of his bonding scent bloomed in the air, she closed her eyes and tried to release all the chaotic recriminations that were tripping and falling around the inside of her skull, circus clowns that she found no amusement in whatsoever.

Fortunately, the contact with Rhage's skin, his body heat, his vital presence was like a Valium without the side effects. Tension slowly left her and those bastards with the rubber noses, the bad wigs and the dumb-ass floppy shoes faded into the background.

No doubt they would be back. But she couldn't worry about that right now.

"It's beating so strongly again," she murmured. "I love the sound of your heart."

Loved also the steady rise and fall of his powerful chest.

And what do you know . . . the sight of all that smooth, hair-less skin over all those thick, heavy muscles wasn't bad, either.

"You're so big," she said as she stretched her arm out and didn't even make it around his torso.

The chuckle that rumbled through him was a little forced. But he followed it up with, "Yeah? Tell me how big I am."

"You're very, very big."

"Just my chest? Or are you thinking of . . . other places?"

She knew that low drawl well . . . was utterly aware of where her mate had gone in his head—and sure enough, as she looked even further down his blanket-covered body, every inch of him was clearly still in working order, near-death experience or not.

Particularly a certain twelve inches. Give or take.

Her eyes went to the door and she wished the thing were locked. There were so many medical people around—okay, only three. But when you were interested in a little privacy, that was three too many.

As Rhage rolled his hips, that telltale thickening under the covers got a stroke that made him bite his lower lip, and Mary felt her body respond with a flush of heat. God, she hated the strange distance that had cropped up between them, that subtle disconnect she had been sensing for a while now: Somehow, even though their love hadn't diminished, they seemed to have been losing touch with each other . . . in spite of the fact that they said their ILYs at all the right times, and slept in the same bed, and didn't imagine being anywhere else with anybody else.

Although come to think of it, when was the last time they'd taken a night off, either one of them? Rhage had been so busy with the war and the attacks on Wrath and his throne—and ever since Bitty and her mother had come to Safe Place, Mary had had a professional preoccupation going that hadn't left her even when she'd been technically off the clock. Hell, worrying about Bitty and Annalye had stuck with her even while she'd been asleep.

In fact, she dreamed of the little girl almost every day now.

Too long, Mary thought. It had been way too long since she and Rhage had focused on each other properly.

So, yes, even though it was a Band-Aid that would no doubt be temporary, and in spite of the public place they were in, and yup, without regard to the fact that Rhage had been dead earlier . . . Mary sneaked her hand under the sheets and moved her palm slowly down her mate's ribbed stomach.

Rhage hissed and groaned, his pelvis rolling again, his arms straightening so that he could grip the bed rails. "Mary . . . I want you. . . ."

"My pleasure."

His arousal was thick and long, and as she circled it, the velvet feel of him and the sounds he made in the back of his throat and the way his bonding scent flared even further were exactly the kind of up-close they needed. This was all about the two of them; nothing else was welcome—not her job, not his, not her worries, not his stress. In that respect, sex was like the best Swiffer in the world, taking away the dust and fallout from Normal Life that had dulled their connection, leaving the love they had for each other as sparkling-fresh as ever.

"Mount me," Rhage demanded. "Get naked and get up on me."

Mary glanced at the medical equipment that was all around his bed and wanted to curse. Talk about blips on a screen. "What about your machines? Things are starting to get really excited."

"Weeeeeeeeeeeeell, that's 'cuz *I'm* starting to get really excited."

"If they go up too much—"

Right on cue, the heart monitor's alarm started going off shrilly. And just as Mary ripped her hand out from under, Ehlena came racing into the room.

"It's fine," Rhage said to the nurse with a laugh. "I'm fine—trust me."

"I'll just check things out—" Except then Ehlena stopped. And smiled. "Oh."

"Yeah, oh." Rhage had the colossal nerve to lie back like a lion

about to get fed. He even winked in Mary's general direction. "So you think maybe we can unplug me for a little bit?"

Ehlena chuckled and shook her head as she reset the machine. "Not a chance. Not until you've had a some more time stabilizing under your belt."

Rhage leaned into Mary and whispered, "I want *you* back under my belt. That's what I need."

The nurse headed for the door. "I'm right down in the OR if you need me. We're about to operate."

Rhage frowned. "On who?"

"There were a couple of injuries. Nothing serious, though, don't worry. Be good, you two, 'kay?"

"Thanks, Ehlena." Mary gave the other female a wave. "You're the best."

As the door eased shut, Rhage dropped his voice. "Unplug me."

"What?"

"Either you do it or I do it—but I need you, *now*."

When Mary didn't make a move, Rhage started blindly for the machines, knocking into a computer on a stand that looked like it cost more than a house.

"Rhage!" Mary started laughing as she gathered his hands and pulled them back. "Come on—"

Next thing she knew, he'd lifted her up and over his hips, settling her right on top of his erection. And yup, as soon as her weight appeared to register, that *beep-beep-beep* thing started speeding up again.

"You can hook me back up as soon as it's done," he informed her. "And even though it'll be a sacrifice, if you only want to give me a handjob, I'll settle for waiting for you till a little later. But I've come close to death once already tonight—don't make your *hellren* die from the wanting."

Mary had to smile at him. "You slay me."

"And you could lay me? Please?"

She shook her head in spite of the fact that he couldn't see her. "You just don't take no for an answer, do you."

"When it comes to you?" Rhage grew serious, his Bahama blue eyes staring blindly at her, his beautiful face growing grim. "You are both my strength and my weakness, Mary mine. So what do you say?

You want to make my whole night? And may I remind you . . . I died in your arms earlier."

Mary burst out laughing, and as she fell forward onto him, she ducked her head into his neck. "I love you so much."

"Ahhhh, now that's what I like to hear." Big hands stroked over her back. "So what's it going to be, Mary mine?"

NINE

Watching from the shadows was not the normal course for Xcor, son of no one.

As a lawless fighter and the deformed, de facto leader of a renegade team of sociopaths, he was more used to action. Preferably with his scythe. Or knife. Gun. His fists. Fangs.

He might not have been descended of the Bloodletter, as he had once believed, but he had indeed been reared by that most cruel of warriors—and the brutal lessons that had been imparted in the war camp by that hand in a spiked glove had been learned well.

Attack before you are attacked had been the first and most important of all other rules. And it had remained his primary operating principle.

There were times, however, when a certain neutrality of action was required, much as inner instincts argued to the contrary, and as he sheltered behind the burned-out shell of a car in the very worst part of Caldwell's underbelly of alleys, he reined himself in. Up ahead, standing just out of the pools of dirty light cast by thirty-year-old street lamps, three *lessers* were exchanging items; a pair of backpacks being turned over for a single satchel.

Given what he had observed of late on the streets, he was confident

that one load was cash and the other black-market wares of the powdered and injectible varieties.

Breathing in, he sorted the scents out and cataloged them. The trio had yet to fade to white, their dark hair and brows signifying their recent recruitment into the Lessening Society—and indeed, that was all one came across in the New World. Ever since he and his band of bastards had made the trip across the ocean from the Old Country, the only enemy they had encountered was this freshly inducted, mostly inferior variety.

Rather lamentable. But where there was a dearth in quality, there was an abundance of quantity.

And the slayers had found themselves a new business venture, hadn't they. This particular threesome was not going to go any further in their drug-dealing endeavors, however. As soon as they finished their little handoff, he was going to slaughter them—

Three different cell phone tones went off, all muffled, all registering only because of Xcor's sharp hearing. Things moved quickly from there. After each of them checked what had to be a text, they argued for a mere moment; then scrambled into a boxy vehicle, the gleaming silver exterior of which was plastered with pictures of tacos and pizza.

As an illiterate, he was unable to read the writing.

As a fighter, he was damned if he were going to let his targets get away.

When the vehicle trundled past him, Xcor closed his eyes and dematerialized onto its top, finding a place in which to settle his frame thanks to a sunken area behind an airshaft of some kind. He had no thought of calling for back-up. No matter where the *lessers* were going or who they would meet up with, if he were overpowered, he could depart without any knowing he was about.

Truer words ne'er were spoken, as it turned out.

The fact that the driver proceeded in the direction of the Hudson River was hardly a surprise. Given the wares they were peddling, one could easily surmise some conflict, armed or otherwise, might require reinforcements in the area below the bridges—or mayhap it was something with the Brotherhood. But alas, that rancid concrete jungle was not their destination. A ramp was soon entered upon, and the highway was surmounted with gathering speed, necessitating that he arrange himself into a tuck and secure his body against the wind draft by wrapping his arms around the base of the shaft and holding on readily.

The ride was rough, although not from uneven terrain, more from the biting cold and the speed. Not long thereafter, however, another exit was taken and the velocity slowed such that he could lift his head and identify a suburban section of abodes that was north of downtown. That populated area did not last. Soon, a more rural area presented itself.

No, it was a parkland or such.

No . . . it was something else.

When at last a left was taken into a property of sorts, he could not tell where he was. A rather lot of empty, overgrown land . . . a rather lot of abandoned buildings. A school? Yes, he thought.

But the place was not for humans anymore.

The scent of *lessers* was in the air to such a penetrating degree that his body responded to the layers of stench, adrenaline pumping, instincts firing up and ready to fight—

The first of the mutilated slayers presented themselves in a scattering across the thick undergrowth, and as the vehicle continued onward, more and more appeared.

Closing his eyes, he calmed himself and dematerialized to the flat roof of a five-story building up ahead of where the truck eventually stopped. Stepping carefully over fallen branches and banks of decaying leaves floating in cold puddles of water, Xcor worked his way over to the edge. The true scale of what had to have been a massive attack on the Lessening Society was evidenced by the acres of carnage in the very center of campus: A great swath of trampled grasses and trees was layered with body parts, half-dead, semi-alive slayers, and a tidal wave's worth of the Omega's black, oily blood.

It was like a depiction of *Dhund* itself.

"The Brotherhood," he said unto the wind.

That was the only explanation. And as he considered what their attack strategy had to have been, he was envious that they had been given the gift of this battle. How he wished it had been for him and his soldiers—

Xcor wrenched around.

Something was moving on the roof behind him. Speaking. Cursing.

In the darkness, and with utter silence, he withdrew a steel blade from his chest holster and sank low on his thighs. Stalking forward in the cold gusts, he tracked the sounds that he was downwind of and tested the air. It was a human.

"—footage! No! I'm telling you, it's some shit!"

Xcor loomed behind the feeble rat without a tail, and remained unnoticed as the human spoke into his cell phone.

"I'm up on a roof—I caught the fuckin' thing on vid! No, Chooch, T.J. and Soz took off, but I came up here—it was a dragon—what? No, Jo, the LSD wore off this morning—no! If it's a flashback, why did I just post it on YouTube?"

Xcor raised his knife over his shoulder.

"No! I'm serious I—"

The human shut up as Xcor struck him on the back of the head with the hilt of his weapon. And as the body went limp and sagged to the side, Xcor took the phone and put it up to his ear.

A female voice was saying, "Dougie? Dougie! What happened?"

Xcor ended the connection, put the phone in his jacket, and leaned over the lip of the roof. The three *lessers* he'd come in with hadn't made it far from their food truck. They seemed dumbfounded by what they were surrounded by, incapable of responding given the magnitude of the losses.

Best he address them first before they took off.

Stepping over the collapsed male, he jumped off the building, dematerializing as he fell, and rematerializing on the ground before he crash-landed and killed himself.

The slayers saw him, and that was exactly what he wanted.

It would make the killing of them a bit more of a challenge.

As the three raced to get back into their truck, he ghosted himself on top of the one in the rear, stabbing it in the chest on a reach around and sending it back to the Omega on a brilliant flash and a *pop!* Next, he lunged forward and grabbed the second one around the shoulders, wrenching it off balance and slitting its throat before casting it aside. The third he captured by the hair just as it attempted to shut itself in the truck on the driver's side.

"No, mate," he growled as he jerked the thing off its feet. "All for one, one for all."

The *lesser* landed flat on its back, and before it could respond, Xcor drove his boot into its face, crushing the bone structure, collapsing the features, rendering the eyes nothing but loose pools of fluid.

Xcor looked over his shoulder. It would be unlike the Brotherhood to leave a mess like this for humans to find. Even though the campus was abandoned, soon enough, random Homo sapiens of the youthful

variety would breach the untidy landscape. Just as the one on that roof had.

Something must have happened during the course of the fighting. A critical injury, perhaps, that precluded clean-up, at least in the short term—

Xcor never saw it coming. Never heard a thing.

One moment, he was fully cognizant of his environs.

And the next, someone or something had done unto him what he had wrought upon that human on the roof.

He didn't even have time for a last thought, so decisive was the blow to his head.

Vishous lowered his arm slowly as he stared down at the massive male who had just collapsed at his shitkickers.

Then he immediately brought his gun back up, two-handing the thing and moving it in a circle around himself.

"Where ya boys at, true?" he said under his breath. "Huh, motherfuckers? Where you at?"

There was no way Xcor, head of the Band of Bastards, had come here alone. No fucking way.

V just wasn't that lucky.

Except nothing came at him. No one counter-attacked. Nobody ran out from a building or from behind a tree with a gun up, shooting. All there was were slayer parts and torsos on the ground, the cold wind hitting him in the face, and a whole lot of quiet.

The sound of a whistle over on the left alerted him to Butch's position. And then there was another from the right. A third from way up ahead.

V whistled back and his brothers came jogging over.

He kept his eyes on Tohr, and as soon as the fighter was within range, V pointed his gun directly at that leather-clad chest. "Stop. Right there."

Tohr pulled up short. Lifted his palms. "What the hell are you doing?"

"Butch, roll him over," V gritted, nodding to the vampire at his feet.

The instant Tohr saw who it was, his hands dropped and his fangs got good and bared.

"Now do you get it," V muttered. "I know it's your right to kill him, but you can't. Do we understand each other. You're not going to off him here, true."

Tohrment growled. "That's not your call to make, V. Fuck you, that fucker is mine—"

"I will fucking shoot you. Are we clear? Stop right there."

Apparently, the Brother wasn't aware of having stepped forward. But Butch and everyone else caught it right away—and the cop approached Tohr cautiously.

"The kill can be yours," Butch said. "But we take him back with us first. We talk to the bastard, get the intel—then he's yours, Tohr. No one else is going to do the final deed but you."

Phury nodded. "V's right. You kill him now, we lose the interrogation. Be logical about this, Tohr."

Vishous glanced around. The four of them had returned to the campus with the idea of stabbing as much as they could back to the Omega and doing what clean-up they were able—but this little discovery changed that immediate goal.

"Butch, you drive him back in the Hummer. Now." V shook his head at Tohr. "And no, you're not going with him as back-up."

"You got me all wrong," Tohr said grimly.

"Do I? Are you aware you have a dagger in your hand? No?" As his brother looked down with some surprise, V shook his head. "Don't think I'm the one with the head wedge. You stay with us, Tohr. The cop's got this."

"I'm calling in Qhuinn and Blay," Butch said as he got out his phone. "I want them with me."

"And this is why I love you," V muttered as he kept his eye on Tohr.

The Brother hadn't put the dagger away yet. And that was fine. Soon as Xcor was on the way out, V was going to make sure that Tohr got to put that murderous impulse to good use.

A moment later, Blay and Qhuinn materialized onto the scene, and both of them cursed when they saw the ugly, scarred face that was staring up sightlessly from the out-cold body.

Butch made quick work of handcuffing Xcor, and then he and Qhuinn footed-and-handed the bastard, carrying him like a sack of potatoes toward the bulletproof, black-on-black Hummer that had been parked behind one of the classrooms. The nasty-looking machine

was actually Qhuinn's second version of the SUV, the first having been stolen when he'd *hyslop*ed it in front of a drugstore the previous winter.

V didn't move a muscle until he saw that the damn thing was headed off the property at pedal-to-the-metal speed.

"It's not that I don't trust you," he said to Tohr. "I just don't—"

Vishous shut up. And went motionless again.

"What is that?" Phury asked.

V had no clue. And that was not good. The only thing he was sure of was that the landscape had abruptly changed in some subtle yet undeniable way, a wave of buffering extending out over the bodies of the slain like a shadow had been cast over the campus.

"Shit," Vishous hissed. "The Omega is coming!"

TEN

Beauty was in the ears of the beholder.

As Rhage ran his hands up and down Mary's thighs, he might have been blind, but he knew exactly how gorgeous his *shellan* was as she sat on his hips and balanced her weight on the palms she'd planted on his pecs.

"So what's it going to be?" he prompted as he rolled his pelvis.

With his erection stroking her core, even through the bed covers and the slacks she was wearing, her reply was husky.

"How can I ever," she whispered, "say no to you?"

God, those words . . . and even more than that, her voice. They made him think of the first night he'd met her. It had been down here in the training center, right after the beast had made an appearance. He'd been blind then, too, and walking down the corridor, looking for a workout to distract him from his recovery boredom. She had come to their facility with John Matthew and Bella, as an interpreter for the boy who'd been mute and needed ASL to communicate.

The second she had spoken to him, her voice had chained him sure as if every syllable she'd uttered had come with steel links. He'd known that moment he was going to have her.

Of course, at the time, he hadn't planned on her being the love of his life. But his bonding had had other ideas, and thank God for that.

Thank God, too, that she'd been willing to have him.

"Come here, my Mary—"

She shifted to one side. "But I'm hooking you back up the instant you finish."

Rhage smiled so wide, his front teeth got a chill. "Fine by me—wait, what? Where are you going?"

Even with his protests, Mary didn't stop what turned out to be a full on dismount, not just an unplug.

"We need to keep this partially discreet." The beeping stopped. "And I'm serious about putting that thing back to work."

Twisting to the side, he reached out in his blindness, grabbing for her waist and pulling her back in his direction. "Come here—"

All thought ended as he felt her hand on top of the covers . . . right over his cock.

The sound that boiled up out of him was part *mmmmmm* and part moan. Her touch, even distilled through the blankets, was enough to kick-start his heart, soft-boil his blood, overheat his skin with a delicious tingle.

And leave him a thin inch away from an orgasm.

The hospital bed's mattress shifted as she stretched out next to him, and her palm moved under the sheet, traveling oh, so very downward. Spreading his legs to give her all the access she wanted, he arched his head back and bowed his spine toward the heavens as she gripped his erection. Shouting her name, he felt the beast surge as well, the dragon riding the crest of pleasure along with him, while still staying leashed.

As if it had learned its good manners.

"My Mary . . ." And then he gasped. "Oh, *yeah*."

She started stroking him nice and slow, and it was strange the way she affected him. The sex made him feel so powerful, so male, so fucking juiced that he wondered how his flesh managed to contain the great roar of erotic heat . . . and yet she was the master of all of him and the entirety of his reaction, utterly in control, dominating him in ways that made him totally weak before her.

And goddamn that was sexy.

"You're so beautiful," she said in a thick voice. "Oh, look at you, Rhage . . ."

He loved the idea that she was watching him, seeing what she was doing to him, reveling in the hold she had on him—literally. And if he couldn't touch her himself, if he had to be a good boy and keep his hands to himself, at least she could enjoy bringing him to his knees and knowing that she alone had the ability to do this to him.

After all, in spite of whatever distance had cropped up between them lately, nothing had changed for him. Mary was the only female he wanted, the only one he saw, scented, couldn't wait to be with.

This was good for them. This sizzling sexual connection was important for them right now.

Especially as she fell into a rhythm that pumped his shaft and squeezed his tip. Faster. Faster still. Until he was panting and the sweet pain of anticipation ripped through his body and his head spun like a top.

Not tired anymore. Nope.

"Mary." He strained on the bed, arching up hard, gripping the mattress on one side and a railing on the other. "Mary, wait . . ."

"What is it?"

As she stopped, he shook his head. "No, keep going—I just want you to do something for me."

"What's that?" she said as she ran her palm back up his shaft . . . and then down . . . and then up . . .

What the fuck had he—oh, right.

"Come here, come closer." When she did, he whispered something in her ear.

Her laugher made him smile himself. "Seriously," she said. "That's what you want."

"Yes." He arched his body again, rolling his hips so that his erection stroked itself in her hold. "Please? And I'll beg if you'd like. . . . I love it when I beg you for things."

Mary shifted up higher on the hospital bed and began to work him in earnest again. Then she leaned in close to his own ear . . .

. . . and with perfect pronunciation said, "Antidisestablishmentarianism."

With a mad barking curse, Rhage came so hard he saw stars, his erection kicking out against her hand, his cum getting things very, very messy underneath those covers. And all the while, his only thought was of how much he loved his female.

How very much he loved her.

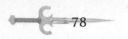

*　　*　　*

Two doors down from Rhage's vocabulary-induced orgasm, Layla was sitting up in her own hospital bed, a giant ball of red yarn on one side of her, the longest neck scarf in the history of the world stretching down to the floor on the other side. In between the two? A belly that was growing so swollen from the twin youngs she carried that she felt as though someone had folded a mattress up and strapped the thing to her torso.

Not that she was in a position to complain. The two were healthy, and as long as she stayed in bed, she knew she was giving them the best chance of survival. And indeed, Qhuinn, their sire, and his beloved, Blay, spoiled her mercilessly down here, as if they both would rather have been the ones to go through the stay-put for her.

Such wonderful males they were.

As she made another turn at the end of yet another row, she smiled as she remembered Blay suggesting that she knit something as that had helped his mother, Lyric, get through her own bedrest with him. It had proven to be good advice—there was something singularly soothing about the click-click of the needles, and the soft yarn between her fingers, and the progress that she could measure tangibly. However, at this point, she was either going to have to cut the thing into segments or give it to a giraffe.

After all, watching *Real Housewives* marathons without doing something, anything productive was positively untenable. No matter what Lassiter contended to the contrary.

Now *Couples Therapy* with Dr. Jenn? That was maybe a different story—although, of course, she didn't learn things relevant to her own relationship. Because she didn't have a male to call her own.

No, she had an unhealthy obsession that had crashed and burned. Which was a good thing—even though the loss of that which she should never have wanted in the first place had caused unimaginable, and unjustifiable, pain.

But one did not fall in love with the enemy, after all. And not just because one was a Chosen.

It was because Xcor, and his Band of Bastards, had declared war upon Wrath and the Brotherhood.

That was why—

"Stop it," she muttered as she closed her eyes and halted her needles. "Just . . . *stop*."

Indeed, she did not think she could bear her guilt and the knowledge of her betrayal of those whom she held dearest another moment. Yet what was another a course? Yes, she had been lied to and then coerced . . . but in the end, her heart had gone where it should not have.

And in spite of everything, had ne'er been returned unto her.

As she heard yet another sound out in the corridor, she glanced at her door and forced herself to get lost in the distraction. There had been a lot of activity in the training center tonight—voices, footfalls, doors opening and shutting—and somehow, it all just made her feel more isolated instead of less so. Then again, when things were quiet, there were fewer cues to remind her of everything she was missing.

Yet she wouldn't have been anywhere else.

Putting her hand on her round stomach, she thought, yes, life as she knew it was of late more inwardly focused than outwardly so—and anytime she got antsy, all she had to do was remind herself of everything that was at stake.

She may never have the love that Qhuinn and Blay shared, but at least the young would be hers and herself theirs.

That was going to have to be enough for her life, and it would be. She couldn't wait to hold them, care for them, watch them thrive.

Assuming she survived the birthing. Assuming all of them did.

As a soft alarm went off on her phone, she jumped and fumbled to silence the chiming sound. "Is it time already?"

Yes, it was. Her freedom had arrived. Thirty minutes to stretch and walk and go for a wander.

Within the confines of the training center, of course.

Pushing the knitting toward the base of the needles, she stuck the tips into her ball of yarn and stretched her arms and her legs, pointed her toes, flexed her fingers. Then she shifted her feet off the bed and eased her weight onto them. The demands of the pregnancy and all of her forced inactivity had led to a certain weakness in her muscles, one that was not cured no matter how much she fed from Qhuinn and Blay—so she had learned to be cautious whenever she stood up.

First stop was the bathroom, something that she was allowed to use readily, but inevitably put off. There was no need to take a shower, as she had done so twelve hours ago during that half hour to be up and around.

No, this was going to be purely investigatory.

What was going on out there?

As she headed over to the door, she smoothed her hair, which seemed to be growing as fast as her scarf was: the blond waves were down past her hips now, and she supposed she should have it cut at some point. Her flannel nightgown was likewise long and loose, rather the size of a flowered tent, and her slippers made a *shhht-shhht-shhht* sound over the bare floor. With her back already aching, and one arm thrown out to steady herself, she felt as though she were centuries older than she actually was.

Pushing open the way out, she—

Immediately stepped back.

Such that her butt hit the closing panel.

Across the way, a pair of males were standing tall and proud, identical expressions of tension marking their faces.

And by identical, she meant exactly the same.

They were twins.

As they focused on her, both recoiled sure as if they'd seen a ghost.

"Watch yourself," came a nasty growl.

Layla whipped her head toward the warning. "Zsadist?"

The Brother with the scarred face stalked over to her, placing his body, with all its weapons, in between her and the two strangers, even though neither of the males had made an aggressive move toward her. Unsurprisingly, it was a very successful block. Zsadist's torso and shoulders were so large she could no longer see the pair—and that was clearly his plan.

"Get back in there with him," Zsadist barked. "Before I *put* you in that room."

There was no argument, and abruptly, the foreign scents dissipated as if they had indeed disappeared from the hall.

"They did naught unto me," she said. "Actually, I think if I'd gone, 'Boo!' they might well have run off."

Z glanced over his shoulder. "I think you should return to your room."

"But I'm allowed to stretch my legs twice a night?"

The Brother gently, but firmly, took her elbow and escorted her back through her door and over to her bed. "Not right now. I'll come tell you when it's okay. We have some unanticipated visitors, and I'm taking no chances with the likes of you."

"Who are they?"

"No one you need to worry about—and they're not staying long."
Z settled her back into position. "May I bring you some food?"

Layla exhaled. "No, thank you."

"Something to drink, then?"

"I'm fine. Thank you, though."

After bowing deeply, the Brother departed, and she half expected
to hear the distant sounds of him pistol-whipping those two soldiers
just for looking at her. But that was the way of things. As a pregnant
female, she was the most valuable thing on the planet not just to her
young's sire, but to every single member of the Brotherhood.

It was like living with a dozen older, bossy, over-protective brothers.

Or Brothers, as was the case.

And ordinarily, she might have challenged even Zsadist. But she
hadn't recognized those big males, and God knew she'd already gotten
into plenty of trouble fraternizing with fighters she didn't know—and
they had to be soldiers. They were built heavy and strong, and they had
been wearing holsters.

Albeit empty ones.

So they were not enemies, she decided or they wouldn't have been
allowed in the training center at all. But they weren't exactly trusted,
either.

Unbidden, an image of Xcor's harsh face came to mind—and the
sting of pain that went through her was so strong, the young shifted
in her belly as if they felt it, too.

"Stop it," she whispered to herself.

Reaching for the T.V. remote, she turned on the big screen across
the way. Fine. She would stay here until those strangers left. Then she
would go and sit with Qhuinn's brother, Luchas, who was in recovery
two doors away and seemed to look forward to her regular visits. Then
perhaps a blather with Doc Jane at her desk, or maybe Blay and Qhuinn
would be back from their shifts by then and they would walk her all
the way down to the classrooms.

Whoever those soldiers were, she doubted the Brothers would let
them stay longer than absolutely necessary. At least going by Zsadist's
reaction.

And all the weapons of which they'd so clearly been stripped.

ELEVEN

No time. Abso-fucking-lutely no goddamn time.

As a rash of evil permeated the air, Vishous took off his lead-lined glove and lifted his glowing palm. Closing his eyes and focusing—because his life, and the lives of his two brothers, did in fact depend on it—he sent out a series of buffering impulses of his own—except the *mhis* he extended was just a pocket in the overall campus landscape, a small section measuring no more than the distance between two inches in front of his face and two inches behind Phury and Tohr's bodies.

Thank God the Hummer was off the property.

"No one move," V commanded as a wavy, iridescent border formed around them all, rather like a child's bubble blown from dishwashing soap.

He had no idea whether this was going to work, but shit knew it had to—the atmosphere was turning a deep shade of malevolence. Hell, even with the *mhis* in place, his skin prickled with a warning for him to *ruuuuuuuuuuuuuuuuuuun!*

And that was when the Omega itself appeared about a hundred and fifty yards up ahead.

Talk about your anti-climaxes. On the surface, the inky transpar-

ent figure in its Clorox-white robes looked about as intimidating as
an animated chess pawn. But that was just going on a visual assessment. Internally, every cell that made up his body, each neuron that
fired in his brain, all the emotions he had ever had or would ever have
started to scream sure as if he were under a dire mortal attack.

Behind him, a soft muttering started, and V glanced over his
shoulder. Phury had started to pray in the Old Language.

"Shhh," Vishous whispered.

Phury immediately canned the talk, but his lips kept moving, the
prayer continuing on. And yeah, V thought of his mother doing her
I-can't-even upstairs—and was tempted to tell the guy he was wasting
his time. But whatever. No reason to rob the brother of his illusion.

Besides, if the *mhis* didn't work? The three of them and what they
did, or did not pray to, were going to moot point it right off the planet.

The Omega slowly made a turn, surveying his "dead," and V
tensed up so hard, he was in danger of falling forward like a plank.
The evil's gaze did not linger on where he and his brothers were standing, however, suggesting that the *mhis* was working—probably at least
partially because the Scribe Virgin's brother was so distracted by the
devastation to his Society.

Shit, that's my uncle, V thought grimly.

And then the Omega went on a float, traveling over the trampled,
black blood–soaked lawn in the same hovering way V's mother ambulated.

Rain began to fall from the sky, the cold drops hitting V's hair and
nose, his shoulders, the backs of his hands. Even though the stuff
tickled his skin, he made no move to wipe it off or shelter himself—
and frankly, yeah, he could have done without the reminder of exactly
how flimsy their optical illusion was. That rain made it through?

Hell, you could pop a newspaper over your dome and get a better
umbrella result.

Fuck.

From time to time, the Omega paused and bent down to pick up
an arm, a leg, a head. It threw whatever it was back on the ground, as
if it were searching for something in particular. And then it stopped
without warning.

A low wail sounded out over the campus, the sound weaving in
and around the empty, rotting buildings without echoing.

And then the Omega extended its palms out straight.

A sucking breeze hit V in the back and pulled his hair into his face and eyes, streaking forward his jacket, too, until the leather began to flap and he had to gather the thing against his body.

All at once, the debris of the slaughter, all those slayer pieces and stains, liquefied into a viscous shadow that pulled into itself, becoming a tidal wave that headed for its master, its home, its core.

The Omega absorbed it all, reclaiming the part of itself that it had given to its inductees during their initiation ceremonies, recalling its essence, reabsorbing everything until the battlefield was as clean as before the attack had been waged, nothing but trampled grass and downed trees to show what the beast and the Brotherhood had done.

When it was all over, the Omega stood in the center of the school's square, turning around and around as if it were double-checking its work. And then, as quickly as it had arrived, the entity disappeared into itself, a subtle flash the only leftover of its presence—and even that was gone a heartbeat later.

"Wait," V hissed. "We wait."

He wasn't about to take for granted that the Omega was up and out of there for real. The problem was, dawn was coming . . . and yup, if the *mhis* couldn't protect the three of them from rain, it wasn't going to do dick about straight-on sunlight.

But they could afford to stay a little longer. Just in case.

Better to be conservative than discovered. Besides, he needed a moment so his one remaining testicle could drop back down into place again.

Fuck.

TWELVE

"I do not believe this is necessary."

Back at the Brotherhood's training center, Assail stared down his body at the dark-haired human who was closing the gash on his calf and ankle with a needle and thread. When the man made no response and did not slow in his ministrations, Assail rolled his eyes.

"I said—"

"Yeah, yeah." The guy poked his needle through skin once more and pulled until the black thread was taut. "You've made yourself perfectly clear. The only thing I'll say back is that MRSA doesn't give a fuck if you're a vampire or a human, and leaving a six-inch open wound on your leg is the definition of stupid."

"I heal rather fast."

"Not that fast, buddy. And can you stop twitching? I feel like I'm working on a goldfish in water."

Actually, he could not. His extremities had their own ideas at the moment, and as he checked the wall clock and calculated how little time there was before dawn, the trembling got worse—

The door to the room swung open and his cousins came back in.

"I thought you didn't want to watch," Assail muttered. And in-

deed, Ehric, the one on the left, was studiously not looking at the fix-it job.

As proficient a killer as the male was, his stomach turned squeamish at clinical matters, a contradiction that could be a source of amusement—but was not, currently.

Indeed, Assail was not in the mood for any manner of levity. He hadn't consented to be brought here to this facility of the Brotherhood's for treatment. What he had wanted to do was go back to his house upon the Hudson and scratch the itch that was quickly turning to a roar.

"When shall you be finished?" he demanded.

"I'm X-raying your shoulder next."

"There is no need."

"Where's your medical degree from?"

Assail cursed and lay back flat upon the gurney. The medical chandelier above him, with its brilliant lights and its microscope arm, was like something out of a science-fiction movie. And as he closed his eyes, it was impossible not to remember coming here with his Marisol, right after he had gotten her free from Benloise . . . the pair of them passing through the extensive gating system, heading underground, entering this stellar facility.

He tried to train his mind elsewhere, however. That thought destination was simply too painful to bear.

"I shall need to depart prior to dawn," he blurted. "And I want our weapons, phones, and other personal articles returned to us promptly."

The doctor did not reply until he had put in his last stitch and tied a tight little knot at the base of Assail's ankle. "You mind telling your boys to step out again for a minute?"

"Why?"

Ehric spoke up. "Zsadist wants us in here. And I am disinclined to argue with the Brother, as I am unarmed and desirous of retaining the blood supply to my head."

The doctor sat back on his rolling stool, and for the first time, Assail read the stitching on the human's white coat: Dr. Manuel Manello, Chief of Surgery. There was a crest and the name of a hospital system below the black cursive writing.

"The Brothers brought you in from the other species for this night?" Assail asked. "How is that possible?"

Dr. Manello looked down at his name. "Old coat. And old habits die hard—don't they."

As the human met Assail in the eye, Assail frowned. "Whatever do you mean."

"Do you consent for me to speak candidly in front of these two?"

"They are my blood."

"Is that a yes?"

"You humans are so odd."

"And you can cut that superior tone, asshole. I'm married to one of your kind, 'kay? And excuse me for thinking you might not want to be called out for your drug addiction in front of a peanut gallery— whether or not they're related to you."

Assail opened his mouth. Closed it. Opened it again. "I know not of what you speak."

"Oh, really?" The man snapped off his bright blue gloves and put his elbows on his knees, leaning in. "You're fidgeting on my table like you have a case of the hives. You're in a cold sweat, and not because you're in any pain. Your pupils are dilated. And I'm pretty sure if I give you your coat back, the first thing you're going to do is make an excuse to go to the bathroom and use the rest of the coke that was in the vial I took out of the inside chest pocket. How'm I doing? Reading your mind correctly? Or are you going to lie like a motherfucker."

"I do *not* have a drug problem."

"Uh-huh. Sure you don't."

As the human got to his feet, Assail did some studious ignoring of his own—no way was he going to look over at his cousins: He could feel their twin stares on him quite well enough, thank you rather much.

At least neither of them said anything.

"Look, it's no skin off my back." Dr. Manello went over to a work-table on which a computer, some pens, and a pad rested. Bending down, he scribbled something and tore the top sheet off, folding it in half. "Here's my number. When you hit bottom, call me and we can help detox you. In the meantime, be aware that prolonged use of co-caine leads to all kinds of fun things, like panic attacks, paranoia, and even full-blown psychosis. You're already in the weight-loss category, and as I mentioned, you're twitchy as fuck. Your nose has also been running the entire time so I'm pretty sure your septum is deviated."

Assail glanced at the wastepaper basket beside him and wondered how all those Kleenexes had ended up in it. Certainly, it could not have been . . . huh. He had a wad of tissue in his hand he had been unaware of holding.

"I am *not* addicted."

"So take this and toss it." The human held the paper out. "Burn it. Roll the thing up and use it to snort your next fix. Like I said, I don't care."

When Assail accepted what was offered, the doctor turned away as if he'd already forgotten about the whole interaction. "So how about that X-ray? And the Brothers will tell you when you can go. Departure is not a voluntary thing, as I'm sure you get."

Assail made a show of crushing the paper and pitching it into the trash with the tissues. "Yes," he said dryly. "I am rather aware of precisely how involuntary all of this is."

Vishous drove the food-service truck back to the compound. Like a bat out of hell.

The thing hadn't been built for speed, and its piss-poor handling reminded him of an old airplane trying to take flight off of a dirt runway—everything vibrated, to the point where you would have sworn you were one sneeze away from total, molecular disintegration. But he kept his foot down on the accelerator—which was what you did when you had, ohhhhhhh, about twenty-five minutes of true darkness left and at least thirty-seven miles of driving to cover. And you really didn't want to abandon possible slayer evidence at the side of the road.

Still, worse came to worst, he and Tohr, who V had insisted ride back with him, could pull over and dematerialize right to the steps of the mansion in a nanosecond: Butch had just texted to report that he'd made it to the training center safely with Xcor. So no one had to worry about Tohr acting out on some bright idea that involved bloodshed and a body bag with the Bastard's name on it.

At least not during these next ten minutes, anyway.

"You saved our lives when the Omega showed up."

Vishous glanced across the front seat. Tohrment had been silent in the shotgun position since the pair of them had driven off the campus about twenty minutes after the Omega had up and disappeared.

"And I wasn't going to kill Xcor."

"You sure about that, true?"

When Tohr didn't say anything further, V thought, Yeeeeeeah, right you weren't gonna murder the motherfucker.

"It's not like I don't get it," V muttered as a dip in the highway helped push the food-service truck's speed north of seventy miles an hour. "We all want to off him."

"I performed a tracheotomy on Wrath. While he was dying in my lap after fucking Xcor shot him."

"Well, and then there was the fact that you had Lassiter driving at the time," V said dryly. "That would have freaked me out just as much."

"I'm fucking serious, V."

"I know."

"Where are we going to put him?"

V shook his head. "Depends on how long the Bastard's passed out."

"I want to work on him, Vishous."

"We'll see, my brother. We'll see."

Or, in other words: abso-fucking-lutely *not*. The aggression rolling out of the brother's pores, even as Tohr tried to make it like he was joe calm-and-in-control, was as big a red flag as anyone ever got.

As they fell silent, V put his hand inside his leather jacket and took out a hand-rolled. Lighting the thing with a red Bic, he exhaled some smoke and cracked the window so he didn't gas his brother.

Urge to kill aside, Tohr had raised a good goddamn question— where the hell were they going to put their prisoner? There were plenty of interrogation rooms in the training center—the problem was, they were of the table-and-chair variety, the kind of thing that had been used, for example, to talk to Mary, John Matthew, and Bella when they'd first come to the facility.

Not luxurious, but certainly civilized.

Nothing that was kitted out for torture.

Yet.

Good thing his love life provided him with ready access to all sorts of straps, buckles, chains, and spikes. And yeah, he was probably going to need some of his larger equipment, too.

"I'll take care of it," he said.

"What? Xcor?"

"Yeah. I got this."

Tohr cursed softly like he was jel. But then the brother shrugged. "That's a good thing. He's dangerous—it's like having a serial killer in the house. We're going to want some seriously strong locks."

Dead bolts weren't going to be the half of it, V thought. Not even close.

THIRTEEN

When Mary woke up, she hadn't a clue what time it was. Lifting her head off Rhage's bare pectoral, she looked around and was surprised to find that both of them had fallen asleep with the recovery room's overhead lights on.

Shoot, she hadn't replugged all the machines. After Rhage's little orgasmic interlude, he'd refused to stop holding her, and she must have passed out against his warm, muscled body. Clearly, Ehlena had figured things out, though—the monitors themselves had been removed. And yes, her *hellren* was still very much alive, his chest rising and falling evenly, that wonderful *ba-bump, ba-bump, ba-bump* of his heart a true testament to his health.

Closing her eyes, she winced as she thought back to the bullet wound, the blood he had been coughing up, that horrible—

"Hey, beautiful one."

As he spoke, she jerked her head up. His half-lidded, blue, blue eyes were so arresting, she wanted to stare into them forever.

"Hi," she whispered.

Moving her hand over, she stroked his cheek, feeling the growth of his blond beard. "You need a shave."

"Do I?"

"It's sexy, actually."

"Then I'm throwing out all my razors. Quick, help me to our bathroom so I can do it now."

She chuckled, then got serious. "How's your eyesight?"

"What eyesight."

"Still blind?"

He made a *hrrumph* sound. "Like it matters? You're here and I can hear you just fine. I can feel you, too." Rhage's big, broad palm rubbed her shoulder. "Hey, I have an idea. Let's go up to our rooms, and after we cancel my subscription to the Dollar Shave Club, we can hit the Jacuzzi. After a bath and a half, we can get in bed and see what comes up. I owe you at least one good ride, remember—and then there's the vig. Ohhhh, that vig—I have a lot to make up for."

Mary laughed a little.

"What," he said with a frown. "What's wrong?"

Pushing herself up from him, she cracked her back on a stretch. Shoved her hair away from her face. Pulled the collar of her shirt into place so it wasn't choking her.

"That bad, huh."

With a grunt of pain, he grabbed for the control buttons, and made the mattress angle higher so he could sit up more properly.

"Talk to me."

As she moved down to the foot of the bed and tried to find the words, Rhage recoiled. "Whoa. Are you—why are you crying?"

"Jeez, am I?" A quick pass of her palms across her cheeks and she found wetness. "Wow. Yeah, sorry about that."

"What's going on? Do I need to kill something for you?"

It was the bonded male's first response to anything that upset their *shellan*, and before she could help herself, she whispered, "The death's already happened, actually."

"Huh?"

For some reason, she thought back to that night, over two years ago, when Rhage, V and Butch had gone and killed a murderous *hellren* so that Bitty and Annalye could live.

"Bitty's mom died last night."

"Ohhhh, *shit*." Rhage sat all the way forward on his own, like he was half a mind to jump out of bed even though there was nowhere to go, no attack to defend her from. "Why the hell didn't you tell me?"

"You were kinda busy dying at the time—"

"You should have told me. Jesus, I made you jerk me off—"

"Stop it. I loved that. We needed that."

As his handsome face grew unbearably tight, and he crossed his arms over his chest like he was pissed at himself, she arched up and kissed him on the mouth. "Thank you."

"For what?"

"Caring about her, too."

"How can I not. What can I do to help?"

Mary sat back and blurted, "I've missed you."

Rhage patted the air between them like he was looking to touch her and she put her face into his hands, letting him feel her cheeks and her jaw, the sides of her throat.

"I've missed you, too," he said in a low tone. "We've been . . . kind of parallel lately. Not apart, but parallel."

"I'm sorry. I know. I've been wrapped up in everything at Safe Place and that really isn't fair—"

"Stop it. You don't ever need to apologize to me for loving your job or wanting to be all-in on what you do. I'm the *last* person who'll ever not get that. You're amazing there, an incredible person who helps everybody—"

Mary dropped her eyes, even though technically there was no stare for her to evade. "Not always. God, not always."

"Tell me. Mary, I don't mean to be demanding . . . but you really gotta talk to me."

As she remembered everything that had happened, her eyes teared up again. "I, ah . . . I got the call at my desk that things weren't going well with Annalye and I took Bitty out to Havers's. I really thought . . . well, when my mom passed, I was with her, and that was important to me—especially later, you know? I mean, when I think of her, and I miss her . . . there's a certain solace that comes with knowing that she wasn't alone when she died. That . . . that she had been with me at the start of my life, and I had been with her at the end of hers." Mary took a shuddering breath. "I mean, Bitty's young . . . there are so many years ahead for her to grapple with it all, you know? And what's been important to me as an adult, kind of seemed like something that would be important to her later. Anyway . . . I didn't mean for it to happen."

"What did?"

Mary covered her face with her palms as the memory sliced through her consciousness like a knife. "When Bitty . . . oh, God, when Bitty took her mom's hand, the female died right then and there. Bitty thought she was responsible. It was . . . *awful.* Not at all what I wanted for either one of them."

I killed her! I killed her!

"Maybe her *mahmen* was waiting for her."

Mary wiped her eyes and dropped her arms in defeat. "That's what I tell myself. Not that it really helps—"

"Mary, when I was shot on that field and dying, I was waiting for you to come to me. It was the only thing I held on to. When you love someone and you're leaving, you wait for your person to come—and it takes a lot of energy, a lot of focus. I'm telling you, Mary, I was waiting for you because I wanted to make my peace with you, but I couldn't hold on for much longer—and although we lucked out and you saved my life, the reality was that I prolonged my suffering just to have that moment with you."

"Oh, God, seriously . . . seeing you suffering like that—it was one of the worst moments of my life—"

As if he were determined to keep her on track, Rhage talked over her. "You need to tell Bitty that, okay? Tell her that her mother died at that moment because Bitty's voice was what she needed to hear before she went to the Fade. She needed to know that her daughter was all right before she left—and I guarantee you, Mary, if you said one word in that room, Annalye knew that you were there with her young, too. And that meant Bitty was going to be safe. Annalye left because she knew it was okay to go."

"I never thought of it that way," Mary murmured. "You have such a good way of putting it. I wish you could say that to her."

"Maybe I can someday. Hell, name the date and time and I'm there."

As Rhage stared across at her, he seemed focused on her even though he couldn't see—and actually, Mary was very sure, in this moment, that nothing else in the world existed for him but her and her problems. Add onto that his ridiculous masculine beauty and that sex drive and the big heart?

"How on earth did I ever get to end up with you?" she whispered.

"I won the lottery."

Her *hellren* reached for her and brought her in close again, tucking her under his chin. "Oh, no, Mary. It's the other way around. Trust me."

As Rhage felt the tension in his *shellan's* body ease, he rubbed her back in slow circles . . . and felt like throwing up.

Not because of the whole beast thing.

"So I know we're still twelve hours away from nightfall," she said, "but I'd like to go into work this evening? Just a little while though, and only if you're—"

"Oh, God, yeah. Bitty needs you." Wonder if there were any Alka Seltzers left? "I'm fine."

"Are you sure?"

Nope. Not at all. "Hell, yeah—I've done this recovery thing how many times? I'm just going to hang down here and sleep it off." Because if he wasn't conscious, he wasn't going to feel like this, right? "And actually, on second thought, you don't need me to tell Bitty anything. You have even better ways of putting things."

"I used to believe that."

"No." He looked down at where the sound of her voice was coming from and took one of her hands in his with urgency. "Mary, you can't second-guess yourself. Listen, you go to war in your own way, and the worst thing a soldier can do is have his confidence fried before he hits the field. Not everything is going to end up in victory, but you've got to start it all off, every time, knowing that your training and your instincts are sound. You didn't do anything wrong. You didn't hurt Bitty on purpose. You certainly are not responsible for her *mahmen* choosing that moment to go unto the Fade—and in fact, there's a lot of evidence to suggest the female left because she felt like her young was in good hands. You need to believe all of that—otherwise, you're going to get stuck in a neutral that isn't going to help anybody."

"Lord, you are always so right."

Meh. Not even close. But like he was going to bring all his wrongs up now, when she had real problems to deal with, with that little girl? He was a selfish prick, but he wasn't *that* much of a douche bag.

Fucking hell, he couldn't believe he'd put his *shellan* through what he had . . . he couldn't live with himself knowing that he'd made Mary essentially watch him fucking die last night—and all for no good fucking reason.

All because he hadn't listened to Vishous.

Actually, no, he thought. It was even worse than that. In fact, he had heard every word the brother had said and had gone out to fight anyway, fully aware of what was waiting for him on the field of combat if the guy was right.

Guess that was the definition of suicidal, wasn't it.

Which meant that he was . . .

Oh, fuck.

As Rhage's head began to implode with a reality that was only now dawning on him, Mary continued talking in a slow, considered way about what she was going to do for the little girl, what staff consults she needed to have, and then there was something about an uncle somewhere . . . and Rhage just let the conversation of hers go on its one-sided way.

In all truth, he was infinitely grateful she felt better and more connected to him. That shit mattered. Unfortunately, he was back to being far away from her again, the inside part of him floating off even as his body stayed where it was.

What the hell was wrong with him? He had everything he wanted in life—and she was in his arms at this very moment. He'd had a death scare and come through it. There was so much to live for, fight for, love for.

So why would he do something like that? Why would he run out into an all-but-guaranteed casket? And why was the distance from her back?

Well, there was one explanation. Something that tied everything up with a big, fat, psychotic bow.

He'd often wondered whether he was crazy. Like, intrinsically so.

His emotions had always been so extreme, jumping from mania to anger, that he'd sometimes worried that one day he was going to spiral off on the top end of one of those pendulum swings, never to return to sanity again. Maybe that had finally happened. And if it had? The last thing Mary needed after what had gone on last night was to learn that he was clinically insane.

Because, shit, why else would he feel so damn weird in his own skin?

Damn it, it was like he'd won the lottery only to find out he was allergic to the cash or some shit.

"Rhage?"

He shook himself. "I'm sorry, what?"

"Do you want me to get you some food?"

"Nah. I'm still full." He retucked her in against him. "I could use a whole lot more of this, though."

Mary snuggled up close, stretching her arm around his shoulders as far as it would go. "You got it."

I tried to kill myself last night, he said to her in his head. And I have no idea why.

Yup. It was official.

He'd lost his mind.

FOURTEEN

"It's up here."

Jo Early eased off on the accelerator of her Volkswagen piece of crap. "Yeah, I know where it is, Dougie."

"Right here—"

"I *know.*"

There was no reason to hit the directional signal. At seven in the morning, there were no other cars around, nobody to care as she went through the off-kilter, paint-flaking iron gates of the old prep school her mother had gone to a million years ago.

Wow. The Brownswick School for Girls had seen better days.

Her mother would *so* not approve of this landscaping at all. Or lack thereof.

Then again, the woman could throw an aneurysm over a single dandelion head in her five-acre lawn.

Driving down the pitted asphalt lane, Jo steered around holes that were big enough to eat her little Golf, and dodged fallen tree limbs— some of which were old enough to rot.

"God, my head hurts."

She glanced over at her roommate. Dougie Keefer was Shaggy from

Scooby Doo—without the talking Great Dane. And yes, his nickname was Reefer for good reason.

"I told you to go to a doc in the box. When you passed out here last night—"

"I was hit on the head!"

"—you probably got a concussion."

Although any neuro consult on the guy would be tough to read because he was usually seeing double. And numbness and tingling was a lifestyle choice in his eyes.

Dougie cracked his knuckles one by one. "I'll be fine."

"Then stop complaining. Besides, half of the problem is that you're sobering up. It's called a hangover."

As they went further into the campus, buildings appeared, and she imagined them with clean, unbroken windows and freshly painted trim and doors that didn't hang at bad angles. She could absolutely see her mother here, with her sweater sets and her pearls, gunning for her MRS. degree already even though this had just been a prep school, not a college.

Twenty-first century mores aside, things had gotten time capsuled in the nineteen fifties for her mother. And the woman had the match-ing shoes and handbags to prove it.

And people wondered why Jo had moved away?

"You're not ready for this, Jo. I'm telling you."

"Whatever. I need to get to work."

"It's going to blow your mind."

"Uh-huh."

Dougie turned to her, the seat belt cutting into his chest. "You saw the video."

"I don't know what I was looking at. It was dark—and before you keep arguing, remember April Fool's this year?"

"Okay, it's October, for one thing." The chuckle he tossed out was so him. "And yeah, that was a good one."

"Not for me it wasn't."

Dougie had decided it would be fun to borrow her car for the day and then send her a photoshopped picture of the thing wrapped around a tree. How he'd managed to focus long enough to get the optical con job done had been a mystery—but it had looked so real, she'd even called her insurance company.

As well as had a breakdown in the bathroom at work as she'd wondered how in the hell she was going to cover her deductible.

That was the thing about leaving your rich parents in the rearview. A five-hundred-dollar, unbudgeted hit could make eating difficult.

With a frown, she leaned into the steering wheel. "What is tha— oh, *crap*."

Hitting the brakes, she stopped in front of an entire tree that had fallen across the lane. Quick check of the clock and she cursed. Even though time was passing, she was not four-by-fouring in the Golf and running the risk of having to call AAA and paying for a tow truck.

"If we're going to do this, we've got to walk."

"Go around it."

"And get stuck in the mud? It rained late last night." She cut the engine and snagged her car key. "Come on. You want to show me, you'd better start hoofing it. Otherwise I'm turning us around."

Dougie was still bitching as they set off on foot, stepping over the downed maple and continuing down the lane. The morning was bitterly cold, and surprisingly so—the kind of thing that made you glad you'd taken your parka on a whim, and pissed that you'd left your hat and gloves behind because in your mind it was "only October."

"Now I know why I don't get up before noon," Dougie muttered.

Jo glanced up at the bare limbs above. She hated being a pessimist, but she had to wonder whether any of the suckers were going to go into a free fall and kill her. "Why did I let you talk me into this?"

He put his arm around her shoulders. "Because you loooooove me."

"Nope." She elbowed him in the ribs. "That's definitely not it."

And yet it kinda of was. She'd met Dougie and his stoner troop through an acquaintance, and they'd taken her in when she'd been in desperate need of a place to crash. The arrangement was supposed to have been a couch-crashing temporary, but then a bedroom had opened up in their apartment, and a year later, she was living in the mid-twenties version of a frat house. With a bunch of recalcitrant man-boys. Who she seemed to be in charge of.

"We're getting close." He put his hands up to his head like it was blown. Which was a short trip. "I mean, body parts everywhere, and the *smell*. Worse than what's in our refrigerator. I mean, we're talking dead bodies, Jo. Dead! Except they were moving! And then that—"

"Hallucination of a dragon. You told me."

"You saw the footage!"

"I know better than this," she said as she shook her head. "Fool me once, shame on you. Fool me twice—"

"Jo. It was real. It was fucking real—I saw a monster and . . ."

As Dougie ran through the litany of impossibility again, Jo focused on the rise up ahead. "Yeah, yeah, you already told me. And unlike you, I still have my short-term memory."

"Chooch, T.J., and Soz saw it, too."

"You sure about that? 'Cuz when I texted them this morning, they said it was a bad trip. Nothing More."

"They're idiots."

As they hit the incline, she smiled and decided maybe she had over-corrected. She hadn't fit in with the stick-up-the-ass society types her parents were so into, but by the same token, hanging out with a bunch of going-nowhere stoners wasn't exactly her bag, either.

Still, they were highly amusing. Most of the time.

And besides, the truth was, she had no idea where she belonged.

"You'll see," Dougie announced as he ran to the top of the rise. "Just look!"

Jo joined him—and shook her head at all the yup, okay, so what down below. "Exactly what am I supposed to be looking at? The trees, the buildings or the grass?"

Dougie dropped his arms. "No, no, this is wrong. No—"

"I think you finally broke your brain, Dougie. But that's what happens when you feed it twelve hits of lysergic acid diethylamide in a six-hour period. At least you thought it was real this time, though, as opposed to that car-meets-tree thing you did for me."

Yup, there was absolutely nothing unusual down below in what had to be the center of campus. No dead bodies. No body parts. And no smell, either. Nothing but more abandoned buildings, more cold wind, and more nothing-weird.

"No, no, no . . ."

As Dougie ran down, she let him go, hanging back and trying to imagine what the place had looked like when it had been operational. It was hard to think that her mother had gone to classes in these buildings. Slept in them. Had that first dance with her father in one of them.

Funny, the past as it had been seemed as inaccessible as the present currently was with both of those people who had adopted her. The

three of them had just never clicked, and although being on her own was tough sometimes, it had been a relief to let go of all those exhausting attempts to fake a bond that had never materialized.

"Jo! Come over here!"

When she cupped her ear and pretended she couldn't hear him, Dougie rushed back up to her with the messianic zeal of a preacher. Grabbing her hand, he pulled her into a descent behind his flapping Army surplus jacket.

"See how everything is trampled over there? See?"

She let herself get dragged over to an admittedly flattened section of the meadow. But a bunch of horizontal long grass and disturbed undergrowth was hardly a scene out of a Wes Craven movie. And it was definitely not whatever was on that video Dougie had insisted she watch over and over again.

She wasn't sure how to explain everything. But what she was clear on? She really wasn't going to give herself a brain cramp trying to reconcile it all.

"You saw what I posted!" Dougie said. "And someone took my phone because they don't want anyone else to see it!"

"You probably just lost the thing—"

"I was up there." He pointed to the tallest of the brick buildings. "Right there! That's where I got the footage!"

"Hey, Dougie, no offense, but I have to get to work—"

"Jo, I'm fucking serious." He pivoted around in a circle. "Fine, explain this. How did everything get crushed here? Huh?"

"For all I know, you and our three roommates ran around in a circle naked. Actually, let's not even go there on a hypothetical."

Dougie faced off at her. "Then how did I get the video? Huh?"

"I don't know, Dougie. Frankly, it's so grainy, I don't know what I'm looking at."

She gave him some time to hop around with all kinds of what-about-this and what-about-that, and then she was done. "Look, I'm really sorry, but I'm leaving. You can come with me or Uber home. Your choice. Oh, wait. No phone. Guess that means walking?"

As she turned away, he said in a surprisingly adult voice, "I'm serious, Jo. It happened. I don't care what the three of them say. I know when I'm high and when I'm not."

When Jo stopped and glanced behind herself, his expression turned hopeful.

"Do you mind if I drop you off at the bus stop on Jefferson? I don't think I have time to take you all the way back."

Dougie threw his arms up. "Aw, come on, Jo—let me just show you over here . . ."

"Bus stop it is," she said. "And remind me of this the next time you drop acid. I want to be prepared."

FIFTEEN

Sometime later, Mary woke up after a good long rest . . . and smiled at her decidedly asleep mate. Rhage was out like a light, his eyes closed, one blond brow twitching, his jaw grinding as if maybe he were dreaming of an argument or a pool game. His breathing was deep and even, and yes, he was snoring. Not like a chain saw, though. Or an unmuffled Mustang revving at a red light. Or even anything close to Butch's wounded-badger routine—which was something you had to hear to believe.

No, the sounds her man let out were more like a Krups coffee pot right as it was finishing a cycle of brewing; the kind of thing that burbled in the background, offering a comforting rhythm of patter that she could sleep through if she wanted to or stay up and listen to if she were stewing again. Come to think of it, his snores were probably the quietest thing about him, considering how heavy his footfalls were, how loud his laugh was, and how much he spoke, especially if he were giving his Brothers a hard time.

All that out-there was just part of what she loved so much about him.

He was always so alive. So very much alive.

Thank God.

As she went for a stretch, she moved slowly against his body so she didn't wake him up and glanced at the clock across the recovery room. Seven at night. Past sundown.

Given how tired he had to be, he was liable to sleep another four or five hours. Probably better that she head out now and come back when he was awake.

"I'm going to head into Safe Place for a little bit," she said softly. "You stay with him. Let him know I'll be back soon, or he can call me?"

She was talking to the beast, of course—and treating that massive, bone-crushing dragon as some kind of social secretary. But it worked. If she had to leave when Rhage was asleep, she always told the beast what she was doing and when she'd be back. That way, Rhage didn't wake up in a cold sweat that she'd been abducted. Murdered. Or had a slip and fall in the bathroom that had knocked her out and left her bleeding all over the marble floor.

Yeah, bonded males tended to jump to conclusions that were just a liiiiiiiiiiiiiiittle over the top.

Mary carefully disengaged herself from Rhage's hold—only to stop when she was halfway free. Staring down at his unmarred, completely intact sternum, she brushed her fingertips over where the gunshot had been.

"I didn't say thank you," she whispered. "You saved him. I owe you . . . so very much."

All at once, Rhage's lids flipped open—but it wasn't him waking up. His eyes were nothing but white orbs, that telltale illumination of the beast's consciousness training on her with total focus.

She smiled and brushed her mate's face, knowing that the dragon would feel her touch. "Thank you. You're a good boy."

A quieter version of the affectionate chuff the beast always gave her reverberated up and out of Rhage's throat.

"Go back to sleep, too, okay? You need your rest as well. You worked hard last night."

One more chuff . . . and those lids started to sink. The beast fought the tide like a puppy, but ultimately lost the battle, the snoring returning, the pair of them both reengaging with whatever versions of dreamland they were in.

Leaning down, she kissed her mate's forehead and smoothed his hair back. Then she padded over to the bathroom and shut the door.

As soon as she turned to the counter by the sink, she smiled. Some-one—oh, who was she kidding, it had to have been Fritz—had laid out complete changes of clothes for the both of them. As well as toothbrushes, a razor and shaving cream, and shampoo and condi-tioner.

"Fritz, thy name truly is thoughtfulness."

And oh, what a shower it was. From time to time, she wondered whether the sounds or scents were going to wake up Rhage, but when she was drying off, she cracked the door and found that, other than having turned to face the bathroom, he remained out cold.

Probably because she'd told the beast what was up.

As she was blowing dry her hair, she wondered where the Volvo had ended up. She had ridden here from the battle in the surgical unit, but surely someone had brought that station wagon back?

Well, she could always take something else to Safe Place.

Fifteen minutes later, she whispered her way across to the door. After a prolonged stare at Rhage, she opened the way out and—

"Oh! God!" she hissed as she recoiled.

The very last thing she had expected to see was the entire Brother-hood standing outside her *hellren*'s recovery room.

Then again, she should have known. Everyone was there, from V and Butch to Phury and Z . . . Blay and Qhuinn . . . Tohr and John Matthew . . . even Wrath and Rehvenge. It was like standing in front of a football squad . . . that was made up of pro wrestlers . . . in full-contact game gear.

Okay that didn't go even far enough to describe the amount of male in the corridor.

"Hey, guys," she said quietly as she pulled the handle and made sure things were closed. "He's asleep right now, but I'm sure he won't mind being woken up."

"We didn't come for him," Wrath said in a low voice.

Mary's brows popped as she looked at their King. "Oh."

Jeez, had she done something wrong? It was hard to know given that Wrath, with his widow's peak and his wraparound sunglasses, always looked pissed off.

The guy didn't have resting bitch face so much as resting I'm-going-to-kill-someone-and-light-their-house-on-fire face.

Swallowing hard, she stammered, "I, ah—"

"Thank you, Mary," the King said as he stepped forward with his seeing eye dog, George. "Thank you for saving our brother's life."

For a moment, she was utterly dumbfounded. And then the King was pulling her into a hard, tight embrace.

When Wrath stepped back, there was something hanging off her shoulder.

A sword? "Wait, what is this?" She jerked into a second recoil. "Why is this—oh, my God . . ."

The weapon was made of ornate gold, from hilt to sheath, and there were gems flashing on it everywhere, white and red. Likewise, the ruby red sash it hung from was festooned with precious stones and metal. It looked old. Old . . . and priceless.

"Wrath, I can't accept this—this is too much—"

"You have performed a service of valor unto the throne," the King announced. "In saving the life of a member of my private guard, you are held in the highest royal esteem—and may call upon me to perform at your direction a benefit of comparable worth at some future time."

She shook her head over and over again. "That is not necessary. Really. It's not."

And suddenly, she felt bad. Very bad. Because she hadn't saved Rhage for these wonderful males who loved him so. Hadn't saved him for herself, either.

God, why . . . why did that one moment have to be contaminated with all the drama with Bitty?

Mary went to take the sword off. "Really, I can't—"

One by one, the Brothers came to her, embracing her with hard pulls, holding on to her until her spine bent and her ribs couldn't expand. Some of them spoke in her ear, saying things that resonated not just because of the words that were chosen, but from the respect and reverence in the tones of those deep voices. Others just made a lot of throat-clearing noises, in the way men did when they were struggling to stay strong and composed in the face of great emotion. And then there was John Matthew, the one she had begun this crazy journey with, the one who had started it all by calling into the suicide hotline she had been volunteering at.

Vishous was the second-to-last of the Brothers to come to her, and as he held her, she caught of a whiff of tobacco. Along with leather. And gunpowder. "We owe you," he said curtly. "Forever."

Wiping her eyes, she shook her head once more. "You give me way too much credit."

"Not even close," he said as he brushed her cheek with his gloved hand. Staring down at her, his diamond eyes and harsh face with its tattoos were as close to tender as she'd ever seen them. "You knew what to do—"

"But I didn't, V. I really don't have a clue where that idea came from."

For a moment, he frowned. Then he shrugged. "Well, whatever. You gave us our brother back. And even though he's a pain in the ass, life wouldn't be the same without him."

"Or you," Zsadist tacked on.

Z was the last to come over, and as he opened his arms wide, for some reason, the slave bands that had been tattooed around his throat and wrists stood out to her.

His embrace was stiff. Awkward. Obviously hard for him as he kept his hips far away from her body. But his eyes were yellow, not black, and as he stepped back, he put his hand on her shoulder.

The scar that ran down the bridge of his nose and around to his cheek moved out of place as he gave her a small smile. "You're really good at saving lives."

She knew exactly what he was referring to—all those sessions the two of them had had by the boiler in the mansion's basement, him talking about the horrific abuse he'd suffered at the hands of his Mistress, her listening and offering comments only when he paused for a very long time or looked to her for some sort of life raft as he struggled in a sea of overwhelming shame and pain and sadness.

"Sometimes I wish I were better," she said as she thought of Bitty.

"Not possible."

When Z fell back in line with his brothers, Mary smoothed her hair. Swiped under her eyes. Took a deep breath. Even though there were a lot of different emotions going through her, it was really good to be around people who loved Rhage as much as she did.

That much she knew to be true and without question.

"Well." She cleared her throat. "Thank you all. But honestly . . ."

As every single one of them glared at her, it was the kind of thing that made you grateful they liked you.

She had to laugh. "Okay, okay, I'll keep it, I'll keep it."

Conversation sprang up among the Brothers, and there was some back slapping, like they were proud of themselves for doing right by her.

With a final wave, she forced herself to continue onward toward the entrance to the underground tunnel. . . with her new sword.

Boy, it was heavy, she thought as she hiked it up further on her shoulder.

Almost as heavy as the weight she felt on her heart.

While Mary walked down the corridor in the direction of the office, Vishous took out a hand-rolled and put it between his front teeth. As he lit the thing, he frowned, thinking about what she'd said to him.

"So Xcor's not conscious," Wrath murmured.

Turning to the King, V exhaled and switched gears in his head. "Not yet. And I checked on him about a half hour ago."

"Where did you put him?"

"Gun range." V glanced at Tohr, who was out of earshot. "And we have an alternating guard schedule. He's tied up to my satisfaction—"

"Do you really use that shit for sex?"

On a oner, the entire Brotherhood looked over at the interruption. Lassiter, the fallen angel, had appeared from out of nowhere, and he was looking somewhat less offensive than usual, his blond-and-black hair pulled back in a braid that went to his ass, his black leathers covering his naughty bits, the gold hoops at his ears, bracelets on his wrists and piercings in his nipples glowing under the fluorescent ceiling lights. Or maybe that was just on account of his heavenly frickin' disposition.

Not.

"What the hell happened to your goddamn shirt?" V shot back. "And why the shits are you off post?"

Goddamn it, he should have known not to put that idiot on guard duty. But at least Payne hadn't left the gun range—and that was something V didn't need to check for himself. His sister was the kind of fighter he'd trust not only with his own life and the lives of his brothers and mate, but with making sure their prisoner didn't so much as sneeze without permission.

"I spilled on it."

"What? You're *eating* in there?"

"No. Of course not." Lassiter sauntered on by to where the scrubs were kept. "Okay, yes. Fine. It was a strawberry milk shake—and I'm just getting a fresh shirt and going back in. Relax."

V took a hard drag. It was either that or put the fucker in a choke hold. "Strawberry? Really?"

"Fuck you, Vishous."

As the angel smiled and blew a kiss over his shoulder, at least the bitch didn't pump his junk.

"Can I kill him," V muttered to Wrath. "Please. Just once. Or maybe twice."

"Get in line."

V refocused. "As I was saying, Xcor is going nowhere."

"I want to find out where the Bastards are staying," Wrath ordered, "and bring the rest of them in. But they've got to be assuming he's been captured. That's what I would do. No body? No witnesses to a death? Safest course is to assume their leader's become a prisoner of war and get the fuck out of wherever they've been staying."

"Agreed. But you never know what you can learn when you push the right levers."

"Keep Tohr away from him."

"Roger that."

V glanced at Tohr again. The brother was standing in the back of the group and looking down the hallway where the gun range was. It felt weird to think in terms of reining the guy in or keeping tabs on him, but it was what it was.

Sometimes emotions were too much for even the most logical of fighters.

Except for him, of course.

He was fucking tight as shit.

"So Assail's two rooms down," V said. "If you're ready to talk to him."

"Take me there, V."

Again, usually it would have been Tohr doing the duty, but V stepped in close and nudged the King forward, leaving the Brothers to reassume various poses and sit-downs as they waited for Rhage to wake up.

After they had gone some distance, the King said softly, "So what do you know about Rhage and his little premature shooting contest."

When V cursed, Wrath shook his head. "Tell me. And don't pretend you don't fucking know something. You were the last one to speak with him."

Vishous considered keeping shit under wraps, but in the end, lying to Wrath wasn't in anybody's best interest. "I foresaw his death and tried to get him to leave the field. He wouldn't and . . . there you go."

"He went out there. Knowing he was going to die."

"Yeah."

"Goddamn it." After Wrath dropped a couple of f-bombs, he switched gears to another happy subject. "I also heard you had a visitor. When you went back to the campus."

"The Omega." Man, he didn't like to even say that name. But like he'd enjoyed talking about Rhage's death wish? "Yeah, my mother's brother took care of clean-up. If his day job as being the source of all evil in the world doesn't work out, he has a second career as a janitor waiting for him."

"Any problems?"

"He didn't even know we were there."

"Thank fuck." Wrath glanced over even though he couldn't see. "Have you talked to your mother lately?"

"No. Nope. Not at all."

"I asked her for an audience. She hasn't acknowledged me."

"Can't help you there. Sorry."

"I'll go up there uninvited if I have to."

V stopped at the door to Assail's recovery room, but didn't open it. "What exactly are you looking for from her?"

"I want to know if she's still up there." Wrath's cruel, aristocratic face got tight. "Going up against slayers is one thing, but we're going to need a wingman with serious power to face the Omega head-on—and I'm not kidding myself. We just knocked out ninety percent of what he has on the earth. He will respond, and we're not going to like whatever it is."

"Fuck me," V muttered.

"More like 'us,' my brother."

"Yeah. That, too." V took another drag to get his shit together. "But you know, if you want me to talk to her or . . ."

"Hopefully it won't be necessary."

Annnnd that makes two of us, buddy, V thought.

Before his mommy issues made him even crankier than he usually was, he rapped on the door. "You decent in there, motherfucker?" He pushed in without waiting for permission. "How we doing, assholes?"

Well, well, well, he thought as he saw Assail sitting cross-legged on the hospital bed. Detox much?

The male was sweating like he was a chicken dinner under a heat lamp, but also shivering sure as if his lower body were in an ice bath. There were circles the color of crankcase oil under both his eyes, and his hands kept going to his face and his forearms, brushing at some kind of lint or stray piece of hair that didn't exist.

"To w-w-what do I owe this h-h-honor?"

Wrath's nostrils flared as the King tested the scent in the air. "You got a monkey on your back, huh."

"I b-b-beg your pardon?"

"You heard me."

V checked out the twin cousins over in the corner and found them as straight-backed and unmoving as a pair of cannons. And just about as warm and fuzzy.

On that note, they kind of didn't annoy him.

"What m-m-m-may I do for you?" Assail asked between twitches.

"I want to thank you for working with us last night," the King drawled. "I understand your wounds are all stitched up."

"Y-y-yes—"

"Oh, for fuck's sake." Wrath glared over at V. "Will you get this cocksucker his drug of choice? I can't talk to him if he's all jonesing for his sin. It's like trying to get someone to focus through an epileptic seizure."

"Looking for this?" V held up a vial full of powder and tilted the thing back and forth, all tick-tock. "Mmm?"

It was pathetic the way the fucker's eyes latched on and bugged out. But V knew what that was like—how you needed the very burn you didn't want, how it became all you could think of, how you withered from the not having of it.

Thank God for Jane. Without her, he'd be walking that stretch of gnawing and ever-empty still.

"And he doesn't even deny how much he needs it," V murmured as he approached the bed.

Dayum, as the poor bastard reached out, it was clear that Assail's hands were shaking too badly for him to hold on to anything.

"Allow me, motherfucker."

Twisting the black top off, V turned the little brown bottle over and made a line down the inside of his own forearm.

Assail took that shit like a pile driver, snorting half up one nostril, half up the other. Then he fell back against the hospital bed like he had a broken leg and his morphine drip had finally kicked in. And yup, from a clinical standpoint, it was a sad commentary on the SOB's state that a stimulant like cocaine was bringing him down.

But that was addiction for you. No damn sense.

"Now, you want to try this again?" V muttered as he licked his arm clean and tasted bitterness. The buzz was not bad, either.

Assail rubbed his face and then let his arms fall to his sides. "What."

Wrath smiled without any warmth, revealing his massive fangs. "I want to know what your business plans are."

"Why is that your concern?" Assail's voice was reedy, like he was exhausted. "Or have you decided that a dictatorship, rather than a democracy, is more suited to your personality—"

"Watch your fucking tone," V snapped.

Wrath kept going as if he hadn't been interrupted. "Your track record is questionable at best. In spite of a more recent trend toward loyalty, you seem to always be on the outskirts of my enemies, whether it's the Band of Bastards or the Lessening Society. And last I checked, you were running a drug ring—something that cannot be done with a mere crew of two, as capable as your henchmen may be. So I find myself wanting to know where you're going to go for your middlemen now that the slayers who you've been working with are out of the black market business."

Assail drew his jet-black hair back straight from his forehead and held it in place like he was hoping that would help his brain get to work.

V braced himself for some bullshit.

Except then the male said in a curiously dead voice, "I do not know. In truth . . . I know not what I shall do."

"You speak no falsity." Wrath inclined his head as he exhaled. "And as your King, I have a suggestion for you."

"Or would that be a command," Assail muttered.

"Take it as you will." Wrath's brows disappeared under the rims of his wraparounds. "Bearing in mind that I can kill you or let you go from this place on a whim."

"There are laws against murder."

"Sometimes." The King smiled again with those fangs. "In any event, I want your help—and you're going to give it to me. One way or another."

SIXTEEN

About halfway to Safe Place, Mary decided she was going to end up with knee-replacement surgery.

As she took an exit off the Northway, she gritted her teeth and punched in the rock-hard clutch of her husband's vintage, rehabbed, brilliant purple GTO—a.k.a. his pride and joy. The light of his life after her. The single most valuable anything he owned since he'd given her his gold Presidential Rolex.

The muscle car started making a coughing noise and then it kicked out a pattern of bass explosions followed by some high-pitched squealing as she moved the gearshift forward and back in the box.

"Third? Third . . . I need, no, second? Definitely not first."

She'd learned that one the hard way when she'd come to a stop at the bottom of the mansion's hill and had nearly knocked her front teeth out on the steering wheel from the jerking and jumping.

"Oh, Ms. Volvo, I miss you so. . . ."

When she'd come out of the mansion, she'd discovered the station wagon wasn't out front in the courtyard with the Brotherhood's other vehicles. But rather than waste time trying to hunt the thing down back at the training center, she'd snagged Rhage's keys and figured,

How hard could it be to take his muscle car in to town? She knew how to drive a stick shift.

It was going to be fine.

Of course, she hadn't banked on the fact that the clutch was like trying to put her foot through a brick wall every time she needed to shift. Or that the gears were so tightly calibrated that if you didn't get the gas in at exactly the right time, all those horses under the hood went buck wild.

The good news? At least fighting with the transmission gave her something other than Bitty-linked anxiety to focus on as she made her way to Safe Place.

Plus Fritz was as good a mechanic as he was a butler.

When she finally arrived at the house, she parked in the driveway, got out, and hobbled around in the dark for a minute, kicking her left leg around until something popped and suddenly she didn't feel as if she were walking like a flamingo anymore.

With a curse, she headed around to the door into the garage, entered a code and slipped inside. As the motion-sensitive lights came on, she put her hand up to shield her eyes, but she didn't have to worry about tripping over anything. The two bays were empty but for lawn-mowing equipment and some old oil stains on the concrete slabs. There were three steps up to the door into the kitchen, and then she put a code in and waited for the dead bolts to begin their sequence of unlocking. She also turned and presented her face for recognition as well.

Moments later, she was in the mudroom, taking off her coat and hanging it up with her purse on the row of hooks above the boot bench. The new kitchen out the back was all busy-busy, stacks of pancakes being made at the stove, fruit getting cut up on the counters, bowls and plates being lined up on the longtable.

"Mary!"

"Hey, Mary!"

"Hi, Ms. Luce!"

Taking a deep breath, she returned the hellos, heading over to give a hug here and there, put her hand on a shoulder, greet a female, high-five a young. There were three staff members on duty, and she checked in with them.

"Where's Rhym?" she asked.

"She's been upstairs with Bitty," the curly-haired one said softly.

"I'll go there now."

"Is there anything I can help with?"

"I'm sure there will be." Mary shook her head. "I hate this for her."

"We all do."

Going to the front of the house, she rounded the base of the stairs and took the steps two at a time. She didn't bother stopping to see if Marissa was in. Chances were good, given the scope of the attack, that the head of Safe Place was taking a little time off to be with her *hellren*.

Being mated to a Brother was not for the faint of heart.

Up on the third floor, she found Rhym asleep in a padded chair that had been pulled over next to Bitty's door. As the floorboards creaked, the other social worker stirred.

"Oh, hey," the female said as she sat up and rubbed her eyes. "What time is it?"

Rhym had always reminded Mary of herself to some degree. She was the sort of female who maybe wasn't the first person you noticed in a room, but never failed to be there when you needed someone. She was on the tall end for height, a little on the thin side. Never wore make-up. Usually pulled her hair back. No male that anyone had ever heard about.

Her life was her work here.

"It's six-thirty?" Mary stared at the closed door. "How'd we do during the day?"

Rhym just shook her head. "She wouldn't talk about anything. She just packed her clothes into her suitcase, got her doll and her old toy tiger together, and sat at the end of her bed. Eventually, I came out here because I thought she was probably staying awake because I was in there with her."

"I think I'll put my head in and see what's going on."

"Please." Rhym stretched her arms up and cracked her back. "And if it's okay with you, I'll head on home for some shut-eye myself?"

"Absolutely. I'll take over from here. And thanks for looking after her."

"Is it dark enough out for me to leave now?"

Mary glanced at the shutters that were still down for the day. "I think—" As if on command, the steel panels that protected the interior from sunlight began to go up. "Yup."

Rhym got to her feet and drew her fingers through her blond-and-

brown hair. "If you need anything, if she needs anything, just call and I can come back in. She's a special little girl, and I just . . . I want to help."

"I agree. And thanks again."

As the other female started down the stairs, Mary spoke up. "One question."

"Yes?"

Mary focused on the oculus window down at the far end of the hall, trying to find the right words. "Did she . . . I mean, she didn't say anything about her mother? Or what happened at the clinic?"

Like something along the lines of *My therapist made me feel as if I killed my mother?*

"Nothing. The only thing she mentioned was that she was leaving as soon as she could. I didn't have the heart to tell her there was nowhere for her to go. It seemed too cruel. Too soon."

"So she talked about her uncle."

Rhym frowned. "Uncle? No, she didn't bring anything like that up. Does she have one?"

Mary looked back at the closed door. "Transference."

"Ah." The social worker cursed softly. "These are going to be long nights and days ahead for her. Long weeks and months, too. But we'll all rally around her. She'll do well if we can just get her through this part in one piece."

"Yes. So true."

With a wave, the female went down the steps, and Mary waited until the sounds of the footfalls disappeared in case Bitty was only lightly asleep.

Leaning into the door, she put her ear to the cool panels. When she heard nothing, she knocked quietly, then pushed things open.

The little pink-and-white lamp on the bureau in the corner was casting a glow in the otherwise dark room, and Bitty's diminutive form was bathed in the soft illumination. The girl was lying on her side, facing the wall, having obviously fallen asleep hard at some point. She was in the same clothes she had had on, and she had indeed packed her battered suitcase—and her mother's. The two pieces of luggage, one smaller and the color of a grass stain, the other larger and Cheeto orange, were lined up together at the base of the bed.

Her doll head and brush were on the floor in front of them, along with that stuffed toy tiger of hers.

Putting her hands on her hips, Mary lowered her head. For some reason, the impact of the room's silence, its modest and slightly thread-bare curtains and bedspreads, its thin area rug and mismatched furni-ture, hit her like body blows.

The barrenness, the impersonality, the absence of . . . family, for lack of a better word, made her want to turn the thermostat up. As if some extra heat from the ducts in the ceiling could transform the place into a proper little girl's room.

But come on, the problems that were ahead were going to have to be solved by a lot more than just functioning HVAC systems.

Tiptoeing across to the bed Bitty's mom had slept in, it seemed fitting to take the patchwork quilt off that mattress and carry it over to the little girl. With care, Mary added the layer without disturbing the sleep that was so very needed.

Then she stood over the child.

And thought back to her own past. After her cancer had made itself known, she could remember very clearly thinking that enough was enough. Her mother had died early and horribly, with much suf-fering. And then she herself had been diagnosed with leukemia and had to go through a very non-fun-filled year trying to beat the disease into remission. The whole lot of it had seemed so very unfair.

As if her mother's hard time of it should have qualified Mary for a tragedy-exemption card.

Now, as she stared down at the girl, she was downright indig-nant.

Yes, she frickin' knew that life was difficult. She'd learned that lesson very well. But at least she had gotten a childhood marked with all the traditionally good things you wanted to be able to look back on when you were old. Yes, her father had died early, too, but she and her mother had had Christmases and birthdays, graduations from kinder-garten and elementary school and high school. They'd had turkey on Thanksgiving and new clothes every year and good nights of sleep where the only worry that might have kept someone up was whether a passing grade was going to happen or, in the case of her mom, if there was going to be enough money for two weeks of summer vacation at Lake George or just one.

Bitty had had absolutely none of that.

Neither she nor Annalye had ever spoken in specifics, but it wasn't hard to extrapolate the kind of violence that they had both been sub-

jected to. For godsake, Bitty had had to get a steel rod implanted in her leg.

And what had it all added up to?

The little girl here alone.

If destiny had had any conscience at all, Annalye wouldn't have died.

But at least Safe Place had come into being in a nick of time. The idea that the resource wouldn't have been available to Bitty when it was needed most?

It was enough to make Mary sick to her stomach.

Rhage woke up in a rush, sure as if an alarm had lit off next to his head. Jacking his torso off the hospital bed, he looked around in a panic.

Except then, as quick as the anxiety hit, it disappeared, the knowledge that Mary had gone to Safe Place calming him down sure as if she'd spoken the words in his ear. And he supposed she had. For a while now, they'd been using the beast as a kind of message board if Rhage was out like a light.

It worked—and you didn't have to worry about having to find a pen.

He still missed her, though. Still worried about his own mental state. But that little girl . . .

Shifting his legs to the side, he blinked a number of times and yup, remained blind after the lid workout. Whatever. He felt otherwise strong and steady—physically that was—and as long as he took things slowly, he was going to make it into the shower just fine.

Twenty minutes later, he emerged from the bathroom buck-ass naked and smelling like a rose. Amazing what a little soap and shampoo could do for a guy. A good teeth brushing, too. Next stop? Food. After the beast came out and then he did his purging thing afterward, his guts felt not so much hungry as hollow—and the best thing he could do was put some low-fiber carbohydrates in there for processing.

Twelve French baguettes. Four sleeves of bagels. Seven pounds of pasta.

This type of thing.

Stepping out into the corridor, he wondered how long it was going to take to find his way to—

"Fucking finally—"

"Couldn't you have put a towel on—"

"Fritz brought you clothes—"

"You're back, motherfucker—"

All of his brothers were there, their scents and voices, their relieved laughter, their curses and jibes exactly what the doctor ordered. And as they embraced him and slapped his bare ass, he had to suck in the emotion.

He was already nakey. #plentyvulnerablethanks

God, in the midst of all the reeeeeunnnnited and it feeeeeeeeels so gooooooood, it was impossible not to get hit with another load of shame for his selfishness and what he'd put Mary and all of his brothers through.

And then V's voice was directly in front of him.

"You good?" the brother asked in his raspy voice. "Feeling back to normal?"

"Yeah. I'm back in working order except for my eyesight." *I'm sorry, too. And I'm scared.* "You know, just a little tired—"

Whack!

The chin shot came out of nowhere, nailing him so hard, his head knocked back and nearly snapped off his spine.

"What the fuck!" Rhage blurted as he rubbed his jaw. "What—"

"That was for not fucking listening to me."

Crack!

The second shot came from the opposite direction, which was a good thing—the swelling would be bilateral, so his face wouldn't look as fucked up.

"And *that* is for going out early and fucking our strategy."

As Rhage brought his brains to level for a second time, he held his jaw with both hands. 'Cuz there was a possibility the lower half of his skull was going to fall off.

The good news was that the double shots cleared his vision a little, the blindness receding enough so that he could make out the hazy blotches of his brothers' bodies and clothes.

"We coulda justh talked thith out," Rhage bitched. "Great, I'm talkin' wif a lispth."

"Where's the fun in that, true?" V grabbed hold of him and hugged him hard. "Now don't *ever* fucking do that again."

Rhage waited for the others to start asking questions. When no one did, he had to guess that V had already told them about the vision thing. Unless . . . well, everybody had seen him run out into that field early and that kind of shit was grounds for a beat down.

"I can thee now," he said.

"You can thank me for that later."

There was a bunch of conversation at that point—which led him to ohhhh-snapping the fact that they had Xcor in custody.

"Tohr kill the fucker yet?" he asked.

"No," came from all fronts.

Then there was a story about the Omega showing up and doing a Mr. Clean at the campus, and V saving the day with some *mhis* action.

"I'll take a thift," Rhage said. "Guarding the bastard, that ith."

"Later." V exhaled some Turkish smoke. "All cylinders first. Then we'll place you."

On that note, the group dispersed, some heading up to the mansion, others hitting the workout room. Rhage went along with the ones who took the tunnel to the main house, but as his brothers went for their beds, he walked through the dining room and into the mansion's kitchen.

God, he wished Mary was with him.

The good news was that there were no *doggen* around, First Meal having not been served thanks to the number of injuries that had been sustained during the attack and all the drama with him. The household staff were no doubt having a rare and well-deserved rest before they resumed their cleaning and tending, and he was relieved not to be fussed over.

As he wandered around Fritz's sacred space, however, he did feel like he should put out an offering or something so he didn't get in trouble with the butler. And on that note, he decided no cooking. He was going to take whatever was readily available and not start thinking independently with the stove or the pantry.

He'd already been punched twice and the night was young.

But first, clothing. He'd been too blind down in the bathroom to see that anything had been left out for him, and he went into the laundry behind the pantry, using his half-assed eyesight and keen sense of touch to locate a set of loose black sweats and a huge sweatshirt with the *American Horror Story* logo on it. Then it was time to get serious about the calories.

Raiding the bread stash, he began to clean it out by putting bags of bagels and sourdough loaves on the counter—but then he thought, *Fuck it*. Reaching under the drawer, he took the thing off its track and carried the whole damn shebang over to the oak table. Step two was to double back to the fridge, get out a pound of unsalted butter and a package of cream cheese, and snag the toaster, unplugging it by pulling the body until the cord gave up the ghost.

A serrated knife and a cutting board later, along with the coffee pot, the sugar bowl, and a small carton of half-and-half, and he was in business. While the coffee percolated, he got to slicing, making mountains of butterable pieces off to the right. The bagels he set up on a Henry Ford, so he could process them through the toaster and into the Phillie zone.

Probably should have gotten a plate. And at least one other knife, but the bigger blade was going to be efficient for spreading.

When the coffee had finished brewing, he took the pot out from under, poured the entire sugar bowl into it, and followed that up with as much of the half-and-half as he could fit in. Then he took a test sip.

Perfect.

He put the thing back on the heat plate and started systematically working his way through the bagels—'cuz, hey, that was close to First Meal–type stuff, right? Next up was anything sourdough because that was as lunch-ish as his options allowed. Dessert was going to be a pecan coffee cake. Or two.

As he chewed along, his teeth were a little loose thanks to V. Mayweather's bare knuckles, but it wasn't a huge deal. And from time to time, he washed things down with drafts off the lip of the coffee pot.

About two thousand calories into the binge, the reality of how alone he was really hit him.

Then again, the room could have been filled with his brothers and he would have felt the same.

Worse, he had the sense that even his Mary's presence couldn't have fixed this isolation for him.

As he sat there, filling his hollow stomach yet unable to do anything about the emptiness that really counted, he thought it would

have been so much easier if he had even a clue as to what his problem was—

Off in the distance, in the dining room, a sound echoed around. And came closer.

It was a flurry of footsteps, like someone was running.

What the hell? he thought as he rose from his chair.

SEVENTEEN

There was a great deal of math to be contemplated when one had an addiction.

As Assail took a seat behind the desk at his glass mansion, he pulled open the long thin drawer that was directly over his thighs and took out three vials that were identical to the one the Brother Vishous had emptied upon his own forearm back at the Brotherhood's subterranean facility.

Math, math, math . . . mostly multiplication. As in, given the amount of cocaine he had, how long would he be able to keep the cravings at bay? Fourteen hours? Fifteen?

He opened up one of the little brown containers and poured its white powder out on the leather blotter. Using a Centurion American Express card, he made a pair of lines, leaned over them, and took care of his business. Then he sat back in his chair and snuffed everything into place.

Truly, he hated the dripping down the back of his throat. The burn in his sinuses. The bitter taste that bloomed in his mouth. And he most especially despised the fact that he didn't really get high anymore. He merely experienced a temporary upswing on this horrible roller coaster he had set himself upon, said respite to inevitably be

followed by a rushing crash—and then, if he did not attend to himself, the clawing, relentless grab of the cravings.

Glancing at the remaining two vials, he found it difficult to believe that he'd fallen into this pattern. The slip and fall had been both the work of a moment and a slow-motion tragedy. He had initially started using to keep himself alert, but what had begun as a habit of practicality now owned him sure as a master had dominion over a servant in the Old Country.

Fates, he had not intended this.

Had not intended rather a lot, of late.

Extending his arm, he woke up his laptop with a stroke on its touch pad, signed in using one hand even though there were capitals involved in his password, and accessed, via encrypted channels, his overseas account. The big one that was in Geneva.

He had several others.

So many digits and commas before the decimal point on the balance. And staring at the line up, he contemplated exactly how much money one needed—even assuming that as a vampire, he would live out ten human lifespans or more.

Assuming his little habit didn't usher him off unto the Fade.

Or in his case, *Dhund* in all likelihood.

Surely he had enough by any practical standard, even in light of recent international finance crises . . . so did he truly have to deal in the drugs anymore? Then again, at the rate he was snorting powder up his nose, he was in danger of becoming his own best customer.

I need your help with the glymera.

As he considered Wrath's proposal, he had to wonder how what the King wanted him to do was any better or worse than making money off the backs of humans and their need for chemical reinforcement. The royal endeavor was something to pass the time, surely. And if he wasn't going to traffic in drugs, he needed to surmount the night hours somehow.

Otherwise he would go insane.

Mostly from missing that female of his. Who had not, in fact, ever been his own.

"Marisol," he whispered into the air.

Why in the hell had he never taken a picture of her? When she had stayed here, in this very house, when he had protected her, with his very life, why hadn't he picked up his phone, pointed it in her direction and snapped a shot? A mere moment of time, a split second, that was all that it required. But no, he had not done such a thing, and now, here he was, on the far side of the divide, with nothing left of her save that which was in his mind.

It was as if she had died. Except she was still on the planet.

In fact, she was down in Florida, where the ocean lapped at the sweet sand and the nights were a balmy mystery even in fucking October.

He knew exactly where she was, precisely where she stayed— because he had tracked her down there. Made sure that she had gotten to her destination with her grandmother safely. Pined for her from the shadows in the most pathetic manner possible.

But he had honored her request. He had let her go. Let her be free of him and this illegal lifestyle they had both participated in.

Cat burglars and drug dealers could co-exist.

A human woman who wanted to be on the correct side of the law and a vampire pusher addict could not.

With a groan, he put his face in his hands and called her to mind. Yes, oh, yes, he could remember her dark hair and her lithe body, her skin and her dark eyes with a certain clarity. But the passage of time . . . he worried he would forget some nuance at first and then ever larger and more significant details.

And the loss of that was a death by inches even as he continued to breathe.

"Enough," he muttered as he dropped his arms and leaned back.

Refocusing on himself, he thought about what the King had laid out for him. It would be a change of endeavor, for certain. But he had enough money. He had enough time. And finding another network of middlemen dealers to farm out his product on the streets of Caldwell and Manhattan abruptly seemed too much like work.

Besides . . . having fought side by side with the Brotherhood? He found himself respecting those males. Respecting their leader, too.

It was quite the about-face for an otherwise avowed Libertarian— rather like an atheist considering the existence of God following a near-death experience.

Plus, he owed Vishous his life; that much he was sure of. As worth-less as his existence was, he would not be sitting upon this chair, in this glass mansion on the Hudson River, feeding his cocaine habit, unless that Brother had thrown him over his shoulder and run like hell.

Twice.

Oh, that beast. Had he not seen it, he would ne'er have believed its existence.

Assail pushed his chair around with his foot such that he could peer out the windows to the river beyond. A subtle chiming rang from the corner of the room where an old French clock was placed. In the background, over in the rear part of the house, he could hear his cousins moving around in the kitchen.

When he decided to use his cell phone, all he had to do was reach into the pocket of his shredded leather jacket. He had neglected to remove the ruined outerwear even though his house was well-heated against the cold October night.

Then again, all he had cared to do when he had arrived back home was sequester himself in private so he could play catch-up with his little problem.

He could not abide doing lines in front of his cousins. Not that he had any intention of altering his behavior for anybody.

Summoning a number up out of his contacts, he hesitated before initiating the call. As his thumb hovered over the screen, he was acutely aware that if he followed through on this, he was going to become something he had always disdained.

An agent of the King.

Or more to the point . . . an agent of another.

With a strange feeling of dread, he gave into the impulse and put the device to his ear, listening to the ringing commence. In the end, he decided to give himself up to Wrath's demand for the simple reason that it seemed like the only good thing he could do with himself.

A right thing.

A positive thing.

He was beginning to feel as if it were about time. And mayhap he was taking a page from his Marisol's book because it was the only way he could be close to her now.

No more drug dealing for him.

Although what he was about to do might well prove to be just as dangerous. So at least he would not grow bored.

"Hello, darling," he said when the call was answered by a female. "Yes, I do need to feed, thank you. Tonight would be preferable, yes. And I have missed you as well. Indeed, very much so." He let her go on a bit as she took his lie and swallowed it whole. "Actually, at your main house, please. No, the cottage does not suit a male such as myself. I was willing to make the accommodation at first due to your *hellren*'s presence, but now that he has taken unto his bed, I find myself unable to make that concession any further. You understand."

There was a long pause, but he knew that she would relent. "Thank you, *nalla*," he intoned evenly. "I shall see you very soon—oh, be in something red. No panties. That is all."

He hung up on her because she was a female who required schooling if one was to capture and hold her attention. Too easygoing? Too charming? She would lose interest, and that couldn't happen until he had acquired what he needed from her.

His next call was to the Brother Vishous. When the male answered, Assail uttered only three words prior to hanging up once again.

"I am in."

"Suuuuure, I'll stay late. No problem. Not like I have anything better to do."

As Jo Early sat behind her reception desk, the rest of the real estate office was empty, nothing but a lingering mishmash of colognes and the strangely depressing Muzak overhead to keep her company. Well, that and the frickin' ficus bushes on either side of her.

Those things dropped their leaves like they were on a constant molt-down—and her OCD just wouldn't let her relax unless the floor was clean. Then again, she didn't have to do stomach crunches at the gym.

Not that she went to a gym.

Checking her phone, she shook her head. Seven o'clock.

The plan, the "favor," she was doing for her boss was to stay here until he brought three contracts in with signatures so she could scan them and e-mail them over to the various buyers' brokers. Why he couldn't feed the things into the machine himself and do a little PDF'ing was a mystery.

And okay, maybe she was part of the problem, too.

Not that she was proud to admit it.

Looking up over the lip of the desk counter, she focused on the smoky glass doors that opened to the outside. The office was located in

an up-market strip mall that had a hair salon where the cuts started at a hundred bucks—and that was just for the men, a boutique that displayed two pieces of barely-there clothing in its window, a glass-and-china shop that sparkled even on gray days, and, at the far end, a jewelry store that the trophy wives of Caldwell seemed to approve of.

Going by the place's pneumatic clientele.

"Come on, Bryant. Come on . . ."

Although really, where did she have to go. Home to Dougie and the crop circle arguments? Now there was a party.

As a telephone rang back where the offices were, she woke up her computer and stared at Bryant's calendar. She put his appointments into Outlook when he texted or called to tell her to. Scheduled things like valid real estate meetings, but also the service for his BMW and visits by the pool man for his place over in that new development. Reminded him to call his mother on her birthday, and ordered flowers for the women he dated.

All the while wondering what he would think if he knew who her parents were.

That little secret was what she soothed herself with when he'd come in on a Monday morning and whisper that he'd been out with a divorcée on Friday and a personal trainer on Saturday and then had a brunch with someone else on Sunday.

Her true identity was armor she used to fight against him. In a war he was utterly unaware of them being engaged in.

Closing out his busy life, she stared at the logo on the screen. Bryant's last name, Drumm, was the second in line—because the firm had been started by his father. When the man had died nearly two years ago, Bryant had stepped into his shoes, as well as his prime office space, in the same way he did everything else—smiling and with charm. And hey, it wasn't a bad strategy. Say what you would about the guy's playboy lifestyle, he could move a ton of real estate and look good doing it.

Caldwell, NY's own *Million Dollar Listing* star.

"Come on, Bryant . . . where are you?"

After a re-visit of her already-twice tidied desk, she checked the floor under the right ficus, picked up a leaf and tossed it, sat back and . . .

What the hell, she went onto YouTube.

Dougie had posted that stupid footage on his channel—a rocking destination with a grand total of twenty-nine subscribers. Of which, like, four were Dougie himself in different sock puppets and two were spammers with low standards. As she hit the arrow to watch the forty-two-second clip all over again, she turned on the speakers. The sound track was right out of amateur-central, a combination of too-loud rustling as her roommate held the iPhone up and a distant, not-so-quiet roaring.

Okay, so yes, it certainly looked like something Jurassic-ish out in the middle of that field. And yeah, there seemed to be a lot of clutter on the ground, but who knew what all that was. It was only a camera phone capturing the footage, and maybe that was just the way the trampled area looked to its lens.

She played things a couple more times. Then sat back.

There were five comments. Three were from Dougie and their roommates. One was a testimonial from someone who was making $1750 a month at home!!!!$$$!!!!!. The last was . . . just four words that didn't make a whole lot of sense.

vamp9120 shit allova again

Left by someone named ghstrydr11.

Frowning, she went on a hunt-and-peck and found vamp9120's channel. Wow. Okay, three thousand subscribers, and what looked like a hundred videos. Firing one up, she—

Laughed out loud.

The guy talking at the camera was like a LEGO character of Dracula, with a point in the middle of his forehead and even pointier canines, facial hair that looked like it had been painted on rather than shaved around, and a swear-to-God, that must be Elvis collar on his shirt. The guy's skin was too white, his hair too black, his red lips right out of a MAC tube. And that voice? It was part evangelist, part neo-Victorian, Bram-Stoker-almost.

"—creatures of the night—"

Wait, wasn't that a line from somewhere?

"—stalking the streets of Caldwell—"

Like the upstate New York version of *The Walking Dead*? When in doubt, drag a leg.

"—preying on victims—"

Okaaaaaaaaaaaaay, moving on. Scrolling down the line-up, she

randomly picked another. And yup, Verily, Barely Vlad was once again face-first in the camera—and this time he had a really good smoky eye going on.

"—are real! Vampires are real—"

Wonder if his pulpit was draped in black vel—okay, wow. That was supposed to be a joke, but as the lens pulled back, it did look like he was leaning on something that was, in fact, covered in black velvet.

Cutting that rant off, she went down to the next video, and told herself after this one, enough was enough. "Oh, hey, Vlad, wassup."

"—testimonial about a vampire encounter." Vlad turned to a guy sitting next to him in a plastic folding chair. Which was total ambiance right there. "Julio? Tell my fans about what happened to you two nights ago."

Talk about mixing it up a little: Julio was the anti-vamp, what with a bandanna Tupac'd on his head, and his Jesus piece, and the tattoos up his throat.

His eyes, though . . . they were bugging and frenzied, all Vlad and then some.

"I was downtown, you know, with my boys, and we was . . ."

The story that came out started off as nothing special, just a gang-banger with his people, shooting up rivals in the alleys. But then things took a turn into Drac-landia, with the guy describing how he ran into an abandoned restaurant—and from there on, things got weird.

Assuming you believed him.

"—guy threw me up on the counter and he was all"—Julio did a hiss-and-claw—"and his teeth was all—"

"Like mine," Vlad cut in.

"'cept his was real shit." Okay, Vlad clearly did not appreciate that, but Julio was on a roll. "And he had a fucked-up face, his upper lip was all fucked up. And he was gonna kill me. He had a . . ."

Jo hung in for the rest of the interview, even through the part where Vlad all but pushed Julio out of the way, as if Dracu-wannabe's sharing threshold had been reached.

Sitting back again, she wondered exactly how far she was going to go with this. And answered that one by heading over to the *Caldwell Courier Journal* site and doing a search on good ol' Julio's name. Huh. What do you know. There was an aritcle written the previous December on gang-related activity in the downtown area—and Julio was front and center in it. Even had a picture of him staring out of the back of a CPD patrol car, his eyes sporting that same stretched-wide thing, his mouth likewise cranked open like he was desperately talking to the photographer.

Nothing about vampires, though.

Scrolling up again, it turned out that the name on the byline was one she recognized.

Matter of fact, Bryant had gotten the guy and his wife a house about six months ago. Assuming she had it right.

A quick search in the client files and, yup, she was correct—

"I'm so sorry I'm late!"

Bryant Drumm came through the glass doors at a dead run, but he didn't look frazzled. His dark hair was in perfect order, his gray-blue suit was closed at the jacket and the papers in his hands were separated into three sections.

So he hadn't really rushed over. He'd been going at his own pace, even as she'd been rotting here.

He put his elbows on the desk and leaned in with his trademark smile. "Jo, how can I make it up to you?"

She held her hand out. "Gimme. And let me go home."

Bryant put the papers in her palm, but then refused to let go when she tried to take them. "What would I do without you?"

As he stared down at her, his focus was locked on and complete—like nothing else existed in the world for him, like he was both captivated by her and slightly in awe. And to someone who hadn't mattered much to her parents, who had been put up for adoption by the people who'd conceived her, who felt lost in the world . . . that was how he got her.

In a sad way that she didn't like to dwell on much, she lived for these little moments. Stayed late for them. Kept plodding along in hopes it would happen again—

His phone rang. And he was still looking at her as he answered. "Hello? Oh, hey."

Jo glanced away, and this time when she tugged, he let her have the contracts. She knew that tone of voice of his. It was one of his women.

"I can meet you now," he murmured. "Where? Mmm-hmmm. No, I've already had dinner—but I'm up for dessert. Can't wait."

By the time he ended the call, she had turned to the side and fired up the scanner.

"Thanks again, Jo. I'll see you tomorrow?"

Jo didn't bother to look over her shoulder as she fed in the pages one by one. "I'll be here."

"Hey."

"What?"

"Jo." When she glanced back at him, he tilted his head to the side and narrowed his eyes. "You should wear that red more often. It looks good with your hair."

"Thanks."

Going back to the scanning, she listened to him leave, the door he went out of whispering shut. A moment later, there was the flare of a powerful engine and then he was gone.

With the knowledge that she was good and alone, she lifted her head and looked at her reflection in the glass entrance. The light from the inset fixtures above streamed down, hitting her hair in such a way that its red and brown tones stood out against the black and gray all around her.

For some reason, the emptiness in the office . . . in her life . . . seemed loud as a scream.

EIGHTEEN

The notes in Safe Place's client files were all still handwritten. Part of it was cost; computers, and networks, and reliable storage were expensive, and with staffing as the priority, funds diverted in an IT direction were just not mission critical. But another part of it was the fact that Marissa, their fearless leader, was old-fashioned and didn't really like things that were important kept in a form she couldn't hold in her hands.

After all, if you were almost four hundred years old, the technology revolution of the last three decades was a blip on your radar screen.

Maybe a century from now the boss would trust the likes of Bill Gates a little more.

And it was kind of nice, Mary reflected. More human, somehow, to see the different handwritings, different inks, different ways people misspelled things from time to time. It was the visual equivalent of conversation, everyone bringing something unique to themselves to the records—as opposed to the entries being made up of uniform, spell-checked, all-the-same typed words.

It did, however, make searching for one particular reference or note more difficult. But then again, re-reading everything from the beginning helped you pick up on things you might have previously missed.

Like uncles, for example.

When there had been no mention of any next of kin on the original intake form, Mary had gone on to read each and every one of the progress notes in Annalye's file, many of which were in her own handwriting. And just as she had remembered, the passages were invariably short and contained little of any use.

Bitty wasn't the only one who had been quiet.

There wasn't a single mention of a brother or any parents. And the female hadn't spoken of her dead mate, either, or of the abuse that she and Bitty had been through. Which was not to say that the violence was undocumented. The medical notes for the two of them had been printed out and attached to the back cover of the file.

After she was done reading it all again, Mary had to sit back and rub her eyes. Like many victims who were afraid for their lives, Bitty's *mahmen* had come in for medical assistance only once, when her child was so hurt, there was no way for the natural healing process to take care of the injuries. The x-rays told the rest of the grim story, showing years of broken bones that had reknitted themselves. For them both.

Closing the file, she traded it for Bitty's. The girl's was thinner as her medical record had been merged with her mom's and she'd given them even less to write down than Annalye had. There had been regular talk sessions, as well as art therapy and creative play and music class. But there was not much to go on.

In a way, everyone had only been waiting for the inevitable—

"Ms. Luce?"

Mary jumped in her chair, throwing out her hands and slapping the desk blotter. "Bitty! I didn't hear you."

The little girl was standing just outside the open door, her small frame looking even smaller in between the jambs. Tonight, her brown hair was down and curling all around, and she was in another one of her handmade dresses, yellow this time.

Mary was struck by a nearly irresistible urge to get Bitty a sweater.

"Ms. Luce?"

Shaking herself, Mary said, "I'm sorry, what?"

"I was wondering if my uncle has come yet?"

"Ah, no. He hasn't." Mary cleared her throat. "Listen, would you come in here for a moment? And shut the door, please."

Bitty did as she was asked, closing things behind her and coming forward until she was standing in front of the desk.

"These are your files, honey." Mary touched the manila folders. "Yours and your *mahmen's*. I've just gone through them again. I'm not . . . I don't see anything about your uncle. There's no mention of him in here? I'm not saying he doesn't exist, I just—"

"My *mahmen* got in touch with him. So he's coming for me."

Crap, Mary thought. Talk about having to tread carefully.

"How did your mother do that?" she asked. "Did she write to him? Call him? Can you tell me how she reached him? Maybe I can follow up with him?"

"I don't know how. But she did."

"What's his name? Do you remember?"

"His name is . . ." Bitty looked down at the desk. At the folders. "It's . . ."

It was physically painful to watch the girl try to come up with what was probably going to be a made-up name. But Mary gave her the space, hoping against hope that there would be a magic solution to all this, some brother who did in fact live and breathe out in the world, and who would be as good to Bitty as she deserved—

"Ruhn. His name is Ruhn."

Mary closed her eyes for a moment. She couldn't help herself. Ruhn was close to Rhym, of course. Just a step over from the intake supervisor's name, a distance that was very easily crossed by a young mind searching for a rescue from a horrible situation.

Talk about needing to stay professional.

"Okay, well, I'll tell you what I'll do." Mary held up her phone. "If it's okay with you, I'll post on a closed Facebook group about him. Maybe someone out there can get in touch with him for us?"

Bitty nodded a little. "Are we done?"

Mary cleared her throat again. "One other thing. Your *mahmen's* ashes . . . they'll be ready to be picked up soon. I was thinking, if you'd like, we could do her ceremony here at the house? I know everyone here loved her very much, and we all love you, too—"

"I would like to wait. For when my uncle comes. And then he and I will do it."

"All right. Well, would you like to come with me to get them? I want to make sure that you have—"

"No. I want to wait here. For my uncle."

Crap. "All right."

"Are we done?"

"Yes."

As the little girl turned away, Mary said, "Bitty."

"Yes?" Bitty glanced back. "What?"

"You can talk to me, you know. About anything. And at anytime of the night or day. I'm here for you—and if you don't want to speak to me, anybody else on staff is here to help you. My feelings won't be hurt. The only thing I care about is that you get the support you need."

Bitty stared at the floor for a moment. "Okay. Can I go now?"

"I'm very sorry about the way it . . . about what happened at the clinic last night. I encourage you to talk about it with someone—and if not me—"

"Talking is not going to bring my *mahmen* back, Ms. Luce." That voice was so grave, it seemed like it should have come out of an adult's mouth. "Talking is not going to change anything."

"It will. Trust me."

"Can it turn back time? I don't think so."

"No, but it can help you adjust to your new reality." God, was she really conversing like this with a nine-year-old? "You have to let the grief out—"

"I'm going now. I'll be upstairs in the attic. Please let me know when my uncle comes?"

With that, the girl let herself out and quietly re-closed the door. As Mary lowered her head into her hands, she listened to the little footsteps go over to the stairs and ascend to the third floor.

"Goddamn it," she whispered.

As Rhage got up from the kitchen table, he wasn't worried that whatever was rushing through the dining room and heading his way was the enemy. He was more concerned that someone in the household was in trouble.

Because there was another sound, layered on top of the footfalls.

A baby wailing.

Before he could get even halfway to the flap door, Beth, the Queen, came tearing into the room, her infant son hanging under one of her arms like a sack of potatoes, her free hand held up as she bled all over herself.

"Oh, shit!" Rhage said as he tripped over his bare feet to meet her at the sink. "What happened?"

His sight wasn't as sharp as it could have been, but there seemed to be a lot of red on the front of her shirt. And he could smell the blood everywhere.

"Can you take him?" she said over L.W.'s yelling. "Please just take him?"

Annnnnnd that was how he ended up holding Wrath's first and only born son under the pits like the young was an explosive device with a fuse that was running out fast.

"Ah . . ." he said as the kid kicked his little feet and wailed right in Rhage's face. "Um . . . yeah, you want to go to the clinic with this?"

As he spoke, he wasn't sure whether he was referring to the cut or the baby.

Moving the screaming bag of Wrath's DNA to the side, he tried to see what was going on—was it her finger? Hand? Wrist?

"I was being stupid," she muttered as she hissed. "I was outside on the terrace, taking him to see the moon because he likes it—and I wasn't looking where I was going. I hit a patch of wet leaves and *whoop!* Feet went right out from under me. He was in my arms and I didn't want to fall on him. Threw my damn hand out, caught it on a flagstone that was cracked and it sliced right through me. Shit . . . this isn't stopping."

Rhage winced as he wondered exactly how long the ringing in his ears was going to last after she took L.W. with her. "What . . . ah . . ."

"Hey, can you just stay with him for a minute? Doc Jane's at the Pit, I just got a text from her. I'll run across and have her look at this. I'll be back in two secs."

Rhage opened his mouth and froze like he had a gun to his head. "Ah, yeah. Sure. No problem." *Please don't let me kill Wrath's kid. PleasedontletmekillWrathskid. OhGodohGodohGod—* "He and I'll be just fine. I'll give him some coffee and—"

"No." Beth shut the faucet off and wrapped her hand in a towel. "No food, no drink. And I'll be *right* back."

The female left at a dead run, skidding out of the kitchen and racing through the dining room—and as she went all Usain Bolt, he had to wonder whether it was because of her hand . . . or the fact that she'd left her child with a total incompetent.

Annnnnnd L.W. was now really crying, like he'd figured out his *mahmen* had left and the hollering that had come before had just been a warm-up.

Rhage squeezed his eyes shut and started back for his seat at the table. But after two steps, he thought of Beth's trip-and-fall and imagined himself flattening the kid like a panini. Going bug-lid, he proceeded heel-toe, heel-toe, as if he were balancing a crystal vase on the top of his skull. As soon as he got within range, he parked it on the chair and stood the kid up on those biscuit feet of his. L.W. wasn't strong enough to hold his body up, but that screaming was straight rock-and-roll.

"Your *mahmen's* coming back." Please, dearest Virgin Scribe, let that female get back here before he was deaf. "Yup. Riiiight back."

Rhage looked around the pair of very healthy lungs and prayed for someone, anyone to come running.

When that passive optimism didn't pan out, he refocused on the red face.

"Buddy, your point's been made. Trust me. I heaaaaaar you."

Okay, if the definition of insanity was doing the same thing over and over again . . .

Turning the little boy around, Rhage laid L.W. back in the crook of his arm as he'd seen Wrath and Beth do—

Fucking hell, that just pissed the kid off more. If that was possible. Next position? Um . . .

Rhage put L.W. up on his chest so that the baby could see over his shoulder. And then he patted his flat palm onto the surprisingly sturdy back. Over. And over. And over . . .

Just like Wrath did.

And what do you know. The shit worked.

About four minutes and thirty-seven seconds later—not that Rhage was counting—L.W. sputtered to a halt, like his tear maker had used up the last of its gas. Then the kid took a ragged inhale and went limp.

Later, Rhage would wonder if things might have been okay had L.W. stopped there. Maybe if the infant hadn't gone any further . . . or maybe if it had started to cry again? Then perhaps Rhage might have been saved.

The trouble was, mere moments later, L.W. wrapped a chubby arm around Rhage's throat, and then he fisted the sweatshirt and held on, getting in close, seeking comfort, finding it . . . relying on it because the little guy was utterly helpless in the world.

Abruptly, Rhage stopped with the patting, freezing exactly where he was even though he was off-balance in the chair. And with a clarity that was shattering, everything about the young registered on him, from the heat in that vital body, to the tensile strength in that grip, to the rise and fall of that little chest. The sniffles were right by Rhage's ear, and so was the soft puffing breath, and when L.W. moved his head, fine, silky hair tickled Rhage's neck.

This was the future, Rhage thought. This was . . . destiny come to rest up against him.

After all, L.W. had eyes that would witness events long after Rhage was gone. And the infant's brain would make decisions Rhage couldn't even comprehend. And the body that was fragile in this nascent state, but enduring in its maturity, would fight and honor and protect, just as his father had and his father's father . . . and all the sires in the blood-line before that had.

Wrath was alive in this boy. And would be in the boy's young. And in their young after that.

Moreover, Beth had given this to him. They shared this. They had . . . *made* . . . this.

Suddenly, Rhage found that he could not breathe.

NINETEEN

Naasha did not keep him waiting.

As soon as Assail was shown into the lady's parlor in her *hellren*'s mansion, a portion of the peach silk-covered wall slid back and Naasha came in from a hidden door.

"Good evening," she said as she struck a pose. "I wore red, just as you asked."

Say what you would about her lack of a pedigree and her gold digger mating, she was a beautiful female, all long black hair with a Marilyn Monroe bust-to-waist-to-hip ratio. Wearing that low-cut dress, and with her size sixes in a set of Loubou's, she was every cock-and-ball's wet dream.

And yet even dolled up and turned out, she didn't hold a candle to his Marisol—in the same way a hothouse flower wasn't nearly as attractive as something that grew, untamed and unexpected, in the wild.

Still, the scent of her went through him in a manner not all that different from the cocaine he'd taken before he'd come here, and his body woke up even as his emotions and soul remained dead and cold. The awful reality was that his flesh needed the blood of a female vampire—and that biological imperative was going to take precedence right here and now over everything else.

Even if under other circumstances he would have given her a pass.

"Do you like?" she said, holding up her arms and doing a slow circle.

As he was supposed to, he smiled, revealing his descended fangs. "It's going to look even better off of you."

"Come here," he commanded.

Naasha sauntered toward him, but didn't come all the way, stopping by a buttercup yellow, antique French sofa that had more pillows than seat space.

"You come to me."

Assail shook his head. "No."

The pout was quick, her thick lips pursing out, gleaming with a color that matched the dress. "You traveled all the way across town for me. Surely you can make it another six feet."

"I shall not cross this room."

As he assumed a bored look, which was not forced in the slightest, her arousal flared. "You are so disrespectful. I should throw you out."

"If you think this is disrespect, you have seen naught from me. And I am more than happy to leave."

"I have taken a lover, you know."

"Have you." He inclined his head. "Congratulations."

"So I am quite well-serviced. In spite of my beloved's infirmity."

"Well, then, I shall take my leave of you—"

"No." She raced around the sofa, moving in until she was so close he could see the pores on her smooth face. "Don't go."

He made a show of looking at her features. Then he reached out and touched her hair.

"Get on your knees." Before she could say anything, he pointed to his feet. "On your knees. Now."

"I've forgotten how demanding you are—"

"Don't waste my time."

As another rush of her arousal hit his nose, he knew she was going to kneel on the Aubusson carpet—and when she reached out to steady herself on his chest, he pushed her hand away so that she was forced to wobble her way down to the floor.

"That's a good girl." He brushed her cheek with his knuckles. Then he grabbed a fistful of her hair and bent her head back. "Open your mouth."

With parted lips, she began to pant, the scent of her sex becoming

a roar in his sinuses, her face flushing with heat, her breasts pumping over the bodice of her dress. With his free hand, he undid the zipper of his fine twill slacks and popped his erection.

Palming himself, he growled, "Do you want to tell me more about your lover?"

Her low-lidded eyes flared with erotic light. "He's such a strong—"

Assail pushed himself in between her lips, stopping her from going any further. And then, using his grip on her hair, he fucked her mouth as she moaned, her hands going to her breasts and squeezing, her knees spreading wide as if, in her mind, he was working himself in and out of her core instead. Or maybe in addition to.

As he manhandled her, it wasn't that he hated her. He didn't even dislike her—she'd have had to be on his radar for him to have any kind of opinion of her one way or another.

What he did hate was that she was not the one he wanted.

And the more he thought about that reality, the forever distance, the loss?

Popping himself free of Naasha's mouth, he led her over to the sofa on her knees, using her hair as a leash. And she loved it. She followed him more than willingly, panting, flushed, ready to be fucked. Which was convenient, wasn't it.

Especially as he bent her over that beautiful French couch, shoved that tight skirting up, and drove into her from behind.

She came immediately, shuddering and bucking under him. And as he yanked her head back once more, she called out his name.

"Shh," he gritted. "Wouldn't want your beloved to hear. Or your boyfriend."

She moaned a bunch of senseless things, so lost in the fucking that her brain had obviously taken a vacation. And in an odd way, he envied her the erotic experience. For him, this was nothing but an expression of base needs, a physical workout with pleasure and blood as an anonymous award.

It held none of the knife-edge pleasure she was so clearly enthralled by. But at least he could use this weakness of hers—to Wrath's benefit.

Baring his fangs, Assail struck the side of her throat, biting hard as he rode her, sucking at her, taking his fill. The taste of her was . . . fine. The feel of her sex gripping and releasing his cock was . . . fine. The strength that she would give him was utterly necessary.

Across the way, in the wavy glass of an antique mirror, he caught sight of him fucking her.

Indeed, he looked as dead as he felt. But he reached into his inside suit coat for his cell phone anyway.

Vishous was heading past the training center's weight room and gym when his cell phone went off, thanks to the training center's Wi-Fi. Taking the thing out of his ass pocket, he put his code in and then smiled at the text.

It was a picture from Assail—of the back of a dark haired female's head as she was bent doggy-style over a sofa. The message below was short and to the point: *I am in.*

Gd job, V typed back. *Enjoy t ride.*

"And bring us back some shit," he said as he returned the phone to its place.

That male's addiction was a potential problem, but it appeared as if Wrath had made the right call with the sonofabitch. Assail looked good, had money, and was a total bastard with the right bloodline. He was the perfect ringer to plant in the *glymera*.

The question was going to be what he found out. And how long he was going to be a good boy and play by the rules.

Any independent thinking on his part and V was going to slit that throat open wider than a garage door. But until that time came, Assail was solidly in the Useful, Allow to Keep Breathing column.

As Vishous came up to the entrance of the gun range, he bent down and snagged a black duffel bag that he'd left at the door hours ago. Heading into the low-ceilinged, musty-smelling space, he called out a *wassup*.

"How we doing?" he said, walking around the shooting booth and proceeding onto the concrete target area.

Blay got up from the folding chair he'd been in, stretching his arms over his head and flattening his palms on the ceiling. "No change."

"But I've beaten this guy twice at gin rummy," Lassiter cut in.

"That's because you cheat."

Vishous glanced over—and shook his head at the angel. "What are you doing here? And why are you in a lawn chair?"

"Lumbar support—"

At that moment, the piece of meat on V's rack twitched—and V had to give the black-and-blond asshole in the tanning position credit: Lassiter was up and out of that thing faster than a blink, gun pointed at Xcor's chest like he was prepared to blow a hole through his heart.

"Easy, cowboy," V said. "It was just an involuntary muscle spasm."

The angel didn't seem to hear him—or maybe he didn't care for anybody else making an assessment for his trigger finger, even if they'd had medical training.

Hard not to approve of the guy. Hard also not to notice that Lassiter clearly wasn't leaving Xcor, as if he trusted only himself to take care of business.

Shit, as long as that angel didn't open his mouth, and provided V didn't think about their little difficulties in the past, you could almost forget how much you wanted to shank the motherfucker.

Going over to their prisoner, Vishous performed a visual assessment on Xcor. When they'd brought the bastard in here, V had strapped him onto the wooden slab table face-up and spread-eagled, locking stainless-steel cuffs on those wrists and ankles and around that thick neck—and what do you know, the guy was right where he'd left him. Color was passable. Eyes were closed. Head wound at the rear of the skull was no longer leaking, having healed already.

"Do you need help?" Blay asked.

"Nah, I got it."

Opening up the duffel, V used what was inside to check heart rate, blood pressure, temperature, and oxygenation. The thing he was most concerned with was the inevitable hematoma from where he'd pistol-whipped the fucker—and its possible complications, which included anything from the inconvenient to the catastrophic. However, without moving him or bringing in some seriously heavy and expensive equipment, there was going to be no way of checking any of that out.

He had his suspicions, though. It was entirely possible the concussion had caused an ischemic stroke due to a blood clot blocking a vessel.

Just their frickin' luck. They capture the enemy and the bastard goes brain-dead on them.

After V had put his toys away and made his notes in the digital file with his phone, he took a step back and just stared at the male's ugly face. In the absence of being able to do a battery of tests, he had to rely on his own observation—and sometimes, even with the heavy-duty equipment, nothing beat a medic's own extraoplation from what he could see.

Narrowing his eyes, he tracked every single breath, each exhale . . . the twitches across the brows and the stillness of the lids . . . the random movements of fingers . . . the skin contractions across the thighs.

Stroke. Definitely a stroke. No movement on the left side at all.

Wake the fuck up, V thought. So I can give you a pounding and put you back to sleep.

"Goddamn it."

"What's wrong?" Blay asked.

If there was no change in status soon, he was going to have to make a judgment call on whether to keep Xcor—or throw his body out with the trash.

"Are you okay?"

V turned to Blay. "What?"

"Your eye is having a seizure."

Vishous rubbed at the thing until it stopped. And then wondered, with everything that was going on, whether he was going to be next on the TIA stroke list.

"Let me know if he regains consciousness?"

"Will do," Lassiter said. "And I'll also tell you when I need my next strawberry milk shake."

"I'm not your butler, true." V put the duffel back up on his shoulder and headed for the door. "And you blow me a kiss again? Ima put an MRI in you, instead of the other way around."

"What happens if I pinch your ass next?" the angel called out.

"Try it and you'll find that immortality, like time, is relative."

"You know you love me!"

Vishous was shaking his head as he pushed his way back out into the corridor. Lassiter was like a head cold, contagious, annoying and nothing you ever looked forward to.

And yet he was glad the fucker was in there. Even if Xcor was little more than a piece of furniture.

TWENTY

Beth Randall, mated of the Blind King, Wrath son of Wrath, sire of Wrath, Queen of all vampires, headed back for the Pit's front door even though Doc Jane was still taping up the bandage on her freshly stitched hand.

"This is great! Thanks—"

V's mate was following along at a jog, the pair of them dodging a gym bag, a duffel . . . a blow-up doll that really, totally needed clothes. "You need to seriously stop!"

"It'll be fine—"

"Beth!" Jane fumbled with her roll of white surgical tape and started laughing. "I can't get this end—"

"I'll do it—"

"What's the hurry?"

Beth stopped. "I left L.W. with Rhage in the kitchen."

Doc Jane blinked. "Oh, God—*go!*"

Beth was summarily shoved out of the Pit with the tape, and she finished the job while bolting across the courtyard, biting the strip off with her teeth and smoothing the sticky stuff onto the white gauze that had been wrapped around the heel of her palm. Taking the steps up to the mansion's grand entrance on a oner, she peeled open the door to the vestibule and put her face into the camera.

"Come on . . . *open*," she muttered as she transferred her weight back and forth on her feet.

Rhage wasn't going to hurt the kid. At least, not intentionally. But holy crap, she was channeling visions of Annie Potts babysitting in *Ghostbusters 2*, feeding an infant French pizza.

When the lock finally was sprung from the inside, she pile-drove into the foyer, bolting past the maid who'd opened the way in for her.

"My Queen!" the *doggen* said as she bowed.

"Oh, jeez, sorry, I'm sorry! Thank you!"

No clue what exactly she was apologizing for as she hightailed it through the empty dining room and pushed her way into—

Beth skidded to a halt.

Rhage was seated by himself at the table and had L.W. up on his shoulder, the baby nestled in close to his neck, that huge arm cradling the infant with all the protectiveness any parent could have shown. The Brother was staring straight ahead over his half-eaten display of carbs and nearly-consumed pot of coffee.

Tears were rolling down his face.

"Rhage?" Beth said softly. "What's wrong?"

Putting the tape roll on the counter, she padded over to the pair of them—and when he didn't acknowledge her, she laid her fingertips on his shoulder. And still he didn't respond.

She spoke a little louder. "Rhage—"

He jerked and looked at her in surprise. "Oh, hey. Is your hand okay?"

The male didn't seem to be aware of his emotions. And for some very sad reason, it seemed appropriate that he was surrounded by the chaos of his meal, open sleeves of bagels and bread scattered across the rough, wooden table, sticks of butter and blocks of cream cheese and smeared napkins all around him.

He was, in this quiet moment, as undone as everything before him.

Kneeling down, she touched his arm. "Rhage, sweetheart, what's going on?"

"Nothing." The smile that hit that handsome face was empty. "I stopped him from crying."

"Yes, you did. Thank you."

Rhage nodded. And then shook his head. "Here, I should give him back now."

"It's okay," she whispered. "Hold him as long as you like. He really trusts you—I've never seen him settle for anyone but Wrath or me."

"I, ah . . . I patted him on the back. You know. Just like you guys do." Rhage cleared his throat. "I've been watching you with him. You and Wrath."

Now he resumed staring across the empty kitchen.

"Not in a creepy way," he tacked on.

"Of course not."

"But I've been . . ." He swallowed hard. "I'm crying. Aren't I."

"Yes." Reaching out, she took a paper napkin from a holder. "Here."

Rising to her full height, she dried under his beautiful teal blue eyes—and thought of the first time she'd met him. It had been at her father, Darius's, old house. Rhage had been stitching himself up at one of the bathroom sinks, working the thread and needle through his own skin as if it were no big deal.

This is nothing. It's when you can use your lower intestine for a belt loop that you have to see the pros.

Or something to that effect.

And then she remembered later, after the beast had come out of him and he'd had to lie down in her father's underground bedroom to recover. She had given him his Alka-Seltzer and soothed him in his blindness and discomfort as much as she could.

How far they had both come.

"Can you tell me what's wrong?"

She watched as his palm went in circles over L.W.'s little back.

"Nothing." His lips stretched into what he clearly meant to be another smile. "Just enjoying a quiet time with your amazing son. You're so lucky. You and Wrath are so lucky."

"Yes, we are."

She had almost died delivering L.W., and in order to save her life, they'd had to remove her uterus. No more biological children for her—and yes, that was a disappointment. But every time she stared into the face of her son, she was so grateful for him that the fact that she wasn't going to be able to chance the lottery again didn't seem like much of a loss at all.

Rhage and Mary, though? They weren't even going to get the opportunity to try. And that was clearly what was on Rhage's mind right now.

"I should give him back to you," the brother said once more.

Beth swallowed hard. "Take as much time as you need."

Back at Safe Place, Mary had just finished posting a message on Facebook about Bitty's hypothetical uncle when there was a knock on her door.

Maybe it was the girl, and they could give the talking thing another try. But probably not—

"Come in," Mary said. "Oh, hey! Marissa, how are you?"

Butch's mate looked drop-dead beautiful as always, her blond hair down and curling perfectly on her slender shoulders as if it had been trained in good manners and wouldn't think of frizzing out. Dressed in a black cashmere sweater and sleek black slacks, she was like the female Rhage in a lot of ways—too physically exquisite to actually exist.

And like Rhage, the outside wasn't nearly as lovely as the inside.

With a *Vogue*-worthy smile, Marissa sat in the creaky chair on the other side of the desk. "I'm okay. More importantly, how are you?"

Mary eased back, crossed her arms over her chest, and thought, ah, so this was not a social visit.

"I guess you've heard," she murmured.

"Yes."

"I swear, Marissa, I had no idea it was going to be that bad."

"Of course you didn't. Who could have?"

"Well, just as long as you know that I didn't mean for things to go the way they did—"

Marissa frowned. "I'm sorry, what?"

"When Bitty and I went to see her mother—"

"Wait, wait." Marissa put up her palms. "What? No, I'm talking about Rhage getting shot on the battlefield. And your saving his life in front of the Brothers."

Mary popped her brows. "Oh, that."

"Yes . . . *that*." A strange look entered Marissa's eyes. "You know, frankly, I'm not sure why you came in tonight. I thought you'd be home with him."

"Oh, well, yes. But with everything that's going on with Bitty, how could I not come in? And besides, I spent all day with Rhage, making sure he was okay. While he continues to sleep at the clinic, I wanted to check on her. God . . . the idea that I made things worse for that girl makes me feel horrible. I mean, I'm sure you know what happened."

"You mean at Havers's? Yes, I do. And I can understand your being upset. But I really think you should have stayed with Rhage."

Mary waved a casual hand. "I'm fine. He's fine—"

"And I think you should go home now."

With a sudden shot of dread, Mary sat forward. "Wait, you're not firing me because of Bitty, are you?"

"Oh, my God—no! Are you kidding me? You're the best therapist we have!" Marissa shook her head. "And I wouldn't presume to tell you how to do your job here. But it's pretty clear that you've had a long twenty-four hours, and however much you want to be there for the girl in a professional capacity, you're going to be even more effective if you've had some R-and-R."

"Well, that's a relief." She sat back. "The not-getting-fired part, that is."

"Don't you want to be with Rhage?"

"Of course I do. I'm just really worried about Bitty. It's crisis time, you know? The loss of her mother is not just a tragedy that leaves her orphaned, it's a huge trigger point for everything else. I just . . . I really want to make sure she's okay."

"You're a dedicated therapist, you know that."

"She keeps talking about an uncle?" As Marissa frowned again, Mary reopened Annalye's file and flipped through the pages. "Yeah, I know, right? I hadn't heard about one before now, either. And I went through everything we have on either of them and there's no mention of any family. I just put up a post for the race on that closed page on Facebook? I'll see if I can find him that way." Mary shook her head as she stared at an entry that had been written by Rhym. "Part of me wonders whether or not I could get the phone records for here to see what calls have gone in and out over the last month? Maybe there's something there? No mail has been returned here. And as far as I know, Bitty's mom never used e-mail."

When there was a period of silence, Mary looked up—and found that her boss was staring at her with an inscrutable expression.

"What?" Mary said.

Marissa cleared her throat. "I admire your commitment. But I think it's best that you take at least the rest of tonight off. A little distance to refocus is best. Bitty will be here tomorrow and you can continue to be her primary staff member."

"I just want to make it right."

"I know and I don't blame you. But I can't escape the feeling that if I had showed up here for work a night after Butch had almost died in my arms? You'd make me go home. No matter what was happening under this roof."

Mary opened her mouth to deny it. Then shut things up as Marissa cocked a brow.

As if the boss knew she'd won the argument, Marissa got to her feet and smiled a little. "You've always been devoted to your job. But it's important that Safe Place not take over your life."

"Yes. Of course. You're right."

"I'll see you at home, later."

"Absolutely."

As Marissa left, Mary intended to do as she was told . . . except it was hard to leave. Even after she got her bag and her coat, and texted for Ryhm to come back in if she wouldn't mind—and the female didn't—she somehow found reasons to delay heading back out to Rhage's car again. First, it was turning over a couple of other responsibilities to another staff member; then it was standing at the base of the attic stairs, debating whether or not to tell Bitty.

In the end, Mary decided not to bother the girl and proceeded down to the first floor. She pulled another pause at the front door, but that one didn't last as long.

When she was finally outside, she breathed deeply and smelled fall in the air.

Just as she was getting into the GTO, she paused and looked up. The light was on in Bitty and her mother's room, and it was impossible not to imagine that little girl waiting with those packed bags for an uncle who didn't exist to come and take her away from a reality that was going to follow her around for the rest of her life.

The trip home took forever, but eventually, she pulled the muscle car into a space in the courtyard between Qhuinn's Hummer II and Manny's Porsche 911 Turbo.

Staring over at the towering gray stone mansion, with its guard-goyles, as Lassiter called them, and its countless windows, and its slant-

ing slate roofs, she wondered what Bitty would think of the place, and figured the girl would probably be intimidated at first. But as scary as it seemed from outside, the people inside made it cozy and warm as a little cottage.

Across the cobblestones and by the fountain which had already been drained for winter. Up the stone steps. Into the vestibule, where she put her face in the security camera and waited.

Beth was the one who opened things wide, and she was balancing L.W. on her hip. "Oh, hey . . . I was about to call you."

"Hey, little man." Mary stroked the boy's cheek and smiled at him, because how could you not? The baby was a tub of cute, an absolute charmer. "Did you need something, you guys?"

As she stepped into the grand foyer, so that L.W. didn't catch cold, she stopped when she saw Beth's expression. "Everything okay?"

"Well, ah . . . so Rhage just went upstairs."

"Oh? He must be feeling better."

"I think you need to go talk to him."

Something in the Queen's voice really wasn't right. "Is there something wrong?"

The female focused on her infant, smoothing his dark hair. "I just think you need to go be with him."

"What happened?" As Beth merely repeated some version of what she'd already said, Mary frowned. "Why aren't you looking at me?"

Beth's eyes finally swung over and held. "He just seems . . . upset. And I think he needs you. That's it."

"Okay. All right. Thanks."

Mary crossed the mosaic floor and took the stairs at a jog. When she got to their bedroom, she opened the door—and was hit with a blast of freezing cold air.

"Rhage?" Putting her arms around herself, she shivered. "Rhage? Why are the windows open?"

Trying not to become alarmed, she went across and closed the sash on the left of their enormous bed. Then she went over and shut the other one. "Rhage?"

"In here."

Thank God, at least he was answering.

Tracking his voice, she went to the bathroom—and found him sitting in the middle of the marble expanse, knees up to his chest, arms linked around his calves, head down and tilted away from her. He was dressed in sweats and as big as ever, but everything about him seemed to have shrunk.

"Rhage!" She rushed across over and crouched beside him. "What's wrong? Do you need Doc Jane?"

"No."

With a curse, she stroked back his hair. "Are you in pain?"

When he didn't answer her or look up, she moved around so that she could see his face. His lids were low and his eyes were unfocused.

He looked as if he had received very bad news.

"Is someone hurt?" One of the Brothers? Layla? Except Beth would have told her that, right? "Rhage, talk to me. You're scaring me."

Lifting his head, he rubbed his face and seemed to realize for the first time she was there. "Hey. I thought you were at work?"

"I came home." And for good reason. What if she had stayed there and he'd been—jeez, Marissa had been so right. "Rhage, what's going on—wait, did someone hit you?"

His jaw seemed swollen, and there were black and blue marks that showed even through his tanned skin.

"Rhage," she said with more force. "What the hell happened to you? Who punched you?"

"Vishous. Twice—well, once on each side."

Recoiling, she cursed. "Dear God, why?"

His eyes traced her features and then he reached up with his fingertips, touching her gently. "Don't be mad. I deserved it—and he made my sight come back sooner than usual."

"You're still not answering my question." She tried to keep her voice even. "Did you two get in an argument?"

Rhage brushed her lower lip with his thumb. "I love the way you kiss me."

"What did you fight about?"

"And I love your body." His hands went down to her shoulders and moved to rest on her collarbones. "You're so beautiful, Mary."

"Look, I appreciate the compliments, but I need to know what's going on," she said, putting her palms over his. "You're clearly upset about something."

"Will you let me kiss you?"

As he stared at her, he seemed desperate in a way she didn't understand. And it was because of the pain that she sensed in him that Mary leaned in.

"Yes," she whispered. "Always."

Rhage tilted his head to the side, and contrary to his usual passion, his lips were soft against her own, brushing, lingering. As her pulse quickened, she almost wished it didn't—she didn't want to be distracted with sex . . . except as he continued to stroke against her mouth, all the chaos in her brain rerouted to an electric feeling of anticipation, his flaring scent, his beautiful body, his male power crowding out everything that worried her.

"My Mary," he groaned as he licked his way into her. "Every time with you . . . it's new. It's never the same and always better than the last kiss . . . the last touch."

His hands drifted downward so that she felt the weight of them over her breasts. And then with a slow draw, he peeled the jacket away, sweeping it off her arms, making her feel her silk shirt and her lacy bra and all her skin beneath her clothes with aching clarity.

Except some part of her spoke up. Her conscience, maybe? Because she sure as hell felt as though she had let him down by being gone when he needed her.

"Why were the windows open?" she asked again.

But it was as if he didn't even hear her.

"I love . . ." His voice caught and he had to clear his throat. "I love your body, Mary."

As if she weighed nothing, he lifted her off the hard marble floor and moved her to the side, laying her on the plush fur rug that was in front of the Jacuzzi. Easing back against the softness, she watched his eyes travel down her throat to her breasts . . . and go lower to her hips and legs.

"My Mary."

"Why do you sound so sad?" she said quietly.

When he didn't answer her, she had a moment of true fear. But then he began to slip the buttons free on her blouse, taking his time, keeping the two halves together even as he tugged the tails out of her slacks. Sitting back, he took the silk between his fingertips and revealed her body to the heat in his gaze and the warmth of the bath's interior.

He shifted himself over and knelt across her thighs. "I love your breasts."

Leaning down, he kissed her at her sternum. On the edge of her bra. On the top of her nipple. A sudden release of the subtle pressure of the cups told her that he'd freed the front clasp—and then the air currents brushed against her bare skin as he moved the fragile barrier off to the sides.

He spent . . . forever . . . caressing her breasts, stroking them, thumbing the tight tips. Until she thought she was going mad. And then he was sucking at her, first one side, then the other. She couldn't remember when he'd last taken his time with her—not that he was ever inconsiderate. Her *hellren* ran on a different Rhage-length, however, which was to say he was all-in, all the time.

Not tonight, apparently.

He kissed his way down onto her abdomen and released her thin belt, the fastener, and the zipper on her slacks. As she lifted her hips, he pulled her pants off and made them disappear, leaving her cream silk underwear behind.

Back at her belly, he splayed his hands wide, until his palms covered her pelvis.

He stayed like that, stroking his thumbs back and forth over her lower abdominals.

"Rhage?" she said in a voice that was choked. "What aren't you telling me?"

TWENTY-ONE

As Rhage knelt above his Mary, he was distinctly aware that she was saying his name, but he was too lost in the clamor between his ears to respond.

Looking down at his *shellan*'s belly, he imagined her growing big like Layla had, her body harboring their young until their son or daughter could breathe on its own. In the fantasy, both his baby and Mary were perfectly healthy before, during and after the birth: she glowed her way through the eighteen months—or was it nine months, for human women?—and the labor was short and painless, and when it was all through, he was able to gather her and their creation in his arms and love them for the rest of his life.

Maybe their little boy would have blue eyes and blond hair, but his *mahmen*'s incredible character and intelligence. Or perhaps their little girl would have Mary's brunette hair and his teal eyes and be a firecracker.

Whatever the combination of looks and spirit, he pictured the three of them sitting down together for First Meal and Last Meal and all the snacks in between. And he imagined he could take the young to give Mary a break, just like Z and Wrath did for their *shellans*, bottle-feeding breast milk to the infant. Or, later, giving little pieces from his plate to a small precious mouth as Z got to do now with Nalla.

In this marvelous daydream, years would pass, and there would be tantrums at three and the first deep thoughts and questions at five. Then friends at ten and, God forbid, driving at fifteen. There would be human holidays and vampire festivals . . . followed by a transition that would terrify the shit out of him and Mary—but because this was a fantasy, their young would make it through and come out strong on the other side. After that? The first heartbreak. And maybe the One.

Which, if he and Mary had a daughter, would be a fucking eunuch.

Either because the sonofabitch came that way as the Scribe Virgin made him . . . or because Rhage took care of that problem himself.

And then much, much later . . . grandchildren.

Immortality on earth.

And all because he and Mary loved each other. All because one night years and years, and then decades and centuries ago, she had come to the training center with John Matthew and Bella, and he had been blind and floundering, and she had spoken to him.

"Rhage?"

Shaking himself, he bent down low and put his lips to her belly. "I love you."

Shit, he hoped she took that huskiness for arousal.

With quick hands, he swept her panties off and spread her thighs. As he brought his lips to her sex, he heard her moan his name—and he was determined as he licked and sucked at her: He would love her even without her having their child. Worship her as any bonded male should. Cherish her, hold her, be her best friend, her lover, her staunchest defender.

There would be a hollow place in him, though.

A small little black hole in his heart for what could have been. What might have been. What he never, ever thought would matter . . . but somehow he would always miss.

Reaching up, he stroked her breasts as he made her come against his mouth.

He wasn't supposed to want young. Hadn't ever considered them—

had even thought that having Mary as a mate was a good thing because he would never be where Wrath and Z had been. Where Qhuinn was.

Where Tohr had gone.

In fact, it seemed wrong to covet the very thing that not only could kill his female if she had been normal and able to bear a child, but what would have doomed them both: if his Mary hadn't been infertile, the Scribe Virgin wouldn't have allowed them to be together after saving her life from the cancer. V's mother would have mandated that, in addition to Rhage keeping his curse, the two of them never to cross paths again.

Balance must be preserved, after all.

Lifting his head, he swept off the *AHS* sweatshirt and what he had on the bottom and moved himself up to mount her—and he was careful as he angled his hard cock to her core. With a gentle roll, he entered her body, and that familiar hold of her, that squeeze, that slick heat, brought tears to his eyes as he imagined, for one and one time only, that the two of them were doing this not to connect . . . but to conceive.

Except then he told himself to stop it.

No more thinking. No more regrets for what would have ruined them anyway.

And there was never going to be any talking.

He would never, ever speak to her about this. She certainly hadn't volunteered for cancer or chemo or infertility. None of it was any of her doing, as far away from an issue of fault as anyone could get.

So there was no way he would ever voice this sorrow of his.

But yes, this was the anxiety he'd been feeling. This was the distance. This was the source of his itch. For the past however long, he had been watching his brothers with their young, seeing the closeness of the families, envying what they had—and burying the lot of it until the emotions had come out unexpectedly in the kitchen with L.W.

Rather like a boil that had festered until it could be contained no longer.

Rhage told himself he should be relieved because he wasn't insane or manic to the point of mental instability. And more to the point, now that he had figured out what it was, he could put this all behind them both.

Just shove it to the back of his head and close the door.

Things were going to get back to normal.

It was all going to be fine, goddamn it.

He was magnificent, as always.

As Mary arched beneath Rhage's thrusting body, she wasn't fooling herself—she knew the sex was just a temporary diversion from what had to be some kind of big issue for him. But sometimes you had to give the person the space they needed . . . or in this case, the sex.

Because, dear Lord, she sensed this was somehow significant to him in a different way than usual. Her mate always wanted her in an erotic way, but this seemed . . . well, for one thing, his powerful hips were capable of driving her across the bathroom floor, but instead they were gently thrusting into her. And also, he appeared to be not so much holding back as holding on, his arms wrapping under her torso so she was lifted off the rug, his body riding hers with a rocking rhythm that was all the more vivid for its poignant restraint.

"I love you," he said in her ear.

"I love you, too—"

Her next orgasm cut off her voice, jerking her up so that her breasts hit the wall of his chest. God, he was so beautiful as he kept going on top of her, the rhythm of his penetrations stretching out the pulsing shocks that kicked through her sex until he was the only thing she knew in the universe, until the past and future disappeared, until all the clutter in her mind and around her heart disintegrated.

For some reason, the silence of those nattering criticisms, the retreat of that incessant worry, the disappearance of the crushing, nightly crucible of wondering if she were doing her job right—and sometimes knowing for sure that she was not—brought tears to her eyes.

Anxiety over Rhage aside, she hadn't known how tightly she had been wound. How heavy the burden had become. How preoccupied she always was.

"I'm sorry," she choked out.

Instantly, Rhage froze.

"What?"

His eyes were strangely horrified as he shifted and looked down at her. And she smiled as she brushed away her tears.

"I'm just so . . . grateful for you," she whispered.

Rhage seemed to shake himself. "I—well, I feel the same way."

"Finish? Inside of me?" She arched up against him. "I want to feel you come."

Rhage dropped his head into her neck and began moving once more. "Oh, God, Mary . . . *Mary* . . ."

Two strokes later he was orgasming, his incredible body tightening up, his erection kicking deeply within her and teeing off another release.

He didn't stop. Not for the longest time. Which was something that vampire males had the ability to do. He just kept orgasming, filling her to overflowing—and still he continued until the releases came so closely together, they became a single pulsing rush.

When he was done, he fell still and drooped, but then he buttressed his weight on his elbows so she could breathe.

God, he was so huge.

She was used to his size to some degree, but as she opened her eyes, all she could see was just part of his shoulder. Everything else was blocked by his bulk.

Stroking his biceps, she said quietly, "Will you please tell me what's wrong?"

Rhage pushed himself back a little farther so he could meet her in the eye.

"You look so sad." She traced his brows. The sorrowful cast to his perfect mouth. The bruises on his jaw. "It's always better if you talk to someone."

After a long moment, he opened his mouth—

Bam! Bam! Bam!

Out in the bedroom, the unmistakable impact of a Brother pounding on the door was not muffled in the slightest.

Rhage twisted around and shouted, "Yeah?"

V's voice carried through into the loo. "We got a meeting. Now."

"Roger that. Coming."

Rhage turned back and kissed her. "I'd better go."

His withdrawal was quick, and his eyes stayed ducked as he helped her up off the rug and over to the shower.

"I wish I were getting in there with you," he said as he cranked on the hot water.

No, she thought, as he wouldn't look at her. You actually don't.

"Rhage, I know you have to go. But you're scaring me."

As he moved her under the spray, he took her face in his hands and stared her dead in the eye. "You don't have anything to worry about. Not now and not ever—at least not about me. I love you til forever and back, and nothing else matters as long as that is true."

Mary took a deep breath. "Okay. All right."

"I'll return soon as the meeting's over. And we can get some food. Watch a movie. You know, do that thing . . . what do the humans call it?"

Mary laughed a little. "Netflix and chill."

"Right. We're going to Netflix and chill."

He kissed her even though it got his face wet, and then he backed off and shut the glass door. On his way out, he threw his sweats on again, but kept his feet bare.

She watched him go. And thought it was amazing how someone could reassure you . . . while at the same time make things worse.

What the hell was going on with him?

When she was finished with her shower, she toweled off, brushed the tangles out of her wet hair, and got dressed in a set of yoga pants and a big black cashmere sweater that nearly came down to her knees. She'd bought the thing for Rhage as they'd headed into the previous winter, and she'd even gotten it in his favorite non-color after a long-standing failure at trying to diversify his wardrobe. He hadn't been able to wear it very often, though, because he'd always overheated with it on.

The weave smelled like him, however.

And as she left their room, she felt as though he were with her—and man, did she need that tonight.

Pausing in front of the King's study, she listened to the deep male voices on the other side of the closed doors.

Down below in the foyer, she could hear *doggen* talking. The floor polisher. The tinkling of crystal, as if the sconces were being taken apart to be cleaned in the sink again.

Without making a sound, she padded across the thick red-and-gold runner, heading for the Hall of Statues. But she didn't go down that corridor, with its Greco-Roman masterpieces in marble and all its bedrooms. No, she was headed for the next floor up.

The door to the mansion's third level was not locked, but it wasn't open, either, and she felt a little like she was trespassing as she opened the way to the stairs and went upward. On the top landing, across from Trez's and iAm's rooms, was the vaulted steel door to the First

Family's suite, and she hit its bell, standing with her face in the security camera.

Moments later, there was a series of clunks as the bars moved free of their holds, and then the heavy panel opened wide. Beth was on the other side, L.W. on her hip, her hair in a braid over her shoulder, those old blue jeans and bright blue fleece the very definition of homey. What was not cozy in the slightest? The incredible glimmer of the gemstones set into all the walls beyond.

Mary had never been in the private quarters before. Few had, other than Fritz, who insisted on doing the cleaning up there himself. But Mary had heard that the entire suite was studded with precious jewels from the Old Country's treasury—and clearly that was true.

"Hey, there." The Queen smiled even as L.W. grabbed onto some hair over her ear and yanked. "Okay, ow. Let's try something else for biceps curls, shall we?"

As Beth untangled that fat little fist, Mary said grimly, "I need you to tell me what happened with Rhage. And don't pretend you don't know what it is."

Beth's eyes closed briefly. "Mary, it's not my place—"

"If the roles were reversed, you would want to know. And I would tell you if you asked me to—because that's what family does for one another. Especially when someone is hurting."

The Queen exhaled a curse. Then she stepped aside and nodded at the sparkling suite. "Come on in. We need to do this in private."

TWENTY-TWO

sually Rhage had something in his mouth during meetings with the King. Tootsie Pops were his favorite, but in a pinch, he'd rock a pack of Starburst, or maybe a thing of Chips Ahoy!—the old-school ones in the blue bag, crunchy, not chewy and no nuts. His stomach wasn't up to handling anything like that, though—and not because of the beast shit.

But at least his vision was even better than it had been after V had hit him.

As the shutters came down for the day, he took up res in the corner by the double doors while his brothers settled in their usual places around the room: Butch and V on one of the spindly French sofas, the pair of them settling into nearly identical, ankle-over-knee poses; Z against the wall in the best defensible position with Phury right next to him; John, Blay and Qhuinn grouped together by the fire. Rehvenge, meanwhile, was in front of Wrath's ornate desk, the leader of the *symphaths* being one of the King's closest advisers, and Tohr was sitting at Wrath's dagger hand due to his position as head of the Brotherhood, a first lieutenant in all things.

Lassiter wasn't around, and Rhage guessed the fallen angel was

watching T.V. somewhere. And Payne, who had taken to attending these sorts of things? She was probably watching Xcor.

'Cuz God knew the female could handle herself, and any male on the planet.

As always, Wrath was the focal point of it all, sitting in the ornate throne his father had used, the Brother's black wraparound sunglasses surveying the room even though he was blind, his hand resting on the boxy head of his golden retriever service dog.

Qhuinn was doing the talking this morning, however.

"—have two people down there getting care, Layla and my brother. Neither of them is in any shape to defend themselves if he gets free, and Doc Jane, Manny and Ehlena are medical people, not fighters."

"With all due respect, Xcor's seriously guarded," Butch said. "Twenty-four-seven."

"If Marissa were carrying your kid, would that be good enough?"

The cop opened his mouth. Then shut it and nodded. "Yeah. Too right."

Qhuinn crossed his arms over his chest. "Personally, I don't give a fuck if he's in a Hannibal Lecter, I don't want him anywhere near that clinic."

As the Brother went quiet, Wrath asked, "What's Xcor's condition now?"

Vishous stroked his goatee. "Still in a coma. Vital signs aren't strong, but they're not slipping. No movement on his right side. I'm thinking stroke."

"But you don't know for sure?"

"Not without dragging his ass to Havers's for a CAT scan. But I don't want to move him across town just to figure out what I'm pretty damn confident of already—and yes, both Jane and Manny agree with my conclusion."

"Any idea how long the coma's liable to last?"

"Nope. He could be waking up now. Or be under for a month. Or go the persistent vegetative state route. There's really no telling. And if he does wake up? Depending on the severity of the stroke, he could be cognitively impaired. Physically fucked. Or completely normal. Or somewhere in between the extremes."

"Goddamn it," Tohr muttered.

Wrath leaned to the side and picked George up off the ground, resettling the dog in his lap. As a cloud of blond fur tufted into the air, the King picked a piece out of his mouth before speaking.

"Qhuinn's right. We can't keep him there, especially if the new trainees are coming in. For one thing, you assholes are going to need the gun range, but more to the point, we sure as shit don't want any of those little fuckers waking up dead at the end of class because our door prize woke up and got out of its cage. The question is, where do we take him? I want him close enough so we can have immediate back-up, but we gotta get him off this property."

There was a bunch of discussion, not all of which Rhage tracked. The truth was, as critical as the issue about Xcor was, the biggest part of his brain was back in that bathroom with his Mary as he deliberately reminded himself how good she felt under him, how amazing her moans were, how much he loved being inside of her.

Nothing was lost between them, or gone from their sex life, if they couldn't reproduce. Nothing.

Really.

"—of Bastards have to be searching all over downtown," somebody said. "Looking for a body or a burn mark."

Vishous cut in. "I have two cell phones that I took off of him. One had a garden-variety password and I got into it no problem—there was nothing except details about drug deals and we all know that's over with. The other unit went dead on me as soon as I cracked its code, and I'm guessing that was Xcor's—clearly, the Bastards have some rudimentary security precautions in place."

"Will you be able to get the cell working again?" Wrath asked.

"Depends on how bad the fry job is and I still need to make that assessment. I may be able to extract some data, but it could be a while."

"The Band of Bastards will not rest until they find Xcor," someone muttered.

Tohr's voice was a growl. "So let me give them his body."

"Not yet, my brother." Wrath glanced over at the guy. "And you know that."

"But if he's brain-dead, there's nothing to interrogate—"

Wrath talked over the male. "I want everyone downtown for the next three nights. Xcor's disappearance will flush the Bastards out of hiding. We got one of them. I want them all."

"We also better keep sweeping for slayers," somebody muttered. "Just because we won last night doesn't mean the war's over."

"The Omega will make more," Wrath agreed. "That's for shit sure."

Butch spoke up. "When it comes to the *lessers*, though . . . I think we're focusing on the symptom, not the disease. We need to take the Omega out. I mean, that's the *Dhestroyer* prophecy, right? I'm supposed to be the one who does it, but I couldn't have absorbed all those down-and-outers at the campus. No fucking way."

V gave his BFFL's shoulder a squeeze. "You do enough."

"Obviously not—how long's it been now? And their numbers are lower, but there was still a shitload coming after us on that campus."

"My mother is so goddamn useless," V bitched as he lit up. "We've been fighting the Lessening Society for centuries and centuries. Even with the prophecy, I've seen no indication that we can eradicate them—"

"I know where we can put Xcor," Rhage cut in.

As all the eyes in the room focused on him, he shrugged. "Don't freak out. But the solution is clear."

Down in the training center, Layla recognized the feeling that had plagued her since the night before.

As she sat on the edge of her hospital bed, she knew exactly what the ringing sense of destination meant, the burn in the center of her chest, the nagging, unrelenting itch.

It just made no sense.

So she had to be misinterpreting things. Maybe this was yet another pregnancy symptom and it just felt like the other thing?

Well, one way or the other, she was going to find out, she thought as she shifted off the mattress and shuffled over to the door. Her most recent twelve-hour wait had passed so it was time to stretch her legs once again—and with no Brothers babysitting her and Qhuinn and Blay in a meeting, she was going to use her relative freedom to the fullest.

Stepping into the corridor, she looked around. There was nobody outside her room. No sounds from the clinic. And the gym and weight room way down the hall both seemed quiet as well.

Ostensibly, there was no one around at all. And that went for Brothers, servants and medical staff. So really . . . how was it possible that she was sensing Xcor's presence down here?

That Bastard couldn't possibly be in the Brotherhood compound.

He was the enemy, for godsakes—which meant if he had infiltrated the property, there would be an attack going on, all hell breaking loose, the Brothers at arms.

Instead? A whole lot of nada, as Qhuinn would have said.

This had to be some pregnancy-related strangeness—

No, she thought. He *was* here. She sensed him in her own blood— which was what happened if you fed someone: an echo of yourself was in them and it was kind of like catching your reflection in a mirror across a distance.

You couldn't mistake it for something else. Any more than you wouldn't recognize your own image.

Picking up the front of her Lanz nightgown—out of habit, rather than necessity because of her big belly—she waddled over the bare floor of the corridor in her slippers, going by the newly constructed ladies' bathroom, the males' locker room, the weight room.

Nothing particularly registered in any of them. But when she got past the gym to the entrance of the pool, she stopped.

Straight ahead. It felt as though he were straight ahead—

"Hey, girl, what are you doing?"

Layla wheeled around. "Qhuinn, hello."

The sire of her young strode up to her, his eyes roaming around her face, her belly. "Are you okay? What are you doing all the way back here?"

"I just . . . it's my stroll time."

"Well, you don't need to be over here." Qhuinn took her by the elbow, steered her around and led her away. "In fact, maybe we should move you back to the mansion for a little while."

"What—why?"

"It's homier there."

In less than a minute, she was back at the door to her room. And she wasn't stupid. He'd been the biggest supporter of her staying down here in the clinic, because it was better for her and the young, safer. Now he was changing his mind?

Heart pounding, head spinning, she knew damn well her instincts weren't lying. Xcor was here somewhere in the training center. Had they captured him in the field? Had he been injured and they'd brought him in as they had that soldier of his?

Qhuinn leaned forward to open her door. "Anyway, I'll just talk to Doc Jane about—"

"Talk to me about what?"

"Speak of the devil," Qhuinn said smoothly as he turned around.

V's mate was coming out of the utility room, a stack of surgical scrubs in her arms. "Look, don't tell Fritz about this, 'kay? But doing laundry clears my head, and sometimes you just need to chill."

Qhuinn smiled for a split second. "I actually came down to see you. I was thinking that Layla might enjoy a visit back to her regular room."

Doc Jane frowned. "At the house?"

"It's so damned clinical down here."

"Ah, yeah, that's the point, Qhuinn." Doc Jane shifted her load, but not her forest green stare. "I know that we've had quite a period of smooth sailing with the pregnancy, and I hope this trend continues. But we can't take any chances, and every night that passes, we're getting closer, not further away, to the big moment—"

"Just for the next twenty-four hours."

Layla looked back and forth between the pair of them. And felt like a lying hypocrite as she said, "I'd feel safer here."

"How long have you been on your feet?" Doc Jane asked.

"I just walked down the hall toward the gym—"

"We can move some equipment to the house," Qhuinn suggested. "You know, monitoring stuff. That kind of thing. Besides, it won't be for long."

Doc Jane shook her head like she couldn't believe she'd heard him correctly. "An OR? You think we can move an OR up there? I don't mean to be alarmist—but she's carrying twins, Qhuinn. Twins."

"I know." Qhuinn's mismatched eyes locked on the doctor's. "I'm fully aware of what is at stake. And so are you."

Doc Jane opened her mouth. Then hesitated. "Listen, I'm going to take these to my office. Meet me there, okay?"

As the doctor took off, Layla stared at Qhuinn. "Who else is down here."

Qhuinn put his hand on her shoulder. "No one, why do you ask?"

"Please. Just tell me.'"

"It's nothing. I don't know what she's talking about. Let's get you settled."

"You don't have to protect me."

Those dark brows got so tight, he wasn't frowning; he was glaring. "Really. *Really?*"

Layla exhaled and put her hand on her belly. "I'm sorry."

"Shit, no, don't apologize." He pushed his hair back, and for the first time, she got a good look at the black bags under his eyes. "Everyone is . . . you know, it's the war. It's so fucking stressful."

Putting his arm around her shoulders, he led her into her room and back to the bed where he set her down as if she were made of porcelain.

"I'll come check on you at the end of my—later. Ah, I'll be back later." He smiled in a way that did not reach his eyes. "Let me know if you need anything, okay?"

As the familiar waves of guilt and fear crested over her, Layla couldn't say anything, her jaw literally locking place and her lips squeezing tight. But what could she do? If she told him that she knew Xcor was here . . .

Well, he'd want to know how. And it would be impossible to lie to him and tell him that it was from her having fed the Bastard all those months before . . . back when she'd been duped by Xcor's soldier into going out to that meadow to take care of what she had assumed was a civilian fighter working with the Brotherhood. She had already confessed her unintentional sin to the King; what she hadn't told anyone was that she had gone on to meet Xcor many times after that—ostensibly to keep him from attacking the compound when he'd discovered its location.

In truth, it was because she had fallen in love with him.

And the fact that the visits had ended? The reality that Xcor himself had been the one to terminate the meetings? That hardly mattered.

The truth was that she had craved that time with him. And that was her treason, regardless of how much she had tried to paint herself as a victim.

"Layla?"

With a curse, she shook herself back into focus. "I'm sorry? What?"

"Are you all right?"

"No. I mean—yes, yes, I am." She put her hands on the small of her back and stretched. "I'm just tired. It's the pregnancy. But everything's fine."

Qhuinn stared at her for a long moment, his mismatched eyes searching her face. "Will you call me? Even if you're just . . . you know, going stir crazy?"

"I will. I promise."

As the door closed behind him, she knew what he was going to do. He was going to go talk to the other Brothers—if he hadn't already done so. And soon, very soon, she was going to find that she no longer sensed Xcor's presence.

Either because she was relocated or he was.

Putting her head in her hands, she tried to breathe and found that it was impossible. Her throat was tight, her ribs were like iron bars, her lungs were burning. She just kept telling herself that getting upset was not going to help things. It certainly wasn't going to be good for her or the pregnancy.

Besides, she wasn't meeting Xcor anymore.

Because that was what happened when you called a male on his feelings. Or at least, a male like him.

And he hadn't attacked the compound—

Unless that was how he'd been captured? Oh, dearest Virgin Scribe, had he brought his soldiers here with arms? Had that been the chaos of the evening before?

Her mind promptly went into a tailspin, her thoughts merging together in patterns that made no sense thanks to too much velocity, and not enough proper reasoning.

Sometime later, she dropped her arms, and glanced across at the bathroom door. It was a hundred miles away. But she did have to pee, and maybe some cold water on her face would help her calm down.

Shifting her legs off the mattress, she steadied herself on her feet and—

Wetness. There was . . . an abrupt wetness between her thighs.

Her hands went to the front of her nightgown as she looked down.

And screamed.

TWENTY-THREE

Upstairs in his glass house, Assail took a shower that lasted nearly a lifetime.

The black out panels had come down over the windows, so it was dark, nothing but the glowing light switches with their little peach-colored toggle heads orienting him. The water was blistering hot, and as he dropped his head back, he swept his hair flat to his skull. His body was in a post-feeding, post-fucking float, even his addiction quieting down.

Although the latter was probably due to the three lines he'd done as soon as he'd come up here.

Strike the *probably*.

He had fucked Naasha a number of times, and roughly, too, so his lower back was tight. His cock was exhausted. His balls, empty and then some.

There was no joy in his heart. None. That was not unusual, however. And the shampoo and soap did naught to make him feel cleaner, likely because the dirt he was coated with was not on his exterior. But he could not say that he was unfamiliar with that, either.

Still, all was not lost. There was work to be done.

When Assail had endeavored to come unto the New World, he

had not made the trip alone. His cousins, Ehric and Evale, had traveled with him, and they had proven to be steadfast and loyal aides throughout his business endeavors. Staying with him here, they had never failed him—and he was going to need them once again.

For something they were rather likely to enjoy.

Naasha, as want would have it, had several friends of hers in a similar situation—females of the *glymera* who were unable to be attended to properly by their older *hellren* and were looking for certain . . . releases . . . that were unavailable to them. And although his cousins had retired to their basement suites by the time Assail had returned home, he was confident that he had volunteered the pair for work they would be quite happy to perform.

Because Wrath had been right.

Things were indeed afoot in the aristocracy.

Assail could sense it sure as a scent upon the night air. He just knew not what yet. Time, and sex, was going to fix that, however.

Stepping out of the shower, he appreciated the thick, warm pile of the bath mat beneath his feet and dried off with a towel heated upon a bar next to the shower enclosure. Indeed, he had purchased the mansion fully furnished from its builder, and all had been considered and attended to in the construction and kitting out of the house. Every luxury provided. Not a penny spared.

The place seemed utterly empty, however, in spite of its three occupants. Rather like the inside of his skin, wasn't it. A thing of refinement and beauty on the exterior, yet soulless inside.

For a brief interlude, things had not been as such. In both cases.

But that time had passed.

Out in his bedroom, he got in between his silk sheets naked and made a mental note to switch them out at nightfall. Although it was not traditional for a male of his station, he had grown used to attending to his own baths and dressings, changing his sheets, washing his clothes. There was a strange comfort to taking care of such simple things, a start and finish to each endeavor from which he derived a certain satisfaction.

And that was how he usually passed the days whilst his cousins slept down below. Tidying up. Scrubbing floors and sinks, toilets and counters. Vacuuming. Polishing. It was a productive way to burn off the cocaine jitters.

Not these particular daylight hours, however. After the feeding, he required rest, not just of the mind, but of the body—

Beside him, his cell chimed softly with the old-fashioned bell ring of phones that were nowhere to be found anymore.

He didn't bother to see who it was. He knew. "I would have called you," he said, "but I didn't want to be rude. It is rather early in the morning for business."

The Brother Vishous didn't miss a beat. Which was rather one of his most predominant characteristics. "What happened? Did you get anything?"

"Indeed, yes. In rather a number of different positions. Naasha was most accommodating."

A dark laugh came over the connection. "With a male like you, I'm sure she was. And we expect you to hit that on the regular until she starts talking."

"She already has." Assail smiled cruelly in the dark. "Tell me, is your Dom reputation just talk or are you truly that perverted?"

"Waste my time with gossip and I'll answer that firsthand."

"Kinky."

"Why do you ask?"

"Your name came up in conversation."

"How."

The fact that that wasn't a question, but a demand was not a surprise. "She was speaking of sexual conquests she had enjoyed. You apparently were one of them, back when she was younger—and she made it clear you had done the conquesting, as it were."

"I've fucked a lot of people," V said in a bored tone, "and forgotten ninety-five percent of them. So tell me what you know—and not about sex. Mine or others'."

Assail was not surprised about the conversation's redirection. "The aristocracy is going to be approaching the King soon. They're going to request his appearance at a private reception for her *hellren*'s nine hundredth birthday—an event that even in good bloodlines is a thing of rarity."

"Are they planning on shooting my Lord again?"

"Possibly. My instincts tell me there is a path being forged." Assail shook his head even though the Brother could not see him. "I'm just not sure by whom. Naasha is more renowned for her horizontal ac-

complishments rather than her mental ones. She is not capable of developing a strategy, whether one of treasonous nature or even for a Last Meal encounter. That is why I believe there is someone guiding her. But again, I know not whom—yet."

"When are you seeing her next?"

"She is having a dinner on the eve and I shall attend with my cousins. I shall endeavor to discover more at that time."

"That's tight. Good job."

"I haven't performed yet."

"Not true. How many times did she come?"

"I lost count after seven."

Another dark laugh came over the connection. "A male after my own heart. And don't knock perversion, you judgmental little fuck. You never know when you might find it appealing. Call me tomorrow."

"We keep this up and I'll talk to you more than I speak with my own *mahmen*."

"Isn't she dead?"

"Yes."

"Some bastards have all the luck."

After the meeting with Wrath and the Brotherhood broke up, Rhage returned to his and Mary's room, and as he opened the door, he was hoping she was asleep—

"Hi."

Okay, right. Mary was anything but in a doze. She was sitting up in their bed, leaning against the headboard, knees tucked to her chest, arms linked around them.

As if she had been waiting for him.

"Ah, hi." He shut the door. "I thought maybe you'd be resting."

She just shook her head. And stared at him.

In the awkward silence that followed, he remembered another night that seemed like forever ago—when he'd walked into this room after he'd taken his edge off with a human woman. Mary had been staying with him, and it had killed her to see him afterward—hell, it had killed him to come back to her like that, too. But at the time, it had been a case of him either giving his body some sex or him mounting Mary and risking the beast coming out while he was inside of her. After all, his Mary had juiced him up so high, so fast that his curse had threatened to emerge

just in her presence alone, and he had been terrified of hurting her. Scared to reveal that part of his nature to her. Convinced that his unworthiness would emerge and ruin everything.

So he had returned here and had had to look her in the face, knowing what he had done with another.

Short of the night he had learned she was dying, it was the single worst memory in his whole life.

Funny, this felt the same in some ways. A reckoning he didn't want, but could do nothing to prevent.

"I talked to Beth," she said grimly. "She told me you sat with L.W. when she was getting her hand treated."

Rhage closed his eyes and wanted to curse. Especially as there was a long pause, as if she were giving him a chance to explain.

"Do you want to tell me why holding L.W. made you so emotional?"

Her tone was even. Controlled. Gentle, might even be apt.

So it made his truth seem especially cruel and unfair. But she wasn't going to let him off the hook, change the subject, push this aside. That was not his Mary's way, not when it came to stuff like this.

"Rhage? What happened down there."

Rhage took a deep breath. He wanted to go over to her by the bed, but he needed to walk around—the churn and burn in his skull required some kind of physical expression or he was going to start screaming. Or punching walls . . .

He just had to figure out how to phrase this so it didn't sound as if he were blaming her. Or catastrophically unhappy. Or—

"Rhage?"

"Just gimme a minute."

"You've been pacing around for over twenty."

He stopped. Glanced across at his mate.

Mary had changed positions, and was now sitting with her feet dangling off the high mattress. She was dwarfed by the size of the bed, but they needed a mattress the size of a football field; he was so big, he couldn't really stretch out on anything smaller.

Shit. He was losing focus again—

"Was it because you . . ." Mary stared down at her feet. Then looked back over at him. "Is it because you want to have your own baby, Rhage?"

He opened his mouth. Closed it.

Stood there like a plank as his heart thundered in his chest.

"It's all right," she whispered. "Your brothers are starting to have families—and watching the people you love do that stirs up things. It brings up . . . wants . . . that maybe people weren't aware of—"

"I love you."

"But that doesn't mean you aren't disappointed."

Backing up so his shoulders hit the wall, he let himself slide down until the floor caught him in the ass. Then he hung his head because he couldn't bear looking at her.

"Oh, God, Mary, I don't want to feel this way." When his voice cracked, he cleared his throat. "I mean . . . I could try to lie, but . . ."

"You've felt like this for a while, haven't you. That's why things have been a little off between us."

He shrugged with defeat. "I would have said something, but I didn't know what was wrong. Until down there in the kitchen when I was alone with L.W. It just came out of nowhere. Hit me like a ton of bricks—I don't want to feel this way."

"It's perfectly natural—"

He drove his fist into the floor hard enough to crack the wood. "I don't want this! I don't fucking want this! You and I are all I need! I don't even like young!"

As his voice thundered in the room, he could feel her staring at him.

And couldn't stand it.

Jumping up again, he pounded around and felt like tearing the paintings off the walls and lighting the drapes on fire and breaking the highboy into kindling with his bare hands.

"I meant it," he barked. "When I told you I would get you a baby if you wanted one, I fucking meant that shit!"

"I know you did. What you didn't expect was to be the one who had the hollow pit in the middle of his chest."

He stopped dead and talked to the Oriental rug. "It doesn't matter. This doesn't matter. It's going to go away—"

"Beth told me something else." Mary waited for him to look over, and when he did, she brushed away a tear. "She said that Vishous came to you before the attack. She said . . . he told you that you were going to die. That he tried to get you to leave the field—but you wouldn't."

Rhage cursed and resumed walking around. Dragging a hand over his face, he found himself just wanting to go back to the early days of their relationship. When it had been easy. Nothing but good sex and greater love.

Not all this . . . life bullshit.

"Why did you go out there?" she asked in a halting way.

He waved away the question. "He could have been wrong, you know. V doesn't actually know everything or he'd be a god—"

"You went out early into the fight. You didn't wait . . . you went out there by yourself. Into a campus full of the enemy. Alone—right after one of your Brothers, who hasn't been wrong yet, told you that you were going to die out there. And then you were shot. In the chest."

Rhage didn't mean to crumble.

It was weird, though. He was upright . . . and then he was down on the floor, his legs collapsing under him at bad angles, his torso following suit in a sloppy fall of arms and shoulders. But that was what happened when a warrior lost his fight—he was nothing more than a gun dropped from a shooting hand, a dagger let loose from a palm, a grenade released, not thrown, into thin air.

"I'm sorry, Mary. I'm so . . . sorry. I'm sorry, I'm sorry . . ."

He just kept saying the words over and over again. There was nothing else he could do.

"Rhage." As she cut into his rambling, his Mary's voice was so sad that the sound of it was worse than that lead bullet through his heart. "Do you think you went out there alone because you wanted to die? And please, just be honest with me. This is too big . . . to just sweep under the rug."

Feeling like utter shit, he put his hands up to his face and talked into his palms. "I just needed . . . to be close to you again. Like it always was. Like it should be. Like it *has* to be for me. I thought . . . maybe if I were on the other side, and you came to me, we could . . ."

"Do what we're doing right now?"

"Except then it wouldn't matter."

"About having a child?"

"Yes."

As they both went quiet, he cursed. "I feel like I'm betraying you in a different way now."

When she inhaled deeply, it was clear she knew exactly what he was referencing—that moment when he had come back to her after that other female. But she recovered quickly. "Because I can't give you what you want and yet you want it anyway."

"Yes."

"Do you . . . do want to be with another wo—"

"God, no!" Rhage dropped his palms and shook his head so hard the thing nearly snapped off his spine. "Fuck, no! Never. Ever. I would rather be with you and never have young than—I mean, Jesus, it's not even close."

"Are you sure about that?"

"Absolutely. Straight up, I am one hundred percent certain."

She nodded, but she wasn't looking at him. She was back to focusing on her feet as she flexed her toes, then separated them out wide, then curled them under and moved them upward.

"It's okay if you do," she said quietly. "I mean, I would understand if you want to be with . . . you know, a real woman."

TWENTY-FOUR

Mary considered herself a total feminist. Yes, it was true that most men could deadlift more than most women—and that was a reality among both humans and vampires—but other than that largely insignificant physical disparity, there was absolutely nothing, in her view, that males could do better than females could.

So it was a bit of an eye-opener to find herself feeling like a total failure when, in fact, she was merely in the position all men were in.

Entities who were born with masculine sex organs could not bear children, and neither could she. See? Total equality there.

God, this hurt.

And it was painful in the strangest kind of way. The sensation was cold; it was a cold emptiness right in the center of her chest. Or maybe it was down lower, even though the metaphor of having a nothing-ness where her uterus was seemed just a little too Lifetime movie.

But that was what it felt like. A hollow space. A cavern.

"I'm sorry," she heard herself mumble. Even though that made no sense.

"Please," he begged. "Don't *ever* say that—"

Oh, hey, look, he'd come over and was kneeling in front of her, his

hands on her knees, his teal eyes staring up at her as if he were about to expire from the thought of having hurt her.

She placed her palm on his cheek, and felt the warmth of his face. "Fine, I won't apologize for that," she said. "But I am sorry for the both of us. You don't want to feel like this and neither do I, yet this is where we're at—"

"No, it's *not* where we're at, because I reject all of it. I'm not going to allow this to affect me or you—"

"Have I mentioned lately how much I hate cancer?" She dropped her arm, aware that she was talking over him, but unable to stop herself. "I really, really, really fucking hate that disease. I'm so glad vampires don't get it, because if you ever ended up with some version of it, I would seriously hate the universe for the rest of my immortal existence—"

"Mary, did you hear what I said?" He took her hand and put it back to his face. "I'm not going to ever think of this again. I'm not letting this come between us. It's not going to be—"

"Emotions don't work like that, Rhage. I'm a therapist, I should know." She tried to smile, but was pretty sure a grimace came out instead. "We don't get to pick how we feel—especially not about something as fundamental as having children. I mean, other than death and who you want to spend your life with, the whole kid thing is the very basis of existence."

"But you can choose what you do about your emotions. That's what you always say—you can choose how you react to your thoughts and your feelings."

"Yes. Except somehow . . . that doesn't seem like a workable plan at the moment."

God, why don't more people knee their therapists in the balls, she wondered. That sanctimonious pile of horseshit about "feel your feelings, but let your nurturing parent control your responses," was really not helpful at a time like this—when you were on the verge of breaking down and your partner was the same, and there was a voice in the back of your head telling you that the two of you were never going to get through this because, Christ, who could?

Oh, and P.S., it was all her fault because she was the one with the lack of fertile eggs—

"Mary, look at me."

When she finally did, she was surprised at the fierce expression on that beautiful face of his. "I refuse to let anything come between us, especially not some dumb-ass pipe dream about having a kid. Because that's what it is. Wrath and Z? Yes, they have young with their mates, but they had to live with the reality that their *shellans* could die—for fuck's sake, Wrath nearly *did* lose Beth. And Qhuinn? Yeah, sure, he's not in love with Layla, but do not tell me he doesn't care about that female with all his heart, considering what she's carrying for the both of them." He exhaled and sat back, bracing his palms against the floor. His eyes drifted to the headboard and roamed around as he traced the carvings. "When I think about it logically . . . as strong as this desire for young is . . ." He shifted his weight and prodded at the center of his chest. ". . . as much as I feel a need for a young specifically with you, what I know to be even more true is that I wouldn't trade any child for you."

"But I'm immortal, remember? You wouldn't have to worry about me on the birthing bed like your brothers do."

His eyes shot to hers. "Yes, but then I wasn't ever going to see you again, Mary. That was the balance, remember? You wouldn't have known that we'd ever been together . . . but I would have. For the rest of my life, I would have known that you were on the planet, alive and well . . . I just couldn't ever see you, touch you, laugh with you again. And if I ran into you? You were going to drop dead on the spot." He rubbed his face. "Your not being able to have young? It's the reason we're together. It's not a curse, Mary . . . it's a blessing. It's what saved us."

Mary blinked back tears. "Rhage . . . "

"You know it's true. You know that's the balance." He sat up and took her hands. "You know that's why we have anything at all. You gave us our future precisely because you can't bear my sons and daughters."

As their eyes met once more and held, she started to say she was sorry again. But he wouldn't have it. "No. I'm not hearing that, Mary. I'm serious. I'm not fucking hearing that. And you know what? I wouldn't change a thing. Not one thing."

"But you want a—"

"Not more than I want you with me, by my side, living with me, loving with me." His stare never left hers, the force of his conviction

so strong, it made his eyes burn. "I'm serious, Mary. Now that I'm thinking about it . . . now that I'm running the math in my head? No. Life without you is a tragedy. Life without our young? That's . . . well, it's just a different path."

Mary's first instinct was to stay stuck in her own drama, the hamster wheel of regret and anger and sadness as seductive and potentially unrelenting as a black hole. But then she tried to reach past all that, tried to somehow get across to the other side.

What helped her to safety?

The love in his eyes.

As Rhage looked up at her, his stare was like the sun, a source of warmth and life and love. Even with all that she couldn't give him? He still somehow managed to look at her as if everything that mattered to him . . . was exactly what he had in front of him.

And in that moment, Mary realized something.

Life didn't have to be perfect . . . for true love to exist in it.

It was just a different path.

The strangest thing happened as those six words came out of Rhage's mouth. It was as if a weight was lifted off of him, everything becoming light and kind of frothy, his heart starting to sing, his soul releasing its burden, the distance that had creeped in between him and his mate just poofing away like smoke clearing, like fog lifting, like a storm passing through and continuing on.

"I wouldn't change a thing." As he spoke the words, he felt . . . free. "Nothing. I wouldn't change anything."

"I wouldn't blame you if you did."

"Well, I don't." He stroked his way up her calves, pulling on her legs so she'd look at him. "I don't at all."

Mary took a deep breath. And then that smile of hers came out, her lips turning up at the corners, those eyes of hers re-lighting. "Really?"

"Truly."

Rhage got to his feet and sat down next to her, mirroring her pose, except his legs were so long, his soles were flat on the floor. Taking her hand, he bumped her with his shoulder once. Twice. Until she giggled and bumped him back.

"You know, you're right," he said. "Talking helps."

"Funny, I was just thinking that was a load of bullcrap."

He shook his head. "It's amazing how everything depends on how you frame it."

"What are you, married to a therapist or something?" As they laughed a little, she shrugged. "You know, I never really thought about children. I was busy getting through college, and then my mom got sick. Then I got sick. By the time I might have started wondering about them, it was too late for me—and there was no dwelling on any kind of loss in my mind. I guess because I always knew the cancer was going to come back. I just knew it. And I was right."

"And then you mated a vampire."

"I did." Except his Mary frowned. "I want you to promise me something."

"Anything."

She turned his hand over, tracing the lines that crossed his palm. "I am glad we're talking—I'm mean, it was inevitable that this was going to come up, and really, in retrospect, I don't know why I didn't anticipate it better. And even though this is tough stuff for both of us, I'm very glad it's on the table and I'm happy you feel better. I just . . . you should be aware that something like this is not going to be fixed in a single conversation."

He wasn't so sure about that. He'd been feeling like his gears weren't meshing, but now? Everything was as smooth as it used to be—and seemed even stronger. "Maybe."

"I guess what I'm trying to say is that I don't want you to be surprised or feel bad if your feelings of disappointment come back. The next time you see Wrath and L.W., the next time Z walks in holding Nalla? You're probably going to get those pangs again."

As he pictured his King and his brother, he shrugged. "Yeah, you're right. But you know what? I'm just going to remind myself that I have you, and that wouldn't be possible under different circumstances. That's going to wipe the slate clean again, I promise."

"Just remember, denial is not a viable long-term strategy, not if you're looking for mental health."

"Ah, but perspective is very much a long-term strategy. And so is being grateful for everything you have."

She smiled again. "Touché. But please talk to me? I'm not going to break, and I'd rather know where you are."

Lifting his hand, he tucked a piece of her hair behind her ear. "Mary, you're the strongest person I know."

"Sometimes I'm not so sure about that." With a shift and stretch up, she kissed him on the mouth. "Thanks for the vote of confidence, however."

"I guess it was just such a surprise," he murmured. "I didn't expect anything like having young or not having them to ever bother me."

"You never know what life's going to throw at you." Now, she was the one shrugging. "And I guess that's the good news and the bad news."

"I meant what I said to you way back when. If you want a young, I'll find one for you. Even if it's human."

Because God knew that vampire young were nearly impossible to adopt. They were too rare, too precious.

Mary shook her head after a moment. "No, I don't think that's ever going to be me. My maternal instinct gets expressed through my work." She glanced over at him. "I would have liked to be a parent with you, though. That would have been a lot of fun. You'd be a wonderful father."

Rhage took her face in his hands, and felt all the love he had for her course through him. He hated that she hurt over this. Would have done absolutely anything to keep her from knowing any pain, whatsoever.

Except sacrifice their love.

"Oh, my Mary, you would have been the most amazing mother." He stroked her lower lip with his thumb. "But you are no less a female in my eyes. You are, and will always remain, the most perfect mate on earth, and the single best thing that ever happened to me."

As her eyes teared up again, she smiled. "How is it possible . . . that you always make me feel so beautiful?"

He kissed her once, and then again. "I'm just reflecting back what I see and know to be true. I'm nothing but a mirror, Mary mine. Now will you let me kiss you again? Mmmmmmm . . ."

TWENTY-FIVE

"You're sure. You're *absolutely* sure."

As Layla spoke, she had a death grip on the sheet that was pulled down around her hips. "I mean, you're completely, totally sure."

Doc Jane smiled and hit some button on the ultrasound machine. As a *whumpa-whumpa-whumpa* filled the dark examination room, the physician turned the monitor toward Layla and sat back.

"Here's Baby A." She moved the wand across Layla's swollen belly to the side. "And here's Baby B."

Whumpa-whumpa-whumpa . . . plus an arm was moving—which was something she could also feel.

Layla collapsed against the pillow. "Blessed Virgin Scribe."

"So, yes, I'm sure," the doctor concluded. "When you stood up, you lost control of your bladder and that was the wetness you felt. It's not uncommon at all—as the babies get bigger, they press on things that don't appreciate it, and there you go."

"Maybe I shouldn't be getting out of bed at all."

Doc Jane removed the reader thingy, wiped it off, and returned the wand to the machine's little holder. Then she typed a couple of notes

on the keyboard and shut the ultrasound down. Taking some tissues, she mopped up Layla's stomach with careful, firm strokes.

"I think you're doing fine. Clinically, everything is where it needs to be. I wouldn't suggest taking up beach volleyball, but I don't think stretching your legs down here twice a day increases your risk for early labor. I really don't want you moving up to the big house, though."

Closing her eyes, Layla told herself to believe the healer. Doc Jane had never steered anyone wrong, and the female did know what she was talking about.

"Layla, if I honestly thought there was something going on, I'd tell you. I treat my patients the way I'd want to be treated, and if there's a threat to your health or that of those babies in there? You'd be the first to know."

"Thank you." Layla reached out and put her hand on Doc Jane's arm. "Don't tell, Qhuinn, okay? I just . . . I don't want to alarm him."

"There's nothing to be alarmed about." Doc Jane gave her a pat and stood up. "So there's nothing to tell him. Hey, guess what—I got two early Christmas presents. I know it's a human holiday, but do you mind if I show them off?"

"Indeed, please do." Layla grunted as she sat up and closed the halves of her robe across her enormous belly. "What are they?"

"Stay here."

Layla laughed a little. "As if I am going anywhere fast?"

As the doctor disappeared through a side door, Layla shifted her legs off the exam table and stared at the ultrasound machine. Even though there was nothing showing on the monitor, she pictured what she'd seen there. The life inside of her. The two lives.

All was well. And that was all that mattered.

"Ta-da!"

Glancing over, Layla straightened. "It's a . . ."

"Neonatal incubator." Doc Jane made like Vanna White, showing off the features of the equipment—which rather looked like a large warming drawer with clear plastic sides. "Climate-controlled. Blue light up here. Ready access. Built-in scale. It's the next-best thing to your tummy and I have two of them."

Layla swallowed. "I should have liked a bassinet."

"Oh . . . shoot." Doc Jane started rolling the thing out. "I'm so sorry. The physician in me—"

"No, no!" She held her hands forward. "I'm just—no, it's good.

Honestly! Safety first—I don't get a bassinet at all if they don't make it after the birth, do I."

Doc Jane laid a hand on the lid. "This is state-of-the-art equipment, Layla. I'm thrilled because we all want those two out and safe, to use Butch terms."

"Thank you." Layla put her palm over her heart. "I really can't thank you enough for everything. I don't want you to think I'm not grateful."

"Let's save the gratitude for when everyone survives and thrives." Doc Jane looked down at the belly she and everyone else was so concerned with. "You're right on the cusp. If you can keep them in a little longer, their lungs will be developed enough so that if you do go early, they'll have a fighting chance. I'll feel better if you can make it another ten days or two weeks—that's all. Then if anything happens? I'm confident we can see them through. After all, although vampire pregnancies are typically eighteen months, according to Havers, at nine months, the lungs can function if they have to."

"That's good news."

"And listen, if we have to bring Havers in, we will. In fact, I think Butch would love to put a bag over the guy's head and drag him here—preferably behind a car."

Layla laughed. "Yes."

Doc Jane grew serious. "There are risks, Layla. But I'm going to do my damnedest to make sure you have both of those young safely."

"That makes two of us."

Doc Jane came over and the two of them hugged. And as the doctor was pulling away, Layla meant to let the female go on about her duties.

Instead, she heard herself say, "May I ask you something? Is there . . . is someone else down here? I mean, aside from Luchas and myself?"

The doctor's face went professionally pleasant, her smile belying a certain distance. "What makes you say that?"

Definitely not a "no." "When I went for my stroll, Qhuinn redirected me away from the shooting range. It seemed like the Brothers were guarding someone down there? And last night I heard a lot of commotion out in the corridor. I know Rhage was recovering from the beast having come out, but wouldn't a prisoner or something like that explain all the coming and going?"

"Actually, Rhage was shot in the chest—and died for a moment on the battlefield."

Layla recoiled. "Oh . . . dearest Virgin Scribe, no!"

"He's fine now, though."

"Thank goodness. He is indeed a male of great worth." Layla narrowed her eyes. "But there is someone else down here, isn't there."

"I'm afraid I really can't comment."

Layla ran her hands over her belly. "The Brotherhood's business affects all of us. And I really resent the idea that just because I'm a female I somehow can't 'handle it.' Protection is fine, but total insulation is an insult."

Doc Jane cursed. "Look, Layla, I get where you're coming from. But if you're worried about your safety, don't be. The male is in a coma right now, and V says they're moving him at nightfall. So you and Luchas will be perfectly safe. Now, you need to eat. Let me call Fritz. And don't be concerned about those babies. You're doing great—"

"What kind of injuries does he have? The male. Who's here."

Doc Jane shook her head ruefully, as if she knew she wasn't going make it out of the room without divulging some information. "He was struck on the head. And it's likely he's had one or more strokes."

"Is he going to die?" Layla blurted.

Doc Jane shrugged. "I don't honestly know. But prisoner or not, I'm going to treat him according to standard medical practice—even though, considering what the Brotherhood will do to him if he recovers, it may be better for him to pass on."

"That's . . . terrible."

"He put a bullet in Wrath's throat. What do you think he deserves? A tap on the wrist?"

"It's all so brutal."

"It's the nature of war." Doc Jane waved her hand in the air as if she were erasing the conversation. "This is getting morbid. And besides, it's nothing either one of us has to worry about. This is out of our hands, and I, for one, am glad."

"Maybe there's a way to rehabilitate him or—"

"You are a very kind female, you know that?"

As the doctor rolled out the incubator, Layla looked around at the tiled room, noting the glass-fronted cabinets full of medicines and wraps, the computer showing a screensaver of bubbles over on the desk, the back-less chair that had been rolled off to one side.

No, she wasn't kind.

She was in love with that Bastard.

Putting her face in her hands, she shook her head at the terrible reality she was in. And also because Doc Jane was right. If Xcor survived his injuries?

The Brotherhood was going to kill him.

Slowly.

TWENTY-SIX

The following evening, Mary got herself into her office clothes and went down to First Meal with Rhage by her side. Like her, he was dressed for work, wearing leathers and a muscle shirt, and carrying a leather jacket in one hand, and a cache of weapons on holsters in the other. His black daggers were already strapped onto his chest, and she could tell by the hard cast to his jaw that he was ready to fight.

In fact, all the Brothers came into the dining room with their autoloaders and their shotguns and their knives with them, too.

There was enough firepower at the table to supply a small army.

Which they were, she supposed as she sat down in her chair.

Rhage pushed her seat in and then took the empty to her left, looping his belts off one side before draping the jacket across the back.

"Oh, good, roast beef," he said as Fritz appeared behind him with a plate.

Actually, make that a "platter." And yes, it was roast beef . . . as in, an entire roast beef for him.

"Fritz, how did you know?" Rhage asked as he looked over his shoulder with adoration.

The old, wrinkled butler bowed low at the waist. "Indeed, I was informed that you had had a bit of a trial of late, and I imagined one would require special sustenance."

"Oh, one does." The Brother clapped the *doggen* on the shoulder and sent the poor guy flailing. "Shit, I'm sorry—"

"Got him," V said as he caught Fritz and stood him upright. "S'all good."

As a fleet of *doggen* came in to serve the rest of the household, Mary put her napkin in her lap and waited for the trays of sausages and bowls of oatmeal and cut fruit to make their way down.

"Danish?" she said, reaching out and snagging a basket that was made of sterling-silver weave. "They smell fantastic."

"Mmmm-hmmm," Rhage answered around a mouthful of protein.

As she pulled back the damask napkin and offered them to her man, Rhage put down his knife and fork and took three, arranging the sweet twists on his platter. Then he picked up his utensils and resumed his careful, measured attack on what had to be an eight-pound roast.

For some reason, as she took her own danish—just one—she thought back to their first meal at TGI Friday's in Lucas Square. Rhage had ordered, like, four plates of food or something—and she'd braced herself for all kinds of stomach-turning gulping. Instead, he'd had the table manners of Emily Post, everything precise and tidy, from the forkfuls he loaded up, to the slices he made, to the way he stopped between almost every bite to wipe his mouth.

Sitting back in her chair, she found herself staring across the table. The mahogany landscape was broad and studded with all kinds of lovely, shiny, sparkly things, and it was strange to think she'd gotten used to the luxury, the help, the standard of living that was so far outside of the way she'd grown up, so beyond anything she had ever expected to be involved in, that she'd always assumed it was only historical fiction.

But she didn't dwell on all the deluxe.

No, she looked at Z and Bella. The pair of them were seated directly across from her, and it was impossible not to watch them as they traded Nalla back and forth, Z choosing morsels off his plate to hand-feed the toddler, Bella dabbing at the chubby chin or tucking a fantastic pink frilly outfit out of the way. From time to time, the parents would lock eyes over the child and a word would be spoken, or maybe just a smile shared.

Mary frowned at the slave bands that had been tattooed on Z's

wrists and neck. They seemed so dark against his tanned skin, an evil stain that was permanent.

She and Z had spent a lot of time in the basement by that old boiler, talking about what had been done to him when he'd been a blood slave. So much abuse. So many scars, inside and out. But he had come through it, triumphed over his past, forged not only a beautiful relationship with the female he loved, but also with the incredible blessing of his daughter.

Jeez, and she was worried about anything that had happened in her own life? Yes, she had had to take care of her mother as the woman died. Yes, she'd had a disease. Yes, she had lost her ability to have children. But that was nothing compared to what Zsadist had been put through, what Bitty had suffered through.

If Z could overcome the torture and the sexual abuse to be a good father to his precious little girl? Now, *that* was strength.

Mary rubbed the center of her chest, massaging the pain that was still dogging her. Sure, she and Rhage had talked things through, and of course she felt good that he seemed to know where he stood. But it was almost as if Rhage's sorrow over their inability to have a family was something she'd caught like a cold. After they had finished talking, after they had made love and then settled into their bed, after he had fallen asleep and commenced that percolating snore of his beside her . . . she had stayed awake all day, listening to the dim sounds of the *doggen* speaking in hushed tones, smelling the faint scent of lemon floor polish, tracking the quiet whir of a vacuum out by Wrath's office.

She had not slept at all.

The question she had never bothered answering just would not stop posing itself over and over in her head. And, Jesus, what a pain in the ass it was. She could have sworn she'd gotten over the whole child thing before it even started.

Yes, her infertility had saved them both, but it did not mean that it wasn't a loss—

"Hey."

Shaking herself, she pinned a smile on her face and resolutely focused on the food that had magically appeared on her plate. Huh, she clearly had served herself and been unaware of it.

"Hey, yourself," she said with determined cheerfulness. "How's your half of a cow going down—"

"Mary," he said quietly. "Look at me."

Taking a deep breath, she shifted her eyes over. He had turned his whole body to her and was looking at her in that way he did, as if everything around him had disappeared, as if nothing else existed but her.

"I love you," he whispered. "And you're the only thing I'm ever going to need."

She blinked hard. And then told herself that if she were smart, she would believe him with every fiber of her being.

That was the way to keep going.

"Have I told you lately," she said roughly, "that I am the luckiest female on the planet?"

Leaning in, he kissed her softly. "You did. Right before we got down to it at daybreak."

As he eased back, looking all self-satisfied, she smiled. And then started to laugh. "You are pretty pleased with yourself, aren't you."

"I don't know what you're talking about." He refocused on his roast beef, the picture of innocence. "But if you really do feel lucky, I have a great way for you to show it."

Mary picked up her own fork and knife and discovered she was, in fact, hungry. "I should send you a card, then?"

Now as he glanced over, his teal eyes were burning. "Nah, words only go so far. And I have nothing planned after work tonight sooooooo . . ."

While he deliberately ran his tongue around one fang, his stare dipped down low, as if he were imagining her sitting in the chair completely naked—and he intended to drop his napkin and go on all fours to find it under the table.

Mary's body started to heat, and her head began to swim, and her skin tingled.

"I can't wait," she breathed.

"Neither can I, Mary mine. Neither can I."

Rhage sent Mary off after First Meal was done, standing on the front steps of the mansion and waving as she and the Volvo disappeared down the hill and into the *mhis*. After she was gone, he stayed there for a moment, breathing the cold air.

It was obvious that all the heavy-duty they'd grappled with was lingering for her, but how could it not? Hell, as they'd headed into the

dining room together, he'd braced himself for another onslaught of his own emotional shit. But clearly, he'd gotten to the root of his problem, processed it—or whatever the term was—and been able to get to a different place. Seeing his brothers with their young hadn't been upsetting; he'd actually been able to help Mary when it became obvious she was having a collywobble.

Being back on track with her felt incredible. Being there for her when she needed him? Even fucking better.

And now it was time to go to work.

When he turned back to face the mansion, he was a deadly machine.

Stalking up the stone steps and through the vestibule, he joined his brothers in the foyer. No one was speaking as everybody got good and armed, strapping twelve different kinds of metal to their chests and their thighs and under their arms.

As he did the duty himself, he was aware of the *doggen* standing on the periphery, worry on their kind, gentle faces.

They were part of the reason this needed to happen.

One by one, the warriors proceeded through the hidden door under the stairs and down into the underground tunnel. As they walked to the training center, they were in formation, breaking up only to pass through the supply closet and the office. Out in the corridor, Doc Jane and Manny were waiting with a stretcher and life-support equipment, and neither of the medical people said a word as everyone went to the target range.

Lassiter had been on guard the whole day, and even though the fallen angel needed sunlight to thrive, he showed no sign of exhaustion or loss of focus as he stood over Xcor's unmoving body.

Certainly made last week's *Punky*-fucking-*Brewster* marathon more forgivable.

"Who's helping me with the transfer," Manny said as he pulled the gurney up to V's worktable.

Rhage, V, and Butch stepped in and released the steel shanks, momentarily freeing Xcor from all tethers—but there were two reasons not to worry: One, the rest of the Brotherhood was standing around with guns up and itchy trigger fingers; and two, the fucker was out cold, not so much deadweight as dead, period.

Only the slight warmth of his bare ankles and the fact that he wasn't completely gray in the face led a male to believe the bastard didn't need a grave and a headstone.

Onto the gurney. Then strapped down with leather this time at the throat, wrists, ankles, thighs, and around the waist. Then the machines were switched, wires being traded from the less portable monitors to ones that were smaller and lighter. The process took a good twenty minutes or so, and the whole time, Rhage stayed right next to their prisoner, searching for signs that Xcor was playing possum—and after eagle-eyeing every inch of exposed skin and all those harsh features? He decided that the bastard had either stroked out completely or had things to teach De Niro.

When it was go time, John Matthew and Qhuinn held open the gun range's door, and Rhage took the feet with V and Butch at the head leading the way.

"Wait!" Manny said.

With a quick shake, he unfurled a white sheet and draped it over Xcor's body and face. "We don't need anyone seeing this."

"Good job," someone muttered. "No reason to scare the young."

The trip down the corridor was fast, and then they were at the steel door that led out to the parking area, with John Matthew and Blay this time holding things open and standing guard. There was an ambulance with human markings all over it parked at the curb, and Rhage released a grunt of relief as Xcor's gurney was rolled into the ass of the vehicle and locked in with them. As he, V, and Butch took seats where they could among all the cupboards and equipment, Z got behind the wheel, and Manny hit the passenger seat in case of medical emergency.

The trip out through the gating system took forever, but then again, it wasn't like they were in a built-for-speed situation. And, because of the way the compound was set up, they had to proceed allll the way out to the main road, hang a right, and go alllll the way around the base of the mountain to the road that led up to the mansion.

The incline was yet another slow go, but halfway to the house, they took a left onto a goat path offshoot. Things got bumpier at that point, and it was a good job the gurney was locked in place on the floor. From time to time, when there was a big hump, or a hard knock that had the three of them going starship *Enterprise* with a lurch to one side, Rhage checked out the machines. Xcor's heart rate, which seemed slow as molasses and as uneven as the dirt lane they were on, never changed. And neither did the low oxygen stats or the blood pressure.

The bastard certainly didn't move. Not independently of the rough ride, at least.

After a forever of travel, which was actually only ten minutes or so, Rhage couldn't stand it anymore and leaned forward to look through the front windshield. Lots of pines in the headlights. More of the rough road ahead. Nothing else.

"You had a wicked good idea," Butch said.

"Doesn't feel right." Rhage shrugged. "But needs must and all that bullshit."

"He'll never get out of there," V sneered, his icy eyes flaring with pure violence. "Not alive, at any rate."

"Good thing you have more than one table." Butch clapped his bestie on the shoulder. "You sick fuck."

"Don't knock it till you tried it."

"Nah, I'm a good Catholic boy. I go that route and my body would incinerate on the spot—and not from hot wax."

"Pansy."

"Pervert."

The pair of them chuckled at their inside joke and then got serious again—because with a squeak of the brakes, the ambulance stopped.

"Let's do this," Rhage announced as the double doors were opened from the outside and the scent of pine trees flooded the sterile interior. "Let's move him into the Tomb."

TWENTY-SEVEN

As soon as Mary walked into Safe Place, Rhym came up to her. "Hey, Bitty has been asking for you."

"Really?" Mary shrugged out of her coat. "She has?"

The other social worker nodded. "Right when she woke up. She didn't want to come down for First Meal, so I took her a tray and told her that I'd send you to the attic when you got here."

"Okay. I'll head up right now, thanks."

"I'm going to take off, if it's okay?" The female covered her mouth as she yawned. "She actually slept—or shall I say, after a bath, she got into a nightgown and headed to bed. I checked on her every hour or so and she seemed to be out like a light."

"Good. And yes, of course—I'll take over from here. Thank you so much for staying with her all day. It just felt like the right thing to do."

"I wouldn't have been anywhere else. Call me if you need me?"

"Always. Thanks, Rhym."

While the female headed for the back of the house, Mary took the stairs in a rush, stopping only to drop her things off in her office before going up to the third floor. When she got to the top landing, she was surprised to find the door to Bitty's room open.

"Hello?" the girl called out from inside.

Mary squared her shoulders and walked forward. "It's me."

"Hi."

Bitty's suitcases were still packed and by her bed, but she was over at the old desk, brushing her doll's hair.

"Rhym said you wanted to see me?"

To herself, Mary added, Any chance you want to talk about something? The mother you lost? The infant brother who died? Your maniac father? 'Cuz that would be great.

"Yes, please." The little girl turned. "I was wondering if you could please take me to my old house."

Mary recoiled before she could catch the reaction. "You mean where you and your *mahmen* used to live? With your father?"

"Yes."

Easing the door shut, Mary went over and almost sat on Bitty's mom's bed. She stopped before she did, though. "What are you—why would you like to go there? If you don't mind me asking?"

"I want to get some more of my things. My uncle doesn't live in Caldwell. If I don't get them now, I may not be able to pick them up when he comes to get me."

Mary glanced around. Then walked around, stopping at the window that overlooked the front yard. Dark, so dark out there—seemingly more so than on a July night when it was humid and warm as opposed to cold and blustery.

Pivoting to face the girl, she said, "Bitty, I've got to be honest with you. I'm not sure that's a good idea."

"Why?"

"Well, for one thing"—Mary chose her words carefully—"the house has been abandoned the entire time you've been here. I'm not certain what condition it's in—it might have been looted. Or suffered roof damage. In which case I'm not sure what we'd find there?"

"We won't know if we don't go."

Mary hesitated. "It could bring up a lot of memories. Are you sure you're ready for that?"

"Location doesn't matter. There is no escape from what I remember. It is with me every waking minute and in my dreams all day long."

As the girl spoke in such a factual way, she didn't miss a stroke of that brush. They might as well have been talking about the schedule of laundry or what was being served down in the kitchen.

"You must miss your *mahmen* a great deal," Mary prompted.

"So may we please go?"

Mary rubbed her face and felt exhausted. "You can talk about her with me, you know. Sometimes that helps."

Bitty didn't even blink. "May we?"

Annnnnnnd that door remained firmly closed, apparently. Great. "Let me talk to Marissa, okay? I'll go find her right now and see what I can do."

"I have my coat." The little girl motioned to the end of her bed. "And my shoes are on. I'm ready to go."

"I'll be back in a little bit." Mary headed for the exit, but paused at the door. "Bitty, in my experience, people either work things in, work them out, or work them through. The latter is the best option, and it usually comes from talking about the stuff we maybe don't want to discuss."

On some level, she couldn't believe she was addressing a nine-year-old like that. But Bitty certainly didn't express herself like someone under the age of ten.

"What do the other two mean?" the little girl said, still working her brush.

"Sometimes people internalize bad feelings, and punish themselves in their minds for things they regret or think they did wrong or badly. It eats away at you until you either crack and have to let it all out or go crazy. Working out means that you avoid what bothers you by channeling feelings into behaviors that ultimately hurt you or other people."

"I don't understand any of that. I'm sorry."

"I know," Mary said sadly. "Listen, I'll go speak to Marissa."

"Thank you."

Walking out of the room, Mary paused at the head of the stairs and looked back. Bitty was just doing what she had been, running that brush down the ratty hair and avoiding the bald spots.

In all the time she had been in the house, she had never played with any of the toys available downstairs in the communal box: the children, when they first came in, were always encouraged to find one or two that they liked and claim them as their own, leaving the

others as joint property. Bitty had been told repeatedly to help herself. Never had.

She had her doll and her old stuffed tiger. That was it.

"Shit," Mary whispered.

Marissa's office was on the second floor, and when Mary went down and knocked on the jamb, Butch's *shellan* motioned for her to come in even as she talked into her phone.

"—completely confidential. No, no. Yes, you may bring your young. No, free of charge. What was that? Absolutely free of charge. For however long you're here." Marissa indicated for Mary to take a seat, and then held up her forefinger in the universal sign for *Hold on, just one second.* "No, it's okay—take your time. I know . . . you don't have to apologize for the tears. Ever."

After Mary lowered herself into the wooden chair across from her boss, she reached out and picked up a crystal paperweight that was in the shape of a diamond. The thing was nearly the size of her palm, heavy as her arm, and she smoothed its facets with her thumbs, watching the light refract out of its depths.

Was this ever going to get any easier with that girl, she wondered.

"Mary?"

"What?" She glanced up. "Sorry, I'm all in my head."

Marissa leaned on her elbows. "I totally understand. What's up?"

Xcor was removed from the training center at around eight o'clock—and Layla saw it all happen.

As soon as her alarm had gone off after sunset, she had gotten out of bed and propped the door to her room open with one of her slippers—such that as she lay back, she could see a slice of the corridor through the crack. And sure enough, the Brothers had soon moved him, just as she had guessed they would: hearing the sound of many heavy footsteps, she had gotten up and stood to the side so that she could see without being noticed.

Eventually, they had paraded by, and Xcor had been with them, lying prone on a rolling table, a sheet covering him from top of head to tip of foot. As they had passed, she had had to press her hands to her mouth. So many machines with him, clearly keeping him alive. And then there were the Brothers, all of them and each fully weaponized, their massive bodies strewn with deadly daggers and guns.

Closing her eyes and holding onto the door jamb, she'd been consumed by the need to rush out and stop them, to beg for Xcor's life, to pray unto the Scribe Virgin for his recovery and his release. She had even marshalled words in his defense, things such as, "He has not attacked us even though he knows our location!" and, "He has never hurt me, never once in all the nights I met him!" and the ever popular, "He's changed from the traitor he once was!"

All of it had served only to confirm her own guilt—and so she had stayed where she was, listening to them proceed all the way down the hall to the parking area.

As the final door had clanked shut and been locked, she had reiterated to herself that she needed to let it go.

She told herself, forcefully, that Xcor was the enemy. Nothing more. And nothing less.

Lurching forward, she returned to her bed, climbing up upon it and tucking her feet under her. With her heart pounding and her brow and upper lip sweating, she tried to control her emotions. Surely this kind of stress was not good for the young—

The knock on her door brought her head around. "Yes?" she yelped.

Had she been found out?

"'Tis I, Luchas." Qhuinn's brother sounded worried. "May I enter?"

"Please." She hefted herself back onto the floor and re-shuffled herself to the door, opening it wide. "Do come in."

As she stood to one side, the male cranked his arms around the wheels of his chair, his forward progress slow, but independent. There had been talk of getting him a mechanized one, but this self-directed momentum was part of his rehabilitation, and indeed, it seemed to be working. Sitting with his knees together and his thin body only a little hunched over, he had all of Qhuinn's handsomeness and intelligence, none of his brother's weight and vitality.

It was very sad. But at least he was getting around now—something that had long been an impossibility for him.

Then again, getting tortured by *lessers* had cost him more than just a finger or two.

When he had cleared the jambs, Layla allowed the panel to shut on its own and once more returned to the bed. Getting up on it, she straightened her nightgown, and smoothed her hair. As a Chosen, it

would have been far more appropriate for her to receive a visitor in one of the traditional white robes of her station, but she no longer fit in any of them, for one thing. For another, Qhuinn's brother and she had long past dispensed with any formality.

"I find it rather impressive that I made it down this far anew," he said in a voice that was a monotone.

"I'm glad for the company." Although she would not be telling him why. "I feel . . . rather caged in here."

"How fare you this eve?"

As the question was posed, he did not meet her eyes—but he never did. His gray stare remained pinned four feet off the floor, its direction changing only when he turned his frail body this way or that in his chair.

She had never before been so grateful for another's dysfunction, for his reticence provided her some privacy as she attempted to control her emotions—although she supposed that didn't reflect well on her character.

What did, though, lately.

"I am well. And you?"

"Well, indeed. I must needs attend to my physical therapy in fifteen minutes."

"I know you shall do well."

"How fare my brother's young?"

"Very well, thank you. They are bigger every night."

"You have been much blessed, as has he. For that, I am most grateful."

It was the same conversation every evening. Then again, what else did the two of them have that was worthy of any kind of polite discourse?

Too many secrets on her side.

Too much suffering on his.

In a way, they were one of a kind.

TWENTY-EIGHT

The Tomb was the Brotherhood's *sanctum sanctorum*, a place where new members were inducted, and old members went after they died—and as such, it was protected from intruders through mechanisms both ancient and modern.

The sturdiest of these, after you breached the cave's mouth, further traveled into the earth some distance and proceeded behind a nine-foot-high slab of granite, was a set of iron gates that nobody was going to get through even with an industrial blowtorch.

Unless, of course, you had the key to the lock.

As Rhage and his brothers came up to the fortification with Xcor on the gurney, Z did the honors with the unlocking and Rhage monitored the interior of the cave, his eyes searching through what was revealed by V's glowing palm.

It was against protocol for anyone to enter the space who was not a Brother, but that was his point about beggars and choosers and all that shit. This was the safest, most isolated place to lock up a seriously wounded, treasonous motherfucker until such time as either he came to and was ready to be tortured, or the bastard kicked it and could be burned on the altar as a sacrifice worthy of all the carved names on the marble wall.

Creeeeeeeeeeeeeeeeeeeeeeeeeeeeeak.

Besides, Rhage thought as he began pulling the gurney ahead again, Xcor wasn't going any farther than the ante-chamber.

At least, not while he was still breathing.

Now there was no need for V's portable glow light. Iron-handled torches came alive with a nod from the brother and shadows started to chase one another over the stone floor and up the rows and rows of shelves, the flickering light darting in and about the countless jars, both those which were centuries old and those that had come from Amazon.com.

It was a display of the Brotherhood's triumphs over the Lessening Society, a collection of souvenirs from kills in the Old World and the New.

In that way, it was appropriate to bring Xcor here.

He was yet another spoil of war.

"This is far enough," Vishous announced.

Rhage stopped and locked the wheels with their foot brake as V shifted a massive duffel bag off his shoulder.

"This battery pack is only going to last ten hours," the brother said.

"Won't be a problem." As Lassiter spoke, his entire body lit up from the inside out, the energy replacing the contours of his flesh. "I can recharge it."

"You're sure you're good alone here during the day?" V demanded.

"I can always step out into the sunlight and top myself off. And before you bitch that that dead fish on the table will be momentarily left unattended, I have ways of keeping track of him."

V shook his head. "I'm surprised you're willing to do this. No Time Warner."

"That's what they make phones for."

"I can almost respect you."

"Don't get emotional on me, Vishous. I left the Kleenex at home. Besides, I have the night off now that the hot potato is safely here. Plenty of time to get busy with the whacker."

"Okay, that sounds dirty," someone said.

"No one but his left hand would have him, are you kidding me?" came a counter.

"Hey, Lass, when was the last time you were out on a date?" somebody else drawled. "Was it before the Punic Wars, or right after?"

"And how much did you have to pay her?"

Lassiter went silent, his strangely white eyes growing distant. But then he smiled. "Whatever. My standards are too high for you bunch of assholes."

As a fresh round of joking flared up, nobody actually relaxed. It was as if Xcor were a bomb with an unknown detonator and a debatable length of time before the boom party started.

"Z and I are on first shift," Phury cut in. "And you guys have work to do downtown."

"Call us and we're back here in a fucking instant." V punched himself in the chest. "Especially if he wakes up."

On that note, Rhage stared down at that ugly-ass face, and imagined those lids lifting. Was the Bastard awake in there? And not as in jump-out-and-attack, but as in conscious in the midst of the coma.

Did the SOB know what kind of trouble he was in? Or was the lack of consciousness the last bit of mercy his fate was ever going to give him?

Not my problem, Rhage thought as he took one last look around, seeking out the jars he had brought here and placed on the shelves, the representations of his own kills. So many. He had been at this war for such a long time—so long that he remembered back when Wrath refused to lead, and the only time the Brotherhood came to this mountain was to deliver these containers to the shelves.

So much had changed, he thought.

Now, not only were they all living in Darius's fancy mansion, but they had new members of the Brotherhood. John Matthew and Blay as soldiers. A medical staff and great facilities. Everyone under the same roof—

"—sides, that way I can polish my nails."

Rhage shook himself back into focus as Lassiter's voice registered. "Wait, what?"

"JK." The angel laughed. "I could tell we'd lost you. Dreaming of what you're going to have at Last Meal? I know I am. Three guesses, and the first two that don't have meat in them don't count."

"You're insane," Rhage said. "But I like that in a friend."

Lassiter put his arm around Rhage's shoulders and led him to the gate. "You have such good taste. Have I mentioned that lately?"

After everyone but Z and Phury filed out, Vishous closed the bars and relocked everything. Then they all stood still for a moment. The

fine steel mesh that was wrapped around the barrier and soldered into place would prevent Phury and Z from getting free. And wasn't that a ball shriveler.

If something went wrong in there, they couldn't get out.

But Rhage told himself, as probably the rest of his brothers were, that there was no way Xcor was going to be anything other than an inanimate object for the foreseeable future—and even if he did come around, he'd be too weak to go on the offensive.

Still, Rhage didn't like this.

But that was the nature of war. It put you in places you hated.

As a subtle vibration went off in Rhage's pocket, he frowned and took out his phone. When he saw who it was, he accepted the call.

"Mary? Everything okay?"

There was static because the reception sucked so he jogged out to the mouth of the cave. As he stepped out into fresh, cold night air, he could hear just fine—and as his mate talked for a little bit, he made a series of uh-huhs and nodded even though she couldn't see him. Then he ended the connection and looked at his brothers, all of whom were clustered around him like they were wondering if something was wrong.

"Gentlemen, I need to help Mary for a little while. Meet you downtown?"

V nodded. "You take care of what you need to. Check in when you're ready to enter the field and I'll give you a status report and an assignment."

"Roger that," Rhage said, before he closed his eyes and began to concentrate.

Talk about not knowing where you were going to end up.

As he dematerialized, he never would have expected to be heading where he was going. But he was not about to let his *shellan* down.

Now or ever.

A simple little gathering for twelve, Assail thought as he was shown into the lemon yellow drawing room he'd enjoyed so much the evening before.

As his name was announced by the same uniformed butler who'd welcomed him then, he stepped forward such that his two cousins could likewise be introduced to the other nine vampires in the parlor. Or, more accurately, the eight females and one male.

Who was not their hostess's mate.

No, the other entity with a cock and balls was not old, infirmed, or unknown. In fact, surprise, surprise, it was Throe, the handsome, disgraced former aristocrat who had previously been a member of the Band of Bastards, but who was now, evidently, making some sort of a return into the *glymera*'s prejudicial velvet fold.

In a perfectly fitted tuxedo, as it were. One that was every bit as expensive as Assail's own.

Introductions over with, Naasha made her way across the room, her black satin gown like water flowing over her body at night.

"Darling," she said to him, holding her pale hands out. On her fingers, diamonds winked and glittered with as much charm and lack of warmth as their owner. "You are late. We have been waiting."

As she curtsied, he bowed.

"How fare thee." Even though he did not care. "You are looking well enough."

Her brows twitched at the almost-there compliment. "Just as you were almost timely."

Assail deliberately stroked the back of the sofa. "These are my cousins, Ehric and Evale. Perhaps you will introduce us to your other guests?"

Naasha's eyes flared as he penetrated the gap between cushions with his forefinger. "Ah, yes. Indeed. These are my dearest friends."

The females came forward one by one, and they were a predictable lot, preened and prettied in gowns that had been constructed precisely for their bodies and jewels that had been purchased or passed down to adorn the precious flesh of noble daughters. Two blondes. Another black-haired one. Three with streaked brown locks. And one with thick white hair.

To him, they were simply variations on a theme he had been bored with a hundred years before—and it was entirely possible that, while he had been over in the Old Country, he had mated with some of their ancestors or even closer relations.

"And this is"—Naasha swept her hand toward the far corner— "my special friend, Throe."

Assail smiled at the male and sauntered over. As he offered his

palm, he kept his voice low. "Change of company. From Bastards to pedigrees. Not much of an improvement, I fear."

Throe's eyes were sharp as daggers. "A return to my roots."

"Is it truly possible to come back after a defection? As significant as yours was, at any rate."

"My bloodline never changed."

"But your character is a bit wanting, it is not."

Throe leaned in. "This from a drug dealer?"

"Businessman. And what do they call males like you? Gigolos? Or mayhap the term 'whore' is sufficient."

"And why do you think you're here? Certainly not for the pleasure of your social company."

"Unlike yourself, I do not need to sing for my supper, I can buy it myself."

Naasha spoke up, her voice filling the parlor. "Shall we adjourn for our meal?"

As the butler eased open a pair of double doors to reveal a dining table as resplendent as any set by royalty, human or otherwise, Naasha linked her arm into Assail's.

In a whisper, she said, "We shall be having dessert down below. In my playroom."

Ordinarily, he would have been unimpressed by such a blatant, I'm-a-naughty-girl come-on and would have commented appropriately. But he had other priorities.

Had Throe defected from the Bastards? Was he infiltrating the *glymera* through an available opening—or three—with an eye toward engineering ambitions against the crown?

Assail was most certainly going to find out.

"I look forward to whatever will be served," he murmured, patting her hand.

Even if the sweets to be consumed were, temporarily, him and his cousins.

After all, orgasms were as good a currency as any . . . and he was quite certain that Naasha and her "dearest friends" were free for the purchasing in that regard.

TWENTY-NINE

"Thank you so much for coming. I was, ah, hoping that we could talk about . . ."

As Jo Early ran lines to herself, she stirred a packet of Sugar In The Raw into her cappuccino, messing up the pretty brown-and-white heart design that had been made in the foam.

The I've Bean Waitin' coffee shop was Caldwell's indie version of Starbucks, a tall-ceilinged, narrow-walled shotgun space with padded chairs and sofas, lots of mismatched little tables, and baristas who were allowed to wear their own clothes under their black smocks. It was one strip mall over from where the real estate office was, a quick trip to make at the end of yet another too-late workday for her too-hot, too-distracted boss.

He'd been in a dark gray suit today. With a bright white shirt and a blue-gray-and-black bow tie that, on him, was about as far away from geek as his Gucci shoes were.

Taking a sip from the rim of the fat white bowl-cup, she gave her little speech another shot. "Thanks for meeting me. I know this sounds odd, but—"

"Jo?"

Jumping, she nearly dumped her 'cino all over herself. The man

standing by her table was six feet tall, with shaggy black hair, black-rimmed glasses, and the kind of skinny-jeaned, tight button-down'd, floppy-jacketed, earth-toned hipster clothes she'd expect to see on somebody ten years younger. But on William Elliot, it all worked.

Shaking herself, she said, "Hi, yes, hello, Mr. Elliot—"

"Call me Bill." He glanced over at the coffee bar. "Let me get a latte, two secs?"

"Sure. Please. Ah, thanks. I mean, that's great. Good luck." Shit. "I'm sorry."

Bill frowned and eased himself down, unwrapping an army-green scarf from his neck, and opening that maroon felt coat. "Is there something wrong with my house or something?"

"Oh, no." She pushed her hair back. "And I didn't mean to bring you here under false pretenses."

Except she kinda had.

"Look, I'm a happily married man—"

Jo put both hands out. "No, God no—this is, this is actually about an article you wrote almost a year ago in December? About Julio Martinez? He was arrested back then downtown as part of a street fight?"

Bill's eyebrows popped up over his glasses. "The gang member."

"That's right, the one who was injured and apprehended in that abandoned restaurant."

As the reporter fell silent, Jo wanted to kick herself in the ass. She should have known better than to get involved in any of Dougie's foolishness—even more to the point, she should have avoided getting anyone *else* sucked into the funhouse.

"You know what?" she said. "I was way out of line. I shouldn't have asked you to—"

"What exactly do you want to know about the article?"

As she met Bill's narrowed eyes, everyone and everything else in the café disappeared; the sounds of hissing steam and brewing coffee, the chatter, the comings and goings, all of it went on the dim. And not because the two of them were sharing a romantic moment.

"Are you aware of the YouTube video Julio's been in?" Jo asked. "And what he said?"

Bill looked away. "You know, I think I will get that latte."

The reporter got up and went to the counter. When he was addressed by name, and a, "Would you like the usual?" she wondered whether it was true that all writers were powered by caffeine.

And it was weird, this place wasn't near his work or his new house. Maybe he'd lived in the area before?

Bill returned with a tall mug that was more beer stein than anything you'd put a latte in, and as he sat down again, she could tell he'd taken the time to get his head back on straight.

"You've seen the videos," she said.

The man shook his head slowly. "I interviewed Julio when he got out on bail, as part of a series on the upswing of gang-related violence downtown. Most of those kinds of kids—and he was just a kid . . . is one, I mean—a lot of them don't say a thing when they're approached. And if they do talk? It's a lot of posturing about territory, their version of an honor code, their enemies. Julio wasn't interested in any of that. He just kept going on about . . ."

"A vampire." For some reason, her heart started pounding. "That's what he was focused on, wasn't he."

"Yeah."

"You didn't mention anything like that in your article, though."

"God, no. I don't want my editor to think I'm nuts—but I did go online, and I saw the videos. Spent about three days doing nothing but watching those things all night long. My wife was convinced I'd lost my mind. Seventy-two hours later, I wasn't too sure I hadn't."

Jo leaned in, her elbow pushing her 'cino forward until she had to keep it from falling to the floor. "Look . . . what are the chances that Julio saw something? And can I just take this moment to say, I *cannot* believe I'm asking that at all."

Bill shrugged and tried out his latte. As he set the tall mug back down, he shook his head some more. "I thought it was crazy at first, too. I mean, I'm into facts—that's the reason I wanted to be a journalist even though it's a dying field. But after I saw everything that's been posted? It's just . . . there's an awful lot of stuff about encounters like that happening in Caldwell. If you audit similar content, even on a cursory level, across the U.S., it's astonishing how so much of it focuses right here in the five-one-eight. Yeah, sure, you get your garden-variety crazies all over the place, like ghost hunters and whatnot. But when it comes to vampires specifically, it's like . . ." He laughed and looked at her. "Sorry, I'm going off the rails."

"No, you aren't."

"Feels like it." He took another draw of his brew. "Why do you ask?"

Jo shrugged. "The night before last, a friend of mine thought he saw something. He managed to get it on video and put it up online . . . but what he said happened is totally impossible, and there were drugs involved on his part. He took me out to this abandoned girls' school—"

"Brownswick?"

"Yes, that's the one." Jo rubbed her nose even though it didn't itch. "He took me out there in the morning to show me the leftovers of some kind of big fight or something. There weren't any . . . at least, not exactly. And I wasn't going to waste any more time on it, but I was bored at work last night—I went online, did a little poking around— kind of what you did. And that's how I found Julio's stuff."

Bill cursed. "I shouldn't ask this . . ."

"Do you want to see the footage?"

"Damn it."

As Bill went quiet, Jo sat back and let the man decide for himself. And she knew exactly how he felt. She wasn't into the dark side or people pretending that one existed.

The trouble was, she couldn't quite let this all go.

"Lemme see," he muttered.

Jo got out her phone, located the video, and turned the little screen around. As he took her cell and watched Dougie's clip, she tracked the flickering of his facial muscles.

When it was done, he handed her iPhone back. Then he checked his watch. After a moment, he asked, "You want to go for a ride over there?"

"Yes," she said, getting to her feet. "I do."

Mary was determined to be careful with her words.

As she waited for Rhage to arrive at Safe Place, she paced around the front living room, dodging the cozy couches and stuffed chairs, straightening a framed pencil drawing by one of the kids, pulling the curtains back from time to time even though her *hellren* was going to text her when he got there.

In spite of the fact that she was alone by all conventional defini- tion, her head was crowded with nouns and verbs, adjectives, adverbs.

And yet even with a countless array of word combinations at her disposal, she remained stuck in *tabula rasa* land.

The trouble was that she was looking to avoid another disaster like what had happened at Havers's clinic, and unfortunately, you couldn't always tell where the land mines were. And what she was going to have to tell Bitty was not—

"Ms. Luce?"

Turning from the window, she forced herself to smile at the girl. "You've come down."

"I don't understand why we're waiting."

"Could you come here for a minute?"

The little girl had on the ugliest black coat you'd ever seen. It was two sizes too big, under-stuffed with down feathers, and molting at the various seams, tufts of white and gray escaping around the stitching. Clearly, the thing had been made in the boys-aged-twelve-to-fifteen vein, and yet Bitty had refused a new one, even though there were coats both new and donated to choose from in all kinds of colors and styles in the back hall.

A sense of exhaustion weighed Mary down, like someone had sneaked up behind her with some chain mail and draped her shoulders in the stuff: the kid wouldn't even accept a toy or a frickin' coat . . . and Mary thought there was a chance in hell she could get Bitty to open up in the slightest? About the most traumatic events in her life?

Good luck with that.

"Sit down," Mary instructed, pointing at a chair. "I need to talk to you."

"But you said we were allowed to go?"

"Sit down." Okay, maybe she needed to work on her tone. But she was so frustrated with the situation she was ready to scream. "Thank you."

As Bitty looked at her from the armchair, Mary gave up sugarcoating anything. Not because she wanted to be cruel, but because there was no other way to phrase these things.

"We can go to your old house."

"I know, you told me."

"But we're not going alone." As Bitty looked as though she were going to throw out a *why*, Mary talked over any protest. "It's just not safe. We are responsible for your well-being, and the two of us going

out alone to a property that has been abandoned in a human part of town for quite some time is simply not going to happen. That is non-negotiable."

Mary braced herself for an argument.

"All right," was what came back at her.

"It's my *hellren*." At that very moment, her phone let out a *bing!* "And he's here."

Bitty just sat in that armchair, with its flower-print fabric and the knit throw hung over its back and the long-necked lamp that peered over one side as if the thing were checking to make sure any inhabitants were okay.

"He's a member of the Black Dagger Brotherhood, and I would trust him with my life. And yours." Mary wanted to go over, kneel down, take the girl's hand. She stayed put. "He's going to drive us there and bring us back."

And he'd already been out to check the house.

On that note, hopefully he wasn't here to say that thing had been razed to the ground. Or looted. Probably should have checked her texts first.

"There is no other way." Mary surreptitiously glanced at her phone. Rhage's message merely said that he was ready when they were. So guess it was thumbs-up. Assuming Bitty was still on board . . . "You don't have to go, but if you do decide you still want to, it's only going to happen with him. It's your decision."

Bitty shifted off the chair in an abrupt way. "Then we go."

She didn't meet Mary's eyes as she walked by, heading for the front door. And as Mary watched the girl, something was triggered in the back of her head. There was no time to tease whatever it was out, though.

Only staff members had clearance to unlock things, and Mary put in a code on the pad to the left of the heavy panels. There was a clunk and a shift, and then she was able to open the way out. Moving to the side, she waited for Bitty to pass by, and then shut and relocked the door.

Rhage was standing at the property line, on the patch of well-mowed but dying grass over on the right. The moonlight made his blond hair flash in the darkness, and did nothing to highlight the black of his leathers and jacket.

Thank God it looked like he'd kept all his weapons hidden.

Bitty stumbled down the steps, her feet tripping over obstacles that were no doubt in her head, and certainly not on the concrete. She kept her chin up, though, even though her stare stayed at ground level.

As Mary fought the urge to put her hand on the girl's shoulder, she felt that flare in the back of her mind again—but she was too concerned about how the meet-and-greet was going to go to worry about it.

Rhage, however, was perfect. He didn't move as they approached him. Kept his hands visible and down by his sides. Inclined his head as if he were doing his very damnedest to appear shorter.

Which was a total losing battle, but very dear of him.

Bitty stopped a good eight feet away and seemed to burrow into that awful coat.

In the meantime, Mary deliberately went up to Rhage and took his hand as she pivoted back around. "Bitty, this is my husband. I mean . . . *hellren*. Rhage, this is Bitty."

For some reason, Rhage's voice made the center of Mary's heart ping as he said gently, "Hi. Nice to meet you."

Bitty just stared at her shoes, her face unreadable. Which was pretty much her standard operating procedure, as the Brothers would say.

"Okay. So." Mary glanced across the lawn. "Let's head over to the Volvo—"

"Actually, we need to take my car," Rhage cut in.

"Ahh—"

Rhage squeezed her hand. "We need to take my car."

When she looked into his face, she took a deep breath. Of course. He had weapons in the trunk, ones that he was prepared to use in addition to whatever was under that jacket of his—and it wasn't like doing a transfer of deadly arms to the Volvo was going to help this awkwardness along.

"All right." Mary nodded toward the GTO. "Bitty, you ready to come with us?"

As Mary stepped forward, the little girl shuffled along behind, keeping her distance.

"So this is my ride," Rhage said as they got to the car. "I'll just unlock this here, and Mary can help you into the back, 'kay? Only have two doors, sorry."

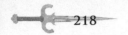

Mary waited for Rhage to open things and go around to the other side before even attempting to put Bitty into the rear. Maybe the girl would like to sit up front? Except then she'd be next to Rhage.

No, the back was better.

Holding the top half of the front seat forward, Mary glanced over her shoulder. "Come on, Bitty—I'll even sit back . . ."

No reason to finish. The girl wasn't hearing it. She wasn't even looking in Mary's vague direction.

Shit.

THIRTY

For most of his nights on the planet, Rhage was only vaguely aware of how big he was. But at the moment, even though he was on the far side of three thousand pounds of steel and engine, he felt like he was an enormous, muckling nightmare.

And OMG, that kid had haunted eyes.

As Rhage waited for Bitty to say something, anything, in response to Mary, he couldn't help but measure how much taller the girl was than the memory he had of her from that horrible night of the rescue. Not that he'd spent much time at all with her—he'd been too busy fighting to have anything more than a foggy recollection of her brown-haired little self cowering in her mother's arms.

Man, he wanted to dig up that father of hers just so he could kill him all over—

"Bitty?" Mary prompted. "We should either go or head back inside."

Rhage was prepared to wait out here all night if that was what it took for the kid to make up her mind, but his mate had a point. This was a safe neighborhood—relatively speaking. Which was to say it was much better than that den of *lessers* they'd attacked at that prep school, but not nearly as secure as inside the house.

"Bitty?"

And that was when the young looked at him for the first time.

The was no shift of her head, no change in her expression, but suddenly the moonlight caught her eyes properly and they flashed.

Later . . . Rhage would reflect that that split second was one of two defining moments in his life. The other being his hearing Mary's voice the first time.

"Is this really your car?"

Rhage blinked. And had to take a moment to make sure he'd heard the question right. "Ah, yes. Yes, this car is mine."

Bitty walked over to the hood and extended her small hand to the GTO's shiny, smooth body. "It's so pretty."

Rhage looked at Mary—who seemed equally flummoxed.

"The, ah, the paint job is custom."

"What does that mean?"

"It was specially made just for her."

Bitty glanced up at him in surprise. "It's a girl?"

"Oh, yeah. Sexy—I mean, hot—er, good muscle cars are always girls. It's 'cuz you gotta take care of 'em like they deserve."

"Muscle car?"

"That's what she's called. She's a GTO. When I got her, she was a wreck, but I had her redone—I brought her back to life. She's old, but she'll blow the doors off any Porsche on the road."

As Mary started making can-it motions with her hand, he clammed up.

Except then Bitty asked, "What's a muscle car? What does it mean, blow doors off?"

"Well . . . would you like to hear the engine? I'm warning you up front, it's loud—but it's supposed to be. There are a lot of horses under that hood."

Bitty recoiled, and yeah, he got an impression of just how sheltered she was, how little she had been exposed to.

"There are horses in your car?"

"Here," he said, holding up the key. "I'm going to start her up—and pump her with some gas. But you might want to cover your ears, 'kay?"

Bitty nodded and clamped her palms on either side of her head like her skull was in danger of popping off her spine.

Opening his door, Rhage got in, left-footed the clutch to the floor, made sure the stick was in neutral, and shoved the key into place. One crank and a little gas—

VROOOM!—*mah, mah, mah-mah-mah*, VROOOM! VROOOM!—*mah, mah, mah-mah-mah* . . .

Bitty walked in front of the car as he continued to pedal the accelerator. After a minute, she slowly dropped her arms and tilted her head to the side.

Over the din, she shouted, "But where are the horses?"

Yanking the parking brake hard, he leaned out. "It's the engine!" he said loudly. "You want to see the engine?"

"What?!"

"The engine!" Reaching for the release, he pulled the lever and got to his feet. "Let me show you."

He was careful not to move too fast as he came to the little girl, and he was very conscious of the way she put her hands in the pockets of her too-big parka and took a couple of steps to the side to keep some distance between them.

Freeing the second latch right in front, he sprang the hood, releasing a sweet, hot breath that was clean oil and fresh gas combined.

Bitty leaned in and seemed to take an inhale. "That smells nice."

Annnnnnnnnnnnnnd that was pretty much when he fell in love with the kid.

Who'd have thought Rhage would be the Bitty-whisperer, Mary marveled as she watched the huge hulk of her husband and the slight body of the girl bend over an engine that was making more noise than a fighter jet.

As Rhage started to point at various things, there was no hearing what he was saying over the noise, but the words, the terms of art, the explanations didn't matter.

The fact that Bitty ended up standing right beside him was all that Mary cared about.

And, oh, boy. If she had loved that male before? This put him straight into heaven territory.

Any avenue in, Mary thought. Anything that could open up the girl, get through to her, reach her in some way . . .

Yes, she wished somehow it had been her to make the connection. Not that she liked admitting such a thing. After all, what could be more selfish, self-serving, and ugly than to feel disappointed that you didn't get to be the savior. But that was a mere passing thought. More than anything, she was sagging in her own skin from relief that Bitty was having a conversation for what seemed like the first time since she'd come to Safe Place.

Rhage lifted his arms, took hold of the hood, and closed it gently. He was still talking as he led Bitty to the open passenger-side door, and as he came around, he spared Mary a quick shrug of, *Are we okay here?*

Mary nodded as discreetly as she could.

"—sure you can," he said as he held the seat back and Bitty scooted into the rear as if she had been doing it all her life. "Anytime you like."

Mary shook herself back into focus. "I'm sorry, what? What's this?"

Bitty sat forward and peered out. "He says I can drive her later."

As Mary's jaw unhinged and she recoiled, Rhage gave her a quick kiss on the cheek. "It'll be fine. We'll just go out to an empty parking lot somewhere."

"You can come with us," Bitty said. "If it'll make you feel better."

Mary looked back and forth between the two of them. "Can you . . . ah, can you even reach the pedals? And it's so powerful—"

"Bitty's going to do great. I'll get blocks for the wheel well if I can't get the seat up far enough."

"He says girls can do anything." Bitty looked at Rhage. "He says, girls are . . . powerful."

"Yup." Rhage nodded. "That's why the fastest and the best cars—"

"—are always girls," Bitty finished for him.

All Mary could do was a little more of the back-and-forthing with her head, as the pair of them clearly waited for her blessing.

"We'll see," she murmured—as she enjoyed a happy little reminder to be careful what she wished for.

"Please?" Bitty prompted.

"Come on, Mary—"

Shooing Rhage out of the way, she put the front passenger seat back into position and got in. "I'm not saying, 'yes,' but if you do drive her, I'm absolutely coming with you two."

"Yes!" Rhage pumped a fist. "That's a yes, Bitty, we got this."

"Yay!"

OMG. Was the girl *smiling*?

With a curse, Mary shut the door—and could have sworn Rhage was frickin' skipping around the car. But then she had to get serious.

Wrenching into the gap between the seats, she said quickly, "Are you okay with this? With him? And I have to ask. It's important."

Bitty didn't hesitate. "I really like him. He's like . . . a big, friendly dog."

As Rhage hopped in and shut his side, Mary started to smile and turned to face the windshield so maybe it wasn't quite so noticeable.

But she couldn't resist reaching over and giving her man's shoulder a squeeze.

And then the three of them were off.

THIRTY-ONE

Over at the Brownswick School for Girls, Vishous was itchy as shit as he slipped into yet another abandoned classroom. With his gun up and ready, and his back flat against the crumbing plaster wall, he scanned the tipped-over chairs with their half-moon tabletops . . . the big desk over by the chalkboard . . . the debris in the corner where part of the ceiling had collapsed.

"Goddamn it."

Moving on to the next room, he only found more of the same: cold air, old mold, discarded, broken furniture, fluorescent light fixtures hanging like broken teeth from up above . . . and absolutely no fucking *lesser* jars.

The slayers had stayed in some of the rooms, typically the ones in the dormitories with mattresses and box springs and windows that were not missing panes—but after no jars were located in any of those buildings, he and Tohr had moved on to the remaining facilities.

As all slayers kept their vessels with them after their inductions, the only conclusion was that the Omega had taken all the hearts with him when he'd gone Merry Maid on the campus the night before last.

Fucker.

Tilting his head to the side, he triggered his communication device by speaking into it. "Nothing here. You find anything?"

"No," Tohr said in V's earpiece. "The Omega must have gotten them all."

"Yeah. Fucking hell."

Beneath his shitkickers, crap that was on the hardwood floor crunched and crackled, but there was no need to be completely silent. And as the image of the Omega in a French maid's uniform and fishnets made V flash his fangs in the dark, he—

Froze where he was.

Cranked his head to the right.

Looked out through the two-out-of-three-ain't-bad set of windowpanes to the stretch of asphalt out behind the building.

Headlights flared into the classroom, shedding a glare of illumination on the rotting shell of prep-school learning before passing over his leather-clad body.

As things were extinguished, he dematerialized over to the glass.

A car had pulled up and parked, and in the glow from the interior dash, he could tell there was a dark-haired man and a red-haired woman inside—

Oh, interesting, he thought as he sensed her.

"We've got company," he said into his communicator.

"And this is my special room."

As Naasha stopped in front of a dungeon door with oak panels thick as tree trunks and hinges big as a male's upper arm, one could have sworn, based upon her affect, that she was about to unveil a marvelous new acquisition, perhaps an oil painting or a marble statue, a car of some vintage or a sterling silver service.

It was none of the above.

Upon a creaking that he supposed was retained on purpose as opposed to being oiled away, a bloodred chamber was revealed. Lit by torches that sizzled on stone walls, and kitted out in swaths of velvet and satin that were like drapes without windows, there was no furniture save bedding platforms that had no pillows, no blankets, just mattresses that were covered with fitted sheets.

Naasha was the first to go in, and as she twirled around, her arms

were held wide as if she were before a grand vista, her eyes seeking his. Behind him, there was an excited twitter from the females—and a flare of arousal from his cousins.

Throe remained silent.

Assail stepped through the jambs. Against the wall by the door, there were a series of make-up stations, no doubt for refreshings for the females after the sessions, and also a series of pegs on which to hang one's clothes. There were two doors over to the left, both painted the dark gray hue of the stone, one with the word *Females* on it in cursive, the other with *Males* written in block lettering.

"And now we have dessert," Naasha said in a husky voice as she reached behind her back and unzipped her gown. "I volunteer to be consumed first."

As the dress fell to the floor, her body was revealed in all its nude glory, her high, tight breasts so very creamy, her smooth sex but a cleft between her long, slender legs. She kept her diamonds on and they twinkled like stars in moonlight, and when she released her hair from its chignon, her midnight locks were a striking contrast to her tan skin.

"Shut the goddamn door," Assail commanded without looking behind himself.

When the creak of those hinges announced that someone had followed instructions, he took three strides over to her. In close proximity now, he watched her ruby lips part and her breasts pump with anticipation.

He smiled at her.

Then he grabbed her by the back of the neck and roughly escorted her over to one of the bedding platforms. Her breasts swayed as he pushed her down on all fours, her sex toward the assembled, her legs not parted enough, so he forced her knees wider by jerking her thighs open. Her core glistened with arousal, her scent like perfume in the air.

"Ehric, Evale," he gritted out. "Drop your kits."

His cousins wasted no time in getting naked, their alacrity as much from their willingness to take orders from him as it was from their having not been with a female for some time.

Both of them were fully erect as he motioned them to come over.

"You," he said, pointing to Ehric. "Here."

He pointed to that slit, and his cousin was on it in an instant, mounting the female from behind, his hips driving in as Naasha groaned and arched her back.

And then all Assail had to do was nod and Evale got with the program, going around and muffling the female's grunts and groans with his rather large anatomy.

"And now you?" somebody proposed to him.

As one of the females sidled up and put her hand on his shoulder, he recognized her as the blonde who had kept her stare on him all through dinner.

"Let us enjoy—"

He pointedly removed her touch. "Get in line for my cousins."

Stepping away, he found a bench over by the bathrooms to sit on, and as he crossed his legs, he watched the show, the females disrobing and feeling one another up, bodies lying out on the platforms, heads and arms intertwining with legs and breasts.

"Do not tell me this is from some misplaced puritanism."

At the dry words, he glanced up at Throe. The male was still fully clothed, but going by the length straining at the fly of his tuxedo pants, that was not going to last.

Assail bared his fangs in a smile. "I have never developed a taste for fast food. It's rather common for my appetites regardless of how noble it wishes to appear."

"That wasn't the case last night." Throe leaned down and smiled, likewise revealing his canines. "I believe you quite enjoyed your time in the parlor."

"Tell me, is Xcor aware of your presence here?"

Throe eased back, calculation narrowing his eyes. "For a businessman, you seem curious about much that does not concern you."

"It's a simple question."

In the background, someone came hard, and Assail glanced over. Ehric and Evale had shifted things around, the pair of them double-penetrating Naasha's well-used sex, one underneath her on his back, the other mounting her on top. A female had joined in and the madam of the house was suckling on a set of voluptuous, pink-nippled breasts.

"Xcor and I have ended our association, shall we say."

Assail refocused on the male. "Breaking up is sooo hard to do."

"His interests and mine did not align any further. He shall not relent in his pursuit of the throne."

"Indeed." Assail carefully tracked the male's features, searching for signs of tension. "And you are now here for how long?"

"I know not. And I care not. I have had an extended, brutal sojourn

in the company of savages, and I crave the civilized in the manner of a starving male."

"Mmmm," Assail said.

Rising to his feet, he faced off with the other male—and reached forward to touch the precisely tied bow at Throe's collar.

As the male's eyes widened in surprise, Assail pushed that body back against the stone wall, holding him in place by the throat.

Then he leaned in chest-to-chest, extended his tongue, and drew it across Throe's lower lip.

Assail laughed as he felt the shudder go through his prey and watched whilst some sort of inner dialogue played out on that handsome face—said conflict being of such note that Throe failed at keeping the reaction to himself.

"You taste like Scotch," Assail murmured as he reached down and cupped that massive erection. "And you feel hungry."

Throe began to pant, much in the manner of Naasha. But he was frozen in place as if he were shocked equally by Assail's actions . . . and his reaction.

"Are you," Assail growled as he hovered above Throe's lips. "Are you hungry . . . for dessert?"

A strange sound came out of the male, half begging, half denial.

And then Throe punched at Assail's shoulders, sending him careening backward onto one of the platforms.

Throe wiped his mouth off on his sleeve and stuck his finger in Assail's direction. "I don't go like that."

Assail allowed his legs to flop to the sides, exposing the arousal behind his fine slacks. "Are you sure?"

Throe cursed and wheeled around for the door. He was gone the next moment, no doubt stomping off to his room, wherever that might be.

Assail sat up and straightened his jacket. That one was going to be fun to crack.

And mayhap in the process, he would learn exactly what Throe was doing here.

He knew in his gut that Wrath and Vishous were correct to be concerned with the *glymera*. Throe was up to something—and the divining of what, in addition to seducing the male out of his sexual comfort zone, was exactly the kind of distraction Assail was after.

This was going to be rather enjoyable.

THIRTY-TWO

As Bill Elliot parked his Lexus behind a non-descript seventies-era building, Jo opened the door on her side and got out slowly. Dilapidation was the name of the game, all kinds of rot and debris and broken things cluttering the flank of the classrooms, like acne on the face of a plain Jane teenager.

"We can walk around from here to the center part of campus." Bill was busy rewrapping the scarf he'd taken off at I've Bean around his neck. "And you can show me where it happened."

As she shut her door, she frowned. The hairs on the back of her neck were standing up like soldiers called to a reveille line, and she looked at the lines of darkened windows. But come on, as if all this talk of vampires wasn't likely to send her adrenal glands into a spiral?

"You coming?"

"Oh, yup." She headed over to him—and had an absurd wish that he was built more like the Rock instead of one of the boys from *The Big Bang Theory*. "So you said you were familiar with the school?"

"My mother went here."

Small world, Jo thought. So did mine.

Their feet shuffled damp leaves out of the way, but did nothing for fallen limbs. Those they stepped over. And when they got to the end

of the asphalt, there wasn't any real difference between the amount of fallen stuff on the grass versus the parking lot.

"What year?" Jo asked as she put her hands into her coat pockets. "Did your mother graduate, that is."

Shoot, they had no flashlights. Just their phones.

Then again, the moon overhead was bright, with nothing but the occasional cloud wisp to mark the dark, cold heavens.

"'Eighty."

"When did the school close?"

"Sometime in the late nineties. I don't know who owns all the land now, but it's a helluva property. I mean, why hasn't someone developed this?"

"Not economically feasible. For one thing, the zoning out here isn't commercial, and second, some of these buildings have to be on the Historic Register, which would restrict their being retrofitted for reuse."

Bill looked over at her. "I've forgotten—you work for a real estate company."

"Two years next month."

"Where did you say you went to school? Or did you?"

Williams College. English lit major with a minor in American history. Accepted into the Yale master's program for English, but couldn't foot the bill on her own.

"Nowhere important." She glanced at him. "How did you know where to park?"

"I used to come here to think when I was at SUNY Caldie. My mom had told me about it, and one day I biked out and just went exploring. I haven't been back in a very long time."

They made it around the side of the building, and just as he'd described, the open area of the campus rolled out before them—which was, yup, still marked with crushed dead grass.

"Jesus . . ." Bill said. "What the hell?"

"Crop circles, Caldwell style, right?"

Bill proceeded ahead of her, and Jo went some distance farther— before she had to stop and look behind herself.

They were being watched. She was sure of it.

"Hey! Wait up," she called out.

As she jogged forward and caught up, he said, "I need to come back in the daytime with a camera."

"Maybe we should just go now—"

"Look at that storage building over there." He pointed ahead. "The roof's been torn off."

"You know, in retrospect, coming during the day would be better. I mean, we can't really see anything—" She sniffed the air. "Is that pine?"

"From the broken rafters. That damage is new."

Sure enough, as they went over to the debris and she picked up pieces of splintered wood, the cuts were all fresh, the yellow insides of the old boards exposed. And asphalt shingles were everywhere around the roof-less shed, littering the crushed ground—

Jo's foot caught on something and she fell to the side, her ankle giving way. As the earth rushed up to her, she threw out a hand and twisted around, saving herself from a total face-plant.

"What the hell?" she muttered as she looked at what had tripped her.

It was *not* a footprint. A giant footprint. Nope.

"Are you okay?" Bill put out a hand—then got distracted by what she'd noticed. "What is that?"

"I'm fine, and no clue." She stood up by herself and brushed her slacks off. "Is it just me or does this feel like a grown up episode of *Scooby Doo*?"

Bill took his cell out and snapped a couple of pictures with the help of his flash. When he checked what had been captured, he cursed. "No, we definitely have to come back during the day."

Jo got down on her haunches and examined the sunken pattern in the ground with the flashlight in her phone. The imprint was deeper and smudged on one side, as if whatever had made it had been pushing off in mid-run.

Bill shook his head. "Does your buddy—Dougie, I think you said that was his name—have resources?"

She glanced up. "You mean, could he have paid to set this all up?" When the reporter nodded, she had to laugh. "He can barely fund his pot-related munchies. No, he didn't do this, and as far as I'm aware, he doesn't know anyone who could."

"Maybe this was made by a four-wheeler." Bill lowered himself down, too. "Skidding out."

Not even close, she thought.

"But what about the roof?" Jo nodded at the topless four walls. "It

wasn't blown off by the wind—there was a little rain recently, but nothing even close to a tornado. And as for an explosion? Nothing is charred and there's no smell of smoke, which you'd expect to find if it had been a bomb."

Bill regarded her steadily. "When you grow up, do you want to be an investigative reporter?"

"I'm twenty-six. By all accounts, I have grown up." Although rooming with Dougie and his ilk might disprove that notion a little. "I really think we should—"

As she stopped talking, Bill looked around. "What?"

Jo searched the shadows, her heart beginning to pound. "Listen . . . I think we need to go. I really . . . *really* think we need to leave."

"Where . . . did my house go?"

As Bitty asked the question from the back of the GTO, Mary leaned forward in her seat—not that the shift of position did anything to change the vacant lot she was staring at.

"Are we in the right place?" Mary got out of the car and held her seat forward so Bitty could join her. "Is there any chance . . ."

Rhage shook his head as he looked across the roof. "GPS says this is the right address."

Shoot, Mary thought.

"There's the ivy bed." The girl burrowed into her coat. "That *mahmen* planted. And the apple tree. And . . ."

The house must have been condemned and torn down at some point, Mary decided, because there was nothing left over, no piles of splintered wood, no chimney's cinder blocks, just saplings and weeds growing in its place. The outline of the driveway, such as it was, had survived, but it would not for much longer with the encroaching vegetation.

As she and Bitty walked forward, Rhage stayed a couple of paces behind them, his looming presence a source of comfort, at least for Mary.

And then she stopped and let Bitty keep going on her own.

Under the moonlight, the girl picked her way around the lot, pausing every couple of minutes to regard the barren landscape.

Rhage's big hand came to rest on Mary's shoulder and she leaned into his body, feeling the warmth of him. It was hard not to measure the vacant, uninhabited property as evidence of the girl's losses.

"I remember the house," Rhage said softly. "Bad condition. Junk in the yard with a broken-down car."

"What did you guys do with the father's body?" Mary blurted. "It's never occurred to me to ask."

"He wasn't, shall we say, in good condition when we left."

"The sun?"

"Yeah. We just left him. The priority was getting Bitty and her mom out. When we came back the following night, there was a scorch mark on the grass. That was it." Rhage cursed under his breath. "I'm telling you, that male was a madman. He was ready to kill anything, anybody who got in his way."

"Her X-rays prove it." As Rhage glanced over, Mary shook her head. "A lot of broken bones—not that she went to Havers when they occurred. Havers said that because she was a pretrans, the healing places still show up until she reaches her maturity. He said . . . they're everywhere."

A subtle growling made her look up. Rhage's upper lip had peeled off his fangs, and his expression was all about protective aggression.

"I want to kill that motherfucker all over again."

Mary gave Bitty as much time as she needed, staying a distance away with Rhage until the girl wandered over.

"I guess my things are gone." Bitty shrugged in that big old parka. "I didn't have a lot of them."

"I'm really sorry, Bitty."

"I was hoping . . ." The girl glanced back at where the house had been. "I was hoping that I could bring some of my old clothes and books to my uncle's. I don't want to be a burden on him. I don't want to get sent away."

Rhage made a small coughing sound. "So I'll go out and buy you what you want. Anything you need to take with you, I got it."

Mary shook her head. "I don't think—"

"It's okay," Bitty cut in. "Maybe I can get a job. You know, when I go to live with him."

You're nine, Mary thought. Damn it.

"How about we head back?" Mary offered. "It's cold."

"You sure you're ready to go?" Rhage asked. "We can stay if you like."

"No." Bitty shrugged again. "There's nothing for me here."

They returned to the GTO, resettling into their various seats, the warmth in the car a balm to cold cheeks and noses.

As Rhage turned them around, the headlights swept over the lot, and Mary thought to herself . . . at some point, this kid was going to get good news. The Scribe Virgin talked about balance all the time, right? So statistically, Bitty was really, totally frickin' overdue.

"I just have to wait until my uncle comes," the girl said as they drove off. "He's going to give me a home."

Mary closed her eyes. And kind of felt like banging her head into Rhage's dashboard.

And as if he were reading her mind, Rhage reached across and took her hand, giving it a squeeze. Mary squeezed back.

"So lemme ask you something there, Bitty girl," he said. "Do you like ice cream?"

"I guess I do. I've had some before."

"Tomorrow night, you got any plans? We could go out after First Meal, before the human shops close up?"

On impulse, because she was desperate to keep any line of communication open, Mary twisted around. "Would you like to do that, Bitty? It could be fun."

When there was a long pause, Mary eased back in her seat and tried to think of another option.

In the quiet, Rhage filled in, "Safe Place has my Mary's cell phone number. If your uncle comes while we're out, they can call her right away and get you. And we can pick a place that's close, like, no more than five minutes' drive." Rhage glanced in the mirror. "I mean, you take baths, right?"

"I'm sorry?" the girl said.

"Like, if you were in the bath and he happened to come, someone would knock on your door, and you'd have to get dry and get dressed and all that jazz. And that would take five minutes, right? So it's just the same. Well, except in one case you need soap and a bath mat, and in the other you get sprinkles and a boatload of hot fudge. If you go that way. Personally, I like to mix and match—I prefer to get a couple of milk shakes, a banana split . . . a sundae or two. Then I top it off with a mocha chip in a cone. I don't know why. I guess that's like the dinner mint at the end of a meal to me. Know what I mean?"

Mary had to turn around again. Bitty was looking forward, her brows super-high, her little face the picture of surprise.

"He's not kidding," Mary murmured. "Even if you're not into the ice cream, watching him eat all that is something to see. So what do you say?"

"They have your number?" the girl asked.

"Absolutely they do. It's a requirement for all staff members. And I keep my phone with me and turned on at all times, even when I'm sleeping—and certainly when I go out into the world."

"And if you're worried about something being missed"—Rhage held up his own phone—"I'll give them my number, too. And my brother Vishous made sure we have the best reception and service in the city. No dead zones. Unless you're around Lassiter, and that's more of a mental thing than anything about cellular networks."

"Um . . . Lassiter?" Bitty said.

Rhage nodded. "Yeah, he's this pain in the ass—oh, shit—I mean, sorry, I shouldn't say ass around you, should I? Or shit. And all those other bad words." He poked himself in the head. "I gotta remember that, gotta remember that. Anyway, Lassiter's a fallen angel who we've somehow gotten stuck with. He's like gum on the bottom of your shoe. 'Cept he doesn't smell like strawberries, he hogs the T.V. remote, and on a regular basis, you think to yourself, Is that *really* the best the Creator could do with an immortal? The guy has the worst taste in television—I mean, the only saving grace is that he isn't addicted to *Bonanza* . . . have you ever watched twelve straight hours of *Saved by the Bell*? Okay, fine, it was probably only seven, and it wasn't like I couldn't have left—my God, I tell you, though, it's a wonder I escaped with my ability to put my pants on one leg at a time still intact. . . ."

It was right about then when it happened. And Mary would have missed it if she hadn't by some stroke of luck picked that moment to turn around again and check to see if Bitty was still listening.

The little girl smiled.

It wasn't some big grin, and she didn't laugh exactly, but the sides of her mouth definitely, totally lifted.

"Will you tell me more?" Bitty asked when Rhage stopped to take a breath. "About the other people you live with?"

"Sure. Absolutely. So my boss, the King? Your King? He has a golden retriever named George that helps him around. Wrath's blind—but he

always knows where you are in the room. He's got crazy senses, that one. He likes lamb, and even though he'd deny it, he seems determined to always finish his vegetables. Like, at meals, you look over—well, see his plates have to all be arranged with the meat, the carbs, and the vegetables in the same place—'cuz, you know, he can't see. Anyway, I can tell he hates those damn veggies, but he eats 'em. Ever since he had his son, L.W. Little Wrath, you know. The kid's how old now?" Rhage looked over. "Mary, can you remember?"

But Mary wasn't really listening to specifics. She was leaning back against the headrest and letting Rhage's prattle of their lives wash over her.

It was the first time in . . . months that she felt relaxed.

"Mary?"

Turning her head to him, she smiled.

I love you so much, she mouthed in the lights of the dash.

Rhage's chest inflated twelve times its normal size, and his I'm-the-*man* expression was so bright on his beautiful face, it was a wonder the entire zip code didn't light up from it.

"Anyway," he continued as he brought the back of her hand up to his mouth for a kiss. "We have a cat named Boo. He came with Wrath's *shellan*, Beth, your Queen. And then one of our doctors has a retired racehorse? And I don't want to think about Vishous owning any gerbils. But I'm not going there, and no, I will absolutely not explain that one. . . ."

Mary found herself closing her eyes as she let the stories and his baritone voice wash over her. For some reason, she remembered a different ride in this car, one very early on in their relationship . . . one where they had put the windows down and blared "Dream Weaver," and she had stuck her head out the window and felt the wind in her face and her hair as they had roared down the road.

It was nice to know, even after all this time, that he still had the ability to carry her away.

THIRTY-THREE

ssail rematerialized at the rear of his mansion, back by the garage. And one after the other, his cousins followed suit, appearing beside him.

"Fates, it is a good job you both remain ambulatory." He approached the kitchen entrance to his home, and entered in a code by the door. As the lock released, he glanced over his shoulder. "I feel quite certain that you are in need of hydration."

All he got back was a mumbled response from Evale—which was a surprise as he was typically the silent one. However, an evening of fucking seemed to have reversed their personalities, draining all conversation out of Ehric, and leaving Evale to be the one who spoke.

Rather amusing, really.

Inside, he removed his coat and tuxedo jacket. They did not have to. Evidently, fully re-clothing had required greater stores of energy than they had had; their outerwear was draped over their forearms, their shirts barely buttoned to the sternum, their white ties stuffed into the pockets of their slacks.

"Food," Evale said. "We require sustenance over that inconsolably small meal."

"Evale, you have the oddest vocabulary."

"Sit, Ehric. I shall endive to service you prior to our retirement."

Assail rolled his eyes. "Endive is a vegetable. 'Endeavor' is the word for which you search. And it is *serve*. Unless you wish to refer to your previous 'endives' this eve?"

Leaving the pair of them to do whate'er they would calorically speaking, Assail proceeded onward to his office. As he took a seat behind his desk, he adjusted his cocaine levels first, and then fired up his computer whilst he placed a call upon his cellular device.

The Brother Vishous answered with, "It's official. I do talk to you more than I talk to my mother. Don't get excited, though, I can't stand her."

"With your warm personality and pleasant demeanor, I cannot *fathom* any kind of estrangement in your life."

"You don't have to jerk me off with the compliments."

"Speaking of such, may I just say that Naasha is a rather pneumatic little female with a taste for exhibition and an all-access policy that does not refer to her *hellren*'s venerable landholdings." After all, when he had tried to leave the dungeon and do a little exploring, she had sent a naked female after him—within moments. "My cousins are happy, if exhausted males, going into daybreak."

"So apart from the fucking, what do you know?"

"Throe is ensconced in the household. He has a room and her affection. He stated to me that he is estranged from Xcor and the Band of Bastards, ne'er to return unto their questionable fold." He had to sniff as his nose ran. "There is something worrisome about that male. I do not trust him."

"When do you go back?"

"She has invited me unto her *hellren*'s epic birthnight celebration. Has the invitation come through to Wrath the now?" He sniffed again, and brushed at the base of his nostrils. "I believe she is intending to present such soon, if it has not already arrived."

There was a *shhhh-cht* and an exhale, as if the Brother were lighting up something. "Not yet. But we'll be waiting. He has no intention of going, but members of the Brotherhood will be there for sure."

"As shall my cousins and I." Assail frowned as something occurred to him. "Pardon me for going a bit off topic, but please allow me to inquire about your armaments."

There was a long pause. And then the Brother's voice, which was already low, bottomed out completely. "What do you want to know."

"Are you in need of any?"

"Why."

"I have contacts with my black market suppliers that could facilitate such purchases."

"Now you want to be an arms dealer? Have your ambitions always pointed you toward lofty pursuits?"

"There is naught lofty about graves, is there? At any rate, consider the offer extended. They contacted me for further business and I declined their kind and generous offer with respect to certain powders and potions. But it did get me thinking that there could still be some exchange of money for goods that Wrath would permit me to engineer."

Vishous laughed in a deep purr. "Always looking for an angle. And will you stop with the coke? You've been sniffing through this conversation like a human in a hayfield."

"I remain loyal to you and your King," Assail concluded. "Contact me as you wish. If I hear anything further or have any further contact with her before next week, I shall call you immediately."

"You do that, true."

Assail ended the call and—

Recoiling, he looked down at the back of his hand. There was a streak of bright red blood across the flesh . . . and droplets upon the white of his starched formal shirt.

Getting to his feet, he went into the nearest bathroom out in the hall and flipped on the light.

"Damn it . . ."

His nose was leaking all over the place.

After cranking the water on, he took a hand towel that he had washed and folded the day before and put the thing under the cool rush. Then he wiped away the blood that was streaming out of his nostrils before applying the cold compress in a pinch and tilting his head back.

He was rather some time with that, all the while standing before the mirror and brushing at the stains on the fine cotton of his shirt. OxiClean, he decided. He would start there, as blood had protein in it. Then he would resort to bleach before throwing the fucking thing out if he had to.

When the exsanguination had been extinguished, he took the towel with him and proceeded to the kitchen.

Whereupon he found his patent-leather shoes faltering.

It was the smell in the air. Rich and spicy, yet delicate as well, the combination of spices exotic to his Old Country palate called out to his stomach, making the thing growl.

Portuguese food. Which had been prepared by an authentic, loving, if slightly belligerent, hand.

He closed his eyes. Marisol's grandmother had prepared he and his cousins many foods prior to her departure and those two had clearly availed themselves of said carefully packaged and frozen entrée packs.

"Would you care to join us?" Evale said as he waited at the microwave. "Or are you just going to stand there in a lure."

Assail shook himself. "I believe the word you are thinking of is *leer*."

"Have you seen your face?" the male asked as there was a *bing*! After popping open the front, he carried a heaping plate of his own to the table. "Hardly welcoming are you."

"Which is the definition of 'leer.' And you should not eat that."

"Why ever not?" Ehric asked as he took his first bite. "Ahhh, 'tis masterful."

"Indeed," his twin agreed. "Mercilessly so."

"Also not the word you want." Assail held off explaining that they should not eat the food because then it all would be gone and the only tie he had left to his Marisol would be— "I shall retire for the day the now."

"Adieu," Ehric said.

"Anew," Evale tacked on.

"That's 'anon,' dear cousin of mine."

Assail proceeded into the laundry whereupon he dropped the bloodied towel in the wash, shrugged out of his tuxedo jacket and removed his dirtied shirt.

Both of his cousins had looked at the stains, but neither had said anything.

Were words really necessary, though.

As Assail passed back through the kitchen bare chested and with his jacket over his shoulders, he said to no one in particular, "I shall endeavor to employ us a proper *doggen*. One who is well versed in the caretaking of a home and all that entails. I tire of doing laundry and vacuuming."

"Are you certain it does not have to do with a dwindling supply of certain frozen foods?"

He glanced at Ehric. "I believe I shall employ you unto Naasha's underground again soon. I prefer you quiet, even if your brother butchers language as if it were a pig upon the slaughter."

Assail proceeded onward to the stairs, and he waited until he had made the corner and turned away from them to massage the ache in his chest.

Would the missing of that human woman e'er ease?

As Rhage waited for his Mary to come home from work, he walked in and around the pool tables in the billiards room, cue in hand, balls in play on the felt, mind . . . back on that vacant lot. That little girl.

Man, destiny could be a real bitch, he thought.

"—talked to him just now." Leaning over the table, Vishous performed a re-rack, getting things set for the next game. "He wanted to know if we needed more guns."

Trying to focus, Rhage frowned. "I thought Assail was a drug dealer?"

"Branching out, evidently." Vishous picked up a chalk square and blued his tip. "What do you think?"

"The new training class is coming in soon, right?"

"Yeah."

"Might make sense to do a test order on some autoloaders."

"That's what I was thinking."

Rhage braced his hip against the table as V bent down and cracked the triangle into pieces. As the colored balls rolled all over the place, Rhage shook his head.

"You see that elephant gun Evale had at Brownswick?"

Those diamond eyes lifted. "Fuck, yeah. We need to get us one of those, true."

"Just on principle. Think of the target practice."

"Yeah, we could strap a small car to Lassiter's back and make him run around by the pool—"

"Hey," the fallen angel called out from one of the sofas. "I'm in here, assholes."

Rhage glanced over at the guy. "You're awake, huh."

The blond-and-black bastard sat up and yawned, stretching his arms over his head. "Time for my shift to start. Shit! I'm late. Gotta go."

As Rhage and V watched the angel take off at a dead run, both of them cursed.

"You know," Rhage muttered, "it's getting really hard to hate him."

"Just think of *Punky Brewster*. Everything will recalibrate." Vishous prowled around the table, his massive body moving like a panther in his leathers and his muscle shirt. "And fuck me, I never thought I'd know that show."

V made quick work of things, all kinds of pockets getting filled—but he flubbed it three strokes later.

"Hollywood? My brother, it's all you."

Rhage tried to refocus, but he just couldn't get Bitty off his mind. After a moment, he looked across the green felt, and was glad that all of the *doggen* were in the kitchen and dining room—and that most of the other brothers hadn't arrived home quite yet.

And hey, he was always glad when Lassiter left a room.

"What," V said. "And do I need to light up first."

"You ever . . ." Rhage cleared his throat. "You ever think about having a kid, V?"

"No. Why?"

As the guy stared back, it was as if Rhage had asked him whether or not he needed a new toaster. Some laundry done. An oil change.

"You don't *ever* wonder what it would be like to be a father?"

"No."

"Never?"

"No." Vishous shrugged. "Not sure why you're asking."

"There've been some kids, you know, coming into this household."

"So?"

"That doesn't affect you at all?" When V shook his head, Rhage frowned. "What about Doc Jane? Does she want them?"

"Okay, first, she can't have any. And second, she's never mentioned it to me. Ever. She's mated to her job—hell, her idea of a romantic birthday present is a new autoclave. And I fucking *love* that about her."

"But what if she changed her mind?"

"She won't."

"How do you know that?" As V just blinked a couple of times, Rhage waved his hand. "Sorry. None of that's my fucking business."

"Is this why you got problems with your Mary? And don't play. It's been obvious—she want kids?"

"No. No, nothing like that." Rhage rubbed the tip of his cue with his thumb, transferring the bright blue chalk to the pad of his finger. "I just was wondering. You know, hypothetically. About other people."

"Look, I don't mean to be dismissive, but come on—I have a god-awful relationship with my mother and had a sadist for a sire. That mother/father business has only ever had bad connotations for me. Besides, I'm about as nurturing as a sawed-off—isn't that the way the saying goes?"

"Like I said, I'm sorry I brought it up."

"You gonna play now?"

Rhage shifted his weight from shitkicker to shitkicker. "I got one other thing to ask you, actually."

THIRTY-FOUR

The last thing Mary did before she left for the day was go to her office and check Facebook on her computer.

Like if she fired the URL up on something other than her phone, the search would give her a different result.

"Okay, let's do this," she muttered as she signed on.

As the machine came to life, she got a front-and-center of the closed, vampires-only group she was looking for—because it had been the last thing she'd been on before she'd gone downstairs to wait for Rhage earlier in the evening.

Hitting refresh, she waited for the Internet connection to show her any new posts, and ended up tilting her head back and looking at the ceiling. Bitty was moving around in her attic room, and Mary fought the urge to go and try to talk to her. But no, it was time to go home, and the girl was tired. Also, Mary had an almost superstitious notion that for once, the pair of them had parted on a relatively optimistic note: Bitty was ready for ice cream after nightfall tomorrow, and Mary was hanging on to that one fleeting smile in the back of the GTO as if it were a lifeline in the ocean.

"Okay, what have we got," she whispered as she focused on the screen.

Nope. Nothing. There were probably only five hundred males and females in the group—mostly females—and the few new posts she saw covered conventional topics that even to human eyes would seem entirely normal.

No one had responded to her query about Bitty's uncle.

She was disappointed, but that was kind of crazy. The logical part of her knew there was no one out there for the girl, but hearing Bitty talk with such desperation about a hypothetical relative? It made you want a miracle to happen.

Shutting everything down, she got her purse and her coat and went out, pausing at the base of the attic stairs.

"Good day, Bitty girl."

About twenty minutes later, she was driving up the *mhis*-covered hill of the compound, going at a slow pace because she didn't want to go off the lane or hit a deer—

"Shit!"

Slamming on the brakes, she yanked the steering wheel to the right, just as Qhuinn's Hummer nearly T-boned her.

The SUV skidded to a halt and all kinds of fighters jumped out and rushed toward her like the Volvo was on fire.

"Mary!"

"Maaaaary!"

Butch ripped her door open. "Mary! Motherfucker!"

She had to laugh at the expression on the cop's face. And on Blay's. And John Matthew's. And Qhuinn's.

Putting her hands up, she said, "I'm okay, I'm okay, I'm okay. Honestly."

"I'm calling Doc Jane—"

"Butch. Seriously." She undid her seat belt and shoved the Bostonian out of the way. "See? And the air bag didn't even deploy. Although I'm getting a little flinchy with all these close encounters. I nearly hit a *lesser* the other night."

That shut all four of them up. And then they just stood there, staring at her as if they were going to synchronize-vomit.

"Boys, you didn't even hit me. I'm fine." She nodded at the dirt path they'd been on. "I didn't even know that was there—where are you coming from?"

"Nowhere." Butch took her elbow and started to try to help her around to the passenger side. "I'll drive you the rest of the way—"

"No." She dug her heels in and nailed him with some serious eye-to-eye. "Butch. There is nothing wrong with me. I want all four of you to take a deep breath—and maybe put your heads between your knees so you don't faint. Close calls happen, we both reacted in time, so let's move along—or I'm going to call Fritz and have all of your bedrooms painted pink. Right after he puts potpourri on your bureaus, and Elsa and Anna pictures up on your walls."

"She means business," Blay said with no small measure of respect.

"Hell, yeah," Qhuinn muttered. "Man, no wonder you can stand being mated to Rhage. He gets out of line, you just whip him right back into shape, don't you."

We're just worried, John Matthew signed. *And we really don't want to tell your hubs that we hurt you. That's all.*

She went over and hugged John. "I know. And I'm sorry if I'm a little bitchy. It's been a long couple of nights. Come on, let's go eat."

Back behind the wheel of the station wagon, she started up the hill, going the same slow speed as before. The Hummer stayed a DMV-worthy six car lengths behind her—and she was very aware of the fighters watching her every move.

Because all four of them were pressed up against the SUV's front windshield, clustered like a bunch of mother hens worried about an errant chick.

They sure filled her rearview mirror with love, though.

Which was never, ever a bad thing.

After they all pulled up in front of the mansion and picked their normal spots in the line up of cars—hers by Manny's Porsche, theirs over by V's new thingamajiggy, whatever it was—she got out with her bag and was prepared to fend off a bunch of how-'bout-a-quick-physical suggestions from the leather-bound peanut gallery.

And what do you know, the pack of four came at her in formation.

Putting up her hands, she said calmly and reasonably, "I can't die, remember? Also, in case you haven't noticed, I'm up and around, speaking in complete sentences—even smiling. See?" She pointed to her mouth. "So how about Last Meal before you all fall over?"

There was a chorus of baritone *fine*s and *whatever*s, and then John

Matthew put his arm around her shoulders, gave her a quick hug and everybody strode up to the vestibule.

Fritz opened the inner door for them. "Greetings! How fare thee all?"

As the butler bowed, and everyone filed in, Mary had to pause. She had walked into the foyer how many times in the last however long, but it had been a while since she'd actually looked at the three-story-high ceiling with its mural of majestic fighters on their war-horses . . . or paused to appreciate the malachite-and-marble columns with their ornate headers and footers . . . or taken a second to listen to the layers of conversation as members of the house came down to gather in the dining room.

Everything seemed over-the-top luxe, and multi-factorial loud, and altogether wonderful, from Z and Bella descending the grand staircase with Nalla to Wrath and George walking across the mosaic floor with Tohr to John Matthew and Xhex wrapped in each other's arms.

Heading into Last Meal, she thought back to what Rhage had told Bitty about the people here, his wonderful, purposely laughable, ver-bally scribbled caricatures of the very real blessings this family had.

Then she pictured him and Bitty leaning over the engine of his car, him taking the time to explain all kinds of things to her, not one bit of this-is-just-for-boys tinting anything, his face open, his eyes kind.

He had been amazing with the girl—

"Mary mine," came a whisper in her ear.

As she jumped and turned to Rhage, she didn't think for a second. She put her arms around him, pulled him down . . .

. . . and kissed the ever-loving crap out of him.

Okay, yeah, WOWOWOWOWOWOWOWOW.

As Mary licked her way into Rhage's mouth, his mind went blank in the best possible way—especially when he reached for her and brought her body close to his, curling his greater height and weight around her. His *shellan*'s lips were soft and warm, and her tongue slipped and slid against his, and her breasts, even though her coat, seemed to be brushing naked against his chest.

"Let's go upstairs," she said into his mouth.

He resumed the kissing while he eyed the staircase. Yeah, so steep, so long—and their bedroom? Shit, it was like, five hundred miles away. More like five thousand.

"C'mere," he groaned.

He ended up shuffling her backward, his hands desperate to get under those clothes of hers—but he couldn't risk that kind of contact. He felt her bare skin? He was liable to take her right there on the mosaic floor.

The pantry was located just off the kitchen and it was about as luxurious and comfortable as a laundry room—with the tragic lack of a washer or dryer that you could put the female you were in love with on and have her at hip height with her thighs spread wide. There were, however, two benes: One, there was a lock on the inside, as if Darius had known what kind of alternate spice might get thrown around among the cans of peaches and jars of pickles; and two, there was a shallow counter four feet above the floor with a good two and a half feet of surface depth that went all the way around the room.

Ostensibly, the thing was there to accommodate the banks of drawers that were under the stacks of shelves.

At the moment? It was the closest thing to Maytag Rhage could get.

"Oh, God, I need you," Mary said as he slammed the door shut, manually turned the dead bolt, and popped her up off the floor.

As she grabbed the bottom of his muscle shirt and yanked it over his head, the thing got caught on his nose, nearly shearing his nostrils off. But like he gave a fuck? And then her shaking hands were clawing at the zipper on his leathers.

"I need you in me, hurry—I *need* you."

"Oh, fuck, Mary, you have me—" The second her hand came into contact with his cock, he arched back and shouted something. Her name? Something about the Scribe Virgin? F-bomb? Again, who the fuck cared. "Let me get you—"

Next thing he knew, she was off the shelf, at his hips, and pushing him back until he slammed into the opposite side of things so hard cans of soup bounced down and rolled across the floor like they feared for their lives.

"Maaaaaaaaaaaaaaaaaary—"

That mouth of hers sucked his erection in deep, and though the warm, wet hold and suction were out-of-this-world erotic, what was even hotter? The sense that she was so fucking desperate for him, she couldn't wait for him to get his pants down and hers off.

She was so damn hungry and greedy to have him she didn't want to waste time.

She *had* to have him.

The bonded male inside of Rhage howled in satisfaction, and the beast surged in a good way under his skin—and oh, yeah, he orgasmed.

God, did he fucking orgasm. And as Mary milked him until he sagged, and then sat back and licked her lips, he felt some part of himself return—a part that had been gone for a while, but that he hadn't really been aware of missing.

She still wanted him. Still needed him. And there was something about that connection that filled him out in a way he'd been previously deflated.

And it was time to return the favor. With a growl, he launched himself at her, taking her down to the hardwood, kissing her and tasting himself as he tore off her slacks, shoved his leathers to mid-thigh, and got her to straddle him while he rolled over onto his back.

Mary sat down hard on his cock and both of them cried out. Then she leaned forward, propped her hands next to his head, and began pumping her pelvis, his erection going in and out of her sex, their bodies slapping together, Rhage's eyes latching onto her as she stared back at him with a combination of fierce determination and utter adoration.

She still had her coat on. The thing was flapping around her, and though he would have loved to see her breasts and her neck, her stomach, her sex, he was too caught up to be any kind of coordinated with his hands and his thoughts.

It was just really fucking awesome to be wanted like this. Ridden like this. Taken like this.

They came at the same time, their hips racking and thrashing, until he somehow ended up rolling her over and mounting her from on top. Thank fuck for that jacket of hers and the cushioning it offered, as it turned out. Grabbing onto one of her ankles, he cranked her leg to her shoulders and went in deep, hingeing his pelvis freely as he banged her across the bare floor of the pantry until they got crammed

in the corner. With a growl, he arched up, held on to the lip of the counter, and got even more leverage.

And the sex just kept going.

And going.

And going . . .

THIRTY-FIVE

As dawn threatened in the East, and the peachy light cast by that unrelenting fireball in the heavens gathered into a thin line at the horizon, Zypher stood by the burned-out shell of a car in one of Caldwell's back alleys.

All around him, the Band of Bastards had gathered, their bodies tense and twitchy, their weapons holstered, but their hands at the ready.

Balthazar spoke up. "This was his last coordinate."

Yes, Zypher thought, they all knew that. Indeed, they had started here at nightfall the evening before, after Xcor had not returned to their new headquarters—which now had to be abandoned. Clearly, their leader had been injured severely in a fight, whether it was here or at some other locale, and one could only assume that he and his phone had been taken into custody either by the Lessening Society or the Black Dagger Brotherhood.

Aye, there was a possibility that he had been wounded and had dragged himself unto some discreet cover for a period of time, only to expire either of natural causes or from sun exposure, his phone going up in smoke with him or being stolen from out of his dead hand—but considering the foes they were facing, it was unwise to rely on such a premise.

Better to assume capture. Torture. And possible information exchange.

"He would not want a memorial," Zypher blurted.

"Aye," somebody agreed. "And he must have entered the Fade in quite a lather."

There was a grumble of laughter—but Zypher wondered if their leader, or any of them, would be granted access to that heavenly sanctuary. For their ill deeds, surely they would be turned away? Sent unto *Dhund*, the Omega's evil playground of eternity?

Either way, as they stood around, he decided that the alley seemed a proper place for this gathering of mourning, the remnants of the old car a fitting grave marker, the lack of specifics an appropriate closing to Xcor's life. After all, although Zypher had worked with the male against the *lessers* for centuries, he could not say that he had e'er truly known his fellow fighter.

Well . . . that was not entirely true. He had been well-versed in their leader's cruelty and calculation, both in the war camp and then later, as they had been travelers with temporary housing, and later still, when they had settled in their castle fortification in the Old Country.

And there had been that one private moment, after Xcor had stabbed Throe—and punished himself for it.

"What do we do now?" Balthazar asked.

After a moment of silence, Zypher realized they were all looking at him.

He wished they had a body. The course would be clearer, then. At the moment, even with all circumstantial evidence pointing them in a certain direction, taking control of the group felt like insubordination.

But there was naught else to do.

Zypher scrubbed his face with his gloved hand. "We must assume our base has been compromised, or soon will be. We must also destroy all cellular devices. Then we will wait a given period of time—before we shall return unto the Old Country. There is a life worth living o'er there."

The castle still stood and remained in their names.

But money. They needed money.

Shit.

"What if he attempts to reach us?" Balthazar asked. "If we do away with our phones, how will he find us?"

"If he has survived, he will locate us."

Leaning to the side, Zypher glanced between two buildings. That glow of dawn was e'er increasing, and if they waited too much longer, they were going to follow a similar fate as this vehicle. As mayhap Xcor himself.

"Let us proceed back to—" He frowned. "No. We shall not go back there."

He wouldn't put it past the Brotherhood to wage an ambush inside the farmhouse even in broad daylight—and not because those males were reckless, but rather because they were that deadly. And if slayers were who had gotten Xcor? Then such an attack was even more a possibility.

Glancing around, he focused on a nearby door. The building it opened into was abandoned, going by the boarded-up windows and the CONDEMNED sign plastered on its brick.

Zypher walked over and slammed his shoulder into the portal. As the metal panel broke free, the lock splintered into pieces, littering the floor of the darkened interior beyond.

The air that greeted him was cold, wet, and smelled like various strains of mold and decay. But the oppressive blackness that surrounded him was good news.

They had no food. Only the weapons and ammunition on their backs. And this was an iffy shelter at best.

It was just like the good old days.

Save for one rather large and noticeable absence.

As his fellow bastards filed in and found places on over-turned crates and stretches of countertops littered with plastic containers, rats scuttled out of the way, squeaking their curses.

"Upon nightfall, we shall return unto the farmhouse, pack up, and determine our course."

Zypher chose a section of floor by the door, wedging himself into a crevice between shelvings such that he was propped up with his autoloader in hand and ready to discharge.

In his long history as a soldier, there had been many days such as this, his body required to catch its sleep on the fly as he rested with one ear and one eye open. And before all that, as a student of the Bloodletter, he had feared for his life when the sun had risen and the trainees had been forced to retire unto the caved war camp until nightfall.

This was a vacation compared to what he and the others had endured.

Closing his lids, he found himself wondering how Xcor had died. And where that troubled soul of his had ended up.

Some questions were destined to remain unanswered . . . and it was strange for him to discover that he most certainly missed their leader—though he found that difficult to admit. Xcor had been as fearsome as the Bloodletter at times; yet his absence was like that of a limb or a crucial organ.

Habits died harder than mortals, however.

And this ennui, tied as it was to centuries of cruelty, was hardly a recommendation for the male's soul.

THIRTY-SIX

"**Y**es, of course. I will get a message to the buyers before the closing next week. Yes, the walk-through is scheduled for Thursday at eight a.m. Is that still convenient? Very good. My pleasure. Good-bye."

Jo hung up the phone, made a note in the client's file, and then checked her personal cell.

She couldn't possibly have read the text right. The damn thing was from Bill:

> You played me well, but not for long. You should have tried this with someone who has no research skills.

What the . . . ? They had parted the night before on good terms, heading back to his car when her sense that they were being watched had become too overwhelming for her to ignore. The plan had been for them to meet up at lunch and head over to the school campus again.

She hit him back. *What are you talking about?*

Returning her phone to the drawer, she tried to look busy as real estate agents walked back and forth in front of her desk without acknowledging her. Which was a good thing. If they stopped to talk to

her, it was usually because they were upset about microwave etiquette in the breakroom, had an IT issue she couldn't help them with, or were acting out their frustration with the current less-than-robust seller's market.

Meanwhile, Bryant had been out all morning, but he had been busy with his phone. He'd sent her fifteen texts, only half of which had been office related. The others had had a strange tone to them: He'd wanted to know why she'd left at seven last night. When she'd replied that he'd told her she was free to head out, he'd asked where she'd gone. When she'd told him that she'd headed straight home . . .

He'd replied, *Are you sure about that?*

Which had been bizarre—

A rattling sounded inside her desk and she ripped open the drawer. Accepting the call that had made the phone vibrate, she repeated, "What are you talking about?"

Bill laughed with an edge. "You didn't tell me who your parents were. Receptionist, my ass."

"I'm sorry?"

"You're Phillie and Chance Early's kid. Their only daughter—I'm sorry—*heir.*"

She closed her eyes and sucked in a curse. "What does that have to do with anything?"

"Look, if you're trying to get your little *Blair Witch Project* wannabe a traditional media boost, you're going to have to find someone else to be your bullshit artist, okay? I don't have time for this."

Jo switched her phone to her other ear, as if that would change the gist of the conversation. "I don't understand—"

"I asked you last night if your buddy, Dougie, had the kind of resources to stage something like all that trampled landscape. You said no—and conveniently left out the fact that *you* do. With your kind of money, you could CGI the crap out of that footage on YouTube, pay people to rough up the center of campus, and then, wow, hey, you hit up a *CCJ* reporter, hoping he's stupid enough to buy into it all and get you some local coverage. Next thing you know, the piece gets picked up by the HuffPost and BuzzFeed—and then it's *Deadline* announcing a movie deal about the "vampires" of Caldwell. How perfectly organic."

"That isn't at all what—"

"Don't call me again—"

"I'm adopted, okay? And I haven't seen those two people you call my 'parents' in at least a year. I don't identify as theirs any more than they support me, and if you want me to show you proof of how small my bank account is, fine—I'm happy to show you my pathetic monthly statement. I asked you what you thought about that stuff on the Net because I'm trying to figure it out myself. Allow me to assure you, however, that *none* of the Brownswick footage is the result of me writing any checks to anybody. So how about you do more than a cursory job at investigating me before you leap to conclusions and jump down my throat. Thanks. Bye."

She nearly threw her phone back in the drawer, but thought better of it—because, hey, people who were worried about covering their rent really shouldn't put themselves in the position of needing to replace their cell—

As the office phone obligingly rang, she grabbed for it and was glad for the distraction.

And while she closed the loop with a buyer about the status of some fire-alarm replacements in a duplex across town, she parallel-processed the whole thing in her head. It was crazy for her to be wasting any more time or effort trying to get to the bottom of those videoes, for one thing. And secondly, she had a very strong suspicion that the reason her brain had gravitated toward this stretch of stupidity was because she was otherwise very bored in her life.

Which that was a problem to be solved not by distraction, but by pulling her socks up and figuring out what the hell she wanted to do with herself.

Yes, she had already decided the socialite existence of the people who had adopted her was a big ol' no. So wha-hey, she'd already narrowed her future down by one option—

When the inside of her desk began to rattle again, she pulled open the door and got her phone back out from the loose paper clips and the pencils she didn't use.

It was Bill. And she thought about letting the call go to voice mail, but knew that was childish. Hitting accept, she said, "I can only assume you're going to apologize right now. Or did you audit my credit score? It's actually not that bad, although remember, that doesn't have to do with net worth, just whether you're as anal as I am about paying bills on time."

The guy had the grace to clear his throat. "I'm sorry. It appears as if I may have jumped to some conclusions that were unwarranted."

Jo rolled her chair around so she was facing the office's logo on the felt wall. Taking a deep breath, she muttered, "You know, it does help, if you're trying to establish yourself as an investigative reporter *par excellence*, that you go a little deeper than mere surface information on someone."

"I just thought . . . well, never mind what I thought." There was a pause. "Do you still want to meet in an hour?"

Jo glanced at her watch. Just to give herself a little time. Har-har.

In or out, she told herself. Fish or cut bait.

If she went with the plan? She was liable to keep getting sucked further into a rat hole that wasn't going to get her any closer to getting off her ass and into a real job—

"Jo?"

As a deep voice said her name, she jumped and swiveled back around. Bryant was leaning on the front counter of her desk.

"Jo?" Bill asked over the phone.

As she looked up into her boss's handsome face, she got an idea of exactly why she might be searching for excuses to stay in a go-nowhere job. And really, eye candy didn't get you far, did it.

"Yes, I'll be there," she said to Bill, and then hung up. "Hey, you're back early."

"Who was that? Your boyfriend?" Bryant smiled as he narrowed his eyes. "You never told me you had one."

"That's because I don't. Did you get that listing signed? I can start on the M.L.S.—ah, why are you looking at me like that?"

Bryant's phone rang in his hand, and her office line rang on her desk, and before he could respond, she went for her receiver, popping the thing off its cradle and going into her scripted greeting.

It was two rings before he answered . . . Bryant actually waited for two rings before he accepted his call—but whatever distraction Jo offered was passed up on as he drawled a "hello," started laughing and then walked away.

Yup, it was so time to fire up the old resume.

"'Keep the change, you filthy animal. . . .'"

As Rhage said the line, he shifted his chin, kissed Mary's forehead, and reveled in their blissful state of total relaxation. In return, she snuggled in closer to his bare chest and yawned so hard her jaw cracked.

"Annnnnnnnnnnnd there goes the pizza guy." Rhage laughed as he put his grape Tootsie Pop in for another suck. "You know, I love the dumb statue that everyone knocks over in the front of the house."

Home Alone. In bed. With his *shellan*, a full belly, and the secure knowledge that his Mary had agreed to let him pick two more movies out for them.

Can you say *Die Hard* and *Christmas Vacation*?

After all, it was coming into her human holiday season, right?

And man, if this wasn't heaven all rolled up on a fluffy white cloud, he didn't know what was. His body was so chilled out he was doing some serious floating on air himself, and none of these cinematic greats he had lined up came with twelve-hanky, foreign-language-proficiency requirements.

Movie night for them could be a thing.

Mary liked valid stuff. He liked pop culture.

Ne'er the twain shall meet. But hey, you had to compromise in a mating. That was the way shit worked.

"What are we watching next?" she murmured.

"Bruce Willis and then Chevy Chase. I'll let you guess what they're starring in."

She propped her head up on his pec. "Are you picking a Christmas theme just for me?"

"Yup. You wanna give me a smooch for being so thoughtful?"

When she leaned up, he took her face between his palms and kissed her deeply. As they parted, he focused on her lips, feeling that old familiar burn roll out where it counted most for a male. "Can I just tell you how much I'm looking forward to our shower before First Meal?"

"Are you now?"

As she smiled at him nice and slow, that rekindle got stoked even more. "Mmmm . . ."

"If you were anyone else," she murmured, "I would wonder how in the world you were going to get aroused again—like, in the next month."

"Oh, I'll be ready for you. Always."

Except then something changed in her. He knew the instant it happened, although he would have been hard-pressed to describe exactly what tipped him off.

"What is it?" he whispered. "Are you thinking about Bitty?"

Before she could answer, he paused the movie with the remote,

ironically right at the point Kevin put his father's aftershave on and screamed at the top of his lungs.

With Macaulay Culkin's ten-year-old self hollering at them from the flat-screen over on the far wall, Rhage brushed his Mary's hair away from her face.

"Talk to me," he said.

She flopped over onto her back. "I don't want to ruin this with more of my heavy stuff."

"Why would you ruin anything?"

"Come on, Rhage . . . I feel like we've finally got things fixed between us, but here I am . . . screwing it up again."

He frowned and turned on his side, resting his head on his palm. "Why would talking about Bitty mess anything up between us?" When she didn't answer him, he drew a circle on her bare arm. "Mary?"

As she finally looked at him again, her eyes were watery. "I need to tell you something."

"Anything." Hell, after the last—what time was it? noonish?— eight hours with her, he felt invincible where she was concerned. "I'm not worried."

"That gunshot wound of yours . . ." She sniffed, and seemed determined to buck up. "When you came back from the beast having been out, and you were lying there on the ground . . ."

She put her hands up to her face and stared at the ceiling as if she were right back there in the middle of that field. And his first instinct was to tell her to stop, put the memory away, never return to that moment.

But she wasn't a coward with her emotions. She never had been.

"I fought to keep you here." She stared over at him. "I . . . I begged Jane and Manny to do something, anything to help you."

"Of course you did. I was suffering—I mean, deal or no deal for the other side, that was no fun for me, I assure you."

"Yes." She looked away. "I didn't want you to suffer."

As his Mary fell silent, he took one of her hands and brought it to his mouth. "Why in a million years do you think your trying to save my life could be a bad thing? I mean, I'm not one of you therapist types, but I'm getting the clear vibe over here that that's what you're trying to apologize for. Which is nuts. Both on a clinical and a practical level—"

"IdidntwanttoleaveBitty."

"I'm sorry, what did you say? I didn't catch it."

Mary sat up, tucking the sheet around her naked breasts. "I could have just met you on the other side . . . but when it came down to it, yes, I freaked out, because you couldn't breathe and you were . . . the dying thing was happening . . . but I also didn't want to leave Bitty. I wanted you to stay so that I could keep helping her. And I'm so sorry, oh, God, Rhage, I'm so sorry."

Rhage blinked a couple of times. "Let me get this straight. You're apologizing to me because you didn't want to leave an orphaned girl who had just watched her mother die to deal with all that alone? Really?"

"I feel like I . . . betrayed you in some way. I mean, the pact about me meeting you on the other side is about your destiny and mine. Together. Just the two of us. But when push came to shove, I fought, but not for us. Not really. Because I knew I could see you again. I fought . . . for someone else. And that just feels really wrong."

Rhage sat up, too, stuffing the comforter around his lap. Put like that, he could kind of see her point.

And yet . . . "Mary, if it helps you in any way, I didn't want to leave my brothers behind. I was mostly concerned about you and me, and what was going to happen to us, but that wasn't the only thing on my mind. There were other people in on it for me, too." He smiled and rubbed his jaw. "Even if one of them happened to coldcock me— twice—right after I got out of bed. Anywho, I can understand what you're getting at, but the way I see it? I don't expect your whole life to revolve around me. I respect your profession, and I love you for every-thing you do at Safe Place. You felt, in that moment, that you had unfinished business you needed to handle. That is something I can totally respect." He frowned. "Well, as long as you intended to actually meet me over there if I didn't come back—"

"Oh, God, yes!" She reached out and pulled him to her mouth. "I swear on my soul. Even if it had meant leaving Bitty alone . . . I would have come to find you. I have *no* doubt about that."

Rhage smiled and cradled her face in his palms again. "Then we're all good. You gotta know, my Mary, your commitment to your job is as much a part of what I love about you as the rest of . . . you know, everything. Don't waste another thought on the whys of what you did.

Focus on how incredibly amazing it is that we're right here, together, and it all worked out exactly as it should have."

She teared up a little. "Really?"

"Yup."

They kissed, slow and sweet this time. And then he eased back and took a long moment just to enjoy her tousled hair, and her sleepy eyes, and her ruby-red lips that were like that because he had been making out with her for hours.

"You feel better?" he said.

She nodded. "Oh, yes. Totally."

"You wanna finish the movie?"

"Yes, I really do."

Rhage smiled once again. "I love it when you lie to me like that."

"It's true!"

As he resettled her in his arms, he shook his head and patted around to find the remote. "Good thing we talked that over. I mean, look at Kevin. He's freaked out that we've been ignoring him. Kid's gonna need some serious therapy if we keep freezing him up like this."

Mary's laughter transmitted from her torso into his own, and God, he loved the feel of it. Then she sighed and got even more comfortable . . . and a few moments later, she was fast asleep, breathing in the deep, even rhythm of someone who had a clean conscience and was at peace with the one they loved.

By the time the burglars were getting tarred and feathered, Rhage was feeling drowsy himself, but he stayed up for the rest of the day. Not because of the movies, though.

Sometimes all the rest you needed came in the form of holding the right person against your body, and feeling her warmth, and knowing that she was not going away.

Not without you, at any rate.

True love, he decided, was all the recharge he required, thank you very much.

THIRTY-SEVEN

Ultimately, Mary chose to go with jeans.

Normally, she was not a 7 for All Mankind girl, but for Bitty's ice-cream trip, she didn't want to wear her blouse-and-slacks professional uniform. The goal was for this to be a relaxed, fun outing, and somehow showing up in a bunch of stuff that needed dry cleaning didn't exactly say Baskin-Robbins, thirty-one flavors with sprinkles on top.

"How do I look?" Rhage said from behind her.

Turning away from their bureau, she did a double take.

"Well?" he said, pivoting in a circle. "Is this okay?"

"That Hawaiian shirt"—she laughed—"was supposed to be a joke."

He pulled out the hem of the tarp-sized eyesore. "It's the only thing I've got that isn't black."

Well, that was true—and talk about mission accomplished. The shirt was about as far away from dour as you could get: which was why she'd bought it. The thing had a hundred variations on teal, green, and sunset peach in an absolutely retina-shattering palm tree–frond pattern.

"I just don't want to be all soldier, you know?"

"That's why I'm doing jeans." She grimaced as she looked down at herself. "Even though I'm not really a fan of them anymore."

"But they love you," he murmured, coming over and wrapping his arms around her. As he slid his hands down to her butt and squeezed, he murmured, "This past day was amazing, by the way."

She put her hands to his chest and played with one of the shirt's pink buttons. "Even though I fell asleep on you?"

"Especially because of that."

They kissed for a while, and then Mary stepped back and gave him the once-over. "Honestly, I think you have to go with what you feel comfortable in."

"This is not it. Someone my size in this much color? I'm like a living, breathing migraine aura."

As he headed back to the closet, she stared down at the jeans—and decided to take her own advice.

Ten minutes later, they left the mansion in all black for him and yoga pants and a red fleece for her.

Stepping out of the vestibule, Rhage put his arm around her and kissed the top of her head. "We're going to have a great time."

"Thanks for doing this. I know you had to switch your shift around."

"Tohr was happy to take over for me. He's really interested in killing things right now."

"Why?"

"Oh, God, too many reasons to count." Leading her down to the cobblestones and by the winterized fountain, he stopped at the passenger side of the GTO and opened her door. "Madam? Your conveyance."

After he got her settled, he got in himself and off they went, barreling down the *mhis*-covered mountainside and shooting off over the winding road that took them to the highway. Safe Place was a good twenty minutes away, but the time passed fast.

Next thing she knew, she was getting out and telling her male she'd be right back.

Mary jogged up the walkway to the front door, put in the code, and then she was in the toasty interior. Heading for the stairs, she—

"I'm here."

At the sound of Bitty's voice, she stopped. "Hey. How are you?"

The little girl was dressed in one of her other shifts, that black parka folded on her lap as she sat with a straight back on the living room sofa.

"Did he really come?" Bitty asked as she got to her feet. "Are we really going?"

"We are."

Bitty went to the closed drapes and pulled them apart. "Oh, he brought his car."

"Yup, just as he said he would. I think you'll find that my *hellren* pretty much always does what he says he's going to."

Mary had already told Marissa about the plan, and gotten a re-sounding approval from the boss, but she wanted to check out properly.

"Can you give me two seconds in my office?"

When the girl nodded, Mary rushed upstairs. Marissa wasn't at her desk, so Mary headed across the hall to send a quick e-mail to all the staff.

She didn't get that far. At least, not immediately.

There was a cardboard box on her desk, one that was about the size of a shoe box, just more square instead of rectangular. An envelope was on top of it, although she knew what was inside before reading anything.

The note was short, but kind. Mary read it twice, and then carefully lifted the lid. Inside, there was a simple brass urn.

A trusted nurse of Havers's had dropped off Bitty's mother's ashes at nightfall, because the female had wanted to spare Bitty any return trip to the clinic. It had been a very kind gesture; the sort of thing that made you blink quick and have to take a couple of deep breaths.

Shaking herself back to attention, Mary went around and signed in at her computer, sent the e-mail, and then hustled back downstairs. Bitty was on the sofa once again, waiting patiently, but she had put her coat on.

"Ready?" Mary asked.

As the girl got to her feet once more, Mary decided to wait to talk about the delivery. The child deserved an easy trip out for ice cream—

"Did you see what was on your desk?" Bitty looked up. "The box?"

"Ah . . . yes. I did."

"It's my mother's ashes."

"Yes. There was a note."

Bitty dropped her eyes to the floor. "A nice female brought them. I was down here waiting already, so I took them. I put them up there because I wasn't sure what I was supposed to do."

"Do you want the urn in your room?"

"I don't know."

"Okay. You don't have to decide anything now."

"I want to save them. You know . . ."

For your uncle, Mary filled in, in her head.

"For my uncle," Bitty concluded. "But I wasn't sure I'd be able to sleep with them upstairs. I mean . . . it's her. But not."

"It's perfectly all right for you to think about it. And change your mind. They're safe in my office. I'll leave them right on my desk. Nothing will happen to them."

"Okay."

There was a pause. "Are you ready to go now?"

"Yes, please."

Mary let out an exhale. "Good. I'm glad. Come on."

Bitty headed for the door, but then stopped halfway there. "Ms. Luce?"

"Yes?"

Those brown eyes flicked up for a split second and then returned to the floor. "Thank you very much."

All Mary could do was blink as Bitty kept on going over to the exit.

"You're very welcome," Mary said in a husky voice.

Standing next to his car, Rhage found himself tucking in his black shirt under his jacket—or rather, re-tucking the thing. Then he ran his fingers through his hair. Man, he needed to get the stuff cut. It was like a blond rug from the seventies, all shagged out.

At least the close shave he'd given himself before leaving the mansion was holding tough. And he was clean. He'd even washed behind his ears and in between his toes.

As the door to Safe Place opened and the females appeared between the jambs, he raised a hand, and got two raised back at him, one from each. Then Mary and Bitty were in front of him, the little girl staring up at him as if he might have been bigger than she remembered. Or blonder. Or maybe weirder-looking. Or something.

Who the hell knew.

"Hi," he said, opening the car door for her. "You ready?"

"Yes." Bitty scooted in. "Thank you."

"Do you know what flavor you're going for?"

"Vanilla?"

Frowning, he put the seat back into position and helped his Mary in. "Huh. Well. That's good."

When he was behind the wheel, he wrenched around. "You know, vanilla is great. It's a good traditional choice. But they'll let you try some of their other flavors before you pick. You might want to give that a shot—or stick with vanilla. Whatever works."

"What kinds of flavors are there?"

"Oh, my God, sooooo many."

He punched the clutch, threw the gearshift into first, but stopped himself before he nailed the accelerator. There was no time constraint here, and he didn't want to paint-mixer the poor kid.

"Hey, is your seat belt on?" he asked, glancing up into the rear-view.

"I'm sorry." Bitty scrambled around, pulling the strap into place across her torso. "I didn't think."

Rhage reached up and put the light on. "Here."

Click. "Thank you."

Easing them out from the curb, he kept to the speed limit. And the traffic laws. And glared at an SUV who swerved out in front of them.

Bessie's Best Ice Cream Parlor was painted bright pink on the outside, and milk-cow black-and-white on the inside. With pink tables and chairs, fifties music piped in from the speakers, and a waitstaff that had poodle skirts for the girls and soda-jerk shirts and pants for the guys, Rhage had always been impressed by how close to right they got the Elvis, goin'-to-the-hop vibe.

As someone who had eaten ice cream in 1950, he remembered firsthand what things had looked like, thank you very much.

And yup, he had chosen the right joint.

Bitty was enthralled by the place, her big eyes roaming around as if she had never seen anything like it—which was, sadly, no doubt the truth. Fortunately, there were only a few human customers: a couple who was over sixty in the corner, a father with three kids in the middle at one of the larger tables, and a pair of teenage girls who were taking selfies with their motor oil–glossed lips pursed out and their ice cream melting off to the side in little paper cups.

Leading the way over to where you ordered, he smiled at the twenty-year-old in her poodle skirt—and then really wished he hadn't.

"Oh!" was all she seemed to be able to say as she stared across the tubs of ice cream in their glass-topped refrigerator units.

"I'd like to try out some samples?" he asked.

And could you please, please, please stop looking at me like that? The only whipped cream you're putting on anything goes on my banana split.

No, not that banana split . . .

And you can skip the nuts—

Okay, come on, was he really arguing with himself over his own innuendos here—

"As many as you like." She actually batted her eyelashes. "What flavors? And you can try the sprinkles out, too. If you want?"

The words were spoken fast and accented by all kinds of leaning over and flashing everything that that little button-down tucked into that big skirt failed to cover.

"Let me ask my wife." He deliberately used the human term. "Mary?"

Mary's smile was easy and relaxed and he loved that about her—she was so confident in herself and his love for her, she never balked, no matter how many females got up in his grille. "I'm fine with chocolate-chocolate chip in a waffle cone."

"Bitty? Would you like to branch out from vanilla?"

The little girl surprised him by stepping in close. "I think . . . yes, could I please try some?"

As Bitty stared up at the human female, the waitress straightened a little, like the dimmer switch on her libido had been cranked down some. "You want me to get you and your dad a sampler? I'll bring it over and you can try 'em at the table."

Everyone froze. Him. Mary.

No, wait, Bitty didn't freeze. "He's not my dad. But yes, please."

The human didn't seem to care one way or the other. She just turned around and got out a little tray with twelve different tiny paper cones arranged in a cardboard holder.

He's not my dad.

The words had come out smoothly and without hesitation, as if Bitty were naming a destination on a map or pointing out a book on a shelf. Meanwhile, Rhage was still stopped in his tracks as the mini-scooping was done, and the tray was set on the counter, and Mary's waffle cone was delivered into her ever-so-slightly trembling hand.

As their eyes met, it was obvious she was worried about him, and he was a little worried, too. He felt like he'd been sucker punched in the gut.

"—table?"

Shaking himself, he looked at the waitress. "I'm sorry?"

"Do you want to take this with you? I mean, I can carry it to your table if you want."

"No, no, it's fine. Thanks. I'll be back to order more and then we'll pay?"

"Sure. Fine."

The *whatever* was silent. Not that he gave two shits.

Over at the table by the rear emergency exit—which he chose out of habit in case, you know, the ten remaining *lessers* in the city of Caldwell happened to bust through that pink door looking for a rocky road—he put the tray down and handed a pink spoon to Bitty.

"Have at it. And then you can tell me what you want in a cone or a sundae, or decide you're full enough."

Bitty just stared at the display of various colors and textures. From the brilliant greens of pistachio and mint chocolate chip, to the beach-sunset coral of some kind of sherbet and the cheery pink of strawberry, it really was a fine representative sample.

"Where do I start?" she asked.

"Anywhere," Mary said as she sat with her cone.

"You want me to go first?" he asked.

"Yes. Please."

Yeah, wow, for the first time in recorded history, he faced off at ice cream and had no interest in it.

"I guess I'll start here," he murmured, spooning up something that didn't register on his tongue in the slightest.

"Is it good?" Bitty asked.

"Ah, sure. Absolutely."

When she leaned in and put her pink spoon into the half he'd left behind, he glanced across at Mary. His *shellan* was focused on Bitty, as if something in the way the little girl tried the dessert might offer some important clue as to how the mourning was going. And it was funny . . . as he looked back and forth between the two, he was amazed as he noticed for the first time that they both had brown hair.

In fact, Bitty looked as if she could be . . .

Yeah. Wow.

He needed to pull back here. After all, there were how many vam-

pires on the planet? And humans? So the fact that the pair of them both happened to be female and both had dark hair as opposed to blond or red or straight-up black was not a huge surprise.

There was, he told himself firmly, absolutely nothing cosmic or preordained about the three of them sitting here in this ice cream shop—other than the fact that the particular kind of dessert served under this pink roof just happened to prove the existence of a benevolent God.

"—please?"

"What?" he said. "I'm sorry. I'm distracted by the menu above that counter over there."

"I think I like the chocolate–chocolate chip the best?" Bitty said.

Rhage glanced at Mary again and then had to look away. "Consider it done. In a cup or a cone?"

"I think . . ."

Waffle, he finished in his head.

"Waffle," Bitty said.

"Roger that."

As he got to his feet and headed back to the human woman in that poodle skirt, he said, Nope. All kids liked chocolate. With chips. In waffle cones.

There was not some kind of destiny at work here.

Really.

Totally.

There wasn't.

THIRTY-EIGHT

The chilly wind swept over the rolling hill, teasing fallen leaves and carrying them over Assail's Bally loafers. Down below, the Hudson appeared static in the night, as if its current had turned in for the evening upon the sun's departure, and the water was relieved to be off the clock. Over to the north, the moon rose, a bright and clean slice of illumination in the deep velvet blackness of the sky.

The cold air bothered his masticated nose, so he breathed in through his mouth. Yet even without full benefit of his sense of smell, he knew when he was approached.

He did not turn about, but addressed the view. "Quite a romantic spot."

Throe's voice was low. "I'm going to kill you."

Assail rolled his eyes and looked over his shoulder. "A gun? Really."

The male was standing directly behind him, an autoloader in his hand, his finger on the trigger. "You think I won't use it."

"Because I kissed you—or because you liked it?" Assail faced the river again. "How weak of you."

"You are a—"

"Your body didn't lie. As much as your brain has a counter-

opinion, we both are fully aware of your arousal. If you have conflict over this reality, that is your issue, not mine."

"You had no right!"

"And you have a very traditional view of sex, don't you."

"I don't want you anywhere near me again."

"Weren't you going to pull that trigger? Or have we moved on from that already? Perhaps because you've realized how incredibly cowardly it is to put a bullet in the back of an otherwise innocent man."

"There is nothing innocent about you. And I do not trust your presence in Naasha's house."

"And meanwhile, you are merely a guest of hers, correct? One who just happens to keep the mistress of the manor warm during these increasingly cold days—whilst her *hellren* sleeps down the hall. Yes, there is nothing unscrupulous about that. So laudable."

"My relationship with her is none of your concern."

"Well, it is and it isn't. You're obviously not satisfying her very well—or I wouldn't have been invited back last night."

"She wanted to show you her toys. Next week, it shall be someone else."

"Does she require you to sleep in the basement? In a darkened room? Or are you upstairs with the grown-ups? By the way, are you going to shoot me? If not, perhaps you'll come over here and address me face-to-face. Or don't you trust yourself."

The sound of crushed leaves circled around. And then Throe appeared on the left, his long black wool coat waving in the wind.

"Is this not a dog park, by the way?" Assail glanced around the rolling earth and then pointed across the river. "That is where I live, as you are aware. I see the humans and their animals on this hillside on warmer nights—"

"Watch yourself."

"Or what?" Assail tilted his head to the side. "What are you going to do to me?"

"Fuck you."

"Yes, please. Or the other way around, should you prefer."

The flush that ran up Throe's throat to his cheeks was visible in the moonlight. And the male opened his mouth as if he were about to offer a staunch rebuke. But then his gleaming eyes dipped down . . . and lingered on Assail's mouth.

"So what will it be," Assail drawled. "Bottom . . . or top."

Throe let out a curse.

And then he up and disappeared into thin air, dematerializing away from the hill—said departure open to only one interpretation: He was more curious than he wanted to admit, hungrier than he could stomach, more desperate than he could bear. The male had come with one agenda, but had not been able to follow through on it because of another.

As Assail stood upon the hill alone, he was surprised at how little he cared about whether or not that trigger had been pulled.

Down below on the water, a vessel floated upstream, propelled by some manner of engine. Its taillight was white, and the red half of its bow lantern was showing. Both bobbed in a lazy way.

It was not his importer contacts. No lights on their craft.

Which reminded him . . . Vishous had come forth with an order for armaments. Nothing exotic, and in a relatively small number.

The Brotherhood was trying him out as a source first—and Assail respected that. His suppliers were not going to be content to provide such small-time numbers for long, however. There was a cost-benefit analysis that was required when one skirted human law, and his contacts were already displeased that his heroin and cocaine orders had dried up so abruptly.

Well, almost all of his cocaine ordering. He still had his own needs to consider.

The pick-up for the guns wasn't scheduled until the following evening, and he found that disappointing.

So much time he had available now. And in truth, although he was committed to doing this job for Wrath, and was looking forward to making Throe compromise all that rigid sexual convention of his, he could not say there was aught that excited or engaged him.

Putting his hands into the pockets of his cashmere coat, he leaned back and regarded the sky, seeing not some version of heaven, but merely vacant, cold space.

For some strange reason, when he righted his head, his cell phone ended up in his palm.

And before he could stop himself, a call was ringing through. Once. Twice. Three times . . .

"Hello?" a female voice said.

Assail's body responded like a tuning fork, his veins vibrating inside his skin, his brain's wiring flushed with a buzz that not even cocaine could get near.

". . . hello?"

Closing his eyes, he mouthed something he was glad Marisol could neither hear nor read upon his lips—and then dropped the phone from his ear. As he ended the connection, he wondered why he kept torturing himself by calling her and hanging up like that.

Then again, he didn't just enjoy torturing others, did he.

After all, enmity, like kindness, started at home.

It was like watching paint dry.

As Vishous lit up another hand-rolled and sat back against the shelving full of *lesser* jars, he watched the torchlight flicker over Xcor's ugly fucking face. He'd started his shift at nightfall, and had sent Butch downtown to work. At this point, it was a waste of resources to have more than one person babysitting for the bastard.

Wake up, asshole, he thought. Come on, open those eyes.

Yeah, file that under NFW. The movement that had been twitching that one side of Xcor's body had ceased during the day, and now the only break in the slab-of-meat inanimation was the rise and fall of the chest. The monitoring equipment—which V had silenced because one, he could see the readouts just fine, and two, the incessant beeping had made him want to go lead-shower on the shit—indicated that, for someone in a deep coma, Xcor's basic functions were doing all right. And meanwhile, the IV was pumping fluids and nutrients into his veins, the catheter was draining his bladder, and that electric blanket was keeping his core temperature up.

V *Really* fucking wished the bastard would come to.

Too much time to think—

As a text chimed, he checked his phone, then got up and strode off, covering the distance to the gate quickly.

Jane was waiting on the far side of the iron bars with their steel mesh, duffels hanging off her shoulders, white coat and blue scrubs insanely erotic even though they were baggy as hell, phone in her hand as she texted someone. Focused on her cell, her short blond hair fell forward and obscured her face, but he could tell she had no makeup on—and for some reason, he took special notice of her blunt, unpolished nails.

She always kept those puppies filed down so she didn't snag surgical gloves on them.

Or internal organs, as it were.

For a moment, he stopped and simply stared at her. She was so buried in her work, she hadn't even noticed him, and man, he just loved that about her. Her mind, that huge engine under her skull, was the sexiest thing about her, the force that challenged him, kept him on his toes . . . and made him feel, every once in a while, as if maybe, possibly, perhaps he wasn't actually the smartest person in the household.

And then, of course, there was her in the middle of that battlefield, *lesser* body parts everywhere, guns and the possibility of devastating chaos as close as the grass under your feet, and her entire focus on saving his brother.

"V?"

The way she said his name suggested she might have tried to get his attention a couple of times.

"Sorry, hey." He freed the lock and opened the gate, standing aside so she could fit in with all that gear. "You want some help lugging that shit?"

"Nope, I got it." She gave him a smile, and then was all business. "How we doing in there?"

Funny, they didn't really hug much, did they. The other couples in the mansion usually did that big greeting thing, but he and Jane? Always too much to talk about.

Whatever, he'd never been into the sappy crap.

After all, anything even remotely pink made him itch. And not just because it might be a sign of a localized skin infection.

"Xcor and I have been arguing." As the two of them walked side by side down the corridor, their shadows sped forward and then fell back as they came up to and passed by the various torches. "He's a Yankees fan, so you can imagine the smack talk. There is some common ground, though. He hates my mother, too."

Jane's laughter was deep and kind of abrupt, an arguably ugly sound that he fucking loved.

"Is that so?" She jacked up one of the duffels. "Any other conversations of note?"

"He has no taste in music. He didn't even know who Eazy-E was."

"Okay, that is just wrong."

"I know. These young kids today. The world's going into the shitter."

At Xcor's bedside—or gurney-side, as was the case—Jane dropped her load and then just stood there, her eyes going over her patient and lingering on the readouts.

"Battery life is stronger than we thought," V murmured as he took a drag. "We still have a couple of hours before we need to do a switch."

"Good—I'll leave the replacements off to the side here."

V backed up and let her have some room as she checked Xcor's catheter, gave him a new bag of saline solution, and administered a number of drugs through his IV.

"So what do you think?" he asked. Not because he didn't have his own opinion, but rather because he loved her to go clinical on him.

As she began rattling off a number of multi-syllabic Latin-derived medical terms, he had to rearrange himself in his leathers. Something about her getting all professional made him want to get all up in her. Probably had to do with the bonding thing—he wanted to mark this spectacular person as his, so the whole world knew they needed to back the fuck off.

Jane was the only female who had ever gotten his attention and held it. And yeah, if he had to wax psychological on the situation, it was probably because her single-minded passion for her job, shit, her relentless commitment to excellence, made him feel a little like he was always chasing her just to keep up.

On so many levels he was a typical predator: The chase was more electric than the capture and consumption.

And with Jane, there was always something to pursue.

"Hello? V?"

When their eyes met, he frowned. "Sorry. Distracted."

"There's a lot going on." She smiled again. "Anyway, as I was saying, I've had a consult with Manny and Havers. We're thinking of maybe opening up his head. I want to watch him for the next twelve hours, but the pressure on his brain is gradually increasing even with the stent I put in this morning."

"Can you operate here?"

She glanced around. "I don't think so. Lot of debris in the air. Light is not great. But more to the point, we're going to need imaging that we just can't get in a cave."

"Well, you let me know what you want and we'll do another transport on him."

"You're the best."

"Yeah, I am. I'd also do anything for you."

As their eyes met, she put her hands in her pockets and backed up until she was leaning against the shelving.

When she didn't say anything, he frowned. "What?"

"So do you want to tell me what's on your mind?"

V laughed softly, and wasted a little time staring at the end of his hand-rolled. In the silence, he debated brushing the question off, but that was because he hated talking about anything even remotely emotional.

"You know, I'd deny I've got a head fuck going on, but—"

"It would be a waste of time."

"—it would be a waste of time."

They both smiled as they spoke the same words with the same tone and at the same time. But then he got serious.

Stabbing his cigarette out on the bottom of his shitkicker, he put the deadie into the empty Coke can he'd been using as an ashtray. To give himself a second longer, he looked at the hundreds and hundreds of jars all around them. Then he glanced at Xcor.

This was not exactly a conversation he wanted to have in front of anyone. But the bastard had about as much conscious awareness as one of the Pit's leather couches. And now and here were better than any other version of later and there that involved the chaotic mansion he and his mate lived in.

"You ever think about having kids?" he said.

THIRTY-NINE

"So will you tell me more about the people you live with?"

As Bitty asked the question from the backseat of the GTO, Mary glanced at Rhage. The three of them were on the way home, all kinds of ice cream in their stomachs, most of the tension gone from the whole "dad" thing. But boy, that had been a difficult moment—well, for everyone but Bitty. She hadn't seemed to care one way or the other.

The same couldn't be said of the two adults with her. Nothing like shining a light on the kid-less issue like that. But at least the rest of the outing had been a wild success.

"More on my people, huh." Rhage looked up into the rearview and smiled. "Lemme see. Who's next. We've covered the King, the animals, and Lassiter. Who actually should be lumped in with the animals, really. So . . . okay, have you ever met a set of twins before?"

"No, never. I wasn't allowed to leave my house."

Rhage blinked. "I'm sorry, Bitty. That must have been very hard."

"My father didn't want us to see anyone."

Mary had to catch herself from wincing.

And as Rhage frowned, she felt him take her hand.

"Lemme ask you something, Bitty," he said.

"Okay."

"How did you learn to read? And you speak really well."

"My *mahmen* was a teacher. Before she mated my father."

"Ah."

Mary turned in her seat. "Would you like to be a teacher, too?"

The little girl's brows lifted. "Yes, I think I would. But I don't know where to go to school for that. My *mahmen* went to school in South Carolina."

Mary tried to show no reaction. "Really? Your mother never said she was from there."

"That's where her parents lived. But they died."

"I'd heard there was a colony down there," Rhage chimed in.

"My father was a migrant worker. He used to move with the seasons, working for humans, until he met her. Then they came up here and he became an electrician for the species. His drinking got bad and that's when things changed. I was born after the bad part happened— or maybe I was the reason for it."

Mary kept quiet, both because she was hoping Bitty would continue, but also because it was really hard to hear any child say something like that. And then she frowned as she recognized that they were getting close to Safe Place.

Glancing at Rhage, she intended to encourage him to keep going—but he subtly nodded, as if he knew exactly what she was thinking.

Maybe if he continued driving, Bitty would keep talking.

Because none of this was in her or her mother's file.

"Sometimes," Mary said, "alcohol can really hurt people."

"My father was the one who hit us. Not the beer he was drinking."

Mary cleared her throat. "Very true, Bitty."

The girl fell silent, and then before Mary could say anything else, she spoke up again.

"May I ask you something, Ms. Luce?"

Mary twisted around once more and nodded as she met the girl's eyes. "Anything."

"You said your *mahmen* had died, right?"

"Yes, she did."

"So where did you do her Fade ceremony?"

"Well, Bitty, it's a . . ." She tucked her hair behind her ears. "The truth is, I used to be human, Bitty."

The little girl recoiled. "I . . . didn't know."

"It's a very, very long story. But I met him and fell in love." She put her hand on Rhage's shoulder. "And then some other things happened. And I've been in the vampire world ever since. My life is here, with you all, and I'm not going back to where I once was."

Bitty's brows drew in tight over the bridge of her nose. "But what happened to your family? Did you bring them with you?"

"It was just my mom and me. And after she died? I had nothing to keep me in that world. Thanks to Rhage . . ." She glanced at him and smiled. "Well, because of him I found my new family."

"Do you have young?"

Mary shook her head. "No, and I can't bear children."

Once again with that recoil. "Ever?"

"No. It just wasn't in the cards for me. But I have my work at Safe Place and there are so many kids there who need my help." Like you, for instance. "So I make my contribution to the future, to young people, that way."

Bitty frowned for the longest time; then she looked at Rhage. "What about you? Do you have young? Before you met . . . well, her?"

Rhage reached out again, his big hand taking Mary's in a warm, strong grip. "I guess I can have them. But if it's not going to be with her, then it's not going to be with anybody."

"My *mahmen* said young are the biggest blessing in life."

Mary nodded through a sudden pain in her heart. "And she was very right about that."

"So, twins?" Bitty prompted.

Rhage took a deep breath, like he was having to force himself back into normal conversation. "Ah, yup. Twins. So, anyway, we have a set in our house. They're identical, but they don't really look anything alike."

"How is that possible?"

"Well, one was taken as a blood slave."

"What's that?"

"It's a practice that's been outlawed by the King. It's where one person holds another against their will, using them as a blood source. Zsadist was scarred during his escape, and Phury, his twin—who was the one who got him out—lost part of his leg in the process. But everything worked out. They're both mated now, and Z has the cutest damn—er, darn—young on the planet. You'd like Nalla. She's a peach of a toddler."

"I think I would like to have young someday."

Mary turned around once again. "And so you will."

"But you can't, right? So what if that happens to me?"

"Well, maybe it could. But I like to believe that if you think positively, positive things happen. So visualize yourself in a happy family, mated to a male who loves you and takes care of you and lets you take care of him. And then see that infant of yours all warm and squirmy in your arms. See her eyes that are like yours, or maybe his hair that's like his father's. Visualize it and think positively, and make it happen."

"And anyway," Rhage chimed in, "even if you can't bear your young, you can maybe adopt one. Or work with kids, like Mary does. There are always ways around things."

"Always," Mary agreed.

They drove along for a little more, and then Rhage headed back to Safe Place. As he pulled up to the curb and put the GTO in park, he cleared his throat.

"So, Bitty."

"Yes?"

Rhage cranked his massive shoulders around so he could look back at the girl. "I have to work tomorrow night, but the night after I have off. Will you have dinner with Mary and me? I want to go out to eat."

"To a restaurant?" Bitty asked.

"Yup. TGI Fridays—ever been?"

"Well, no, actually."

"So what do you say?"

Annnnnd this is just one more reason to love him, isn't it, Mary thought.

Getting out, she popped the top half of her seat and held it forward.

Bitty looked up at her. "Is that okay, Ms. Luce?"

"Absolutely."

"Then yes, please."

"Great!" Rhage clapped his hands. "Oh, my God, you have to totally get the brownie sundae. It's amazing."

Bitty stood at the curb for a moment. Then she lifted her hand in good-bye. "Thank you. For the ice cream."

"Can't wait for dinner!"

Mary put the seat back into place, leaned in and planted her palm on the still-warm leather from where she'd been sitting. "I'll see you back home?"

"Mmm-hmm."

Stretching forward, she kissed him on the mouth. "I love you."

"Love you, too, my Mary." Rhage tugged her down for another kiss and lowered his voice. "Baths are fun. Did you know that?"

As a smile hit her face and stayed there, she cocked a brow. "Oh, really?"

"I think I'll run one and get in it right before Last Meal. Come find me?"

"Does this mean we're eating in our room again?"

"God, I hope so."

She laughed as she straightened out of the car. "I'll be home regular time, okay?"

"And you know where to find me!"

As she stepped away, she found Bitty staring back and forth between them. And then the car was roaring and Rhage skidded the tires, leaving tracks.

Mary laughed. "Such a show-off."

"What does that mean?"

"He's trying to impress us with his driving." The pair of them started for the house. "Guys do that. They can't help it."

Coming up to the front door, Mary entered the code, and as she opened things wide, the scent of chocolate-chip cookies wafted into her nose.

"Wow. Twice this week with the Toll House."

She wanted to suggest to Bitty that they follow the sounds of laughter and talking back to the big kitchen and hang out with everyone, but the girl went directly to the stairs. Hoping for some other opening, or chance to talk, Mary followed her up to the second floor, and stopped on the landing in front of her office.

"You're going to head for the attic?" she said. "I'll be here doing paperwork if you need anything. Or, you know, if you want to go make cookies?"

Bitty shrugged out of that big, puffy parka. "I think I'll sit in my room. But thank you."

"Okay. Well, good-night."

"Good-night—"

"I'll be here. Until just before dawn."

"Thank you."

Mary stayed where she was, in front of the open door to her office, as Bitty went to the stairs—

It happened so fast. One moment, the girl was walking away. The next, she had turned around and rushed back across the distance.

Her arms went around Mary quick as a breath and held on for no longer than that.

And then Bitty was gone, ascending to the attic without sparing another word or glance.

Mary stood where she was.

For quite some time.

Okay, so then *that* happened, V thought as his words hung in the air between him and Jane.

You ever think about having kids?

As his mate went really still and very quiet, he cursed under his breath—but that was not the kind of inquiry you could take back. Even if there was a half-dead enemy lying on a gurney between the pair of you.

And the two of you were, like, surrounded by a thousand hearts in jars.

And it was in the middle of a worknight for both parties.

Holy shit, had that really come out of his mouth.

Oh, and P.S., he was so hitting Rhage again when he saw the brother next. Even though this wasn't technically Hollywood's fault. All the guy had done was pose the question because, clearly, it was something on his own mind.

V was still gonna punch him, though.

"Wow," Jane said slowly. She rubbed her nose and tucked her blond hair back. "That's a surprise."

"Look, forget I ever said anything—"

"No, I won't. And are you asking because you want them or because you want to know what I think?"

"I want to know what you think."

And yeah, it was maybe weird that it hadn't come up before now, but it had been clear Jane couldn't have any, biologically speak-

ing, when they'd commited to each other, and a lot of shit had been going on since then.

"Well, how do you feel?" she said.

"I asked you first."

"Is this a game of chicken? Or an intimate conversation?"

They both fell silent. And then at the same time they said, in exactly the same tone:

"It's not a priority for me."

"It's not a priority for me."

As V laughed, Jane did, too, and he got the impression that as the tension flowed out of his body, something similar was happening for her, her stance loosening, her exhale one of relief.

"Look," V said, "L.W. and Nalla are cute and all. But I'm interested in them because they're a part of Wrath's and Z's lives, not because I want something like that for us. Unless, you know, it became a big deal for you."

"Well, I can't have kids. I mean, I'm technically dead." She rolled her eyes. "Can I just tell you, every once in a while, when I say something like that, I get existential whiplash? Like, how the hell did this become my life—not that it isn't a miracle or anything. But jeez."

"And you're mated to a demi-god."

"Did you just promote yourself?"

"Maybe. Can you blame me?" As she laughed, exactly as he'd intended her to, V got serious again. "Adoption is difficult in the vampire race, but it can be an option."

"True. Very true." Jane shrugged. "But you know, I was never one of those women who planned out her wedding or saw rainbow mobiles over the cribs of babies. Not that I've seen many babies in cribs." She frowned. "Holy crap. I've actually . . . I don't think I've ever seen a baby sleeping in a crib."

"And you're not a freak because of that. I can tell what you're thinking."

"Yeah." She rubbed the back of her neck. Then shook herself as if clearing away thoughts that she refused to buy into. "I mean, of course, I'm not. Just because women can be mothers doesn't mean they have to be."

V had to smile a little. But then he shook his head. "I don't think there's anything wrong with us. And actually, I hate that I just felt the need to say that."

"Compatibility is the issue. If one of us wanted them and the other didn't? Then that's a problem."

Jane came over to him and put her hands on his shoulders. And it was funny: Ordinarily he couldn't stand people getting very close to him. Not because of some kind of horrific abuse—although his father's partial castration of him hadn't been a party, granted—but because tons of contact and closeness was just too much sensation for his brain to process.

With Jane, though, he never felt crowded.

Same with Butch.

Maybe because the two of them seemed to understand the overload thing with him.

"You look worried," she said as she brushed his hair back and traced the tattoos at his temple with her forefinger.

"I don't want anything to come between us. Ever."

"That's up to you and me, though, right? So why be anxious?"

"Rhage and Mary have been going through a time."

"Over having babies? Are they okay now?"

"Yeah. I think so."

"Good." She leaned her head to one side. "And as for you and me? We can't predict the future. No one can. So we talk and we sort things out and we keep going. Together. I can't fathom, right now, a scenario where all of a sudden some biological clock starts ringing and I have a compelling need to do the parent thing. I guess, for me, I don't feel like anything is missing in my life. There are no hollow spaces that require filling. I have you, I have my work, and I reject the notion entirely that all women are destined to be mothers. Some of us are and some of us aren't, and the awesome thing is, we get to choose. Same goes for men. So yeah, we just keep talking and everything is going to work out—no matter what the outcome happens to look like."

Vishous stared down from his greater height, and somehow felt smaller than she was. "You always make sense."

"I don't know about that. But I do try to look at everything from all angles and be logical as much as I can—"

"I don't think I can be a father, Jane."

His mate shook her head. "I know where you're going with that. Your parents are not you—and besides, that's the wrong way to put it. The question is, Do you *want* to be a father?"

He tried to imagine being weighed down as Wrath and Z were,

constantly worrying about some little creature and whether it was killing itself. Yeah, sure, there were good parts to the experience; the joy on his brothers' faces was very real. But, God, the work.

Was he using that as an excuse, though?

Whatever. "Definitely not right now. No, I do not want to be a father right now."

"So that's what we go with. And if it changes, we address it. Same for me."

"I would never want anything on this planet to hate me as much as I hate my parents."

There. He said it.

"Lot of reasons to support that position," Jane whispered as she stroked his face. "And I am so very sorry."

"Don't tell me I should go talk to Mary about it, okay? I'm not interested in that shit, true?"

"You know where she is if you need her. And I don't have to tell you that she would be available to you anytime if you asked." Jane brushed his hair back. "And I have to say this. As awful as your mother can be . . . without her? You and I wouldn't be together."

He frowned, thinking of when he'd found Jane in that crumpled Audi at the side of the road. None of his life-support measures had done a goddamn thing. She had remained unmoving as he had tried to bring her back.

For some reason, the image of his mother up on that bedding platform resurfaced and wouldn't be stuffed back down underground. The shit lingered . . . like it was a message of some sort.

"I really trust you," he heard himself say to his *shellan*.

"And I love you, too, Vishous."

FORTY

"Okay, I might have thought you were joking about this."

As his Mary sank down into a Jacuzzi full of bubbles, Rhage reached out through the warm, frothy swirl and ohhhhh, yeaaaaaah, there it was, his mate's body all slippery and smooth, from the curve of her waist to the flare of her hips—and so many other things.

"Gimme, gimme, gimme."

Leaning back against the wall of the tub, he pulled her to him, splitting her thighs and settling her right on top of his bobbing, bright-idea cock. He didn't enter her, though. There was time for that later.

"How long have you been waiting for me?" she asked as she put her arms around his neck.

"Hours and hours."

Her breasts were obscured and revealed, obscured and revealed, as the level in the tub recalibrated itself to her presence, and Rhage licked

his lips at the sight of her glistening nipples and the bands of suds that remained on her skin.

It reminded him of a bikini top that had failed in the most miraculous of ways.

"I thought you went downtown to fight after ice cream?" she said.

"Oh, I did." He shifted his palms around and cupped her breasts, moving them together while he thumbed those nipples, wiping them free. "Yup."

Mary moaned in the back of her throat, and she seemed to struggle to collect her thoughts—especially as he lifted her up to his mouth and sucked one of her tips in, flicking it with his tongue. Under the surface, his erection kicked like a bull and his hips surged.

"What did you say?" he murmured as he moved to her other breast.

Squeezing her, kneading her, he found himself thinking, yes . . . yes, he remembered this back from their earlier nights, when he couldn't wait to get home and get her naked, when Last Meal was second priority, because his Mary was the only sustenance he really needed.

"I honestly can't—oh, right, how long did you wait for me."

"Years."

"That's"—she gasped—"not possible."

"Are you kidding me? I got home about ten minutes ago."

Mary laughed. "And that was forever?"

"Waiting for you? In this tub alone? Hell, yeah."

And *fighting* would not have been a word he'd have used to describe what he'd done in those alleys. More like foot patrol.

No slayers had been out and about—and that was not a good sign. The question was where the next wave of the Omega's troops was going to come from. Who the *Fore-lesser* was going to be. How long the lull was going to last.

The enemy was going to be back. That had been the nature of the war for aeons and aeons. And sometimes the quiet periods were harder to get through than the battles.

A subtle glint at the window beside them caught his attention. It was the automatic steel shutters coming down to protect the mansion's interior from sunlight.

And provide privacy, too.

Using his superior strength, he lifted Mary from the water until one of her knees was on a stack of fluffy white towels next to his head and her other leg was fully extended and propped against the floor of the Jacuzzi. As she balanced herself by holding the molding of the window, her breasts swayed forward.

So much dripping.

So much warm water and so many trails of tiny bubbles sluicing off her skin, trickling down her stomach, her hips, her thigh.

Her sex.

Extending his tongue, he nestled his face in there, licking at her in a lazy way, wishing he'd not gone with the damn bubbles, because they masked her taste some. Pulling her onto him, he worshiped her with his mouth, hearing her groan his name, feeling her orgasm—

Something slipped, her foot on the inside of the tub probably, and talk about applecart over; her body went off balance, and he slid down, and the next thing he knew, he was underwater, and she was laughing, and there was a tidal-wave splash out onto the marble.

"Oh, no!" Mary said. "I'd better clean that up—"

"Not yet, female."

With a growl, he put her under him, her buoyancy in the deep tub bringing her up to his body. "Wrap your legs around me."

As she did, he reached between them and angled himself and then—

"Oh, yeah," he gritted out.

They worked together to create the friction, him wrapping his arm around her waist and pumping her up and down, her rocking herself by pushing and pulling with her legs against his pelvis. So good, so tight that he didn't even notice the suds in his face, or the fact that he kept having to readjust his grip on the tub's lip.

Annnnnnnnd there was one other thing he kind of ignored.

There might have been some more over-the-gunnels splashing.

Just as he was starting to come inside of her, as his balls tightened and that sharp-knifed pleasure kicked his cock and made him punch his hips over and over again . . .

There was the not-so-dulcet sound of pounding out on the bedroom door.

"Rhage! Yo, Rhage!"

"Not now," he barked as he continued to pump and Mary's release had her locking tight against him.

"Rhage! What the fuck!" came another voice.

"Not now!" he yelled back.

"Rhage!"

More pounding. Like, with multiple fists.

With a last jerk of the pelvis, he went still with a curse. "Mary, I'm so sorry."

She laughed and put her face into the crook of his neck. "It's not your fault—"

So much more pounding on the door—to the point where it was clear there were a number of Brothers out there. And as multiple males kept calling his name, he cursed again.

"You stay here," he muttered.

Withdrawing his cock, the warm bathwater was a piss-poor substitute for Mary's core, and he was in a really bad mood as he stood up and kicked one leg out to put a foot on the marble—

Three. Fucking. Stooges.

All three hundred pounds of him went ass-over-elbow, the water on that smooth stone turning the floor of the bathroom into an ice-skating rink. Arms pinwheeling in thin air, body contorting, something in his spine cracking—

Boom! He didn't so much land as detonate, all kinds of pain lighting off in explosions in his arm, his shoulder, his back, his ass, and one of his legs.

"Rhage!"

For a moment, all he could do was stare at the ceiling as he got his breath back. And then Mary's face was in his line of vision.

"Ouch." And then he sneezed for some reason—oh, right. He had bubbles up his nose—and fuck, that hurt. "I mean, like . . . really *ouch.*"

Meanwhile, the cast of thousands outside was still going batshit at their door. And yeah, there was a lot of water.

"Mary, do me a favor?"

"You want me to get Doc Jane?"

"Not unless all this wetness under me is my blood," he said dryly. "Can you please put a bathrobe on before they break that door down?

I love my brothers, but if even one of them sees you naked, I'm going to kill him. After I get out of traction, that is."

When Mary was sure that Rhage was fairly okay-ish, she stood up and carefully walked over to where one of Rhage's thick terry-cloth bathrobes was hanging on a hook. She figured he'd like her in that the best because it smelled like him, and it had so much surface area, it would cover her from collarbone to ankle with yards to spare.

Then she went across to the archway–

Well, waded across, she amended, as water literally splashed up onto her feet. Shoot, this was out of the realm of towels, and seriously into the wet-vac zip code.

"This is bad, this is really bad," she said.

"I'll be fine—ow. Fuck, I think I broke my arm."

"We're never doing that again. Ever."

"Sex?!" he sputtered. *"What?"*

She pivoted back around to the sight of him buck-ass naked, covered with vaguely pinkish bubbles, in the midst of a giant pool of water, with an expression of total, abject, and enduring horror on his face.

Mary burst out laughing so hard, she had to reach out and steady herself on the wall. "Oh, my God, I need to stop—"

"Tell me we're still having sex—"

"Of course! Just maybe not in the tub with that much water!"

"Jesus, don't scare me like that. You'll give me a damn aneurysm."

"You may already have one. And can I let them in now?"

Rhage grunted as he sat up, the tattoo on his back writhing as if the beast were feeling a little beaten-up, too. "Fine, but I don't know what they're bitching about. Jeez, you spill a little water and everyone has a fucking cow."

"Try a swimming pool's worth."

It was a relief to get out onto the carpet, where the traction was good and she didn't have to think about exactly how she was stepping.

"I'm coming! You can stop pounding now!" she hollered over the din.

When she got to the door, she found that it had been locked. No doubt Rhage had willed the dead bolt into place—which made her smile.

Opening things up, she faced off with—

"Wow." Okay, there were a lot of Brothers out there. "It's a convention."

Butch was in the front of the pack, a glass of what had to be Lagavulin in his hand, a wry smile on his face. John Matthew was behind him, along with Blay and Qhuinn. V. Zsadist. And Phury. And Tohr.

"What are you two doing in there?" someone asked.

"Don't answer that, Mary!" Rhage shouted.

"Did you think there was a fire in the pantry?"

"I'm coming!" Rhage said.

"I think he already did," somebody else muttered.

A collective *oooooooooooow!* rose from the group as Rhage appeared behind her.

"That arm is wicked bad," Butch said. "I mean, it's like you have a second elbow."

As Mary glanced over her shoulder, she recoiled, too. "Oh, Rhage, you need to get that set."

Rhage glared at the group. "Just gimme a Band-Aid, I'll be fine. Now will you give us some privacy?"

Butch shook his head. "Okay, one, no, we will not, because where do you think all that water is going? And two, you are on your way to the clinic—"

"It's fine!"

"Then why are you holding it with your free hand?"

Rhage looked down at himself as if he'd been unaware of what he'd been doing. "Oh, shit."

Mary patted his shoulder. "I'll go with you, okay?"

He stared at her, and dropped his voice. "This was not how I envisioned the session ending."

"They'll be other opportunities—"

"Just not in water," came the collective response.

Striding back to the bathroom, she snagged a towel and returned, wrapping it around her mate's waist and tucking the end in so the thing stayed put.

Getting up onto her tiptoes, she whispered, "If you're a good boy, I'll play nurse and patient with you after you get your cast."

Rhage's laugh was low and a little evil, his eyes going half-lidded and hot. "Deal."

FORTY-ONE

As night fell, Rhage was, yet again, back down in the clinic, sitting shirt-less on an exam table, his leather-clad legs and shitkickered feet dangling free off one end. His weapons were over on a chair, and as soon as he got this cast sawed off, he was going to catch a quick meal in the cafeteria that had been set up for the future trainees and go to work.

Mary had left early for Safe Place so she could get ready for a staff meeting—although she'd offered to stay for the buzz cut. Man, thank God he'd fed a week ago from one of the Chosen, and his body could heal a simple fracture like that in a matter of twelve hours. He'd heard humans had to live with these plaster deadweights for weeks and weeks.

Insanity.

When a knock sounded on the door, he called out, "Come on in, Manny. I'm ready to get this—oh, hey, V. Wassup."

His brother was dressed to fight, black daggers strapped to his chest, a newspaper folded up under his arm by one of his twin forties. "How's that arm?"

"You're coming to free me from my cage of plaster?" Rhage knocked on the thing with his fist. "Or whatever it's made out of."

"Nope." V settled back against the door. "I got no news and bad news, what do you want first?"

"You didn't find shit on Bitty's uncle, did you."

When his brother shook his head, Rhage released a tense breath, his whole body easing up with a relief that was all wrong. And then he had to tell himself not to get ahead of things. He and Mary were *not* adopting Bitty.

Really.

Yeah, 'cuz that would be crazy. Especially as he was basing the compatibility and interest on the kid's part on the fact that a pair of chocolate-chip waffle cones had been ordered and consumed the night before at Bessie's Best.

Vishous shrugged. "I checked every database, every contact down South that the Brotherhood has. I'm not saying there aren't families under the radar, but there was nothing I could come up with that matched Bitty's name, her mother's, her father's or the name of the uncle."

Gripping the edge of the table, Rhage stared past the tips of his shitkickers to the linoleum floor.

"You and Mary thinking of taking her in?" As he glanced up in surprise, V gave him a well-duh. "It's cool if you are. I mean, you were talking about kids the other night, and then asking about an orphan's family situation. That math ain't complex, true."

Rhage cleared his throat. "You say nothing about this. To anyone."

"Yeah, 'cuz I'm such a fucking gossip."

"I'm serious, V."

"Come on, you know me better than that. And I know what your next question is going to be."

"What's that."

"You need to go talk to Saxton. He'll be able to tell you what the requirements are to adopt her. I think in the old days, the King had to sign off whenever nobility was involved—and even though Bitty is a commoner, you, as a member of the Brotherhood, are aristocracy. I think a lot of that had to do with inheritance issues, but again, Saxton would know the ins and outs."

Okay, that was good advice, Rhage thought. He hadn't even con-sidered that there might be paperwork involved, and how naive was that?

Oh, and yeah, it wasn't like he'd spoken about all this to Mary. Or Bitty.

Shit. He was already so far ahead, wasn't he.

"Thanks, V." Feeling awkward, Rhage nodded at the rolled-up copy of what had to be the *Caldwell Courier Journal*. "What's your other news? And I'm surprised you're not online, my brother. Was it you or Egon Spengler who said that print is dead?"

"Both of us. Around the same time, actually." V unfolded things and flashed the front page of the *CCJ*. "Fritz was the one who picked this hard copy up."

Rhage whistled under his breath and held out his good hand to take the thing. "Annnnd we're back in business."

The headline read in bold letters, "Ritual Murder Scene at Abandoned Factory," and lengthy columns of text were accompanied by pixilated photos of blood and buckets next to a broken-down manufacturing line of some kind. Rhage scanned the print and flipped to the interior to finish the article, the scent of the ink and the sound of sloppy pages flapping against one another making him think of days gone by.

He shook his head as he put the paper back together. "Not a very big scale, though."

"Only twelve to fifteen new recruits. Clearly, there were some in the pipeline, and maybe the Omega hurried up the induction. But that's not a huge scale."

"Nope. We're making progress."

"I want to be there when the last one is poofed out of existence."

Rhage narrowed his eyes. "The only way that's going to happen is taking out the Omega."

"I've been thinking about how to do that." V took the newspaper back. "Trust me—"

A round of rapping on the door cut the brother off.

"Come in, Manny," Rhage said. "Let's get this—"

"Oh, hell, no," V muttered as the panel was thrown wide.

Lassiter stood between the jambs in a yellow slicker that was big as a circus tent, an umbrella popped open over his head, and a pair of wellies on his feet. His legs were bare. Which was not a good sign.

"No, I do not want to buy a watch," Rhage said, "so you can keep all that closed, buttercup."

"Watches?" Lassiter came in, or tried to—the umbrella got caught on the jamb. "Screw that. I heard you had a little trouble with your Jacuzzi early this morning."

He tossed his Mary Poppins back out into the corridor and did a *ta-da!* with something yellow in his palm. And then the bastard started to sing. Badly.

"Rubbbbber duuuuucky, you're the one. . . . You make bath time looooots of funnnnnn. . . ."

V glanced over. "Are you shoving that up his ass or am I?"

"We can take turns," Rhage shouted over the singing. "Hey, can I get a doctor in here!"

If he could just have his cast removed, it would make the beatdown of the angel so much easier. Plus the medical staff could help clean up the Lassiter pieces.

#perfect

When Mary got to Safe Place, she peeled off her layers in her office, put her purse on the floor by her chair, and signed into her computer.

Every night when she arrived, she checked that Facebook page—because she'd had to discipline herself not to do it on her phone or else run the risk of Internet vapor lock. And every night, right before the update hit the screen, her heart stopped and she held her breath.

She told herself it was because she desperately wanted to send the girl to some white-picket-fence situation in South Carolina with a dog, a cat, and a parakeet, and a set of mystical, Hallmark grandparents who turned out not to be dead.

The only trouble with that altruistic fantasy?

When yet again there was no word on the uncle, Mary found herself sagging in her chair and letting out the breath in her lungs with relief.

Which was about as professional as her unconsciously trying to drive the kid to the mansion that first night after her mother's death.

The truth was, however . . . that sometime in the past few days, a shift had happened in her heart. She had begun to think that—

"Ms. Luce?"

Mary sat up with a shout. "Oh, Bitty. Hi, how are you?"

The girl stepped back from the doorway. "I didn't mean to startle you."

"That's okay. I was just about to head up and check on you."

"Do you mind if I come in?"

"Please."

Bitty was careful to close the door without making a sound, and Mary had to wonder if that was the result of having tiptoed around her father for so long. Tonight, the girl had her hair in a ponytail and a blue sweater on over the dress she'd worn two evenings before. Her shoes were her other pair, the ones that were brown and came up to her ankles.

"I need to tell you something."

Mary indicated the chair opposite her. "Have a seat."

When Bitty did, Mary rolled around so that she was free of the desk and they were facing each other without any obstacles. Crossing her legs, she steepled her fingers.

The girl stayed silent, her eyes traveling around the walls of the office. There wasn't a lot to look at, other than a couple of drawings done by some of the kids and a map of Lake George that Mary had hung up because it reminded her of summers when she'd been young.

It was not a surprise when that stare drifted over to the box with Annalye's urn in it.

"Whatever it is, Bitty, we can deal with it."

"My mother lied," the girl blurted. "I'm not nine. I'm thirteen."

Mary was careful to show no surprise. "Okay. Well, that's all right. That's perfectly fine."

Bitty looked over. "She was afraid I wasn't young enough, that there was some kind of age limit to staying here or receiving help through the healer's clinic. She told me she was worried about us getting separated."

"You can live here until you transition, Bitty. It's not a problem."

"She tried to pick the youngest age I could pass for."

"It's all right. I promise."

Bitty looked down at her hands. "I'm really sorry. That's why she told me not to talk very much and to play with that doll. She didn't want me to give it away."

Mary sat back and took a deep breath. Now that she thought about it, the timing of everything made better sense if the girl was older. Vampire females went through their needings every ten years or so and Bitty's mother was pregnant when they got here—and those young were usually carried for about eighteen months. So Annalye would have conceived when Bitty had been eleven, give or take. As opposed to seven.

What was worrisome, though, was how tiny the girl was. For an eight- or nine-year-old, she was a good body weight. That was not true for someone who was thirteen—even if you took into account the fact that the biggest growth spurt happened to young vampires during their transition.

"I'm really sorry," Bitty said as she hung her head.

"Please don't feel bad. We understand. I just wish we'd known so we could have put her mind at rest."

"There's something else."

"You can tell me anything."

"I lied about my uncle."

Mary's heart started pounding. "How so?"

"I don't think he's coming for me."

"And why's that?"

"She talked about him from time to time, but it was always in the past. You know, what they used to do when they were kids. She did it to distract me when things got bad with my father. I guess I just . . . I just wish he were coming for me, you know?"

"Yes. I do."

"He's never actually met me."

"How does that make you feel?"

"Really alone. Especially because my *mahmen* is gone now."

Mary nodded. "That makes a lot of sense to me."

"My *mahmen* and I . . . we took care of each other. We had to." Bitty frowned and stared at the box on the desk. "She tried to get us away from him three times. The first one was when I was an infant. I don't remember that, but it didn't go well. The second time . . ." Bitty trailed off. "The third time was when my leg was broken, and she took me to Havers because it wasn't healing. That was when I got the pin put in—and then we went home and . . ."

Rhage, V and Butch went and got them out.

"I like your *hellren*," Bitty said abruptly. "He's funny."

"A total stitch."

"Is that a human phrase?"

"Yup. It means he's a crack-up."

Bitty frowned again and looked over. "So you were really human? I thought that you couldn't be turned into a vampire."

"I'm not. I mean, I haven't been." Mary flashed a smile. "See? Nothing pointy."

"You have pretty teeth."

"Thank you."

Bitty's eyes returned to the cardboard box. "So she's really in there."

"Her remains are."

"What happens if I don't bury her right now? Does she . . . is that wrong? Is it bad?"

Mary shook her head. "There's no rush. Not that I'm aware of, at least. I can double-check with Marissa, though. She knows all your traditions inside and out."

"I just don't want to do anything wrong. I guess . . . I'm responsible for her now, you know. I want to do the right thing."

"I totally understand that."

"What do humans do with their dead?"

"We put them in the earth—or at least, that's one option. That's what I did with my mom. I had her cremated and then buried."

"Like mine."

Mary nodded. "Like yours."

There was a pause and she stayed quiet so that Bitty had the space to feel whatever she was feeling. In the silence, Mary took a good look at the girl, noting the reed-thin arms and legs, the tiny body beneath the layers.

"Where did you put her in the ground?" Bitty asked.

"In a cemetery. Across town."

"What's a cemetery?"

"It's a place where humans bury their dead and mark the graves with headstones so that you know where yours are. From time to time, I go back and put flowers by her site."

Bitty tilted her head and frowned a little. After a moment, she asked, "Will you show me?"

FORTY-TWO

"𝕴 did not expect your call."

As Assail spoke, he pivoted around and smiled at Naasha. "Not so soon, at any rate."

This eve, Naasha had chosen to receive him at her *hellren's* abode in a dark and dramatic study full of leather-bound volumes and furniture that reminded him of humans' private gentlemen's clubs. Tonight, and she had dressed herself again in red, perhaps to match the velvet curtains that hung down like arteries from the ceiling—or perhaps because she believed he enjoyed her in the color.

"I found myself bereft of your company." As she spoke, she enunciated the words with deliberation, her glossy lips pursing and releasing the syllables as if she were giving them a blow job. "I could not sleep this day."

"From checking on your mate's health through the hours of sunlight, no doubt."

"No. From aching." She came forward, crossing the thick red carpeting without making a sound. "For you. I am starved."

When she stopped in front of him, he smiled coldly. "Are you now."

She reached out and stroked his cheek. "You are quite an extraordinary male."

"Yes, I know." He removed her touch, but kept hold of her wrist. "What is curious to me is why my absence is so troubling, considering that you already have a cock under this roof."

"My *hellren* is infirmed, if you recall," she said in a remote tone. As if he were the last thing on earth she wished to speak of.

"It was Throe to whom I referred." Assail smiled again and began to rub his thumb o'er her flesh. "I beg of you, what is your relation to him?"

"He is of distant blood to my mate."

"So you have taken him in out of charity."

"As is proper to do."

Assail put his arm around her waist and drew her to his body. "You are not very proper sometimes, are you."

"No," she purred. "Does that turn you on?"

"It certainly turned you on two eves ago. You enjoyed my cousins very much."

"And yet you did not participate."

"I wasn't in the mood."

"Tonight?"

He made a show of looking over her face. Then he stroked her long hair back, moving it over her shoulders. "Mayhap."

"And what would it take for you to get in the mood."

As she arched her body against his, he pretended to find her captivating, closing his eyes and biting his lower lip. In truth? He might as well have been stropped by a dog.

"Where is Throe?" he asked.

"Jealous?"

"Of course. In fact, I am consumed."

"You lie."

"Always." He smiled and bent to her mouth, running one of his fangs across her bottom lip. "Where is he?"

"Why do you care?"

"I like threesomes."

The laugh she let out was husky and full of a promise he had no interest in. What he did care about was getting back down into that basement of hers—and that would be literally, not figuratively. Although if he had to fuck her to get there, he would.

She had clearly not wanted him to explore the other evening. And that made him wonder if she hadn't something to hide.

"Alas, Throe is not in this evening." She turned about in Assail's arms and drove her ass into his pelvis. "I am by myself."

"Where has he gone?"

She glanced over her shoulder, a sharp look in her eyes. "Why e'er do you focus on him so?"

"I have appetites that you cannot service, my dear. Much as your wares appeal."

"Then mayhap you shall call your cousins in?" She resumed rubbing herself against him. "I should like to welcome them again."

"I do not fornicate with my blood relations. However, if you should like to?"

"They do have a way of filling a female up. And mayhap I am too much for you to handle alone."

Doubt it, he thought. But his cousins herein was a good idea.

Keeping an arm around her, Assail spun her back to face him, took his phone out, and a split second later, a discreet chiming sound from the front of the mansion was heard on the far side of the closed study doors.

"Ask and you shall receive," he murmured as he kissed her hard and then disengaged her from him, giving her a push toward the exit. "Answer that yourself. Welcome them properly."

She hurried off with a giggle, as if she liked being told what to do—and God, he couldn't help but think of Marisol. If he had ordered his lovely cat burglar around like that? She would have castrated him and worn his balls for earrings.

A burning in the center of his chest made him reach for the vial of coke in the inner pocket of his Brioni suit jacket, but it wasn't actually his addiction calling his hand to home for once.

The extra dose made his head hum, but that was going to work for him.

He had a lot of ground to cover tonight.

"Okay, where are you, where are you . . ."

As Jo drove ever deeper into Caldwell's main, mostly failing, industrial park, she leaned into her VW's windshield and wiped the sleeve of her jacket on the glass to clear the condensation. She

could have cranked on the defroster—except the damn thing wasn't working.

"I need another month before I can pay for that," she muttered. "Until then, I'm not going to breathe."

As she thought about Bill confronting her on her parents' wealth, she had to laugh. Yes, it was true that principled stances were laudable. They rarely paid the bills, however—or fixed broken blowers that smelled like an electrical fire when you turned them on.

You did tend to sleep better at night, though.

When her phone started ringing, she grabbed for it, checked the screen, and tossed the thing back to the seat. She had other stuff to worry about other than Bryant's after-hours demands. Besides, she had left his dry cleaning right where he'd told her to, on the front porch of his condo.

"Okay, here we are."

As her headlights illuminated a flat-roofed, one-story building that was long as a city block and paneled in gray metal siding, she entered its empty parking lot and continued down toward its unadorned entrance. When she pulled up to the glass doors and the sign that had the name of the factory blackened out with layers of spray paint, she hit the brakes, killed the engine and got out.

There was yellow police tape in a circle all around, the fragile barrier whistling in the wind . . . a seal plastered on the door crack with the words CRIME SCENE in big letters on it . . . and evidence of a lot of foot traffic having been in and out, a path carved in the leaves and debris by shuffling feet and equipment that had been rolled or dragged along the ground.

Man, it was dark out here. Especially as her headlights turned themselves off.

"I need to get that carry permit," she said out loud.

When her eyes adjusted, the graffiti on the building became visible again, and the pitted parking lot reemerged in her field of vision. There was no ambient city glow going on out in this part of Caldwell; too many abandoned buildings, the business park having failed when the economy went into the crapper seven years before.

Just as she was getting antsy and thinking of calling Bill, a car came over the rise and entered the lot as she had.

As Bill pulled up next to her, he put his window down and leaned across some other man. "Follow me."

She gave him a thumbs-up and got back in her car.

Around they went, down the long front and the shorter side of the building. The facility's rear door was even less fancy than the front; it didn't even have a sign. The graffiti was thicker here, the signatures and angled line drawings layering one upon another like people talking over each other at a party.

Jo got out and locked her car. "Hey."

The guy who emerged from Bill's car was a little bit of a surprise. Six feet, maybe taller. Prematurely gray hair, but the hot kind, like Max's from *Catfish*. Dark heavy glasses, as if being ocularly challenged and having a sense of style were prereqs for hanging with Bill. The body was . . .

Well, very good. Broad shoulders, tight waist, long legs.

"This is my cousin, Troy Thomas."

"Hey," the guy said, offering his hand. "Bill's told me about you."

"I can imagine." She gave him a shake and then nodded over at the rear entrance. "Listen, you guys, there's a seal on this door as well. I'm not feeling good about this."

"I have clearance." Troy pulled out a pass card. "It's okay."

"He's in the CSI unit," Bill explained.

"And I need to pick up some equipment, so this is authorized. Just please don't touch anything, and no pictures, okay?"

"Absolutely." Jo dropped her arm when she realized she was about to swear, palm-to-heart.

Troy led the way, cutting through the seal with a box knife before inserting his card in a CPD electronic padlock.

"Watch your step," he said as he opened the door and flipped on the lights.

The shallow hall had two-toned carpet: cream on the outsides of the footpath, a mucky gray/brown where work boots had trodden. Streaks of dishwater gray grit lined the wall vertically, denoting leaks in the ceiling. The smell was something between moldy bread and sweat socks.

And fresh copper.

As they walked forward, there were cans of drooling paint to step over, some tools, and a couple of drywall buckets, all of which seemed to suggest the old owners, or maybe the bank that had repossessed the place, might have taken a stab at some renovation—only to give up when it proved to be too costly.

There were two offices, a reception area, a unisex bathroom, and a pair of steel doors, next to which were hard hats covered in dust hanging on hooks.

"Let's go through over here. It's easier."

Heading to the left, Troy led them to a third option, standing aside once again as they went through a much narrower door. On the far side, he hit not a light switch, but something that looked like a fuse-box pull.

With a series of bangs, huge panels of lights came on one after another in a cavernous manufacturing space that was mostly vacant, nothing but empty brackets bolted into the floor and great grease shadows on the concrete indicating where machines had been.

"The massacre happened over here."

Jo popped her eyebrows. Yes, it most certainly had, she thought as she caught sight of the pools of coagulated blood, once bright red, now browning with time's passage. There were more of those drywall buckets here and there, and when she walked across and got a closer view of everything, she put her hand over her mouth and swallowed hard.

"It's just like the farm," Bill commented as he wandered around.

"Like what farm?" Jo said as she shook her head at the gore. "God, this was so violent."

"You remember—almost two years ago? There was a scene just like this one only ten times more blood."

"No bodies," Troy interjected. "Again."

"How many people do you think died here?" Jo asked.

"Ten. Maybe twelve?" Troy came around and crouched down next to a series of swipes through the blood on the floor—as if someone might have tried to escape but had slipped and fallen. "We can't be sure. This place has been on the market for a year or two. The bank stopped using the security cameras five months ago when a lightning strike knocked them out during a spring storm. We've got nothing."

"How do you get rid of that many bodies?" Jo wondered. "Where do you take them all?"

Troy nodded. "The homicide division is looking into all of that."

And as for the vampire angle? she thought to herself. Those types usually took blood, right? They didn't leave it behind in five-gallon lots.

Not that she was about to pose that one to Troy. Way too crazy.

She glanced over at Bill. "How many other mass murders or ritual whatevers have taken place in Caldwell in the last ten years? Twenty years? Fifty?"

"I can find out," he said as their eyes met. "I'm thinking the exact same thing you are."

FORTY-THREE

"It's so peaceful out here. So beautiful."

As Bitty said the words, Mary glanced over at the girl. The pair of them were strolling down one of Pine Grove Cemetery's miles of paved lanes. Overhead, the moon was giving them more than enough illumination to see by, the silvery glow landing on the tops of fluffy pine boughs and also the elegant bare limbs of maple and oak trees. All around, headstones, statues, and mausoleums dotted the rolling lawns and shores of man-made ponds, until you could almost imagine you were walking through a stage set.

"Yes, it is," Mary murmured. "It's nice to think that all this is for the ghosts of the people buried here, but I believe it's more for the folks who come to visit. It can be really hard, especially in the beginning, to come visit a family member or a friend who's passed. I mean, after my mother died and I put her ashes in the ground, it took me months and months to come back. When I finally got here, though, it was easier in some ways than I'd thought, mostly because of how lovely it is—we're going over there. She's right there."

Stepping off onto the grass, Mary was careful where she trod.

"Here, follow me. The dead are in the front of the markers. And yes, I know it's weird, but I hate the idea of trampling anyone."

"Oh!" Bitty looked down at a beautiful headstone inscribed with a Jewish Star of David and the name Epstein. "I beg your pardon. Excuse me."

The two of them wended their way in farther, until Mary stopped at a rose-colored granite marker with the name Cecilia Luce carved upon it.

"Hi, Mom," she whispered, getting down on her haunches to pick a fallen leaf off the front the headstone. "How are you?"

As she ran her fingertips over the engraved name and the dates, Bitty knelt down on the other side.

"What did she pass from?" the girl asked.

"M.S. Multiple sclerosis."

"What's that?"

"It's a human disease where the body's immune system attacks the coating that protects your nerve fibers? Without that sheath, you can't tell your body what to do, so you lose the ability to walk, feed yourself, speak. Or at least, my mom did. Some people with it have long periods of remission when the disease isn't active. She wasn't one of them." Mary rubbed the center of her chest. "There are more options for treatment now than there were fifteen or twenty years ago when she was first diagnosed. Maybe she would have lasted longer in this era of medicine. Who knows."

"Do you miss her?"

"Every day. The thing is . . . I don't want to freak you out, but I'm not convinced you ever get over a death like that of your mother's. I think it's more that you get used to the loss. Kind of like getting in cold water? There's a shock to the system in the beginning, but an accommodation happens so you don't notice the chill as much as the years pass—and sometimes, you even forget you're in the tub at all after a while. But there are always memories that come back to you and remind you of who is missing."

"I think of my mom a lot. I dream of her, too. She comes to me in dreams and talks to me."

"What does she say?"

As a cold breeze rolled through, Bitty tucked some hair back behind her ear. "That everything is going to be okay, and I'm going to have a new family soon. That's what got me thinking about my uncle."

"Well, I think that's lovely." Mary let herself sit back on her butt, her thigh-level coat a barrier to the damp ground. "Does she look healthy in your dreams?"

"Oh, yes. I like that most. She's with my baby brother, the one who passed as well."

"We gave your mother his ashes."

"I know. She put them in her suitcase. She said that she wanted to make sure they came with us if we were told to go."

"It might be nice to put them together at some point."

"I think that's a really good idea."

There was a long pause. "Hey, Bitty?"

"Mmm?"

Mary picked a little stick off the ground and bent it up and down to give her fingers something to do. "I, ah, I wish I'd known how worried your mom was about the resources at Safe Place. I would have worked really hard to reassure her." She glanced over at the girl. "Are you worried about any of that?"

Bitty put her hands in her coat pockets and looked around. "I don't know. Everyone's really nice. You especially. But it's scary, you know."

"I know. Just talk to me, okay? If you get scared. I'll give you my cell phone number. You can call me at any time directly."

"I don't want to be a burden."

"Yeah, I guess that's what worries me. Your mom didn't want to be one, which I can absolutely respect—but the end result was that things were much harder on her, and you, than they had to be. Do you know what I mean?"

Bitty nodded and fell silent.

After a while, the girl said, "My father used to hit me."

Deep in the grungy heart of downtown, Rhage ran through an alley, his shitkickers landing on the asphalt like thunder, his autoloader up, his rage in check so that it was an engine that drove him on, not a disaster that flipped him out.

As his target darted across another street, he stuck to the fucker like glue, that sickly sweet *lesser* smell like the vapor trail of a jet across the night sky, easily trackable.

It was a new recruit. Probably from out at that abandoned factory.

He could tell because the thing was all panicked, tripping and slipping before scrambling away in a mess of arms and legs, no weapons on him, no one coming to his rescue.

He was a lone rat without a mischief.

And as the slayer fell for the umpteenth time, his feet knocked out from under him by what looked like a carburetor, he finally didn't get up again. He just held his leg to his chest and moaned, rolling onto his back.

"No, p-p-p-please, no!"

As Rhage pulled up to his prey and stopped, for the first time in recorded history, he hesitated before the kill. But he couldn't not stab the fucker. If he left the damn thing on the streets, it was just going to heal up and find others of its kind to fight with . . . or it was going to get discovered by a human and end up on some fucking YouTube video.

"Nooooooo—"

Rhage shoved the thing's arms out of the way and buried his black dagger right in the center of that now-hollow chest.

With a flash and a *pop!*, the slayer disappeared into thin air, nothing but a greasy stain of the Omega's blood on the pavement and an acrid burn left behind—

Rhage jerked around, switching his dagger for an autoloader. Flaring his nostrils, he sniffed at the air and then let out a growl.

"I know you're there. Show yourself."

When nothing moved in the shadows at the far end of the alley, he took three steps back so that he had cover in the doorway of an abandoned tenement building.

In the distance, sirens howled like stray dogs, and on the next block over, some humans shouted at one another. Closer by, something was dripping off the fire escape behind him, and there was a rattling higher up, as if the gusts coming from the river were agitating the scaffolding's tenuous hold on the brick.

"You fucking pussy," he called out. "Show yourself."

His natural arrogance told him he could handle whatever this was all by himself, but some vague unease he couldn't put a name to had him signaling for back-up by triggering a beacon located on the inside of his jacket's collar.

It wasn't that he was frightened—fuck, no. And he felt stupid the second he'd done it.

But there was another male vampire hiding over there, and the only thing he knew for sure? It wasn't Xcor.

Because they knew where that bastard was.

The rest of those sonsabitches were an open question.

FORTY-FOUR

Naturally, getting Naasha naked was the work of a moment. In fact, she volunteered for it.

As soon as Assail and his cousins stepped into that sex dungeon of hers, she began peeling herself out of her red dress, kicking the haute couture out of the way as if the thing were worth nothing more than a paper napkin. She left her high heels on, however, and her basque.

Ehric's and Evale's arousals were instantaneous, a one-two punch of sexual aggression that made the female laugh in that husky way of hers.

She didn't go to either of them, however. She approached Assail.

Leaning in, she pressed herself against his chest and put her arms around his neck. "I am in need of you first."

Silly female. She confessed too much, transferring her power to him.

But that was a good thing.

Setting her aside, he tugged at the knot of his Hermès tie, loosening the silk. As he removed the length, she did a little spin and went across to one of the bedding platforms, lying out flat and stretching her arms over her head. With her body forming an erotic S-curve on the

mattress, one breast popped out of its cup and her bare sex gleamed as she parted her legs.

Assail prowled over to her, all-fouring up her body until he sat on her pelvis, trapping her. Stretching the tie out between two fists, he stared down at her.

"You are so trusting," he murmured. "What if I did something bad with this? No one would hear you scream or struggle, would they."

For a moment, fear flared in her eyes. But then he smiled.

"It is a good thing I am a gentlemale, is it not." He leaned down with the silk. "Close your eyes, my darling. And not to sleep, no, not to rest."

He covered her eyes with the tie, knotting the silk into place. Then he looked over his shoulder and nodded for his cousins to descend upon her. They were, as ever, more than obliging, ridding themselves of shirts and slacks, getting naked before they reached out to touch and lick, stroke and penetrate.

As Naasha began to moan, he dismounted, grabbed the nearest wrist—Ehric's, as it turned out—and scored it with his own fangs. Drawing the welling blood to Naasha's mouth, the female gasped and latched on, nursing at the vein as her body began to writhe in ecstasy.

Obviously she was not living off the blood of her *hellren*—and Assail assumed that was why she required the likes of Throe's company. But vampires, particularly horny ones, oft enjoyed partaking whilst in the midst of pleasure, even if they were otherwise well fed. Like alcohol or drugs, the drinking amplified everything in a most satisfactory way.

With his cousin's blood in the air and on her tongue, she was so distracted, Assail was able to get over to the door without her being aware of his withdrawal. Reaching into his coat, he took out a tiny old-fashioned oil can, the kind with the poppable bottom and a short-necked nose.

Pocka-pocka. Pocka-pocka. Up above.

Pocka-pocka. Pocka-pocka. Down below.

The lubricant didn't smell like much because he'd loaded the thing with brand new Pennzoil 10W-40 for motorcars—and after his ministrations, the massive door opened in utter silence. With a sly smile, he slipped out of the playroom and re-closed the heavy panels. Replacing his oil can into the pocket of his cashmere jacket, he looked both ways. Then he proceeded to the left, following the path Throe had taken the previous evening.

The basement walls and floor were made of rough-cut stone, with electrical lights tacked onto wooden ceiling beams casting dim shadows. He tried every door he came to and discovered storage room after storage room, some filled with lawn-care equipment from the forties and fifties, others with travel trunks from the turn of the twentieth century in them, and yet another with festival decorations that had wilted and spoiled in the damp and mildew.

No sign of Throe's quarters, and that was truly not a surprise; he would not deign to stay down here in this window-less land of forgotten utility objects. No *doggen*, either, the house clearly having been modernized, with the supplies and sundries of the servants moved up to higher levels. No wine cellar, but then he would imagine that that, too, would have found a home on the first floor, closer to the hub of social activity.

All of which was why she had kitted that space out as she had.

There was privacy to be had down here.

Mayhap, like him, she did her own sheets from those bedding platforms? Perhaps not. The female probably had a trusted maid.

At the very far end, a second set of stairs appeared as the corridor took a turn, the stone steps so old they had wear patterns in them.

Ah, so this was where Throe had run off to.

Moving quickly, Assail was almost upon them when he came to a final door—which was reinforced like that of Naasha's dungeon, as opposed to the flimsier ones of those storage areas.

The Master Lock upon it was fresh and shiny, and of the sort that required a specific key. On a whim, he patted around the molding, in the event such a thing happened to be hanging up on a nail or a hook, as some were wont to do. Alas, no. Whate'er was on the far side was something that was precious.

Or not for prying eyes.

Taking the stairs, he was quiet as a draft as he ascended to a door that, blessedly, appeared to be unlocked. He listened for a moment, confirmed that there was nothing on the far side, and opened the way with care.

It was the butler's pantry, going by all the glass-fronted cupboards full of dishes, and the silver closet that was paneled in green felt and stacked with great stores of gleaming sterling.

Although he did not know the layout of the house, he was well familiar with the necessaries of great manors, and sure enough, an unadorned staff stairwell with bald wooden steps and a functional handrail was not far. As he continued onward to the second floor, he was forced to stop halfway up and flatten himself against the wall as, upon the landing above, a maid passed by with a load of laundry in a wicker basket. When she was gone, he closed the distance and sneaked out behind her into the staff section of the bedroom wings.

Following his instincts, he whispered to a wide door, one that was broad enough to accommodate all manner of ins and outs—and indeed, on the other side, the hallway became splendiferous, crystal and brass sconces lighting the way, thick wool carpeting cushioning the foot, antique bureaus and tables marking windows that no doubt had views of the gardens.

He ducked into every bedroom, and each appeared to correspond to a given sex, done in alternating masculine or feminine schemes.

He knew when he got to Throe's from the aftershave that scented the air.

Now, he went inside and shut the door behind himself. Fortunately, the maids had already been through and done their tidying up, the bed made, a fresh stack of towels set in the bathroom, new flowers on the writing desk. There were few in the way of personal effects, which would be in line with a former soldier of few resources and much mobility. The closet was filled with clothes, however, many of which had tags on them, indicating new purchases.

No doubt by the lady of the house.

Back out in the room proper, he went through the drawers of the Chippendale highboy and found nothing. No weapons. No ammo. At the antique desk, he searched for papers, phone records, mail. There were none.

Pausing by the bed, he observed the paintings that hung on the silk wallpaper.

"There you are, little one."

With a purr of satisfaction, he went across to a small framed landscape—that just happened to be ever so slightly off center.

As he removed it, the burnished face of a wall safe was revealed.

The dial was flat and red, and there were many numbers from which to spin one to another.

Where was his cat burglar when he needed her, he thought as he put back the painting.

There were no doubt ways he could get inside if he chose, but he was ill prepared for such an endeavor, and he did not want to run out of time with the fun that was transpiring downstairs—his cousins were a hardy pair, but the fucking was not going to last forever.

Measuring the gold-leafed frame of the picture, he made certain that it was exactly as off-kilter as before, no more nor less, and then he went back across the Oriental—feeling rather glad that the short-napped, multi-colored expanse would not reveal his tracks.

With a final look around, he put the doorknob to use and re-emerged out in the corridor—

"May I help you?"

As Rhage waited for the male vampire down the alley to respond, he glanced up to the roof of the building across the way. Vishous had just dematerialized to that vantage point—but the brother stayed quiet and motionless.

Refocusing, Rhage called out again, "Show yourself or I'm coming to get you. And you won't live through that, motherfucker. I guarantee it."

Beneath his skin, the beast surged, his curse coiling and unfurling restlessly in spite of all the sex he'd been having. Then again, his instincts were at a roar. Having already been shot in the chest this week, he wasn't looking to beat the Brotherhood's record for near-death experiences.

"'Tis I, yet I am unarmed."

The sound of the aristocratic voice echoed around the grungy tenaments, and then a moment later, Throe stepped out with his palms up and facing outward, his body tense.

"Do not shoot." The male performed a slow circle. "I am unaccompanied."

Rhage narrowed his eyes, searching for other signs of movement in that dark corner. When there were none, he zeroed in on Throe again. No weapons were visible, and the male was not dressed for fighting—unless he was looking to bitch slap Zoolander: The bastard's threads were as nice as Butch's, his overcoat tailored like a fine suit, his shoes gleaming even in the low light.

"Looks like you've had a makeover," Rhage muttered. "Last time I saw you, your clothes weren't that good."

"My prospects have improved since I have left Xcor's employ."

"Word had it you weren't employed, you sonofabitch. Conscripted is more like it."

"I had a debt to repay, 'tis true. But that is done now."

"Well, we're not hiring. Not assholes with your résumé, at any rate."

"May I put my arms down? They are getting rather tired."

"Up to you. I'm a trigger-happy douche bag, though, so you might want to watch where you choose to put your hands."

There was the sound of someone landing on two feet, and Throe wrenched around. As Vishous stepped out of the darkness right behind the guy, Rhage laughed.

"You don't like being sneaked up on, huh." Rhage likewise left his cover, keeping his gun up and ready. "Imagine that. And why don't you hold the fuck still while my brother searches you."

Vishous pounded his way around Throe's torso and down his legs, giving the guy's crotch a good honk. As Throe's high-pitched squeak drifted off, the brother stepped back, but kept his forty pointed at Mr. Neiman Marcus.

"So if you're not with Xcor, what are you doing out here?" V demanded. "You're wearing too much cologne and you're unarmed."

"I was hoping to run into one of you."

"Surprise!" Rhage quipped. "Now what do you want."

"Did you send Assail to check up on me—or is he acting independently?"

V laughed in a hard burst. "Say what?"

"I have perfect enunciation." Throe glanced at V. "And you are no more than three feet from me. So one can assume you heard me well enough."

As V bared his fangs, Rhage shook his head. "You might want to rethink the attitude. My brother's looking like he wants to turn you into confetti."

"Well?" Throe pressed. "Did you send him to seduce me? You'd have more luck with a female—not that you would find aught out from the effort. I am retired from all conflict."

"You risked your life," V said, "to send this message, true?"

"I thought it would mean more if it were in person."

"You vastly overestimate your appeal. Or the significance of your sexual orientation."

Rhage spoke up. "Why don't you get the fuck out of here. I'd hate for a private citizen such as yourself to get injured out here in the field."

"Real fucking pity." V lifted his gun muzzle so it was on a line with the male's head. "Tick tock."

"Bye-bye, asshole." Rhage made a little waving motion. "Have a nice life. Or not. Who gives a fuck."

Throe shook his head. "You are wasting your time if you are looking into me."

"I'ma count this down," V said. "On the count of three, I shoot. Three."

Throe was out of there just as V let off a round about two feet to the left of where the bastard had been standing.

"Shoot," V remarked in a bored tone. "Missed."

"Man, this is such a shitty part of town," Rhage said as he went over to his brother. "You meet the worst kinds here."

"So Assail is going above and beyond the call of duty. I'll have to tip him—in his thong, evidently."

Rhage nodded and then pointed to the blast spot on the asphalt. "I got a *lesser*, by the way."

"Congratulations. You want another—"

"Why aren't you looking me in the eye, V?"

"We're in the middle of the field. I'm busy."

"Uh-huh. Right."

Vishous frowned, and still avoided him. But then in a low voice, the brother said, "I talked to Saxton for you."

Rhage recoiled. "About Bitty?"

"Is that her name? Well, yeah. Anyway, I got the paperwork together. You don't have to do anything with it, but it's on your bureau in a folder. Later."

Justlikethat, the brother dematerialized out of the alley, and Rhage knew better than to think that the pair of them would ever speak of it again. And man, that was so V—the SOB was capable of great kindness and empathy, but always at arm's length, as if he were afraid of getting too entangled in emotion.

He was always there for the people he loved, though.

Always.

"Thank you, my brother," Rhage said to the thin air where the male of worth had stood. "Thank you as ever."

Taking a deep breath, Rhage told himself that he needed to chill. Just because V couldn't find the uncle, and there was now a blank set of adoption forms waiting for him back home, didn't mean that anything was going to happen with Bitty.

He hadn't even talked to Mary yet.

And, hello, the girl had agreed only to go out for ice cream and then dinner with them. That didn't mean she was even interested in having a new family or something.

He *really* needed to chill the fuck out.

FORTY-FIVE

Sitting beside her mother's grave, Mary held her breath as she waited for Bitty to say something further. In the silence, the words the girl had spoken hung in the cold air between them.

My father used to hit me.

"It can be so hard to talk about things like that," Mary murmured. "Did your father ever . . ."

"No. Actually, I don't even have any memories of him. He died when I was two in an accident. My mother was the only parent I had."

"My *mahmen* was all I had, too. But sometimes I didn't feel that close to her. It's hard to explain."

"There was a lot going on in your house."

"I used to get him mad at me on purpose. Just so he wouldn't . . . you know, go after her." Bitty shrugged. "I was faster than he was. I had a better chance."

Mary closed her eyes and kept her cursing to herself. "I'm very sorry."

"It's okay."

"No, it really isn't."

"I'm cold," Bitty said abruptly.

"Let's go back to the car then." Mary got to her feet, respecting the change in conversation. "I'll turn the heat on."

"Do you want to stay longer?"

"I can always come back." She wanted to take the girl's hand, but knew better. "And it is cold."

Bitty nodded, and together they walked around the graves, the ground soft underfoot until they got to the lane. As they came up into the Volvo, the girl hesitated.

Mary glanced over as she opened the driver's-side door. "Do you want me to take the long way back to Safe Place?"

"How did you know?"

"Just a lucky guess."

As they followed the main lane out to the iron gates of the cemetery, Bitty murmured, "I never knew Caldwell was so big."

Mary nodded. "It's a good-size city. Have you ever seen downtown?"

"Only in pictures. My father had a truck, but my mother wasn't allowed to drive it. When we came to Havers that one time, she took it when he'd passed out. That was why . . . other things happened. You know, after we got back."

"Yes." Mary looked into the rearview. "I can imagine."

"I would like to see it. The downtown."

"Do you want to go now? It's really pretty at night."

"Can we?"

"You bet."

At Pine Grove's entrance, Mary hung a left, and headed across the 'burbs for the highway. As they passed neighborhoods full of human houses, most of which were dark, Bitty had her face pressed against the window—and then came the stand-alone shops, and farther on, strip malls that were nothing but glowing signs, empty parking lots, and closed-up spaces.

"This is the Northway." Mary hit her directional signal. "It'll take us through safely."

Up the exit ramp. Into what little traffic there was at ten o'clock at night.

And then there it was on the horizon, like a different kind of sunrise, the city's skyscrapers dotted with lights in random patterns.

"Oh, look at that." Bitty sat forward. "The buildings are so tall.

When *mahmen* took me over the river to the clinic, she made me hide under a blanket. I didn't see anything."

"How did . . ." Mary cleared her throat. "How did you get food? You lived in a pretty rural area—there wasn't much within walking distance, was there?"

"Father would bring home what he wanted. We got what was left."

"Have you ever, you know, been to a supermarket?"

"No?"

"Would you like to go to one? After we drive through here?"

"Oh, I would love to!"

Mary kept the speed at fifty-five as they went through the forest of buildings, the highway much like the lanes of the cemetery, fat curves bringing them close to the vertical stacks of countless offices before turning in another direction for yet another view of steel and glass.

"Not all the lights are off."

"No." Mary laughed. "Whenever I drive around here at night, I always make up stories about why someone forgot to hit the switch before they left. Were they rushing to meet someone for an anniversary dinner? A first date? The birth of a baby? I try to make it good things."

"Maybe they have a new puppy."

"Or a parakeet."

"I don't think a fish would be worth the rush."

Annnnnnd that was the silly discussion as Mary made the wide loop through Caldwell's financial district to hook up with a four-lane motorway that took them back in the direction they'd come from. The Hannaford she was heading for was about three miles away from Safe Place, and when she pulled into its parking area, there were only a few straggler shoppers going in and out of its brilliantly lit entrance, some with bags, others with carts, the ones yet to buy empty-handed.

After she parked, Mary and Bitty got out.

"Are you hungry?" Mary asked as they walked toward the automatic doors.

"I don't know."

"Well, let me know if you want anything."

"There's food back at Safe Place."

"Yup, there is."

Bitty stopped and watched the doors opening and closing. "That is so amazing."

"Yes, I guess it is."

As they stood there together, Mary thought . . . God, how many times had she gone in and out of an entrance like this, head buzzing with lists of things to buy, or stuff she was worried about, or plans that were coming later? She'd never given much thought about how cool it was that the doors regulated themselves, riding back and forth on little runners, neither too fast nor too slow as they were triggered by people.

Through Bitty's eyes, she saw what she'd taken for granted in a totally different light.

And *that* was so amazing.

Without thinking, Mary put her hand on the girl's shoulder—it just seemed like such a natural thing to do that she failed to stop herself. "See up there? There's a sensor—when a person comes into the eye's field of recognition, that's what makes them go. Try it out."

Bitty stepped forward, and laughed as the glass parted for her. Then she inched back. Leaned in and waved her arms until they separated again.

Mary just hung on the periphery . . . a big smile on her face, her chest full of something so warm that she couldn't bear to look at it too closely.

Standing just outside Throe's bedroom, Assail turned about to confront the female who'd made the inquiry of him—all the while wondering what level of complication this was going to result in.

But it was only the maid who had been transporting laundry as he had come up the mansion's back stairs—and the *doggen's* eyes were wide and a bit frightened, hardly a suggestion of trouble even though his presence had been discovered where he should not have been.

Assail sought to reassure her by offering an easy smile. "I'm afraid I am a bit lost."

"Forgive me, sire." She bowed deeply. "I thought that the mistress's guests were arriving closer to dawn."

"I am early. But there is naught to worry about. Are the main stairs that way?"

"Indeed." The maid bowed again. "Yes, sire."

"Problem solved. You have been most helpful."

"My pleasure, sire."

He paused before he pivoting away. "Tell me, how many are expected?"

"There have been six bedrooms prepared, sire."

"Thank you."

Striding off, he left her in the hall, making a show of pretending to take note of the decor as he strolled with his hands in his pockets. As he approached the main stairwell, he glanced back. She was gone— and given her station in the household, it was unlikely she would say anything to anyone. Maids were little more than washer/dryers who needed to be fed—at least in terms of the hierarchy of staff.

She was more likely to be rebuked for interrupting the butler, even though she had news that was pertinent to the household.

Assail proceeded down the main stairs on a saunter. After all, the best disguise in a situation like this was to be out in the open—and he was prepared, his story set.

Alas, he ran into no other servants and no one else as he went to the rear of the house and reconnected with the staff stairs that he had previously ascended. Taking them back down to the basement, he stopped in front of the padlocked door.

Now that he was less rushed, he discovered a scent lingering in the air. It was one that he could not immediately place, but he did not tarry to suss it out.

Continuing on, he proceeded to the mistress's dungeon and sneaked back in. Things had progressed with admirable efficiency, his cousins swarmed over the female's naked flesh, blood marking skin and mattress alike, their cocks and her sex slick with orgasms. That Hermès tie was still in place over her eyes, however.

Such well-performing cousins he had—

The door opened wide mere moments after his return, and Assail looked over his shoulder.

"Well, well, well," he said with a smile, "madam's favorite houseguest returns."

Throe was none too pleased, going by the tight brows and tension in his body. "I was not aware you were coming."

"The cellular phone is an incredible device. It allows one to call others and to receive calls from others, resulting in meetings taking place."

The mistress of the house moaned and arched as Ehric traded places between her legs with his brother.

Throe's eyes narrowed. "I don't know what you're doing here."

Assail indicated the sex that was ongoing. "This is not enough of a rationale? And if you are so concerned about my presence, do speak with your madam. This is her show, is it not?"

"Not for much longer," the male said under his breath.

"Busy with plans. Such a surprise."

"Watch and learn." Throe's eyes glinted with malice. "This household is about to be transformed."

"Do tell."

"Enjoy her while you can."

Throe departed, closing the door behind himself with no sound at all. Thanks to Assail's ministrations.

As Assail turned his attention back to the bedding platform . . . he had the distinct impression a funeral was coming. The question was whether it was the master's or the mistress's first.

FORTY-SIX

Layla sat up on her elbows as Doc Jane began wiping off the clear lubricant from her big belly. This previously scheduled exam had turned out to be well-timed—even though she'd just had one, the double-check was reassuring.

"Yup, everything's fine." The physician smiled as she helped bring the pink robe's two halves back in place. "You're doing really well."

"Just a little longer. And then I can relax some, right?"

"You betcha. Soon enough, those two sets of lungs will be at a point where we can handle them better." Doc Jane looked across the exam room. "Any questions from the dads?"

From over in the corner, Qhuinn shook his head as he twitched in the chair and rubbed his mismatched eyes. Beside him, Blay massaged the male's shoulder.

"We were wondering about the feedings," Blay said. "Is Layla getting enough from us?"

"Her levels have been looking great. What you all are doing is working just fine."

"What about the delivery?" Blay asked. "How do we know if . . . I guess we don't know if it'll be okay, do we."

Doc Jane sat back on her rolling stool and crossed one knee over the other. "I'd like to tell you that we can predict anything about what will

happen, but I can't. I will say that Manny and I are all set, Havers will be on standby, and Ehlena has assisted at over a hundred deliveries. We are ready to help nature take its course—and when they're out, I have two incubators here, as well as breathing assistance equipment that's like nothing I've ever seen before. I understand, and I'm glad, that you all are open to anyone lending a vein if it comes to that. And the good news is that the babies are tracking perfectly at this moment in time. We're prepared, and that's the best position we can be in. Bear in mind, though, that there could be months and months left to go. The two-week mark from now is just the bare minimum for survival. I'm hoping they stay where they are for another six months, at least."

Layla looked down at her belly and wondered how much more space she had to give. She already felt as though her lungs were crammed up under her collarbones and her bladder was somewhere south of her knees. Whatever it took, though. Whatever the young needed.

As Qhuinn and Blay got to their feet, there was some lighthearted conversation, something about Rhage and Mary flooding their bathroom, and then there were hugs good-bye as the males left.

Doc Jane sat back down on her stool. "Okay, so what do you want to ask me?"

"I'm sorry?" Layla pushed her hair back over her shoulder. "About?"

"You've been my patient for how long now? I can read you—which Qhuinn and Blay probably could, too, if they weren't so worried about you and the babies."

Layla fiddled with the fluffy lapel of her robe. "It's nothing about the pregnancy. I feel better about everything there."

"So . . ."

"Well, ah, Luchas and I were wondering." Layla smiled in what she hoped was a nonchalant way. "You know, he and I don't have a lot to talk about down here. Other than how big I'm getting and how hard PT is for him."

Doc Jane nodded. "You two are both working really hard."

"So how is the prisoner doing?" Layla put her hands out. "I know it's none of my business—well, our business. We're just curious. And I didn't ask in front of Qhuinn and Blay because they want me to exist in a bubble where nothing worries me and, you know, there is no ugliness to speak of in the world. I just thought maybe you could tell Luchas and me what's going on with him now that he's been moved. Has he recovered from his strokes?"

Doc Jane shook her head. "I shouldn't have said anything."

"Is he still alive?"

"I'm not going to answer that. I'm sorry, Layla. I know you must be curious, I get it. But I just can't go there."

"Can you at least tell me if he lives?"

Doc Jane took a deep breath. "I can't. I'm sorry. Now, if you'll excuse me? Time for me to have something to eat."

Layla lowered her eyes. "I apologize. I don't mean to force the issue."

"It's all right—and don't worry about anything other than taking care of yourself and those kidlets, okay?" Doc Jane patted her on the knee. "Do you need help getting back down the corridor?"

Layla shook her head. "No, thank you."

Shifting off the table and onto the floor, she rearranged her robing, left the exam room and started the shuffle back to where she stayed. As a prevailing guilt dogged her, she told herself it was what happened when you made bad choices—

From out of nowhere, her belly tightened front to back, to the point where she stopped and sagged against the corridor wall. A moment later, though, the invisible band was gone as if it had never been, nothing lingering in its place—and she suffered no dreaded loss of bladder control, either.

It was fine.

"You guys okay in there?" she whispered to her belly as she stroked it in a circle.

When someone kicked as if they were answering, she was incredibly relieved.

Doc Jane was correct: She needed to focus on what she was doing here—eating well, sleeping well, and making sure she wasn't responsible for anything going wrong that was within her control.

Besides, it was better for everyone if she let this Xcor thing go.

On so many levels.

As she resumed her rocking walk, she cursed. Why did she have to have the same conversation with herself over and over again?

After Vishous left Rhage in the alley, he rematerialized on the mansion's front steps, grabbed a set of car keys from Fritz and took Qhuinn's Hummer back down the mountain. Cueing up the sound system, he

mellowed out with some old-school Goodie Mob, cranking "Soul Food" before he slid into some 'Pac. He didn't light up. That would be rude.

See, he was a fucking peach. A real stand-up motherfucker.

When he got to the road at the base of the compound's property, he hit the accelerator and roared toward the twin bridges downtown. Twenty minutes later, he headed over the river, took the first exit on the far side and proceeded onto a thin road that followed the shore to the north.

Assail's glass house was on a peninsula that jutted out into the Hudson, and V pulled into the rear parking area by the banks of garage doors. As he killed the lights and the engine, he remembered a different night when he had come here, all kinds of chaos reigning—especially after Wrath had been shot in the fucking throat.

Goddamn nightmare.

The back door opened and Assail stepped out of the modern mansion, dressed like he was going to a French restaurant for dinner—except for the fact that his tie was hanging out of one of his side pockets.

"You ready for me?" V asked as he lit up.

"Always. But you're going to want to pull in, if you do not mind."

On cue, one of the garage doors began to roll up, revealing a brightly lit interior with a van, a black Range Rover, and a spot for Qhuinn's whip.

"Gimme a minute," V said as he took another drag.

Assail laughed. "Alas, I am in need as well. For something different, however."

The male turned away, as if the dirty little secret he stroked off by sniffing up one nostril and then the other was going to be cooooompletely missed.

V smiled through his own exhale. "That monkey's riding you so hard, true."

Assail tucked his vial back into his jacket's inside pocket. "Cannot you smoke in the vehicle?"

"Not my ride. And hey, at least your little problem doesn't need an air freshener."

As the male rubbed his nose, once . . . twice . . . and again, V frowned as he caught a scent on the air. "You got a bleed there, buddy."

Next thing you knew, Assail had taken that perfectly nice silk tie, which was the color of the inside of a cantaloupe and covered with some kind of pattern, and pressed it to his schnoz. Because it was either that or ruin that fancy-schmancy shirt and jacket of his.

Vishous lifted one shitkicker, stabbed his hand-rolled out on the tread, and put the smudged butt into the pocket of his leather jacket.

"Back up, asshole." He shoved the guy against the SUV, forced his jaw up and took over holding the tie in place. "How often does this happen?"

As Assail made some kind of a sound, V rolled his eyes and pinched the SOB's nose. "Whatever, this is your lucky night. I'm a medic, and I'm going to look in there as soon as you stop doing this imitation of a golf sprinkler. And you can shut it unless it's a thank-you."

The two of them stood out there in the cold for a while. From time to time, Assail muttered some shit, which came out sounding like Pee-wee Herman, but V ignored him.

"Here, hold this," V muttered. "And don't move."

V put the guy's fingers where his had been. Then he ducked into the Hummer and got the Swiss army knife that Qhuinn kept in the cup holders up front. Back at his patient, he snagged his phone, turned on its flashlight, and moved Assail's hand out of the way.

Using the flat part of the biggest knife blade as a separator, he looked into the nostrils that had been worked so hard.

Clicking the beam off, he wiped the blade on his leathers and snapped it back in its slot. "You have a nicely perforated septum. Do you have trouble sleeping? Any of the cast of thousands you're fucking tell you you snore?"

"I sleep alone. And I do not sleep much."

"You have trouble breathing? Any sense of smell left?"

"I can smell. And I haven't thought about breathing."

"Well, my advice, not that you'll hear it, is to stop with the snorting. Or you can make shit so bad in there that surgery is not only your sole option, but possibly ineffective."

Assail stared off into the forest without focusing.

"Not so easy, is it." V shook his head. "Creeps up on you."

Crossing his arms over his chest, Assail crushed the bloodstained tie in his fist. "I find myself in a curious prison. One of my own manufacture, as it were. The trouble appears to be that whilst I was constructing it, I was wholly unaware of the bars I set around myself. They have proven to be rather . . . enduring, as it were."

"How much are you doing? For real."

It was a while before the guy answered. And when Assail finally did, it was clear the delay had been a result of the enormous addition and multiplication involved in the math.

Talk about carrying the ones and the fives.

Vishous whistled softly. "Okay, I'ma be straight with you. Although your average vampire has a tremendous leg up on humans when it comes to health, you can still blow your heart up doing that much. Or your brain. At the very least, at this level, you're going to get seriously paranoid, if you aren't already, and no wonder you can't sleep."

Assail rubbed under his nose, and then looked at the blood that had dried on his fingers.

"When you're ready," V said, "call us. You're going to want to detox under medical supervision and we can do this discreetly. And don't waste my time or yours denying the extent of your problem or trying to pretty this shit up. You got yourself an ugly parasite, and if you don't get on top of it, it's going to get on top of you. Your grave, specifically."

"How long?"

"Do you have before you tach out and wake up dead?"

"Does the detox last?"

"Depends on how well it's managed. The physical withdrawal isn't life-threatening, but the psychological shit is going to make you wish you were dead."

Assail remained silent for quite a while, and since V itched for a cigarette, he gave in and lit one up.

"I know about addictions." V glanced at the glowing end of his hand-rolled. "Thank God vampires don't get cancer, true? So I'm not judging you. And you know where to find me when you're ready."

"Maybe I am getting paranoid."

"How so?"

"I was at Naasha's house before I came here."

"And?"

The male shook his head back and forth. "I had this sense of impending death in that house."

"That *hellren* of hers is in poor health."

"Indeed." Assail glanced over, his silvery, moonlight-colored eyes flashing. "But it wouldn't surprise me if he was helped into his state of ashes. Or at least that was what I was thinking earlier."

"Inheritances are powerful things."

"Aye." Assail shook himself as if he were pulling back from an internal ledge. "Would you care to pick up your guns the now?"

Vishous exhaled a stream of smoke away from the guy. "That's why I'm here."

"Please move your vehicle inside when you're ready. We shall load you up there."

As Assail looked over, V cut him off. "I got your money—don't worry. And the medical advice is free."

"Such a gentlemale you are, Vishous."

"Not even close. Now let's get this over with."

FORTY-SEVEN

As the Brotherhood household gathered for Last Meal in the grand dining room, Mary went over and sat next to Marissa. "You mind if we talk a little shop before we eat?"

Marissa put her wineglass down and nodded with a glowing smile. "I'm sorry I left work early tonight, but Butch took me out for a date."

"Oh, you guys deserve it! Where'd you go?"

"Nowhere special. Just a pizza place in the suburbs. He was right—it was the best pepperoni-and-onion I've ever had. He's helping V unpack some supplies and then he'll be here just for the conversation as I am. It was so good to just have a little time off together, you know?"

"Totally. Rhage and I are going out tomorrow night, actually." Mary cleared her throat. "Which is part of what I need to talk to you about. I've finally made a breakthrough with Bitty."

"You did?" Marissa leaned in for a quick hug. "I knew you could do it! That's wonderful. There's so much for her to process."

"Yes." Mary eased back. "But there's something I want to have checked out. Medically, that is. It's not emergent or anything . . . it's just that she's thirteen, not nine."

As Marissa's brows jumped in surprise, the female murmured, "Are you sure?"

Mary went into everything, including what Bitty had said about her mom telling her to lie about her age, and the visit to the grave site and the supermarket.

Marissa frowned. "You took her to your mother's grave?"

"She wanted to see it. She asked to. Her treatment is going to have to involve more than just sitting in a chair talking. She's incredibly intelligent, but she's led a life that has been so remote, so full of violence that if she's got any hope of getting through her grieving in one piece and transitioning into the world, she's going to need exposure."

"There are group field trips to accomplish things like that."

"She'd never been to a supermarket before." As Marissa recoiled, Mary nodded. "She didn't know what automatic doors were. She'd never seen downtown. She didn't tell me at the time, but when Rhage and I took her for ice cream last night? She'd never been in a restaurant or a café before."

"I had no idea."

"No one did." Mary looked at the thirty-foot-long dining room table with all its finery. "She and her mother kept quiet because they were afraid. And the thing is, I'm worried about Bitty's health. I know that she had treatment at Havers's for that broken leg, and there was a work-up at that point. But that was a while ago. I want someone to take a look at her sometime soon, and I want to bring her to the clinic here, not to Havers's."

As Marissa started to protest, Mary put her hand up. "Hear me out. Her mother just died there. You think she needs to head back to that facility anytime soon? And yes, it can wait a month or two, but you've seen how frail she is. Even if you assume vampires are under-developed compared to humans of similar age until the change, she's alarmingly small. Ehlena has a great background with young vampires, Doc Jane has a perfect bedside manner, and we can easily bring Bitty into the training center, do the work-up there, and take her out again as soon as it's over."

Marissa fiddled with her fork. "I can see the logic."

"We can even do it tomorrow night if Doc Jane has some time. We're taking Bitty to dinner with us."

"You and Rhage?"

"It's just like the ice cream trip. She really likes him." Mary smiled. "She calls him a big friendly dog."

Marissa's frown did not inspire confidence. And neither did the period of silence that was filled with talk from other people as folks filed into the room in pairs and small groups.

"Marissa. I know what I'm doing here. And more to the point, the proof that I'm on the right track with her is the fact that she's finally opening up. She's been with us for how long?"

"Look, I'm not qualified to tell you how to do your job—and I guess that's my problem. I'm a manager, I make the trains run on time. I do not have a master's in social work—so I'd like to talk to some of the others. You're very good at your job, and I can't argue with the results, especially in Bitty's case. But I don't want you to get in over your head—and I'm a little worried about that."

"How so?" Mary put her hands up. "I admit I might have treated the situation with her mother's passing in a different way if I'd known—"

"You're taking an orphan out for ice cream. To your mother's grave site. To dinner with your mate. You don't think there's a possibility that you're doing this for reasons that are personal in nature?"

"Lemme see. Come on, lemme see."

Out in front of the mansion, Rhage elbowed Butch's body to the side so he could check out what was in the back of the Hummer. When he got a gander at the display of hardware, he laughed under his breath.

"Not bad." He picked up one of the Glock autoloaders out of its egg-carton padding and ran a check on it, popping out the clip, pumping the trigger, assessing the weight and sight. "How many did you get?"

V popped a second steel briefcase. "There are another eight in here. Sixteen total."

"What was the price?" Butch demanded as he snagged another weapon and put it through the same workout.

"Ten thousand." V opened a black nylon duffel and showed off the boxes of ammo. "There's no discount on them, but there are also no numbers, and we didn't have to worry about dealing with legit human channels."

Rhage nodded. "Fritz has got to be on some kind of watch list by now."

"What else can we get from them?" Butch asked as he palmed up a third, the sound of metal-on-metal rising from his quick hands.

"Like they have a catalog or some shit?" V shrugged. "I'm thinking ask and ye shall receive."

"Can we BOGO some rocket launchers?" Rhage asked. "Or, I'm telling you, we could use some anti-aircraft guns."

Butch punched Rhage's biceps. "If he gets anti-aircraft, I want a cannon."

"You two are a pair of fuck sticks, you know that?"

Rhage took the duffel with the ammo, and Butch took the two suitcases so V could lock up and light up. They were about halfway across the cobblestones when V hesitated. Wobbled. Shook his head.

"What's doing?" Butch asked.

"Nothing." The brother kept going, taking the stone steps two at a time and opening the vestibule's door. As he put his puss in the security camera, he muttered, "Just hungry."

"I feel you on that one." Rhage rubbed his belly. "I need food stat."

The comment was casual. The look he and Butch shared was not. The reality, however, was that even Brothers could be hypoglycemic, and not everything was an emergency. Going by the cop's grim expression, he was going to be on it, though, when he and V went back to the Pit for the day.

"Where you want this stuff, V? In the tunnel?"

When Vishous nodded, Rhage took the suitcases from Butch and walked the load behind the grand staircase to the hidden door to the tunnel. Unlocking things by entering the code, he placed the load of metal and lead on the landing and triple-checked that things re-locked as he shut the panel once again. With Nalla crawling, nobody took any chances with guns or ammo, even when the shit was separated.

Doubling back, he headed for the dining room.

Inside the beautiful space, there was lots of chatter and laughing, with people everywhere, and *doggen* making sure drinks were served before they brought out the food. Mary was over by Marissa, and at first Rhage started to go around to them, but then he caught the tension and backed off, taking his normal chair across the way.

Meanwhile, Mary was leaning into her boss, speaking urgently. Marissa nodded. Then shook her head. Then spoke. And now it was Mary's turn again.

Had to be about work.

Maybe even about Bitty?

Manny pulled up a chair. "How we doing, young man?"

"Hey, old fart. Where's your better half?"

"Payne's having a lie-down. I tired her out, if you get what I mean."

The two pounded knuckles, and then Rhage went back to trying to look as if he weren't lip-reading. Which, P.S., wasn't going that well.

"Cabbage nightmare, juicing machine cassette player," Mary said.

"Movie magic twelve times a day." Marissa took a sip from her wineglass. "Then tennis with the can-can. Peanuts and Philly steak, bagel bagel cream cheese."

"Saran wrap?"

"Toothpaste."

"Garage bay, Christmas bikini wannabe Grape Nuts with Dr Pepper."

"Fuck me," he muttered. And considering how many food references his brain was pulling out of their mouth positions, he was *so* ready to eat.

Mary eventually got up and the two nodded. Then his *shellan* came around to him.

"You okay?" he asked as he pulled out her chair.

"Oh, yes. Yes." She smiled at him and then sat down and stared at her empty plate. "Sorry. I'm just . . ."

"What can I do to help?"

Turning to him, she rubbed her face. "Tell me that everything's going to be okay?"

Rhage pulled her into his lap and ran his palm up and down her outer thigh. "I promise you. Everything is going to be fine. Whatever it is, we'll make it fine."

The *doggen* of the house filed in with silver trays of roast beef and potatoes, chicken and rice, and some steaming veggies and sauces. As Mary shifted back onto her own seat, he was bummed, but he understood where she was coming from. He would just end up feeding her until she was stuffed while he starved—and then he would wolf everything that wasn't nailed down before dessert came.

They'd been through this before.

"Sire," a *doggen* said behind him. "There is a special preparation for you."

Even though he was worried about his Mary, Rhage clapped his palms and rubbed them. "Fantastic. I'm ready to eat this entire table."

A second member of the staff removed his charger and pushed his silverware setting wide. Then a large silver platter with a cloche was placed in front of him.

"Wassup, Hollywood?" someone said. "Our food not good enough for you?"

"Yo, Rhage, you get your own cow or something?"

"I thought you were on Jenny Craig," another voice called out.

"I think he's eating Jenny Craig—and that shit is just wrong. Humans are not food."

He gave everyone the middles, and popped the lid—

"Oh, come on!" he barked as laughter exploded in the air. "Seriously? You guys are serious. *Really.*"

A snorkel and a diving mask had been arranged with care on a porcelain platter, little sprigs of parsley and lemon wedges tucked in around the edges.

Mary started laughing, and the only thing that saved his brothers was that she threw her arms around his meatheaded neck and kissed him.

"That's a good one," she said against his mouth. "Come on, you know it is."

"You flood one goddamn bathroom, and suddenly, it's a theme—"

"Shh, just kiss me, okay?"

He was still grumbling, but he did what his *shellan* told him to. It was either that or ruin his appetite . . . . by commiting murder.

FORTY-EIGHT

"You realize that he's married."

It was around midday that Jo jumped in her receptionist chair and frowned. Bryant was leaning on the counter over her desk, his face dead serious, his bow tie so perfectly done, it looked like it was a sculpted piece of plastic rather than anything made from silk.

"What are you talking about?" She handed him a file. "And this is for your one-thirty."

"Bill. He's married."

"What are you—excuse me?"

"Look." Bryant made a show of running his manicure around the edges of the legal-size folder. "I saw you, okay. At a stoplight. You were in his car. I just don't want you to get hurt."

For the first time in recorded history, Jo sat back and really looked at the guy. Funny, his aura was actually a good eraser of some minor flaws that she'd missed before: His eyes were a little too close together; his upper lip had a curious overhang; that nose had a bump at the end.

"I'm only worried about you," he concluded. Like an older brother.

Jo crossed her arms over her chest. Come to think of it, his voice had a reedy quality that was kind of grating.

"Hello?" he prompted. As if he'd banked on a specific reaction and was determined to get it. "Jo. Did you hear what I said?"

It was definitely time to move on, she decided. Polish up her résumé. Get on Monster.com and the *CCJ* website. Do something else.

She had spent a good year and a half mooning over this narcissist, living off of a wink or an implication from him, bending over backward to make his professional and personal lives run smoothly—and, ultimately, checking her libido at the door because this one-sided sexual tension with a jerk was a safer bet than trying to find a real guy of her own.

"I'm giving you my two weeks' notice."

"What."

"You heard me."

"Wait, are you crazy? You're quitting because I tell you your boyfriend has a wife? When you already knew it? The closing was here in this office. You met her—"

"It's got nothing to do with Bill. He and I are working on a story together." Okay, that was a stretch. "I just need more than you can give me."

"Is this about the real estate exam? Fine, if you insist on taking it—"

"It's really not anything like that." She glanced at her computer. "And it's noon, so I'm taking lunch."

With quick work on the office phone, she routed the main number to voice mail, picked up her purse from the floor, and walked around the partition. Bryant moved into her path like he wanted to argue, but she just shook her head.

"You'd better start looking for a new receptionist if you want me to have any time to train her."

"Jo. You are acting in a really unprofessional way."

Dropping her voice, she said, "You have me lie to the women you're dating so they don't find out what a douche bag you are. I pick up your dry cleaning. Make your haircut appointments. I've taken your car in to be serviced how many times? And don't get me started on your condominium association's complaints for your noise violations, your pool boy, your HVAC issues and the bug man. All of *that* is unprofessional. But don't worry. You'll find yourself another sucker. Men like you always do. It's just not going to be me anymore."

Jo walked out the glass doors and into the October sun—which

was too weak to move the temperature much, but was bright enough to make her take out her Ray-Bans.

Getting in her VW, she was not surprised that Bryant didn't come after her—no doubt he was onto the next dinner date crisis. Or maybe he was checking his hair in his private bathroom. Or who the heck knew what he was doing. One thing she did know? It wasn't going to have anything to do with her.

It never had been about her, at least not on his side. And the stuff he'd said about Bill? That was just a self-protective reflex because she was a good lackey and he didn't want her slipping away.

But as she'd said, there would be another. No doubt.

As Jo drove off, she looked at the real estate office in her rearview and thought of Bill and his cousin Troy. They were nice enough guys, but not really anything that truly caught her eye.

When was she going to meet a real man?

Whatever. She needed to find a job, and then there was the whole vampire thing to spin her wheels about.

Taking out her phone, she called Bill. "I'm heading out to the farm now if you want to meet me."

"You ready to turn in?"

At the sound of Rhage's voice, Mary jerked on the sofa, kicking the blanket that had been pulled over her legs onto the floor. Sitting up, she glanced around the billiards room, and then looked at Rhage, who was leaning over her.

"I fell asleep. Where did everyone go? Is the tournament over?"

He nodded as he sat on the coffee table and balanced his pool cue on his forefinger. "Butch won. The bastard. He and V just headed to the Pit."

With a big yawn, she pushed her hair back. The massive T.V. over the fireplace was muted, some kind of Steven Seagal throwback movie from the early nineties showing him punching out a bunch of guys on a city street.

"I think that was what was on when I crashed," she said idly as she pointed to the screen

"Actually, that was three movies ago." Rhage stroked her cheek. "This is a different one, but don't feel bad. They all look the same. You going to let me carry you up?"

"I can make it myself."

"I know." He put the cue aside and offered her a hand. "The question is, will you stop me from picking you up?"

She smiled. "No."

Rhage drew her off the sofa, and the next thing she knew, she was in his strong arms and he was striding in between the pool tables. Out in the foyer, she yawned again and got comfy for the trip.

"You are too good to me," she murmured.

"Not even by half."

Up on the second floor, he stopped in front of the closed door of their room, and she bent down and opened the way in for them. With no effort at all, he took her over to the bed and laid her out on her side of the mattress.

"Can you brush my teeth for me?" she asked. "That is the real question."

"You got it."

As he went to turn away, she laughed. "That was a rhetorical."

"I was going to bring you your brush and a glass of water." He put his hands on his hips and stared down at her. "Unless you're determined to make it to the sink?"

Boy, he was a fantastic-looking male specimen, she thought as she measured his enormous shoulders and bulging arms, his flat stomach and lean pelvis, those long, powerful legs. And then there was that blond hair, those brilliant Bahamian blue eyes, that bone structure that seemed drawn by a master artist as opposed to something that had been born into this world.

"Mary?"

"Just admiring the view."

"Oh?" He pivoted and flashed his ass. "You like?"

"Very much. How 'bout you take that shirt off for me?"

Glancing over his shoulder, he narrowed his eyes. "Are you coming on to me?"

"Why, yes, I believe I am."

He turned back around, grabbed the front of his muscle shirt, and growled, "Say please first."

"Pleeeeeeeeeeeeease—"

Riiiiiiip. And then his bare chest was on display, all that musculature throwing shadows in the dim light from the lamp on the bureau.

Rhage moved his hand down between his legs, gripping the hard

length that had made a very serious appearance in the front of his leathers. "You want to see something else?" he drawled.

"Yes," she breathed.

His fingers were slow on the button fly, teasing her as he revealed his erection inch by inch until it popped free and jutted straight out at her.

Mary reached down herself and disappeared her pants, spreading her legs as he stood back and stroked himself.

"Come here," she said.

Rhage was up on that bed of theirs, up on her, in the work of a moment, and she guided him to her, bringing his head to her core. With a moan, she wrapped her legs around his ass, and he moved with force, joining them, rocking against her with increasing speed, going hard until the bed creaked and the pillows got bounced off and the duvet waded up beneath her.

As she grabbed onto his back, she felt the beast surge under her nails, the tattoo rising up and creating a pattern in his skin as if it wanted to get out.

"Mary," Rhage said into her neck. "Oh, fuck, *Mary . . .*"

At the sound of his hoarse voice, an orgasm hit her like a lightning strike, the pleasure making her call out as he punched his pelvis into her again and again while he ejaculated.

When they finally went still, she stroked his spine, petting the beast, which surged under her touch. And it was so strange. In moments like this, even though it was crazy, it seemed like the three of them were together.

"Would you like to come shower with me?" Rhage asked as he nuzzled her throat. "I can think of some fun things to do with the soap."

"Really? Do tell."

"Cleanliness is next to godliness—isn't that the human expression?"

Mary yawned and stretched, feeling him still inside. "I have an idea. You get started and I'll be right in."

"Perfect."

After a couple of lingering kisses, Rhage pulled out and got up. Ditching the leathers from his lower legs, he walked buck naked into their bathroom.

Talk about a view.

He was like a walking Greek statue.

The shower came on, and she caught a whiff of the shampoo they used, and then the soap . . . and then the conditioner.

Motivating herself, she stretched once more and got out of bed. By the time she made it into the bathroom, Rhage was leaning back under the spray, rinsing his hair. With a quick strip, she took off her shirt and then she was in with him, his slick, aroused body glistening in the light from the mirrors.

"There she is," he murmured as he pulled her in close.

It was a while before they got out, and by the end of it, her legs were so loose, it was a good thing she didn't have far to go. Wrapped in Rhage's robe, she padded over to the bureau to take out her pearl earrings while he went to the laundry hamper in their walk-in closet with the clothes they'd left everywhere.

She'd taken one of the studs out when she noticed the folder. "What's this?"

"What's what?" he said from the closet.

Opening the front cover . . .

. . . she felt the breath leave her lungs.

FORTY-NINE

When Rhage came out of the walk-in, he was feeling really damn good about life. Yeah, sure, the cop had prevailed at pool again, but after what his Mary had just treated him with? He was the true winner.

That shower sesh had been straight-up Olympian, top-of-the-mountain, land-speed-record stuff.

Walking out, he . . .

. . . stopped where he was.

Mary was sitting in the chair beside their bureau, her little pink feet on the carpet, her body engulfed by his bathrobe, her head down with her damp hair hanging forward. In her lap, open wide, was a folder that Rhage didn't recognize.

But he knew what she was looking at.

Rhage went back into the closet and pulled on a pair of nylon track pants. On second thought, he added that *AHS* sweatshirt he'd worn the other night. Coming back out, he walked over to the bed and sat down.

Mary looked up when she got to the last page. "What is this? I mean . . ." She shook her head. "I think I know what it is. I just . . ."

Rhage gripped the edge of the mattress and leaned into his arms. Strangely, the antiques in the room, the heavy drapes, the pattern in the carpet, it all became much too clear, everything around him sharpening to the point that he winced.

"I didn't ask Saxton to print all that out," he blurted.

"Adoption papers? That's what these are, aren't they? I mean, I'm not completely versed in the Old Language, but I can catch the drift."

"Look, we don't have to do anything with them. It's not like . . . I mean, I'm not suggesting we adopt her. I asked Vishous if he could help find her uncle—yes, I know you didn't tell me to, but I thought if any of my brothers could help, it was him. He went into some databases kept at the Audience House and found nothing. Checked some other places, too. There was no trace of anything, no family, no uncle. And, ah, I talked to him about you and me and the kid thing. He was the one who brought up the adoption process and then followed through with it on his own."

Mary closed the folder and laid her hand on it. When she didn't say anything further, he cursed. "I'm sorry. Maybe I should have talked to you first about my going to Vishous—"

"Marissa thinks I'm over-involved. With Bitty, that is. That's what we were going back and forth about before Last Meal. She thinks I'm crossing professional lines, making it too personal."

"Wow."

"And even though I argued with her . . . she's right. I am."

Rhage's heart skipped a beat from dread. "What are you saying?"

There was a long period of quiet. And then she shrugged. "I've been around a lot of young people. Not just at Safe Place, but also before, when I was working with my autistic kids." She looked over. "Do you remember when I was staying at Bella's? And I told you I didn't want to see you anymore?"

Rhage closed his eyes, memories of that horrible confrontation coming back to him. For some reason, he remembered the quilt in that guestroom she'd been sleeping in, that handmade quilt with its blocks and slices of color. Mary had been on the bed when he'd come in. And even though she had been just across the way from him, he'd felt as if they were a world apart.

"Yes," he said roughly. "I remember."

"I was in so much pain that I couldn't imagine bringing anyone down with me. I was blocked off, closed up, ready to go lose the battle

that I really wasn't interested in fighting anymore. I pushed you hard. But you came anyway. You came and . . . and in you, I saw a beacon I couldn't turn away from."

I'm not okay.

In his mind, he heard her say those words. Felt her body nearly tackle his as she ran out of that house after him as he'd stood there, holding the moon in his palm just as she'd shown him to.

"I guess I've felt as though Bitty was like me. I mean, for the last however long I've known her, she's been completely closed up. Even when her mother was around, she was like this insular little creature, watching, pushing people away, closing herself off. And after the abuse, and then the deaths? I never blamed her. I just wanted desperately to reach her. It was like . . . well, in retrospect, I think I've been trying to save my old self."

"She really opened up last night," Rhage offered. "At least, I felt like she did. I wouldn't know, though—"

"That was my point to Marissa. I don't know if the normal proto-cols of treatment would have reached her. And she is responding. I took her to my mom's grave. Then we bought M&M's at the local Hannaford. She is just beginning a very hard journey and I don't want to stop helping her."

"Is Marissa reassigning you?" he demanded.

"No, she just thinks I'm emotionally involved—and I am, I admit it. Bitty's special to me."

Rhage glanced down at the folder, which Mary had brought to her chest and held in place—in a way that he wasn't sure she was aware of.

"Mary."

When she finally looked up, he felt like he was leaping off a cliff. The good news? If he had to be flying through mid-air with anyone, he could think of nobody better than his *shellan*.

"We could give her a good home."

As Mary's eyes grew watery, he got up and went to her, kneeling down in front of his *shellan* and putting his hands on her legs.

"You don't want to say it, do you," he whispered.

She took a shuddering breath. And then shook her head. "It wasn't supposed to happen for us. We were just talking about it. It's not . . . supposed to happen for us. The parent thing."

"Says who?"

Mary opened her mouth. Then it shut as she held those papers

even harder to her heart. "I was okay with it. I really was. I really . . . with me never being a mother."

As her tears started to fall, Rhage reached up and wiped his love's face. "It's okay if you can't say it. Because I'll say it for you. You would be . . . the most wonderful *mahmen* to that little girl. Bitty would be so lucky to have you in her life."

The words he spoke seemed to crush her in some way, and he knew exactly how she was feeling. He had been prepared to come to terms with missing out on a huge part of life, because among the many blessings he had been given, being a father was not among them. And yes, it was a sort of cruelty to have that door that he had so resolutely closed get knocked on so soon.

But there was one thing he knew for damn sure.

If by some miracle they were called upon by fate to step up to the plate for that little girl? He was going to be there without hesitation. And he knew without asking that his Mary was going to be the same.

Parents.

It would be a miracle.

Mary was surprised by the great, yawning chasm of pain that had opened up in the center of her chest.

And as she thought about it all, she decided, yes, it was entirely possible that she might have been sublimating the whole child-less thing . . . self-medicating an unacknowledged agony with honest good works that served those who needed help during their most vulnerable moments.

With a shudder, she leaned forward and Rhage was there to catch her as she fell off the chair and into his lap on the floor. As his arms wrapped around her and held her close, she hugged that folder full of papers as tightly as she could.

It had been too terrifying to admit to herself, or to Rhage, the idea that had been kindling in her heart over the last year. But a maternal yearning had taken root at some point along the journey with Bitty— although Mary had been careful never to infringe or intrude upon the true mother/daughter bond, or even acknowledge her feelings in her own mind.

She had, however, from time to time, wondered what the little girl would do if she were left alone in the world.

And yes, there might have been an occasional daydream about bringing her into their lives.

It was no doubt why, on the night of the death, Mary had driven toward the compound and the mansion instead of Safe Place.

But she had known that such feelings were not appropriate or professional, so she had said nothing, done nothing, acted no differently than she did around the other young she worked with.

Her heart had been on another page, though.

Easing back, she looked up into Rhage's handsome face. "What did Vishous say about the uncle?"

Even though she'd thought she'd heard him tell her that V had come up with nothing also.

"He said he could find no one by that name. And no formally recorded details of Bitty, her mother, or any family, either." Rhage wiped beneath her eyes with his thumbs; then dried her tears on his sweatshirt. "She really is orphaned."

They were quiet for a while. And then Mary said, "It won't all be fun trips to the ice cream parlor."

"I know."

"And she might not want to come live with us."

"I know."

"But you like her, right? She's special, right?"

"Very." He laughed in a short burst. "I think I decided I wanted to adopt her when she ordered that waffle cone."

"What?"

"Long story. But it just . . . it kind of feels like it's supposed to be."

"That's what I think."

Rhage moved around so that he was leaning back against the wall, and she settled in between his legs, easing up against his chest. Maybe they should have moved over to the bed. It would have been more comfortable, after all. But the sense that some tremendous shift was occurring in their lives made it seem safer to stay on the ground—just in case the earthquake happening for both of them on an emotional level translated into the physical world somehow.

The damn thing would level the mansion into a pile of rubble.

"This is going to be a process, Rhage. It can't happen overnight. There are going to have to be things we need to do, together and apart, to make sure this is real."

But all that was just rhetoric.

In her heart, as far as she was concerned, the decision had been made.

Mary sat up and twisted around. "Do you want to be her father? I mean, I know where I stand—"

"*It would be my honor and privilege.*" He placed his dagger hand over his heart as he spoke in the Old Language. "*It would be a duty that I would seek to fulfill all the nights I am upon this earth.*"

Mary took a deep breath. And then cursed. "We're going to have to explain to her what . . . I am. What you have."

Oh, God, what if his beast and her . . . existential situation . . . precluded them from being prospective parents? And who made that decision? And where did they go to figure out how to do this?

With a groan, she fell back against Rhage's strength. And it was funny . . . as she felt the pads of his muscles all around her, she knew that he would stand beside her for however long it took, never ducking from a challenge, pressing on with purpose and focus, going until they crossed the finish line.

That was just how he was made. He didn't quit. Ever.

"I love you," she said as she stared straight ahead.

"I love you, too." He tucked her hair behind her ear and massaged her shoulders. "And, Mary . . . it's all going to be okay. I promise."

"They might not let us have her. Even if she wants us."

"Why?"

"You know why. We're not exactly 'normal,' Rhage."

"Who is?"

"People who are alive in the conventional sense. And don't have a beast who lives inside their body."

As he fell silent, she felt bad, as if she'd ruined something. But they needed to be realistic.

Except Rhage just shrugged. "So we'll get counseling. Or some shit."

Mary laughed a little. "Counseling?"

"Sure. What the hell. I can talk about how I feel about the beast. And maybe he can eat a couple of counselors so he can internalize their constructive comments. I mean, jeez, acupuncture the fuck out of me and maybe the dragon will turn into a bunny or a titmouse or—"

"A titmouse."

"Yeah, or like, a gopher. It could end up like a giant purple gopher who's, like, a vegetarian." As Mary started laughing harder, he stroked her arms. "What about a Cavalier King Charles spaniel."

"Oh, come on—"

"No, no, I got it. I know what it's going to be."

Mary rolled over in his lap and smiled up at him. "Be gentle. I've had a rough morning. Well, except for the shower part. That wasn't hard at all."

Rhage held up his forefinger. "Okay, first of all, something was hard in there. And you know that firsthand." As she laughed again, he nodded. "Uh-huh. That's right. And as for the beast's alter identity—how about an enormous purple jack-alope."

"They don't exist!"

"Fine. A snape."

"Also doesn't exist."

"Then I could make the dreams of snape hunters worldwide come true." Rhage smiled. "Who could turn us down then. After I pull a public service like that?"

"You're absolutely right." She stroked his face. "We need to put the acupuncture/jack-alope plan into immediate effect."

Rhage scrunched down and kissed her. "I love it when we're on the same page. I just love it."

FIFTY

When night fell, Layla was largely nonplussed. One of the disadvantages of living in the training center underground was that she was unable to set her internal clock to the rhythms of the sun and moon. Time was just numbers on a clock face, meals appearing when they did, visitors and traffic coming and going in random patterns that eventually meant little in terms of night and day.

Her sleep had fallen into a cycle of six hours of wakefulness followed by three hours of fitful dreams. Repeat, ad nauseam.

Usually.

This evening, however, as the electronic clock showed a glowing red eight followed by a sixteen after the two vertical dots, she closed her eyes with a purpose beyond that of sleep.

She had agonized over this since her resolution after the ultrasound. Had run the yes's and no's through her brain until she thought she would go mad.

In the end, she had made up her mind, for better or for worse.

Probably for worse. Because that was just how things always went for her when it came to Xcor.

Taking a deep breath, she found that everything irritated her. The

sheets felt itchy. The pillow under her head was not in the correct position, and her moving it up and down didn't help. The weight of her belly seemed enormous, an entity separate from the rest of her body. Her feet twitched as if someone were tickling them with a feather. Her lungs seemed to only partially inflate.

Take out the "seem."

And the darkness of her room amplified everything.

With a curse, she discovered her eyes had opened themselves, and she wished she had tape so she could make her lids stay shut.

Concentrating, she forced herself to breathe slowly and deeply. Relaxed the tension in her body starting at her toes and going to the tips of her ears. Calmed her mind.

Sleep arrived in a gentle wave, submerging her beneath common consciousness, setting her free of the aches and pains, the worry and fear.

The guilt.

She gave herself a moment to enjoy the weightless float. And then she sent her core self, her soul, that magic light that animated her flesh, not just off the hospital bed and out of the room, not just down the corridor and free of the training center . . . but out of the realm of earthly reality.

To the Sanctuary.

Given her pregnancy, it was unsafe for her to travel to the Other Side in her physical form. This way, however, she covered the distance with grace and ease—plus, even as she left her body, she could sense her flesh back under the sheets and was thusly able to continuously monitor her corporeal incarnation. If aught were to occur, she could return in the blink of an eye.

Moments later, she was standing on resplendent green grass. Overhead, the milky sky provided illumination from no definable source, and all around in the distance, a forest ring established the sacred territory's boundaries. White marble temples glowed pristine and fresh as the night they had been called into existence so many millennia ago by the Scribe Virgin, and brilliantly colored tulips and daffodils were like gems spilled from a treasurer's satchel.

Breathing the sweet air, she could feel a recharging happen, and it reminded her of her centuries spent serving the mother of the race up here. Back then, all had been white, no shades or variation in anything, not even shadows thrown. The current Primale, Phury, had changed all that, however, freeing her and her sisters to live lives down below, to experience the world and themselves as individuals, instead of as cogs in a homogeneous whole.

Unconsciously, she put her hands to her belly—and had a fright. Her stomach was flat, and she panicked—only to sense her body's function down on Earth. Yes, she thought. The flesh was with young; the soul was not. And this representation of her was a moving mirage, both existent and nonexistent.

Gathering the folds of her ceremonial robe, she ambulated across the rolling expanse, passing the Primale's private quarters where the impregnations used to occur, and continuing on until she stood on the threshold of the Temple of the Sequestered Scribes.

A quick look around confirmed what had been true not just since her arrival this moment, but for such a time since the Primale had released them all: As beautiful as the Sanctuary was, as much as it had to offer in terms of peace and refreshment, it was as empty and abandoned as a useless factory. A gold mine with no more veins to plunder. A galley with bare cupboards.

For her purposes, this was good.

And in her heart, it was bittersweet. Freedom had led to an abandonment, a cessation of service, an end of the way things were.

Change, however, was more the nature of destiny than anything else. And much good had come from it—although perhaps not for the Scribe Virgin. Who knew how she felt, though, as none had seen her now for how long?

With a solemn prayer, Layla entered the scribing temple and regarded the simple white tables with their bowls of water, their inkwells, their parchment rolls. In the lofty space, no dust drifted from the rafters to cloud the sacred reading pools or fade the edges of things— and yet it seemed that the observation of the race's history, which had once been a sacred duty, was now an abandoned endeavor unlikely to be e'er resumed.

And that seemed to make the temple decayed in some way.

Indeed, it was hard not to think of the great library, which stood not far from here, and picture all of its shelves that were filled with volume after volume of carefully recorded passages, those sacred symbols in the Old Language put to parchment as the scribes had played

witness to the goings-on of the race in these very bowls. And there were further records there: of the Black Dagger Brotherhood and their lineages, of the Scribe Virgin's dictates, of the decisions of the Kings, of the observances of the calendar festivals, and the traditions of the *glymera*, and the respect that had been paid to the Scribe Virgin.

In a way, the lack of any further history record was a death of the race.

But it was also its rebirth. So many positives had come out of the shift in values, with the rights of females being recognized, and the abolishment of blood slavery, and freedom for the Chosen.

The Scribe Virgin had all but disappeared into the spiritual vacuum, however, as if the worship of her had been a sustenance that now, having been removed, had left her diminished into incapacity. And yes, Layla missed parts of the old ways, and worried about their having no spiritual leader at a time of such unrest . . . but fate was larger than not only her, but the race as a whole.

And indeed, its creator.

Walking forward, she went to one of the tables and pulled out a white chair. As she took a seat, she arranged her robing and offered up a prayer that what she was about to do would be in service to a greater good.

Any greater good.

Oh, shoot. It was impossible to argue that what she was about to do wasn't purely self-serving.

Bowing her head, she placed her hands on the bowl, cupping the vessel with reverence. With as much clarity as she could muster, she pictured Xcor's face, from his narrowed eyes to his misshapen upper lip, from his brush-cut hair to his thick neck. She imagined his scent in her nose, and his imposing physical presence before her. She pictured his veined forearms and his blunt, callused hands, his heavy chest and his strong legs.

In her mind, she heard his voice. Saw him move. Caught his eye and held it.

The surface of the water began to move, concentric circles forming to the beat of her heart. And then the swirl started.

A picture appeared, rising out of the depths and stilling the animation of the crystal-clear liquid.

Layla frowned and thought, That makes no sense.

The bowl was showing her shelving, rows and rows of shelves that were stacked with . . . jars of all kinds. There were torches flickering, orange light strobing over what appeared to be a dusty underground environment.

"Xcor . . . ?" she breathed. "Oh . . . dearest Virgin Scribe."

The image she received was as clear as if she stood over his recumbent body. He was lying beneath white sheets on a gurney in the center of the hall of shelves, his eyes shut, his skin pale, his arms and legs unmoving. Machines beeped next to him, ones that she recognized from her own room at the clinic. John Matthew and Blaylock were seated on the stone floor next to him, John's hands moving as he said something.

Blay just nodded.

Layla willed the picture to change so that she could see what was in front of, and behind, where Xcor lay. If she progressed deeper into what turned out to be a cave, she eventually came out into a vast ceremonial space. . . .

The Tomb.

Xcor was in the ante-hall to the Tomb.

Layla willed the image to return to that of John and Blay, and she heard Blay say, "—pressure is going down. So no surgery. But he doesn't look like he's waking up anytime soon."

John signed something.

"I know. But what's the other option?"

Layla asked the bowl to show her the way out, and the image provided a progression in the opposite direction until there was a terminal gate of stout build with steel mesh over its bars—as well as a lock that looked strong enough to keep out even the most determined of invaders. Then she was in a cave's belly, the stone walls shorn by hand or nature, or perhaps a combination of both.

Finally, she was stepping free into a forest of many pines.

Zooming out, she noted the landscape getting smaller and smaller . . . until she caught the glow of the mansion.

So he was still on the property. Not that far away.

Releasing the bowl's edges, she watched as what she had been shown disappeared as if it had never been, the water resuming its clear and anonymous character.

As she sat back, she thought for a good long while.

Then she rose to her feet and left the scribing temple.

She did not return to Earth, however. Not immediately.

*   *   *

"I feel like we're going to get in trouble for something."

As Mary took a seat next to Rhage in the mansion's library, she patted his knee. "You know that's not true."

"Do I look okay?"

Leaning back on the silk sofa, Mary regarded her mate. "Handsome as ever."

"Will that work in our favor?"

"How can it not?" She kissed his cheek. "Just remember not to come on to her. She's your best friend's wife."

"As if. She's fine-looking and all, but so are most of the major appliances in Fritz's kitchen, and I have no interest in humping any of them."

Mary laughed and gave him another squeeze. Then she resumed feeling like her head was going to explode. "So. Yeah. Anywho . . . you know, I've never paid much attention to this room before. It's nice."

As Rhage gave her an *mmm-hmmm*, she glanced around at the shelves of books and the crackling fire and all the rich jewel tones of the carpets, drapes and throw pillows. There was a desk to write at. Sofas to curl up on with a specimen from the collection—or your Kindle, if that was the way you went. A number of oil paintings. And then all kinds of knickknacks that Darius had collected when he'd been alive, from special seashells to rare stones to fossils.

"I can't breathe."

As Rhage put his head between his knees, she rubbed his shoulders, comforting herself as she comforted him, too. Probably wasn't going to help to tell him she was feeling suffocated as well. And a little nauseous.

Marissa came rushing in ten minutes later. "I'm so sorry! I'm sorry I'm—oh, hey, Rhage."

"Hi." Rhage cleared his throat and lifted his palm. "Ah . . . hi. Yeah."

Marissa looked back and forth between them. Then she seemed to compose herself, and closed the doors. "I'd wondered why you wanted to meet here. Now I see."

"Yeah," Rhage said. "I can't . . . well, you know. Go to Safe Place. Which you know . . . because you run it. And—I really need to stop talking here, don't I."

Marissa came over toward the fire, her extraordinary beauty seeming to attract all the illumination and warmth from the hearth. As she took a seat on an armchair, she crossed her legs like the perfect lady she was.

Her face was remote, but not cold. She seemed braced.

This was not going to go well, Mary thought with dread.

"So . . . thank you for meeting with us." Mary took Rhage's hand. "I'm not going to beat around the bush. Rhage and I have been talking, and we'd like to explore the possibility of adopting, or at the very least, fostering Bitty. Before you say no, I'd like you to consider that I have a clinical background in—"

"Wait." Marissa put her hands out. "Wait, this is not about . . . you wanting to quit?"

"*What?*"

Marissa put her hand over her heart and sagged in her seat. "You're not quitting."

"No, good God, where did you get that idea?"

"I just thought that I'd offended you during that conversation before Last Meal. I didn't know whether I'd put my foot in it—I mean, I'm only trying to do right by Bitty and I—" Marissa stopped short. Shook herself. "Did I hear you say *adoption?*"

Mary took a deep breath. And, man, did she squeeze her *hellren's* hand. "Rhage and I talked about it. We want to be parents, and we want to give Bitty a loving home, a place to call her own, a support system that's more than just professional. As you know, I can't have children . . . and Bitty truly is an orphan. Even Vishous couldn't find her uncle."

Marissa blinked a couple of times. Looked back and forth between the pair of them again. "This is . . . extraordinary."

Rhage leaned forward. "Is that good or bad?"

"Good. I mean . . ." Marissa sat back and stared at the fire. "It's wonderful—it's fantastic. I'm just not sure what we need to do."

Wait, was that a "yes"? Mary thought as her heart jumped.

"Bitty gets to have an opinion about it," she said, trying to keep cool. "She's old enough to have an opinion. And I know that it's not going to be easy—the adoption process or the parenting. So does Rhage. I guess, though . . . this kind of all starts with you, you know?"

Without any warning, Marissa burst up out of her seat and threw her arms around first Mary, then Rhage. When she sat back down, she fanned the tears in her eyes.

"I think it's a *really* great idea!"

Okay, Mary started getting a little misty. And she could not look at Rhage—because if he were tearing up, and she was pretty sure he was, it was game over.

"I'm really glad you're behind us," Mary said roughly. "Although I don't know if we're suitable—

Marissa's elegant hand sliced through the air. "I am not worried at all about you two being good parents. And please don't take any pauses on my part as being unsupportive. I've just never had to do anything like this."

Rhage spoke up. "Saxton knows the legal procedure. He got us some paperwork. I think I need an audience in front of the King as a member of the aristocracy—"

Mary put her hands up, all whoooooa. "Wait, wait, we need to have a formal assessment of us both, first. And we have to do even more due diligence on her mother's family—and her father's. And we have to ask her if she's even interested in all this. It's very soon after the death of her mother. I don't want her to think that we're crowding out her blood family or trying to replace someone who will never be replaced. We need to move slowly and be flexible and remain calm. There's also one potential problem."

"What's that?" Marissa asked.

When Mary glanced at Rhage, he cleared his throat. "I eat people. I mean . . . the beast. You know. It eats things. That shouldn't, you know, be eaten."

"He's never been a danger to me," Mary interjected. "But we can't pretend his dragon isn't a factor in all this. Whoever makes the determination of fitness, whether it's you or Wrath or someone else, needs to be fully aware that we come with a three-story-tall, purple-scaled, *lesser*-eating monster."

Rhage raised his hand like he was in class and waiting to get called on. When they both just looked at him, he dropped his arm awkwardly. "Ah, he's never actually consumed anything but *lessers*. Although I do think he tried to eat Vishous." Her *hellren* winced. "Okay, fine, from what I heard, the other night he chased V and Assail into a cabin, which he might have taken the roof off of, and he mighta tried to eat them— but he did *not* succeed."

"Thanks to me," Mary pointed out.

"He listens to Mary. It. Does. I mean." There was a pause. "Shit."

Mary shrugged. "Anyway, we're aware that we're not the most

conventional of prospective parents. But I will promise you . . . if we get the chance, we will love that little girl with everything we've got."

"Ditto," Rhage said. "Completely ditto."

Marissa let out a soft laugh. "Annnnnnnnnnnd this is exactly why I'm not worried about the two of you adopting anything or anyone, whether it's a dog out of a shelter or a child from Safe Place."

Mary exhaled in relief.

Meanwhile, Rhage took a page from Marissa's book and started fanning himself. Then he braced one arm on the coffee table as if he were worried he was about to pass out. "Is it hot in here? I feel like it's hot—I think I'm going to—"

Mary jumped up and raced for one of the French doors. As she popped it open, she said, "He gets a little light-headed sometimes. You know, when he's relieved. Breathe with me, my love. Breathe with me."

Marissa moved across and sat next to Rhage. As she picked up a throw pillow and started flapping it up and down next to that handsome, badly flushed face, she laughed.

"We'll figure it out. Somehow, some way, we'll figure all this out, okay? And hopefully at the end, Bitty will get to come home with you both."

As Mary grabbed another cushion and joined in the effort, she looked into the eyes of the Brother she loved . . . and tried to see the future in his features. "I hope so. God, I hope for that so much it hurts."

FIFTY-ONE

"You want to know what?"

As V posed the perhaps understandable question, Assail switched his cell phone to his other ear and put his coffee mug into the dishwasher. The *doggen* he had hoped to interview this eve—so that his cousins would cease and desist all frozen meals—had had to reschedule. So that meant he remained Mr. Clean-up.

"Master Lock," Assail explained. "I need to know how to release a Master Lock. And it has to be in such a fashion that the thing remains functional thereafter."

The Brother laughed with a hard edge. "Yeah, my first piece of advice would be to shoot the bitch off—and that is not going to help if you want it to keep working. What exactly are you trying to get into?"

"A secret."

"Sounds kinky. And how old are we talking? The lock, not the secret."

"New."

"Okay, yeah, I got something for you. Where are you—"

A subtle chime cut in, and Assail took the cell phone away from his ear. "Ah, yes, here she is. And I'm at home, Vishous."

"I'll be there in two mins. In your backyard."

"I shall look forward to your audience." Assail clicked over. "Hello, darling—"

Weeping. Naasha was weeping openly, and Assail knew the cause without the explanation.

"Whatever has happened," he said as he walked over and opened his back door.

The chilly air irritated his nose, but he willed the sneezing away as all kinds of stuttering and snuffling came across the connection.

"He's dead. My *hellren* . . . is dead."

Of course he is, Assail thought. And I know why.

"I am so sorry, darling. What may I do for you in your mourning."

The female sniffed a number of times. "Please come?"

"I shall. Give me ten minutes?"

"Thank you. I am heartbroken."

No, you are his heir, he thought as he ended the call. And your lover is engineering all of this—and you are next in line for the coffin, dearest.

From out of the darkness, a huge form appeared upon the lawn, and Brother Vishous triggered the security lights as he walked forth unto the house.

"There's been a death of some note," Assail announced. "It appears as if Throe's mistress's *hellren* has passed."

"Oh, really."

"I am not paranoid yet, it appears. Accurate is more like it." He met Vishous halfway across the lawn, and the pair clapped palms. "I knew that he was not long for this world. The question is how he passed—and I intend to find out."

"There is a killer under that roof."

"Indeed. And I shall let you know what I discover."

"If you need back-up, we gotchu. And if you happen to find evidence of murder? I'll be happy to put the 'death' in the sentence."

"Agreed."

"Oh, and if you're still interested in the Master Lock, this is what you need." Vishous gave him a silver tool that looked like a miniature screwdriver. "Use this like a key. It should work."

"My thanks."

Vishous clapped him on the shoulder. "You're proving worth the skin you walk in, true."

"I'm not sure whether that's a compliment or not."

"Smart of you."

Poof! the Brother was gone, leaving nothing but a cold breeze behind. And in the wake of his departure, Assail turned back to his house, and called out, "Gentlemales? I am leaving."

Ehric stepped into the open doorway. "Where to?"

"Naasha's. She has had a change in station, as it were. Her *hellren* has passed—or been murdered, as may well be the case."

"Interesting. Let us know if you require us?"

"I shall."

Closing his eyes, Assail dematerialized and traveled in a scatter across the river to Naasha's *hellren*'s estate. As he re-formed at the front entrance, he walked directly to the portal and opened it right up, eschewing any knocking or ringing.

Throe was standing in the foyer, and as he caught sight of the door opening, he frowned and then recoiled. "What . . . what are you doing here?"

Assail shut the heavy weight behind himself, and then teased his pocket square back into optimal position. "I have been invited here."

"Then you should enter properly—by engaging the bell. You don't live here."

"And you do."

"Yes."

Assail crossed the distance to stop before the other male; whereupon he reached out and ran his fingertips down the lapel of Throe's admittedly sharp black suit. The fucker was handsome . . . one had to give him that. Of course, he was also morally corrupt and about as trustworthy as a viper underfoot.

And wasn't it true how that mix went together so very often.

"My dear boy," Assail murmured, "if you do not know why I have been summoned, you are either blind or naive."

Throe slapped Assail's hand away. "I'm not your 'boy.'"

Assail leaned in. "But you'd like to be, wouldn't you."

"Fuck you."

"All you have to do is ask nicely and I'll consider it. In the meantime, you might remind yourself that your mistress is going to be looking for her next victim—I mean *hellren*. And as numerous as your charms are, I believe you are missing one important criterion. Last I heard you were poor. Or at least what passes for poor by her standards. However, I do not have that problem, do I. Mayhap that is why she called me to her?"

As Throe bared his fangs and seemed prepared to offer a rebuke, the sound of hurried footfalls came down the winding staircase.

"Assail!"

Opening his arms wide, he accepted the fragrant, carefully tended-to tackle that hit him, and as he held Naasha close to his body, he met Throe's eyes. Throwing the gentlemale a wink, Assail deliberately moved his hand down to the female's ass and squeezed.

Naasha inched back. "The solicitor is coming. Will you stay whilst I meet with him?"

"But of course. In this, your time of need, I am e'er at your service."

"They have taken my mate's remains away." Outing her silk handkerchief from her bodice, she blotted cheeks that were dry and tended to eyes that were neither red rimmed nor smudged. "He is to be cremated this eve. And then we shall have the Fade ceremony. He always said he wished to be fade on the property."

"Then that is what you need to do for him in his final repose."

"I have sent my houseguests away. It seemed improper to have them under this roof whilst such arrangements are being made." More of the dabbing. "I am so very alone. I shall need you now more than ever."

Assail bowed as he felt Throe seethe. "My pleasure."

"Perhaps you shall sit in with me and the solicitor—"

Throe spoke up. "No, I will be there to support you. This needs to be private."

"He does have a point," Assail murmured as he stroked her cheek with the backs of his knuckles. "And I am happy to tarry herein for however long it takes. Provide me with a parlor and I shall amuse myself with something from your library, perhaps?"

There was a chiming from the front door, and the butler materialized out of a back room. As the *doggen* hurried forth to answer the summoning, Throe cocked a brow—as if to point out that this was indeed how proper guests were to be received.

And then Saxton, the King's own solicitor, strode into the mansion.

Saxton was more suited to the Regency *ton* than to modern life in

many ways, his thick blond hair curled back off his face, his suit hand-made for him by an expert, his cashmere coat and Louis Vuitton brief-case suspending him between the polar opposites of fashion dandy and industrious lawyer.

"Mistress," he said with a bow. "My condolences for your loss."

Cue another round of dry-eyed theatrics and hankie waving—and as the drama hit, Assail stepped out of the conversation, although he did catch Saxton's eye. As they nodded to each other discreetly, Assail had the distinct impression that the attorney knew exactly why he was in the household.

Ah, Wrath. Fingers in everyone's pie—and that was a good thing, Assail was coming to believe.

"Allow me to show my friend into the study," Naasha said. "And then we shall have our meeting in the library. My *doggen* will take you there the now and accept your orders for refreshment. Throe shall be joining us as an adviser of mine."

Assail was careful to take formal leave of Saxton, as if the two did not know each other at all. And then he was following Naasha into a room that smelled like potpourri and wood smoke. As she closed them in together, the pair of sliding doors were as ornate as full-cut statues and had as much gold on them as the Bulgari necklace the female had at her throat.

She walked over to him. Sniffling delicately. "Will you relieve me in my mourning?"

"Always."

He pulled her against him, because she wanted him to. And he kissed her gently so that he didn't smudge her matte red lipstick—also because she wanted him to.

"My darling," he said as he passed a light hand over her coiffed and cascading curls. "Do tell me. How did you find out your beloved had passed?"

As she spoke, he memorized every word she said: "I went in to greet him before his First Meal was served. He was lying back in his bed, as peaceful as can be—but he was cold. So very cold. He was gone. In his sleep—which is a blessing."

"A good death. A fine death for a worthy male."

She kissed him again, licking into his mouth—and he could taste Throe on her, smell the scent of the other male all over her.

"Be here when I am finished?" she said with a hint of command.

Assail's inner dominant balked at the order, but his logical side overrode the instinct. "As I said, I shall wait for however long it takes."

"The will has many provisions."

"And I have naught else to do than attend upon you."

She positively glowed at that—and it was all he could do not to roll his eyes. But then she was dancing out of the room, ready to go find out all that she was to inherit.

"Bye for now," she quipped before sliding the doors back into place.

As the clipping of her high heels on the marble faded, he looked around at the ceiling. No security cameras that he could see, but that was just the most obvious place to put them.

Before he attempted to depart the study, he had to know if anyone was watching.

FIFTY-TWO

"Fritz . . . how to describe Fritz . . ."

As Rhage came up to a stoplight, he hit the brakes on the GTO and looked into the rearview. Bitty was in the back and staring forward with a rapt expression, like whatever he was about to say was the single most fascinating thing she was ever going to hear.

For a moment, his heart pounded. He couldn't believe there was even a possibility that he might get a chance to . . .

Focus, he told himself. There was a long haul ahead before it was time to get sentimental.

But, God, if it happened, he was going to be having a lot of conversations with the little female.

"Rhage?" Mary prompted.

"Sorry, right." The light turned green, and cued his brain into forward motion along with the car. "Okay, so Fritz looks like that guy from *Raiders of the Lost Ark*, you know, the one who got his face melted off. Except not that scary—and nothing actually falls away."

"What is *Raiders of the Lost* . . . what?"

Rhage sagged in the driver's seat. "Oh, my God, listen—we're going to have to work on your education. There's so much—have you seen *Jaws*?"

"No?"

He thrashed back against the headrest. "No! Oh, no, the humanity!"

As Bitty started to giggle, Rhage threw out a hand to Mary. "Hold me, I have to ask the big one."

"I'm here for you, honey."

Rhage looked into the rearview again. "Do you even know who John McClane is?"

"No?"

"Hans Gruber?"

"Um . . . no?"

"Maaaaaaaaaaaaaary, hold me!"

Mary started laughing and shoving him back into position. "Drive the car!"

With the girls laughing, he shook himself and pulled it together. "We'll work on all that later. Anywho, Fritz is . . . he's older than God, as the humans say. And he gets flustered if you try to do anything. He won't let you clean up after yourself, he stresses if you try to fix yourself any food, and he has an obsessive need to vacuum. But." He held up his forefinger. "He bought me my own ice cream freezer. And I'm telling you, that absolves a multitude of sins."

Mary turned around. "Fritz is the kindest force on the planet. He runs the staff and takes care of everybody and everything in the house."

"How many people live there?" Bitty asked.

"Counting *doggen*?" Mary got quiet for a moment. "Jeez, I'm thinking thirty? Thirty-five? Forty? I don't really know."

Rhage cut in. "The most important thing is that—"

"—there's a lot of love."

"—there's a movie theater with its own candy counter."

As Mary shot him a look, he shrugged. "Do not underestimate the importance of Milk Duds in the dark. Bitty, tell me you've had Milk Duds?"

When the girl shook her head with a grin, he threw his hands up. "Man, I got things to teach you, young lady."

Up ahead, Lucas Square appeared in the distance, the glow of all the shops and neon signs bright as noonday. And talk about hopping. There were pedestrians everywhere on the broad sidewalks, humans strolling arm in arm on dates, families scrambling along, clutches of teenage girls and saunters of teenage boys passing this way and that.

"Is it Friday?" he asked as he pulled into one of the open-air lots.

"I think so—no, wait, it's Saturday." Mary took out her phone. "Yup, it's Saturday."

"No wonder it's so busy."

It took him a while to locate a suitable spot, and he rejected a number of them for either having truck-crowding issues, cockeyed SUV-itis, or minivan creep. Finally, he found a vacant berth that was next to a planting area and docked his baby close to the curb.

"Yes, he's always this choosy," Mary said as she got out and popped the seat forward for Bitty.

"Hey, I take care of my females." As their door was shut, he reached across and locked it manually, then he got out himself and used the key on the driver's-side handle. "Ain't no human going to ding my panels."

They fell in line together, Bitty between them. TGI Friday's was up ahead on the corner, and as a group of noisy humans came rushing out of its doors, Rhage frowned.

"Hey, Bitty?" he said casually. "So you've never been in a restaurant before?"

"No."

Rhage stopped and put his hand on a shoulder that shocked him because it was so thin and small. But he had another concern at the moment.

"It might be kind of loud, okay? Lot of talking, you might hear babies crying, people laughing in bursts. There are going to be servers running around with big trays of food—lot of different smells and sounds. It can be overwhelming. Here's what you need to remember. If you have to go to the bathroom, Mary will go with you so you don't have to worry about getting lost or being alone. And if you find, at any moment, that it's too much, we leave. I don't care if we've gotten the menus, put in our order, or just picked up our forks. I'll put a hundy on the table and we're"—he snapped his fingers—"outta there."

Bitty stared up at him. And he worried that he'd gone too far or—

The kid hit him with her little body and held on tight. At first, Rhage didn't know what to do and just held his arms out to the sides and looked at Mary in a panic. But as his *shellan* put her hand to her mouth and seemed like she was composing herself, he hugged the girl back lightly.

As they stood there together, Rhage found himself closing his eyes. And saying a silent prayer.

Mary could only shake her head. She'd thought that she'd fallen in love with Rhage before. Thought she loved him with all her heart. Thought that he was her soulmate, her center, her never-gonna-get-better-than-this.

Yadda, yadda, yadda.

Seeing him curl his enormous body around that little girl as he hugged Bitty back?

Well, what do you know, not only did it turn out her ovaries had a little spark left in them—the suckers might as well have exploded between her hip bones.

When the three of them started walking again, Rhage kept one hand on Bitty's shoulder. Like for the both of them it was the most normal thing in the world—even though Rhage had to tilt to the side and the pair of them bumped into each other until they got their strides on a par.

As they closed in on the restaurant, Mary glanced around and ID'd the other families—and she couldn't help but open the fantasy door for a split second and pretend that her little unit was just like all the others. That they were a mom and a dad and a daughter, going out to dinner to talk about silly stuff and serious stuff and nothing at all—before they headed back home to a safe place together.

Rhage jumped ahead to open the door, and inside, the restaurant was exactly as he'd described it, noisy and busy and teeming with life. Fortunately, Bitty seemed more curious than nervous, although she stuck with Rhage as he went up to the hostess stand and asked for three in a booth, if possible.

The brunette who was behind the cash register took one look at him—and what do you know, no waiting for Rhage. As the young woman smiled with all her teeth and did a little shimmy as she pulled a trio off the pile of menus, Mary shook her head in apology at the other twelve people in line.

"Right this way!"

The hostess hipped her way through the different sections of the place, taking them to the far side where there was, in fact, a booth that

had just been cleaned off, its surface still wet, no silverware rolls put out yet. The latter was taken care of immediately as Rhage and Bitty sat on one side and Mary took the bench across from them.

"Enjoy your meal," the hostess said to Rhage.

Before anyone could say a word, a blonde with short hair and a lot of eye makeup came by with waters on a tray. Her expression was a combination of bored and harried—until she saw who she was serving.

Mary just smiled and shook her head as she opened her menu. As she checked out the enormous variety of food offered, she was dimly aware of some conversation happening, but she didn't bother with any of that.

When they were alone, Rhage opened his menu. "Okay, what do we got—"

"Do they always do that?" Bitty asked.

"Do what?" He turned a laminated page. "Who?"

"The human females. Stare at you like that."

Rhage picked up his water glass for a test sip. "I don't know what you're talking about."

"It's like they want to order a meal of you?"

Water. Went. Everywhere. As Rhage coughed and fisted his chest, Mary had to laugh. Also had to unroll her fork, knife, and spoon and do a little mop-up.

"Yes, they do," Mary said. "They get sucked into the Awesome Zone and can't pull out."

Rhage dragged in a breath. "I don't know . . . what either of you are talking about."

Bitty turned to him. "You don't see how—"

"I don't notice them." Rhage looked the girl straight in the eye. "My Mary is the only female I see. That is the way it is and ever will be. The others can trip over themselves all they like, they will never match up to what I have been blessed with, and I will never, ever have anything to do with them."

Bitty seemed to consider that for a moment. Then she picked up her own menu with a little smile. "I think that's really nice."

"So, what do you feel like having?" Mary asked. "Both of you."

"I'm in a steak kind of mood." Rhage turned another page. "And also Mexican. And chicken. And I think I gotta rock some potatoes."

Mary leaned across to Bitty. "Good thing there are only three of us. We're going to need the table space for his plates."

"I don't know what to get," the girl said. "I've never seen . . . so much."

"Well, I'm willing to share." Mary closed things up and put the sheath on the edge of the table. "But I'm just going to get a big salad."

"I'm still working on my list." Rhage nudged Bitty with his elbow. "I think you should get at least one thing on your own. You deserve to have your own plate—plus I can eat whatever you don't finish."

When the waitress came back, she had eyes only for Rhage—and it was funny; Mary could remember being insecure about that sort of thing in the beginning of their relationship . . . especially in light of that one episode. Now, though? It truly didn't bother her. Rhage had not lied. These women could literally strip down to their hey-how're-ya's in front of him and he would have no more interest in them sexually than he would a sofa.

Amazing how your mate could make you feel cherished without actually saying a word to you.

"So what are you thinking?" the waitress asked Rhage.

"First, my ladies. Bitty?"

The girl seemed to panic. "I don't know. I don't—"

"You mind if I make a suggestion?" Rhage asked. When she nodded, he said, "Have the mac-and-cheese side with the broccoli side and the crispy chicken fingers with the honey barbecue sauce. Simple. Easy on the stomach. Not a lot of confusion with the old taste buds."

Bitty seemed to brace herself. Then she looked at the waitress. "May I please have that?"

The waitress nodded. "No problem."

"My Mary?"

Mary smiled. "I'll have the grilled chicken Cobb salad please, with no avocado and no bleu cheese—for dressing, just ranch or something like that would be great. On the side."

"We have ranch." The waitress focused on Rhage, her eyes clinging to his face, his shoulders, his chest. "And you?"

"Well, I do believe I'll start with the buffalo wings and the loaded potato skins. Then I'd like the hibachi chicken skewers, the New York strip with the half rack of both the barbecue ribs and the Memphis-rubbed, the strip done medium, and I'll finish with the triple-stack

Reuben. Oh, and I think I want the all-American burger, too. Medium, as well. Oh, and ranch with the wings, please. On the side."

As he closed the menu, he seemed to be unaware that he was being stared at.

"Yes?" he said to the waitress.

"Are you—are you waiting for more people?"

"Nope." He gathered the menus and handed them over. "And may I have two Cokes, please? Ladies?"

"Water's good for me," Mary said. "Bitty? Water or a soda? Water? Okay, she'll take water—and then I think we're done. And very hungry, as you can see."

As the waitress walked off with a set of wall-eyes, Bitty started to giggle. "You're not going to really eat all that, are you?"

"Heck, yeah." Rhage put out his palm. "Wanna bet me?"

Bitty shook his hand. "But what happens if I lose?"

"You have to finish what's left."

"I can't do that!"

As the pair of them went back and forth, Mary just watched them, the huge, impossibly beautiful male with the small little sprite of a girl as comfortable with each other as you could get.

"Mary?"

She shook herself. "What?"

Rhage reached his hand across the table. "Bitty's asked how we met."

As Mary clasped his palm, she had to smile. "Oh, you wouldn't believe it."

"Tell me?" the girl asked, sitting forward. "Please?"

FIFTY-THREE

When Assail was satisfied that there was no closed-circuit, or otherwise, monitoring in the study, he went to the carved door panels and cracked one open. Hearing nothing, he stepped out into the foyer and stood stock-still, listening for sounds of voices or footsteps.

"A coast that is clear, indeed," he murmured, looking all around.

He was about to head toward the grand staircase when there was a shriek from the closed room across the way.

"—untrue!" Naasha bellowed, her volume barely dimmed. "Then it is a forgery of his signature! This is an abomination!"

Bad news? he wondered with a smile. Perhaps a long-lost relation had just come into a windfall in the will?

He jumped back into the study and closed the door most of the way just as she burst out into the foyer and stomped her way toward the stairs. Throe was on her, though, taking her elbow in a rough grip and wheeling her around.

Jutting himself forward, the male said in a low tone, "You *must* listen to the rest of the provisions. Yes, I realize this is a shock, but we can't fight what we don't know the full story of. You will go back in there. You will stop yelling. And you will let Saxton finish the presen-

tation. When he has concluded, we shall ask him what your rights may be and who will adjudicate your contesting of the will. Then we shall engage a solicitor of our own. But you will *not* run out of there half-cocked and hysterical. Not if you want to get the money you're due. Do you understand what I am saying to you."

The voice that came out of the female's well-greased throat was nasty as a growling dog's. "It's supposed to be mine. I spent the last twenty years listening to him complain. I have *earned* every penny of that money."

"And I shall help you get what is yours. But that shall *not* happen if you do not control yourself. Emotion is not welcome here."

There was a little more back-and-forth. And then Naasha squared those padded shoulders of hers and stalked back into the meeting.

One had to feel sorry for Saxton.

Although there was no dwelling on that now.

Assail wasted no time when they closed that door. He popped out of the study, re-shut things, and hit the stairs at a dead run. As he got to the second floor, he went down the hall farther than he had before, to a grand bedroom suite, the door of which was open. The moment he smelled astringent in the air, he knew he was in her *hellren*'s room—and what did one know, but the bed had been stripped, the pillows stacked in the center of the mattress, the whole of it looking well-worn.

He took out his camera phone and started snapping pictures. He had no idea what might or might not have been out of place, but that was for later perusal.

Stains. On the mattress.

High up on the mattress, not where one would expect them from a loss of bladder control.

The pillows were likewise marked.

A quick whiff told him it was not blood, nor urine. But what was the substance?

Into the bathroom. Medications everywhere, bottles with caps on cockeyed or not at all. A walker. A cane. Depends.

He was in and out of the suite in under seven minutes, and he paused at the head of the stairs. Two ways to get to the basement. The back fashion, which he had traveled the previous night . . .

No, he would use the other set of steps this time.

Closing his eyes, he dematerialized to the first floor and ghosted under doorways until he presented his physical form at the top of the front stairs to the cellar.

His ears gave him no reason to be worried, so he opened the way and stole into the darkness. Using his phone's flashlight to navigate, he stuck to the sides of the rough-cut steps, the damp, cold air stinging his sinuses.

Down at the bottom, he continued on apace, passing by Naasha's playroom. He did not like the amount of noise his leather-soled shoes made on the stone floor, but there was naught to be done about that— and presently, he came up to the door with the Master Lock on it.

That smell was still in the air, he thought, as he took out Vishous's tool and inserted it where the proper key would go. Manipulating the slice of metal around, the lock went loose, and he sloughed the thing off its perch.

Without checking to see what precisely he was getting into, he slipped inside and shut himself in.

In the utter blackness, there was a shuffling sound in the corner. And a rattle of . . .

Chains?

Breathing. Something was breathing over there.

Assail pointed his phone in that direction, but the little beam reached no farther than a couple of feet. Putting the cell away, he palmed one of his guns and patted around the exposed beams next to the door.

When he found the light switch, he flipped it—

And recoiled in horror.

A naked male was chained on the bare stone floor in the corner. Chained and trembling as he curled in upon himself, ducking his head and holding onto his skeletal legs, his long hair the only covering he had.

The smell . . . the smell was of an old meal that had been left on a tray just within reach of him. Facilities, such as they were, were beside him, a mere hole that opened into the earth. There was also a hose, as one might find in a garden, hanging on a peg. And a bucket.

As long as Assail would live, he would ne'er forget the soft chiming sounds that rose up from the male's tethers as that scrawny body shook.

Assail took a step forward.

The whimpering was of that of an animal.

"I shall not hurt you," Assail said roughly. "Please know . . . I . . . whate'er are you imprisoned herein for?"

Even though he knew.

This was a blood slave. He was staring at a blood slave—there were even . . . yes, there were the tattoos: one around the throat, and a pair on the wrists.

"How may I be of help?"

There was no reply, the male merely tightening himself even further, the bones of his elbows seeming to break through his skin, his ribs like claw marks down the sides of his torso, his thighs so small that his knees seemed as great swollen knots.

Assail looked around, although that was daft. What was in the room was there and unchanged.

"I need to get you out of here."

Wrenching around, he pictured the way out. "I'm getting you . . ."

What could he do? Carry the poor male?

Assail went further into the dungeon. "Here now, be of ease. I am not about to harm you."

He was cautious as he approached, and he was very aware that his brain had lit up like a switchboard, all kinds of thoughts swirling and disturbing him.

"My dear male, you mustn't fear me." He made his voice stronger. "I am here to rescue you."

The slave's head lifted a little. And then some more.

And finally, the male looked at him with terrified, red-rimmed eyes that were sunken so far into his skull that Assail wondered how much longer life could be sustained.

"Can you walk?" Assail demanded. When there was no response, he nodded down at those legs. "Can you stand? Can you walk?"

"Who . . ." The word was so reedy, it was barely a syllable.

"I am Assail." He touched his chest. "I am . . . no one of importance. But I shall save you."

The slave's eyes began to water. "Why . . ."

Assail leaned down to touch the male's arm, but the slave's autonomic jerk was so violent, he retracted his hand immediately.

"Because you are in need of saving." As he spoke in an utterly raw tone, he felt in some way as if he were addressing himself. "And I . . . I am in need of a good deed to prove myself."

Glancing over his shoulder, he calculated the distance up to, and out of, the grand home's front door. The time that had elapsed since he had left the study. The amount of ammunition he had on him. The calls that would have to be made to his cousins. To Vishous.

To anyone.

Shit. The chains.

No, he could handle them.

Reaching into the holster under his arm, he took out the nine millimeter he'd brought with him and then retrieved its silencer from his jacket pocket. With quick twists, he screwed the equipment into place on the muzzle.

"I need you to move." He indicated the way toward himself. "I need you away from the wall."

The slave was still trembling, but he attempted to comply, dragging himself on all fours from the place he habitually curled up—indeed, one could see the imprinted shadow on the stone of both the floor and the wall as the male vacated the area.

All at once, sweat broke out over Assail's body, beading upon his upper lip and across his brow—and his heart abruptly thundered.

"Stop it—" As the male froze, Assail shook his head. "No, I'm speaking with myself. That was not directed at you."

The chains were anchored to the wall via a ring that was thick as a male's thumb and as wide as a neck—and which was bolted into the stone.

Any bullet was going to ricochet around. But what choice did he have?

Leaving the slave here was certainly not an option.

"You're going to have to—here, will you allow me to touch you?"

The male nodded mutely, and braced himself for the contact. With quick work, Assail lifted him up—

Fates, he weighed not a thing.

The chains rattled as they moved over the floor—likewise, the male's teeth chattered as he moaned, there being some obvious soreness.

When they were as far away as possible, Assail put the slave down and stepped in front, shielding the male with his body. Then he took aim and—

The bullet didn't make a sound as it was discharged, but it pinged around the cell, hitting rock faces until it buried itself somewhere far from its intended target. Assail took a moment to see if he'd been hit. Then he checked on the slave.

"You all right?" When he got a nod, he went over to inspect the ring. "Close, but not quite there, damn it."

His aim had been good, but the metal was stout. He daren't take another shot, however.

Grasping onto the thing, he moved the injury he'd imparted upon the metal to the bolt and put all his weight and strength into the pull. Grunting, straining, he was curiously desperate as he sought to break the hold.

After much struggle, there was a high-pitched whine, as if the metal were cursing him, and then he stumbled back, the ring in his hands, his loafers slipping out from under him.

The landing hurt like a bitch, but he did not care. He was on his feet and back at the male a split second later.

Shrugging out of his suit jacket, he wished he'd thought to take a proper coat with him, but as he'd just been dematerializing over, he'd assumed there would be no need for more appropriate cold-weather wear.

"Let us put this upon you."

That proved better in theory than reality, the chains not lending themselves to sleeves or lapels. In the end, he put the thing back on just so he did not leave it behind.

Wrapping the chains around his own neck—twice on account of their length—he picked up the male and managed to hold him up with only one arm. Then he proceeded forward to the door.

The slave was the one who opened the way out for them both.

Which enabled Assail to keep his gun up.

He left the light on. Soon enough the household would realize the slave was gone, and he didn't want to waste time futzing around with shutting things back up.

The far worse outcome would be to find that the meeting with Saxton was over, and Throe and the mistress of the house were looking for him.

Past the sex dungeon. Up the stairs.

The slave reached for the door handle again.

"Slowly," Assail said between breaths. "Let me listen."

No sounds. At the nod, the male opened the way fully and Assail broke through at a fast walk, his heart thundering, his legs curiously numb even as they functioned appropriately.

Quickly, quickly, fleet of foot and keen of ear, he raced through the various pantries and ante-rooms until he came up to the foyer. Pausing before he stepped out into the space, he prayed to the Virgin Scribe, the Fates, destiny, fucking anything, that the vast open area would not just be empty, but remain so as he made a mad dash to the front door.

After that? He would have to run far enough to find some safety and call his cousins. Then the Brotherhood.

Blood slavery had been outlawed by the King—so there might well be a legal way of seizing this living, breathing chattel who should never have been property. But Assail wasn't leaving the male behind just so that he could show up with a bunch of Brothers, head down to the basement, and find out that Naasha had disappeared the slave into a grave because something had tipped her off.

Just let there be a way out of this house, he thought. *Please . . .*

"Through the front door," he whispered. "We're going right out the front door. You ready? Try to hang on to me."

The male nodded over and over again and tightened his hold a fraction.

"Here we go."

Assail broke out into the space, moving fast, the chains clanking, his cargo slipping, all that dirty, damp hair slapping—

He had to stop dead not even halfway to their goal.

FIFTY-FOUR

"Please," Bitty said. "Please tell me how you met?"

Mary glanced at Rhage and wondered which one of them was going to take a stab at it. When he nodded at her with a smile, she shrugged and rubbed his hand.

"Okay, so—" she started. "It was a—"

"Dark and stormy night," Rhage jumped in.

"Well, it certainly was a dark night." She thought back to what seemed both forever ago and two seconds back. "I had been doing some work with this helpline. You know, for people who needed a little advice." Okay, it had been the Suicide Prevention Hotline, but editing that out seemed appropriate. "And this person kept calling in. I eventually met with him, and my next door neighbor recognized him for what he really was—a pretrans caught in the human world. Long story short, I ended up going with them to the Brotherhood's training center to translate—"

"John Matthew can't speak verbally," Rhage said. "And she knows American Sign Language. She helped him communicate."

"So there I was, wondering *where* I was—"

"When I came down the hall. And it was love at first sight for us."

"Okay, he was blind at the time—"

Bitty spoke up in alarm. "Why?"

Mary glanced at Rhage, and they both froze. "Ah . . ."

"It's a long story," he said.

The waitress came back with Rhage's two Cokes. "Let me know if you need a refill, okay?"

"Thank you." Rhage took a draw off one of the big/talls as the woman went on to the next table. "Anyway, I couldn't see, but the instant she spoke? I was in love."

"What did you think of him?" Bitty asked.

Mary ducked her eyes as a smile wide as the table hit her face. "Well, at first I was overwhelmed. There's a lot of him to go around, as you know. And I didn't know where I was or who he was—and I couldn't figure out why he was giving me so much attention."

"It's because you're beautiful. That's why—"

"Anywaaaaaaaaaaaaay." Mary batted away the compliment—and then stopped herself as she wondered what kind of impression that would have on a young female. "I, ah . . . thank you."

Was she blushing? Why, yes, yes, she was.

Rhage got up and leaned all the way over, giving her a kiss. "That's more like it."

Mary tried to hide her fluster behind taking a sip of her water. "So we dated—our first date was actually right here in this restaurant."

"Really?" Bitty said.

"At that table—"

"At that table—"

As they both pointed across the way, Mary finished, "Right over there. And yes, he ordered this much, too."

Rhage sat back as the waitress delivered his appetizers. "Oh, thank you—and listen, we don't need to wait if our entrées are ready. Just bring 'em all out. Mmmm, wanna try some, Bits?"

"It does smell good." The little girl edged closer. "Yes, please."

"Get your fork and dive in. The potato skins are awesome. Bacon is the source of all goodness."

As the two of them danced their way around the plates, Mary thought back to those early days: Rhage asking her to say "antidisestablishmentarianism" in the training center's corridor. Him meeting her here and staring across the table as if she were the single most captivating thing he'd ever seen. Him showing up at her house at four in the morning . . .

"Penny for your thoughts?" Rhage asked.

"I—ah . . ." As Bitty also looked at her, Mary wondered how much to say. "Well, to be honest, I was thinking about the moment you found out . . ."

Mary stopped herself. She didn't want to talk about her own illness, her own strange situation to Bitty. There was just too much already going on.

Rhage got somber. "I know exactly what you're remembering."

Mary crossed her arms and braced them on the tabletop. Leaning in, she said to Bitty, "When he came to my house the first time, I didn't expect him. I'd woken up at four a.m., and I was opening a can of coffee—I sliced my thumb pretty deeply. Of course, I didn't find out until later—well, I didn't know he was a vampire at that particular moment."

Bitty shook her head. "I keep forgetting that you're human. What did you . . . were you surprised?"

Mary laughed in a burst. "You might say. It was a while before I found out. He ended up . . . spending a day with me. He couldn't leave because of the sunlight, but he didn't want to tell me why—and then there was . . ."

She remembered him disappearing into her bathroom. And reappearing eight hours later, unaware that he'd been gone so long.

"Well, we had a lot of things to get through. I pushed him away a lot."

"So what got you together?"

Mary looked at Rhage. "Oh, it's a very long story. What matters is that it all worked out in the end."

"And look, here's dinner!" Her *hellren* all but got up and rushed the waitress over. "Perfect!"

Rhage helped usher the plates back and forth, trading empty ones for full ones, and then he arranged the constellation of calories he'd ordered in a semi-circle around him and Bitty.

"Anything that I have is yours," he said to the girl. "Don't be shy."

As Rhage tucked in, he seemed wholly unaware of how Bitty stared at him, as if she were realigning something in her mind.

"I know," Mary found herself saying. When the girl looked over, she murmured, "I couldn't believe he was real, either. But I swear on my mother's soul that he is the very best male I've ever met—and when he says he'll never hurt you or let anything hurt you? He means it."

Bitty glanced back at Rhage. And then said, "May I try some of your steak?"

Oh, she knew just what to say, Mary thought with a smile.

And sure enough, Rhage's chest puffed up—because he was exactly that kind of male who liked to provide. In fact, it was better than actually eating, to him.

"Let me give you the best part of this," he said as he took his fork and knife, and began making a surgical assessment of the honking huge piece of meat. "The very, very best."

As Assail froze with the blood slave in his arms, the male who was in the middle of Naasha's foyer turned around—and Saxton nearly jumped out of his skin when he saw what had rushed into the space.

Fortunately, the King's attorney recovered quickly. And even had the presence of mind to keep his voice down. "Whatever are you . . ."

Assail swallowed hard. "Help me. Please."

Saxton patted at his jacket—and then took out the Holy Grail as far as Assail was concerned. "My car is outside—I had shopping to do this night, and thank the Virgin Scribe for that. Take it—but be quick. They asked me to step out as they argued. I don't know how long they'll be. Go! Go now!"

The solicitor lunged for the front door and held it wide as Assail hustled across the foyer, zeroing in on the cold night air that streamed into the mansion.

"I'll delay them," Saxton said. "For as long as I can."

Assail paused for but a heartbeat as he took the key and stepped over the threshold. "My debt to you. For e'ermore."

He didn't wait for a response. He tore out, and would have leaped down the shallow steps if he'd been able. And dear God, those chains, those dreadful chains, they chimed and threatened to cut off his air supply as he crossed the distance to the BMW 750i.

He all but threw the male in the back.

No time to waste. Free of the weight, he bolted around to the driver's side, jumped in, and started the engine. The temptation was to floor the accelerator, but he didn't want to risk squealing out and causing attention to be garnered. He took off with alacrity, but no undue speed, and was soon cruising away, the mansion fading in the rearview mirror as he proceeded down a long, descending driveway.

Now, he was the one who was shaking as he took out his phone.

He used Siri to place the call. And when it was answered, he cut off the *hello*. "Vishous, I need medical help. Now. Where are you? Okay. Right. I can be there in fifteen minutes. Please. Hurry."

Ending the connection, he tilted the rearview downward so he could see into the backseat. "Hang on. We're going to get you help. Tell me, what's your name?"

"I . . . don't know," came the weak response.

Stopping at the end of the drive, Assail went right, but did not take any deep breath that they were free. It was going to be a while for that. "Stay with me. You must . . . stay with me—you're too close to safety to quit now. You stay with me!"

Aware that he was yelling, he forced himself to ease off on his voice.

"Do not die on me," he muttered as he found himself lost.

Where was he going? Where . . . ?

Vishous had told him to go to the northeast part of town, to—

He took his phone out again and hit up Siri once more. When Vishous answered, Assail didn't recognize his own voice. "Where am I going? Tell me . . ."

Vishous started to speak.

"I can't hear you . . . I can't . . . see . . ." Assail wiped his eyes. Fates, was he crying? "Help me . . ."

"Where are you?"

"I don't know."

"Look for a sign. Look for a sign, Assail."

Assail's blurry eyes rose to the rearview, to the shivering naked male on the leather seats. Then he looked out the front windshield.

"Montgomery Place. The sign says . . . Montgomery Place."

"Take a left. Now."

Assail did what he was told without argument, wrenching the wheel, skidding on the pavement, cutting off a car in the opposite lane. As a horn sounded, Vishous kept talking.

"Two miles up, there's a high-class shopping center. It's got a real estate office in it. Hair salon. Restaurants. A jeweler's. Go around to the back. I'll be at the far end."

Assail nodded, even though the Brother couldn't see him.

And as he didn't end the call, Vishous said calmly, "You got this, my man. Whatever it is, we'll handle the shit."

"All right. All right." Assail looked back at the male again. "Stay with me. . . ."

"I'm not going anywhere," Vishous murmured. "I'm only going silent for a sec as I dematerialize. Okay, I'm back."

Assail didn't say anything further as he leaned in to the wheel and waited for the—how many miles did he have to go? two?—shopping center to appear. And then there it was, its glowing signs and mostly empty lot a beacon of hope, a symbol of salvation.

"I'm here, I'm here."

He punched the accelerator, shooting beside the real estate office and skidding around to the rear of the building. The back was all utilities and Dumpsters, staff parking and loading docks for the stores. The BMW gathered speed, surging ahead like a missile.

In the headlights, at the far end, a single dark figure was standing with feet planted.

Assail stomped on the brakes, and then relented as he heard a clunking and a groan of pain from the back seat. As the car jerked to a stop, he got out without putting the engine in park and had to duck in again to toggle the gearshift.

"What are you doing with Saxton's car—"

He cut off the Brother. "Help me—"

"Have you OD'd—"

Assail ripped open the rear door. "Help him! Please!"

He had to wipe his eyes again—indeed, they were leaking all over the place.

Vishous took out a gun and approached the open car, peering in. "What. The. *Fuck.*"

"He-he-he—" Shit, he couldn't speak. "I found him. Behind the lock. He was in the basement. I couldn't leave him."

The male cowered away from Vishous, retracting his spindly body into the far side of the backseat, that stringy hair all over his thin arms and boney back.

"Shit." Vishous straightened and looked over. "I can't even start treating him here. We gotta bring him in. Christ—the chains—okay, get in—not behind the wheel. I'm driving. You can explain on the way."

Assail stumbled togo around to the passenger side in the front. But

then he stopped, re-thought things and slid into the back with the male. Taking off his jacket, he laid it over the slave's nakedness.

"It's all right." The car began to move, streetlights flaring in the dark interior as Assail tried to get a hold of himself. "We're going to be . . . all right."

FIFTY-FIVE

ayla returned to Earth and regained consciousness in her physical form, her eyes opening to focus on the low ceiling of her hospital room. Her hands went immediately to her belly, and as she shifted her legs and took a deep breath, there was movement there, reassuring, strong, vital movement.

She'd left the light on in the bathroom with the door mostly closed, as was her habit whenever she tried to sleep, and her stare gravitated to the illumination. Then she looked at the clock. Eleven thirty-four p.m.

She had been up in the Sanctuary for quite a while.

When she had proceeded from the Temple of the Sequestered Scribes to the library, it had taken her a while to find what she was in search of. And then she had studied the particular volume for some time. As well as others.

Pushing herself up higher on the mattress, she rubbed her temples.

She should not have gone into Xcor's history.

Then again, if his story had been different, if his true sire's identity had proven to be that of another, it wouldn't have mattered as much, she supposed. Such a shock. Indeed, she had even cross-referenced what she had found, going into the sacred annals of the Black Dagger

Brotherhood, pulling out volumes, searching for some inconsistency, some contradiction in the sire's records.

There had been nothing of the sort. In fact, there had been a confirmation.

And now she could not un-learn what she had discovered.

With a groan, she sat up further, swung her legs off the side, and noted that her ankles were so swollen, it was as if her calves ran directly down into her feet.

She should not have gone hunting for any information.

For now what did she do? How did she explain why she had looked?

Pushing herself onto her feet, she pulled her nightgown down and moved her hair back behind her shoulders. With a curse, she took one step forward—

Wetness. Down the insides of her legs again.

Great. Just what she needed in the middle of all this.

Waddling forward, she was preoccupied with Xcor and irritated with her bladder. But at least she could take a shower and relax knowing that everything was okay with the young. And didn't they make adult diapers for this sort of thing?

She was pivoting around to shut the bathroom door when she looked back—

Blood. Blood on the floor . . . bloody footprints on the floor.

Lifting her gown, there was blood on the inside of her legs.

As she screamed, someone came running—and Ehlena burst in.

The nurse took one look at what was going on—and immediately went into professional mode. "Come with me. Back to bed. Back to bed we go."

Layla was dimly aware of the female taking her by the arm and depositing her back on the mattress.

"The young—what about the young—"

"Hold on, I'm calling for Doc Jane." Ehlena hit the summoning button. "I'm just going to hook you up to the machines, okay?"

Everything happened so fast. Wires set upon her, monitors engaged, Doc Jane rushing in. The ultrasound rolled into the room. Manny arriving. Qhuinn and Blay nearly breaking down the door as they came in.

"The young," she moaned. "What about the young . . . ?"

*   *   *

It was as the wind blew o'er the land.

Consciousness returned to Xcor in the manner of a gust that traveled around and over a landscape, bypassing some things, rustling others, penetrating through still more. Accordingly, he was aware of many aches, and yet there were great patches of numbness, too—he could feel measures of agony and stretches of tingles . . . twitches and jerks . . . but then nothing at all in great swaths of his flesh.

Smell registered with acuity, however.

The scent of dirt confused him.

Behind his closed eyes, he oriented himself as best he could using his ears and his nose. He was not alone. There was the scent of one— no, two other male vampires with him. Further, they were speaking in low tones—well, one of them was. The other said naught that Xcor could ascertain.

He did not know them. Or, more accurately, he did not recognize them as being his soldiers—

The Brotherhood. Indeed, yes, he had scented them before. When the Brotherhood had come to speak unto the *glymera* at that meeting of the Council.

Had he been captured?

Hazy details of the night came back to him. Of him being in that alley next to that burned-out car shell. Of him following a food truck . . . following where? Where had he gone?

Was this a dream?

Images filtered across his mind's eye, but they did not stay long enough for him to grasp—

"He's frowning," the male voice said. "His hands are moving. Are you awake, bastard?"

He could not have answered if his life depended upon it—and in fact, his life did depend on it. If he had been captured, the how's and where's were—

Campus.

He had not followed the food truck. No, he had been on top of the vehicle, riding through the night as the slayers he had been hunting had proceeded out of downtown, past the suburbs, unto an abandoned college or preparatory school's campus.

Whereupon he had witnessed the aftermath of a great battle, a devastating loss for the Lessening Society.

Waged by the Brotherhood.

He had found a human. Upon a roof.

And then he himself had been struck upon the back of the head.

How long had he been unconscious? His body ached all over, not as if it had been beaten, but rather as if it hadn't been used in a while.

"Are you finally awake?" the voice demanded.

Finally . . . ? Yes, it must have been some time that he had been unconscious. In fact, he felt as though he had been lying in this position for a prolonged period.

What was that beeping—

Ringing. All of a sudden there was ringing—cell phones going off. The male who had been doing the speaking answered.

"What? When? How much? Oh, God . . . yes. Right away. Can Lassiter come and sit with him? Where is he? We'll both come then." There was a pause. "John—yes, it's happening now and they need us for blood. We have to go. I don't want to leave him, either, but what are we going to do? No, I don't know where Lassiter is."

There was some shuffling, as if they were gathering up supplies.

"No, they want both of us. She's in labor. The young are coming and it's too early."

Layla!

Without thinking, Xcor's lids popped open. The two fighters had turned away and were leaving, thank the Fates, so they caught him not.

"I'm terrified, too," the one with the red hair said. "For her, for Qhuinn. And he'll be fine. He's going nowhere."

The sounds of their footfalls decreased until there was a clanking, as if a gate or perhaps some chains were being moved. And then there was a repeat of all that.

Xcor blinked wildly. When he went to sit up, he found that, indeed, he was not going anywhere. There were steel bands at his wrists and ankles, and even around his waist. Moreover, he was too weak to do much more than hold his head up.

Craning around, he saw that he was surrounded by vessels of some description or another . . . they were jars, jars that were set upon shelves that ran from floor to ceiling. In a cave? And yet there was monitoring equipment keeping tabs on his bodily functions that were of complex and electronic nature.

"Layla . . ." he said in a voice that cracked. "Layla . . ."

Collapsing back against the bedding he was strapped down on, his will to escape and go to her was great though he knew not where she was or even where he was. His body had other plans, however. As night eclipsed the illumination of the daytime hours, darkness descended upon him once again.

Owning him.

His last thought was that the female he both loved and feared needed him, and he wanted to be there for her . . .

FIFTY-SIX

On the way out of TGI Friday's, Rhage stopped by the hostess stand. Or rather, he was forced to come to a halt because the human woman who had seated him got in his path and wouldn't move.

"Did you have a good meal?" she said as she pressed something in his hand. "That's our customer service number. Give us a call and let us know how your meal was."

The wink she gave him told him all the hell he needed to know and more about what a dial to those digits would get him—and it sure as shit wasn't going to be a survey.

Not one without kneepads, at any rate.

He put the folded piece of paper back into her palm. "I'll tell you right now. My wife and I had a wonderful time. So did our . . . er, friend. Thanks."

As he pivoted away, he put his arm around Mary and drew her in close. Then he did the same to Bitty before thinking about it.

They left all together, squeezing through the double doors.

Outside, the night had gotten even colder, but his belly was more than full of food and he was really happy—and it was amazing how that kind of mood created its own warmth, independent of the weather.

Hell, it could have been sleeting and he would still have looked up to the dark sky and gone, *Ahhhhhhhh.*

As they were about to step off the curb and head for the car, a minivan pulled up and a mother and a daughter rushed over together to get in. Man, talk about a gene pool. The two of them had identical brown hair, the tween's in a ponytail, Mom's cut jaw-length. They were nearly the same height and both dressed in blue jeans and sweatshirts. Faces had the same bone structure, from the round cheeks and flat forehead to a stick-straight nose that he imagined some humans asked for in plastic surgery offices.

They were neither ugly nor beautiful. Not poor, but not rich. They were laughing, though, in exactly the same way. And that made them both spectacular.

Mom opened the door for the daughter and shooed her in. Then she leaned inside and quipped to the kid, "Ha, I so did win the bet! I totally did—and you're doing the dishes all week long. That was the deal."

"Moooooooom!"

The mother shut things on the protest and hopped into the front seat next to what had to be her husband or partner. "I told her, don't bet against me. Not when it comes to *Godfather* quotes."

The guy turned around to the daughter. "No way, I'm not touching this with a ten-foot pole. You know she's memorized the movie, and yes, the correct wording is, 'No Sicilian can refuse any request on his daughter's wedding day.'"

The mother shut her door and the pale blue minivan pulled away.

For a moment, Rhage imagined what that trip home was like— and he found himself in a big fat hurry to do the same. Take Bitty home, that was.

And also argue about *The Godfather*, if that was the way things went. Or what Play-doh tasted like. Or whether it was going to snow early or late in the season.

"We good?" he asked as Bitty hesitated. "Bitty?"

"I'm sorry," the girl said softly. "What?"

"Come on, let's get to the car."

It felt really good to walk his females back to the GTO, and even

better to drive them along the streets, obeying the traffic laws. Staying in his lane. Not taking the bait when a pair of douche bags in a Charger pulled up next to him at a stoplight and pumped their engine like the thing was an extension of their cock and balls.

He just motored along.

When his cell phone rang, he let it go to voice mail. Soon enough they'd be at Safe Place and he could—

The thing went off again.

Taking it out, he frowned. "I've got to get this." Accepting the call, he put the cell up to his ear. "Manny?"

The surgeon was in full urgent-mode. "I need you back here right now. Layla's hemorrhaging. The young are coming—we need veins for her to take. Can you dematerialize?"

"Shit," he hissed as he hit his blinker and pulled over. "Yeah. I can come in."

Mary and Bitty both looked at him in alarm as he hung up and wrenched around. "Listen, I'm so sorry. There's an—" He stopped as he glanced at the girl. "I have to go back home."

"What's happening?" Mary asked.

"Layla." He didn't want to go into it. Not with what Bitty had just gone through. "They need some help. Can you drive her back? I have to ghost out right now."

"Absolutely. And I'll come directly home—"

"Can I go with you guys?" Bitty asked.

There was a moment of *ummmm*. And then Mary turned around to the rear seat. "I'd better take you back to Safe Place. But someday maybe you can?"

"Are you going to be okay?"

It took Rhage a moment to realize that the girl was talking to him. And as he met eyes that were wide and anxious, a strange jolt went through him.

"Yes. I'll be fine. I just need to help a friend."

"Oh. That's okay, then. When do I see you again?"

"Anytime you like. I'll always be right around the next turn for you." He stretched an arm back and brushed her face with his hand. "And we're going to have to watch *The Godfather*. Parts one and two. Not three."

"What's all that?" she asked as he opened his door and got out.

"Only the best movies ever made. Be good."

Mary was already out and coming around the front of the car, and they met at the grille between the headlights, embracing each other for a second.

"I love you," he said as he gave her a quick kiss.

"Me, too. Tell them I'm coming home?"

As he met Mary's eyes, he put himself in Qhuinn's position—times one billion. Then he shook himself back into focus.

"I will." He took her face in his hands and kissed her again. "Drive safely?"

"Always."

With a nod, he closed his eyes, took a deep breath—and then he was out of there, traveling in a rush of molecules over the human neighborhoods . . . and then across the farmland . . . and going farther, to the foothills that turned into the mountains.

He re-formed at the front entrance of the mansion, shoving his way into the vestibule, putting his face into the security camera.

As he waited for someone to open up, his heart was pounding for all kinds of reasons. But mostly because of the way Bitty had stared at him.

Funny how you could be transformed by someone.

The door broke open and Fritz was on the other side, looking worried. "Sire, how good to see you. All are going down to the training center. We are in the midst of preparing victuals in the event any can eat."

Rhage had a strange impulse to hug the *doggen*—and he might have followed up on it except Fritz would have passed out from the breach of protocol.

"Thank you. You're so on it. That means everything."

Rhage strode fast and hard over the mosaic depiction of an apple tree in bloom—and he was almost to the hidden door under the grand staircase when he stopped and looked back.

"Fritz?"

The butler skidded to a halt in the archway of the dining room. "Yes, sire?"

"I know this is god-awful timing. But I need you to buy something for me. Right away."

The ancient butler bowed so low his jowls nearly hit the polished

floor. "It would be a relief to do something for anybody. One feels so helpless."

Behind the wheel of the GTO, Mary felt like time had run backward—that somehow she and Bitty had gotten stuck in a warp where they were back nights ago, heading for the clinic across the river.

And it was not just because of Layla and what was happening at home. In the rear seat, the girl had retreated into herself, her eyes fixed on the window beside her, her face a mask of composure that was all the more alarming because Mary had learned exactly how engaged and cheerful she could be.

"Bitty?"

"Mmm?" came the response.

"Talk to me. I know there's something going on—and yes, I could beat around the bush or pretend I haven't noticed, but I think we're beyond that. I hope we're beyond that."

It was a long while before the girl answered.

"When we left the restaurant," Bitty said. "Did you see the human *mahmen* and daughter?"

"Yes." Mary took a deep breath. "I saw them."

As the silence resumed, Mary glanced into the rearview. "Did that make you think of your *mahmen*?"

All the girl did was nod.

Mary waited. And waited. "Do you miss her?"

That was what did it. All at once, Bitty began to cry, great sobs racking her little body. And Mary pulled over. She had to.

Thank God they were in a good part of town, and in a section where there were lots of bakeries and stationery stores and locally owned pet shops. Which meant plenty of parallel-parking spots right on the road that were empty.

Putting the GTO in neutral and pulling the hand brake, Mary twisted all the way around until her knees were tucked into her chest.

Reaching out a hand, she tried to touch Bitty, but the girl shrank away.

"Oh, sweetheart—I know you miss her—"

The girl wheeled back, tears streaming down her face. "But I don't! I don't miss her at all! How can I not miss her!"

As Bitty covered her eyes with her palms and sobbed, Mary let her be even though it killed her. And sure enough, after an agonizing wait, the girl started talking.

"I didn't get that! What that human and her *mahmen* had! I didn't get . . . bets and laughing. . . . I didn't get going out to dinner or a friendly pick-up in a car by my father!" When she sniffed and wiped her cheeks with the heels of her fists, Mary fished in her bag and took out a pack of Kleenex. Bitty took the package and then seemed to forget she had it. "My mother was scared—and hurt and running for cover! And then she was pregnant and then she got sick and—she died! And I don't miss her!"

Mary turned off the engine, opened her door and got into the back. She was careful to lock them both in the dark car, and as she settled beside the girl, the ambient light helped her see the anguish and the horror on Bitty's face.

"How can I not miss her?" The girl was shaking. "I loved her—and I should miss her. . . ."

Mary reached out, and it was relief to pull Bitty over and hug her close. Stroking her hair, she murmured soft words as Bitty wept.

It was impossible not to tear up herself.

And it was hard not to whisper platitudes like, "It's going to be all right," or, "You're okay," because she wanted to do something, anything to ease the girl. But the truth was, what Bitty had been exposed to growing up was not all right, and kids and people from those environments were not okay for a very, very long time, if ever at all.

"I've got you," was all she could say. Over and over again.

It seemed like years until Bitty took a shuddering breath and sat back. And when she fumbled with the tissue packet, Mary took the thing from her and broke the seal, teasing out a Kleenex. And another.

After Bitty blew her nose and collapsed against the seat, Mary unclipped the girl's seat belt to give her a little more room.

"I didn't know your mother all that well," Mary said. "But I'm very sure, if she could have had those kinds of loving, normal moments with you, she would have taken them in a heartbeat. Violence is all-pervasive when it's in the home. You can't get away from it unless you leave, and sometimes you can't leave so it colors everything. Do you think maybe it's more that you don't miss the suffering the two of you went through? That you don't miss the fear and hurt?"

Bitty sniffled. "Am I a bad daughter? Am I . . . bad?"

"No. God, no. Not at all."

"I did love her. A lot."

"Of course you did. And I'll bet if you think about it, you'll realize you still do."

"I was so scared all the time she was sick." Bitty fiddled with the tissues. "I didn't know what was going to happen to her and I was worried really about myself a lot of the time. Is that bad?"

"No. That's normal. That's called survival." Mary tucked a piece of hair behind Bitty's ear. "When you're young and you can't take care of yourself, you worry about those kinds of things. Heck, when you're older and you can take care of yourself, that's also what you worry about."

Bitty accepted another tissue, putting it on her knee and smoothing it flat.

"When my mom died?" Mary said. "I was angry at her."

The girl looked up in surprise. "Really?"

"Yup. I was bitterly angry. I mean, she had suffered and I had been there by her side for a number of years as she had slowly declined. She hadn't volunteered for any of it. She hadn't asked to get sick. But I resented the fact that my friends didn't have to nurse their parents. That my buddies were free to go out and drink and party and have a good time—be young and unattached, unburdened. Meanwhile I had to worry about tidying up the house, buying groceries, making meals—and then as the disease progressed, cleaning her up, bathing her, getting coverage when the nurses couldn't come in because of bad weather. And then she died." Mary took a deep breath and shook her head. "All I could think of after they took her body away was . . . great, now I have to plan the funeral, deal with the bank account stuff and the will, clean out her clothes. That's when I really lost it. I just broke down and cried, because I felt like the worst daughter in the history of the world."

"But you weren't?"

"No. I was human. I am human. And grief is a complex thing. They say there are stages of it. Have you ever heard of that?" When Bitty shook her head, Mary continued. "Denial, bargaining, anger, depression, acceptance. And all that's largely what people go through. But there are so many other things mixed into it as well. Unresolved issues. Exhaustion. Sometimes there is relief, and that can come with a lot of guilt. My best piece of advice? As someone who has not only walked this road, but also helped other folks through it? Let your thoughts and feelings come when they do—and don't judge them. I can guarantee that you are not the only person who has had thoughts they didn't like or emotions that felt wrong. Also, if you talk about what's going on for you, it is absolutely possible to move through the pain, fear and confusion to what's on the other side."

"And what is that?"

"A measure of peace." Mary shrugged. "Again, I wish I could tell you that the pain goes away—it doesn't. But it does get better. I think of my mom still, and yes, sometimes it stings. I think it always will—and honestly? I don't want that grief to disappear completely. Grief . . . is a sacred way of honoring those we love. My grief is my heart working, it's my love for her and that's a beautiful thing."

Bitty patted the tissue on her knee. "I didn't love my father."

"I don't blame you."

"And sometimes I got frustrated that my mother didn't leave him."

"How could you not have?"

Bitty took a deep breath and exhaled long and slow. "Is that all right? Is all this . . . all right?"

Mary leaned and took both the girl's hands. "It is one hundred percent, absolutely, positively okay. I promise."

"You would tell me if it wasn't?"

Mary's eyes didn't waver. "I swear on the life of my husband. And what's more? I completely understand where you're coming from. I get it, Bitty. I totally get it."

FIFTY-SEVEN

Assail had no clue where they were. As Vishous drove the BMW like a bat out of hell through the streets of Caldwell, and then out into farmland, Assail paid little attention to what they were passing by. All he cared about was measuring the breathing of the slave.

"Stay with me," he whispered.

Before he knew what he was doing, he had reached out and taken the male's cold hand. Rubbing it between his palms, he tried to will some of his body heat, his life force, into what lay so motionless beside him.

God, he hated those chains.

When he finally looked up out of the windows—because he was losing his mind with worry and wondering why the trip was taking so long—he frowned. All around, a fog had rolled in—or rather, visibility had decreased as if there were a mist in the air, even though the telltale pale cloudiness was absent from the landscape.

"You're going to be safe here," Assail heard himself say as they came up to the first of the training center's gates. "They shall endeavor to care for you here."

After all the stop and go, they arrived at the last leg of the trip, a descent that took them underground. And then they were in a park-

ing structure as fortified and large as any in the municipality of
Caldwell.

Vishous pulled directly up to a steel door. "I've called ahead."

Assail frowned, wondering when the Brother had gotten on the
phone. He hadn't noticed. "How do we get him—"

He didn't have to finish the sentence. That portal burst open, and
a gurney appeared along with the female called Doc Jane and another
Brother pushing it forth. Assail recognized the fighter—it was the
stocky one with the odd, human name. Also known as the *Dhestroyer*.

The healer already had blood on her loose blue shirt.

As Vishous bolted out from behind the wheel, he talked as he ran
about and opened the rear door. "Male, unknown age. Unknown vitals. Malnourished. Unknown psychological and physical trauma."

Assail stumbled to his feet and raced around to help extricate the
male who was shaking with fear once again. "Let me!" he barked. "He
does not know you!"

Although in truth, the slave knew Assail no better. He did, however, have the advantage of having extricated the imprisoned.

"Here now," he said to the male. "I shan't leave you."

Assail reached in and picked the slave up, pivoting and laying him
out upon the gurney. Immediately, the healer further covered his nakedness, and the dignity that afforded the patient made Assail have to
blink quickly a number of times.

"Hi, my name is Jane," the healer said, staring directly into those
terrified eyes. "I'm going to take care of you. No one is going to hurt
you here. You're safe, and we're not going to let any harm come to you.
Do you understand what I'm saying?"

The slave looked at Assail in a panic.

"It's okay," Assail said. "They are good people."

"What's your name?" the healer was saying as she put her stetho-
scope into her ears. "I'm sorry, what was that?"

"M-m-markcus."

"Markcus. That's a good name." She smiled. "I'd like to listen to
your heart, if that's okay? And I'd like to run an IV into your arm so
we can get some fluids into you. Would that be all right?"

Markcus looked at Assail again.

"It's all right," Assail said. "They're going to make you feel better.
I promise."

Things moved so fast after that. An IV was started, assessments

were made, and then they were on the move, entering the sophisticated facility with its medical rooms and its provisions—and all sorts of people.

Indeed, the entire Brotherhood seemed to be milling about.

The chains got everyone's attention, the whole of the variable crowd in the corridor turning toward the sound of clinking as the healer rushed them along and those links of metal skipped on the floor.

"What the hell?" someone said.

"Oh, God . . ." came another voice.

The fighters split down the middle, parting to let them through. Except for one member of the Brotherhood.

It was the Brother Zsadist. And as he saw the male on the gurney, he turned so white that it was as if he had died suddenly even as he remained standing in the center of the wide hallway.

The Brother Phury stepped up to him and spoke in a low tone. Then he hesitantly touched his brother on the arm.

"Let them pass," Phury said. "Let them take care of him."

When Z finally moved aside, Assail followed along as they ended up in an examination room with a large chandelier in the center, and glass-fronted cabinets all around the edges.

Vishous held him back to the periphery. "Let them work. And tell me what the fuck happened?"

Assail was aware that his lips began to move and he was speaking, but he had no clue what he was saying.

Something must have made sense—and been accurate—because Vishous said, "I swear, she deserves to die if she did this."

Doc Jane turned to Vishous. "Can you help with these chains?"

"On it."

Vishous stepped forward, removing the black leather glove on his hand. Reaching out, he clasped one of the lengths—and a brilliant glow gathered in his palm, heating the links, disintegrating them such that the weight fell free to the floor with a clank.

Assail rubbed his face as the Brother went around to each of the four points, releasing so much of the weight. The bands around the wrists and ankles stayed in place, but at least the heavy links were off.

When Vishous came back over, Assail said in a low tone, "Is he going to live?"

The Brother shook his head. "I have no idea."

FIFTY-EIGHT

Qhuinn stood in the corner of the operating room, his eyes locked on Layla as Manny performed yet another internal exam on her, the male ducked in between her spread thighs, a sheet covering what was going on to preserve her privacy.

"It's too soon . . ." Qhuinn shook head and tried to keep his voice down. "It's too soon—this isn't supposed to be happening now. Why is this—it's not supposed to be happening. Jesus, this is too early. What the fuck—the ultrasound said it was okay."

Not happening, his brain insisted. This had to be some kind of a dream.

Yup, any minute, he was going to wake up and find Blay next to him in their bedroom—and he was going to take that deep, relieved breath you got to suck in when you realized that the bogeyman who'd been terrorizing you was in fact nothing but a figment of your imagination. Or maybe a backed-up chili dog.

"Wake up," he muttered. "Wake up now. Wake the fuck up. . . ."

Blay was, in fact, beside him. But they were not horizontal, and they sure as fuck were not back up at the big house in their suite of rooms. His male was, however, supporting the shit out of him: the only thing keeping him standing was Blay's strong arm was around his waist.

Manny retracted his hand from under the sheet and snapped off his bright blue glove. Then he got up and motioned for Qhuinn and Blay to come over to the bedside.

The fact that Layla was still conscious was testimony to how strong a female she was, but oh, God, she was pale. And there was so much blood, filling the pan under her bottom, scenting the air like a stain in the oxygen molecules themselves.

Manny put his hand on Layla's shoulder and addressed her. "The bleeding is slowing. That's good news. But now both of them are showing signs of fetal distress, with the boy's heart rate beginning to fluctuate as well. Moreover, I remain particularly worried about the little girl, what with her being the smaller of the two of them. I strongly recommend that we do a Cesarean section—"

"But it's too soon!" Layla looked at Qhuinn in a panic. "It's too soon—"

Manny took the female's hand. "Layla, you've got to listen to me. The babies are struggling—but more to the point, you are not going to make it unless we get them out."

"I don't care about me! You said that the bleeding is stopping—"

"It's slowing. But we're running out of time and I need you as strong as possible when I put you under."

"I don't care what you do to me! You need to keep them inside—"

Layla hitched a breath as another contraction hit her, and Qhuinn rubbed his face. Then he motioned for Manny to step away with him.

Lowering his voice, Qhuinn said, "What the fuck's going on?"

Manny's eyes were steady in the midst of all the panic, a harbor in the thrashing sea of emotions. "I've spoken with Havers. There's nothing that can be done to keep the pregnancy going. On ultrasound, it's obvious that the placenta is separating from the uterus. It's exactly what happened to Beth—this is extremely common, especially with multiples, and the cause of most maternal and fetal deaths in your species. Layla hasn't done anything wrong—she did everything right. But the bottom line is, the pregnancy is failing and we're at the decision point where we need to save her life, and try to save theirs."

There was a pause. And Qhuinn ran the words that had been spoken to him back and forth in his head. "What about their lungs? We need another couple of nights—"

"We have special breathing apparatuses from Havers that can help them. We've got the right equipment. If we get them out, I know the protocol and so do Ehlena and Jane."

Qhuinn scrubbed his face and wanted to vomit. "Okay, all right. We're going to do it."

Shoring himself up, he went to Layla, stroking her blond hair back from her clammy face. "Layla—"

"I'm sorry! I'm so sorry! This is my fault—"

"Shh, shh, shh." He continued to run his hand over her head to soothe her protests. "Listen to me—no, listen me. Hear what I'm saying—there is no fault in this. And your life matters. I can't lose . . . I'm not going to lose everyone in this, okay? It's in the Scribe Virgin's hands, all of this. Whatever happens, it's what is meant to be."

"I'm so sorry. . . ." Her eyes clung to his, tears pouring out of the far corners, wetting the thin white pillow under her head. "Qhuinn, forgive me."

He pressed a kiss to her forehead. "There is nothing to forgive. But we need to do this—"

"I don't want to lose your young—"

"It's *our* young." He glanced over at Blay. "We did this together, and no matter the outcome, I'm at peace, okay? You did the absolute best you could, but at this point, we need to move forward."

"Where's Blay?" Another contraction hit her and she gritted her teeth, straining in the pain. "Where is—"

Blay came over. "I'm right here. I'm not leaving."

At that moment, Jane came in. "How are we?"

"Layla," Qhuinn said. "We need to do this. *Now.*"

As Layla lay on the gurney, her body outside of her control, her youngs' futures in doubt, she felt as though she were in a speeding car, heading for a sharp turn on a slick road. The metaphor was so apt that every time she blinked, she felt the careening velocity, knew the ringing screech of the tires, braced herself for impact as she went into a flipping, tire-over-roof accident that was surely going to kill her.

In fact, the pain of the impact was already with her, emanating from the small of her back in a steady hum, and then peaking in contractions that racked her belly.

"It's time," Qhuinn said, his mismatched eyes burning with a will so fierce she was momentarily reassured.

It was as if he were prepared to go to battle with death for her and the young.

"Okay?" he prompted.

She looked at Blay. And when the male nodded, she found herself nodding back. "Okay."

"Can we feed her?" Qhuinn asked.

Jane stepped in and shook her head. "We need her stomach empty for the anesthesia. And we have to put her under, there's no time for an epidural."

"Whatever you . . ." Layla cleared her throat. "Whatever needs to be done to save the young . . ."

She remembered when this had happened to Beth, what had had to be done to save her and L.W. If it turned out Layla could have no more young? Then so be it. She would have two. Or . . . perhaps one.

Or mayhap . . . none.

Oh, dearest Virgin Scribe, she prayed as she started to weep. *Take me. Leave the young and take me instead.*

Turning her head, she looked through her tears at those two neonatal medical cribs that had been rolled in and put against the wall. She tried to picture the young in them, small but alive.

She could not.

Moaning, she was struck by an absurd impulse to just get up and walk out, as if this were a movie she could depart from because she didn't like the plotline. Or a book she could close because she didn't care for the direction in which the author had taken the characters. Or a painting she could abandon with her brush because the scene she had intended to depict had turned into a mess.

Suddenly, there seemed to be people everywhere. Vishous had come in, his goateed face covered with a surgical mask, his street clothes hidden beneath a large sterile yellow suit. Ehlena was there. Qhuinn and Blay were suiting up. Manny and Jane were speaking back and forth in a kind of shorthand that didn't register.

"I can't breathe . . ." she groaned.

Abruptly, some kind of alarm went off, the shrill sound separating out from the generalized beeping of the machines that were monitoring her and the young.

"I can't . . . breathe. . . ."

"She's arresting!"

Layla had no idea who said that. Or even if it had been a male or a female that had spoken.

A strange feeling came over her, as if she were submerged in lukewarm water that muffled her sight and her hearing and caused her body to become weightless. The pain also drifted off, and that terrified her.

If she was hurting, she was still alive, correct?

As the abyss came up and claimed her consciousness, like a monster devouring prey, she tried to shout for help, to beg for the lives of her young, to apologize once again for transgressions only she knew about.

No time, though.

There was no more time left for her.

FIFTY-NINE

Assail sat in a fairly comfortable chair in a room that was of a rather nice temperature—and yet felt as though his skin was being burned off his bones.

Across the shallow space, the slave he had rescued was on a hospital bed, looking more like a pretrans than a full-grown adult male. Sheets and blankets had been set upon his naked form in order to warm him. Nutrients and fluids were being introduced into his veins via tubing. Various machines assessed the performance of his organs.

He was asleep.

Markcus had fallen asleep. Or passed out.

And so Assail sat in the hospital room of a total stranger, as incapable of leaving as if his own blood were under those covers, hooked up to those monitors, resting on that mattress.

Rubbing his arms, he wanted the sensation of heat to stop in his own flesh so he could concentrate more fully on Markcus's health. But he had already removed his suit jacket and taken off his tie. Next stop was naked.

It took him a while to realize what the problem was.

With a curse, he extracted his vial of cocaine, and held it in his

palm, looking at the brown transparent belly and the black screw on top.

He took care of his gnawing need quickly, feeling embarrassed that he had to snort the drug no more than a matter of feet away from the male.

How long before Naasha discovered what had been taken from her? he wondered.

And how could she have done that to another? Especially considering she had a stable of vital young males to service not only her sex, but her blood needs.

Indeed, every time Assail closed his eyes, he saw that cell, smelled that stench, re-lived bursting into that underground prison.

Where had she stolen him from? Was his family looking for him?

How long had he suffered down there, naught but a meal to be tapped into?

The diagnosis thus far was malnourishment, a kidney infection, fluid in the lungs and a sinus infection. But the medical staff had indicated there were further tests to be done.

The horror of it all made it difficult to breathe, and Assail had to sit forward in the chair.

Outside, he heard the Brothers talking and pacing in the hall. Clearly, someone was injured seriously, given the anxiety level, but he had not asked and no one had offered an explanation. Further, Vishous had had to go be of aid to whatever emergency was being dealt with, although he had promised to return—

The knock was soft.

"Do come in," Assail murmured, even though he felt as though he had no right to invite or disinvite visitors for Markcus.

It was a while before the door opened even a little.

"Hello?" Assail called out.

When he saw who it was, he recoiled.

Zsadist was a Brother he had long heard tales of. After all, such was the warrior's history and behavior that his reputation, even in the New World, had traveled to ears all around the Old Country. And yes, the male's scarred face was something to fear, the ragged, badly-closed old wound distorting his upper lip whilst his narrowed eyes glowed with malice. Standing just inside the room, with his nearly shaved head and his tremendous body, he appeared to be exactly what gossips had suggested he was—a sociopath to be avoided at all costs.

Assail had learned, however, that things had changed for him, of late. That he had mated. Had a young. Retracted from the murderous rage that had defined him ever since he, too, had been held against his will.

In fact, as his yellow eyes locked on the male upon the bed, he crossed his arms over his chest, rather as if he were seeking to comfort himself.

"I found him . . ." Assail had to clear his throat. "Chained to the wall."

Zsadist walked slowly to the bed and stared down at Markcus. He stayed there for the longest time, barely blinking, only the rise and fall of his chest and an occasional twitch of his eyebrows suggesting he was not a statue of some sort.

Assail could imagine what memories had perhaps come for him.

Those slave bands around the Brother's neck and wrists seemed black as the evil that had put the ink into his skin.

"His name is Markcus," Assail offered. "That is all I know about him."

Zsadist nodded. At least, Assail thought he did. Then the fighter spoke. "Let me . . . help. In some way. In any way?"

It was on the tip of Assail's tongue to say that there was naught to be done. But then a curling fury licked into his chest.

Assail was not a savior. Never had been. His interests had always been his own and no one else's. He was also not one to form attachments, quickly or permanently.

But Assail found himself narrowing his eyes on the Brother. "Exactly how far does that invitation extend?"

Instantly, that yellow stare flashed black, those eyes becoming soul-less pits of *Dhund*. "As far as is required. And then a hundred thousand feet farther."

"Even if it puts you in conflict with the King? For the manner I shall be seeking to exact justice does not involve edicts or resolves. And it will not be with Wrath's permission."

"There will be no conflict."

Assail's first thought was to rise out of his chair, ask for further arms, and proceed immediately back to that house.

But no, upon further reflection, that was not strategic enough. And not violent enough.

"I pray that you mean that, kind gentlemale."

"I am not gentle or kind."

Assail nodded. "Good. And worry not. I sense the outlet you are in search of, and I shall provide it to you, posthaste."

Back at the library in Naasha's *hellren's* vast mansion, Throe took the female by the shoulders and gave her a shake. "*Listen* to me. You *must* listen to me."

Even as he sought to quell her incessant ranting, he had to confess, though only to himself, that he was likewise frustrated beyond measure. He had wasted how long in this household? Bedding her, catering to her, seducing her into a false sense that they were in some kind of enduring relationship. And all along, she had assured him of the fealty of her "beloved" *hellren*. Spoken of how the money would flow like wine all over her when the old male finally passed. Related to Throe her love for him regardless of her mated status or her other lovers.

Assail had entered the picture, however—and that bastard's presence had created such a flush in between Naasha's thighs that Throe had had to act earlier than he would have liked: The proper sequence would have been first to change Naasha's own will, naming Throe her next of kin—under the guise that he would be mating her as soon as the mourning period for her current *hellren* had passed. And then for Throe to arrange for the death of the old male. Followed by a "suicide" for her.

Whereupon Throe's coffers would be set and he could use the funds to imbed himself in the *glymera* properly and set up a strategy for taking Wrath off that ridiculous elected throne he had created for himself.

Assail, that fucking slut, however, had changed the order, forcing Throe's hand such that forgeries were going to become necessary. It was either early action, though, or him running the risk that Naasha's rather oily affections could transfer to her newest suitor, upsetting the applecart all over the market square, as it were.

Throe had seen the way she looked at Assail.

Had felt the pull to that male himself, goddamn them both.

And, now, this mess.

That old *hellren* of hers had left everything to a distant relation, a male whose name Throe did not recognize.

"Naasha, my love," Throe said urgently. "I need you to be logical."

This looked so bad. That solicitor waiting out in the foyer, no doubt coming to all kinds of conclusions that were both accurate and unhelpful. Her falling apart to anger. Him getting increasingly frustrated.

Taking another tactic, Throe walked over to the ornate desk and placed his hand upon the stack of papers that Saxton had brought with him. "This. *This* is your only focus. Anything other than successfully challenging these provisions is an unacceptable distraction."

"I have been shamed! To be forsaken like this is an abomination! It is—"

"Do you want to be reasonable? Or poor? Your choice is now." That shut her up. "Imagine all of this gone, yourself surrounded by none of this, your clothes, the jewels, the servants, this very roof o'er your head—gone. Because that is what is going to happen unless you get some control over yourself. The abomination is not what your *hellren* did to you. The abomination is your letting it happen. Now, I am going to get the attorney back in here. You are going to shut up and listen to what he says. Or you can continue to prance and stamp around here, wasting time and strategy, just so that you can enhance your victim status—to absolutely no cash avail."

It was rather like zipping up a ballgown, he reflected. All at once, a composure stilled her and transformed her face from flushed and crazed to, if not placid exactly, certainly something far more evenkeeled.

Throe walked back over to her. Taking her shoulders, he kissed her. "That is my female. Now you are ready to proceed. No more outbursts. No matter what else is contained therein, you will allow the solicitor to finish this presentation. We do not know how to fight if we do not know what we have to fight against."

For the Virgin Scribe's sake, let this stick, he thought.

"Now, I shall bring him back in, yes?" When she nodded, he stepped back. "Be aware of all you have to lose. That can be remarkably clarifying."

"You are right." She took a deep breath. "You are very strong."

You have no idea, he thought as he turned away.

Back at the double doors, he opened them—

Sniffing the air, he frowned and glanced around the foyer. Saxton was over by a Flemish painting, inspecting the depiction of dewy flowers upon a black background, his hands clasped behind his back, his lean torso tilted forward.

"Are we ready then?" the solicitor asked without looking up. "Or does she need even more time to compose herself? It has been over an hour."

Throe looked about. The doors of the parlor and the study were all in the same positions they had been in. There was no one rushing anywhere. All looked . . . as it had.

But why was there a prevailing scent of fresh air all around . . . fresh air and . . . something else.

"Is there aught wrong?" Saxton inquired. "Do you wish me to return at another time?"

"No, she is ready." He stared at the attorney, searching for some sign of . . . he knew not what. "I have calmed her."

Saxton straightened. Adjusted his tie. And came over in a gait that was unhurried. Totally natural. Without any airs.

"Mayhap she shall allow me to finish this now." Saxton stopped. "Although, if you'd prefer, I can just leave the papers and the two of you can go through them. My verbalizing the provisions, or not, shall not change a thing."

"No," Throe said smoothly. "It is best that she have an opportunity to ask questions. Do come in again, and please pardon our delay."

As he stepped to one side and indicated the way, his instincts pricked and refused to be quieted. "In fact, perhaps it is better if you take a moment with her privately. Mayhap my presence is the problem."

Saxton inclined his head. "As you wish. I am here to serve—or not—at her behest."

"We are ever in your debt," Throe murmured. In a louder tone, he said into the room, "Naasha, darling, I shall go see about some victuals. Perhaps that will be of aid to this tedious process."

He waited as she placed her hand across her bosom and sighed dramatically. "Yes, my love, I am feeling weakened from the news."

"But of course."

Shutting the doors behind the attorney, he sniffed the air again. Too fresh. And too cold. Someone had opened a door or a window.

Striding across to the front entrance of the manse, he opened it wide—and stepped out to regard the parking area.

Saxton had come in a car. He'd seen the male arrive from up in his bedroom.

Wheeling around, he strode back into the house and went directly to the study doors, sliding one side back. "Assail," he snapped.

Alas, the room was empty.

SIXTY

Quuinn held his breath as the anesthesia was administered to Layla and a dark brown, pungent-smelling antiseptic was splashed across her round belly. And he further did not breathe as Manny, Jane, Ehlena, and Vishous clustered around the operating table, two on each side, their gloved fingers picking up and trading instruments back and forth.

You could scent the blood in the air as the cut was made, and Qhuinn felt the floor go into a wave pattern under his feet, sure as if the tile had liquefied.

As Blay's hold bit into his arm, it was hard to tell whether that was because the male was worried about Qhuinn fainting, or because he himself was likewise unsteady. Probably some of both.

How did it come to this? Qhuinn wondered silently.

But as soon as the thought hit him, he shook his head. What the fuck had he assumed was going to happen with two young in there?

"Is she all right?" he barked. "Are they alive?"

"Here comes one," Blay said roughly.

"Baby A," Manny pronounced as he handed a little purple bundle to Ehlena.

There wasn't even a chance to look at the kid. The nurse moved fast, rushing the infant over to one of two triage beds that had been set up.

Too silent. Motherfucker—it was too damn quiet.

"Is it alive!" Qhuinn yelled. *"Is it alive!"*

Blay had to hold him back—but then again the lunge forward was ridiculous. Like he could do anything to help any of this? Oh, and as if he wanted the nurse to be thinking about anything other than saving that infant?

But Ehlena looked over. "Yes, he is. He is alive—we just need to keep him that way."

Qhuinn took no comfort in any of that. How could he when the entity she was intubating and giving drugs to looked like some kind of tiny alien. A tiny, fragile, wrinkly alien that had nothing in common with the fat babies he'd seen born to humans on T.V. from time to time.

"Jesus Christ," he moaned. "So small."

The infant wasn't going to survive. He knew it down to his soul. They were going to lose him and—

"Baby B," Jane announced as she handed something over to Vishous.

V steamed by with the young, and Qhuinn gasped.

The daughter—his daughter—was even smaller. And she wasn't purple.

She was gray. Gray as stone.

All at once, the memory he had taken with him when he had serviced Layla during her needing came back to him. It was from when he had nearly died himself, and had gone up unto the Fade, and had faced off at a white door in the midst of a foggy white landscape.

He had seen an image on that door.

The image of a young female with blond hair and eyes that were shaped like his—eyes that had changed color before him from the precise shade of Layla's to the mismatched blue and green of his own.

With an animal's cry of pain, he bellowed into the OR, screaming with an agony he had never felt before—

He had guessed wrong. He had . . . been wrong. He had misinterpreted what he had seen.

The vision on the door had been not the prediction of a daughter to come.

But a daughter he had lost in birth.

A daughter . . . who had died.

SIXTY-ONE

As Mary sped through the underground tunnel to the training center, the slapping sounds of her rushing feet echoed out in front of her, an auditory shadow seemingly in as much of a hurry as she was to get where she was going. When she came to the door that opened into the office's supply closet, she put in the code and burst through into the shallow space beyond, passing by the shelves of pens and pads, the back-up flash drives and stacks of printer paper.

Out in the office, she pulled up short. Tohr was sitting behind the desk, staring at a computer screen that had all kinds of rainbow-colored bubbles obscuring the DailyMail.co.uk home page.

He jumped as he noticed her and then scrubbed his face. "Hey."

"How are they?"

"I don't know. They've been in there for what feels like forever."

"Where's Autumn?"

"She's out at Xhex's hunting cabin. It's my night off and she was getting it ready for us to . . . you know." He checked his watch. "I've been debating on whether or not to call her. I was hoping for news first, so she wouldn't worry. Well, good news, that is."

"You should tell her what's going on."

"I know." His eyes returned to the monitor. "I, ah . . . I'm not handling this very well."

Mary went around the desk and put her hand on the male's huge shoulder. The tension in that big body was so great, she felt as though she'd laid her palm on a knot. Made out of granite.

"Tohr, I don't think you should be alone. And if I were her, I'd be really upset if you didn't let me support you."

"I just . . ." Now he looked at the office phone. "I'm back in the old days, you know."

"I know. And she'll understand that. Autumn is one of the most understanding people I've ever met."

The Brother glanced up at her, his deep blue eyes boring into her skull. "Mary, am I ever going to be all right?"

In that moment, she was transported back to sitting with Bitty in Rhage's GTO—and she thought, Yes, that is what everyone wants to know, isn't it. Am I okay? Am I loved? Am I safe?

Will I get through this?

Whatever the "this" was, be it death or loss, confusion or terror, depression or anger.

"You're all right already, Tohr. And I really think you need to call your *shellan*. You don't need to protect her from your pain. She knows exactly the burdens you carry—and she picked you with all of them. There is nothing here that will shock her or make her think you're weak. I will guarantee, however, that if you try to keep this from her, it's going to make her feel like you don't trust her or you don't think *she* is strong enough to handle things."

"What if the young don't make it? What if—"

At that moment, a scream . . . a horrible, masculine scream . . . racked what seemed like the entire training center, the sound so loud it rattled the glass door, a sonic boom of mourning.

As Tohr scrambled out of the chair, Mary bolted for the exit, ripping it open.

It was not a surprise to see the entire Brotherhood gathered once again in the vast corridor. It was also not a shock that every single one of the males, and their mates, was staring at the closed door of the main OR. It was further apt that all of the Chosen and the directrix, Amalya, stood among them looking equally panicked.

No one said anything. It wasn't as if that scream of Qhuinn's didn't explain enough.

Mary went to Rhage, slipping her arm around his waist, and as he looked at her, he pulled her in close.

When there was nothing further for a moment, people began to mill. Soft talk broke the silence. Tohr took out his phone with hands that shook as he sat down on the concrete floor like his legs had fallen out from underneath him.

"Oh, God," Rhage said. "This is . . ."

Unbearable, Mary thought.

To lose a child, no matter how premature, no matter the circumstances, was an agony like no other.

For the first time in his adult life, Vishous froze in the midst of a medical emergency. It was only a split second, and he came back online an instant later . . . but there was something about the little lifeless body in his palms that stopped, literally, everything about him.

He would never forget the sight of it.

Wouldn't forget, either, the scream that Qhuinn let out.

Shaking himself into focus, however, he snapped back into action to do the one thing that might possibly help. With steady hands, he got a small tube down the infant's throat, slid a mask over the face and hooked the breathing apparatus up to a piece of medical equipment that was not human, but strictly for vampires. When he initiated the flow, a fortified, oxygenated saline solution went into the young's lungs, flushing out the sacs, blowing them open . . . and then sucking out the liquid, which was sent into a filtering system that would clean it, reoxygenate it, and send it back in.

Using his thumb, he pressed into the achingly tiny chest, massaging the heart with a rhythm.

Bad color. Really wrong color. Goddamn gray of a headstone.

And the young was lax, nothing moving, the arms and legs that were scrawny and wrinkled as a hatchling's flopping loose from shoulders and hips.

The eyes were open, the all-white orbs showing no pupils or irises because the little girl was so fucking premature.

"Come on, wake up . . . come on . . ."

Nothing. There was nothing.

Without thinking, he shouted over his shoulder, "Payne! Get me fucking Payne—RIGHT NOW!"

He didn't know who responded to the command. He didn't fucking care. All that mattered was that a millisecond later, his sister was right next to him.

"Wake her up, Payne," he barked. "Wake this kid up—I am *not* having this on my conscience for the rest of my goddamn life. You wake up this fucking kid right fucking now!"

Okay, yeah, his delivery sucked. But he didn't care—and neither did his sister, evidently.

And she knew just what to do.

Extending her open hand directly over the infant, she closed her eyes. "Someone hold me up. I need—"

Qhuinn and Blay were on it, each of the males taking one of her elbows. And, shit, V wanted to say something to the pair, offer some kind of . . . anything . . . but there was nothing that could be helped with mere words here.

"Payne, you gotta do this."

As the aching syllables hit the airwaves, it was a shock to realize that he had spoken them, that it was his voice that was cracking, that he, the one male on the planet who never begged, ever, for anything, was the person uttering the shaky—

Warm.

He felt a warmth.

And then he saw the light, the glow that, unlike the destructive force that he housed in his palm, was a gentle healing power, a rejuvenating force, a blessed, miracle-giving benediction.

"Qhuinn?" his sister said roughly. "Qhuinn, give me your hand."

Vishous got the fuck out of the way, although he had to still hold the breathing mask in place because the infant was too premature for even the smallest one Havers had.

Qhuinn extended an arm, and, shit, the male was shaking so badly it was as if he were standing on an agitator. Payne took what he put out, though, and laid it under her glowing palm so that the energy had to pass through his flesh to get to the infant's.

The brother gasped and jerked in response, his teeth beginning to chatter, his flushed face instantly paling.

"I need another set of hands over here," Vishous barked. "We need to keep Dad off the floor!"

Next thing he knew, Manny was by Qhuinn, the human jacking a hold on the guy around the waist.

As energy began to leave him and channel into the young, Qhuinn started to breathe hard, his chest pumping, his mouth falling open, his lungs clearly burning—

The infant changed color in the blink of an eye, all that was matte and gray and the terrible hue of death going red and pink.

And then the tiny hands, the impossibly tiny, but nonetheless perfectly formed, hands twitched. And so with the legs, the feet kicking once, twice. And so with the belly, the hollow pit expanding and contracting along with the beat of the machine.

Payne didn't stop. And Qhuinn lost his footing, only Blay's strong arms and Manny's extra support keeping his body from the floor.

Longer, Vishous thought. Keep going longer. Bleed the well dry if you have to. . . .

And that was exactly what his wonderful sister did. She kept pumping energy from herself into and through Qhuinn, where it was magnified and focused, and thereafter funneled into the young.

She kept going until she passed out cold.

Qhuinn wasn't far behind her.

But Vishous couldn't worry about them. He just kept his eyes on the young, looking for signs that the life force wouldn't hold . . . that the gray would return and signal death's renewed grip on the little thing . . . that the miracle would be but a short, cruel respite. . . .

Don't you do this, Mother, he thought. Don't you do this to these good people.

Don't take this life from them.

SIXTY-TWO

Rhage was probably crushing Mary with the hold he had on her, but she didn't seem to notice. Good thing, as he doubted he could have loosened his arms.

All around him, he was both dimly and achingly aware of his brothers, their mates and the Chosen, the household and community standing together in the midst of the tragedy on the far side of a door that was too flimsy to contain all the ensuing grief.

Rhage just couldn't help thinking about Bitty. God, if he got the chance . . . if he and Mary got the chance, he would never rest from protecting that little girl. Making sure she got the life she deserved, the education she needed to be independent, the grounding to know that she was never without a home, no matter how far away she traveled.

"It's so awful," Mary whispered. "So terrible. There's just been too much death around here lately—"

The door opened wide and Blay exploded out of that OR like he'd been shot from a cannon.

"She's alive!" he yelled. "They're both alive! They're alive! And Layla is stable!"

There was a moment of total silence.

As if everybody who was in the corridor kind of had to reprocess everything, switch to a different track, change to another gear.

"And Qhuinn's out cold on the floor!"

Later, Rhage would think it was bad timing that the cheering started up right after that little update—but who the fuck cared?

Blay was engulfed in bodies, everyone shouting and crying, hugging and slapping palms, cursing and laughing and sputtering and coughing as details were demanded and given once, twice, many times. There was just so much noise, so much life, and Rhage was right in there with the best of them, feeling like the lottery had been won, the gift given, the semi-trailer truck sailing by instead of striking one of their own.

Doc Jane was the next one out, and she peeled her mask off her face as everyone cheered for her. But unlike the new dad, she was careful to shut the door behind herself, holding it in place.

"Shhhh," she said with a laugh. "We have a lot of patients in there. I need two gurneys to come through here, can you guys make some room? Oh, thanks, Ehlena."

The nurse had obviously exited through the other door, and was doing a push-and-pull with the rollers. People milled to get out of the way, but Blay was still getting hugs, which led to a little bit of a delay.

"How can I help?" Rhage asked Doc Jane.

"Well, right now we're good. Everyone's okay—we just need to move some patients around."

Rhage took the doctor's arm before she turned away. "Are we really out of the woods with the young?"

Those forest green eyes held his. "As much as we can be right now. It's going to be a long couple of nights, but that water ventilation system of Havers's saved both their lives. We owe him."

Rhage nodded and let the female go. And then he was going over to where Mary and Tohr were hugging and waited his turn. He just wanted to feel his *shellan* against him once more.

As Mary pivoted toward him, he held out his arms. It was so damned good to have her jump into them, and he lifted her off the floor.

"You ready to give it a shot?" he said into her ears. "You ready to be a parent with me?"

"Oh, Rhage." His *shellan*'s voice caught. "Oh, I hope so."

"Me, too." Putting her back down on the ground, he frowned. "What?"

"Ah . . ." Mary looked around. "Where do you think we can get a little privacy for a sec?"

"Come with me."

Taking her by the hand, he led her away from the crowd, going past the locker room and the weight room to the entrance to the gym.

"Ladies first," he said as he held one of the steel doors open.

The security lights softly illuminated the vast space, and the exit signs over the doors glowed red like little hearths.

"I've forgotten how big it is in here," Mary said as she broke away, put her arms out, and circled around, going *Sound of Music*.

Rhage hung back and just watched her move, her body lithe and beautiful to him, stirring him in places that were going to get greedy fast if he didn't look away.

"I can turn on some lights," he murmured, hoping for something to do.

"I like it dim like this. It's romantic."

"I agree."

As his cock kicked behind the leathers he'd thrown on for dinner, he shook his head. Clearly, they had something important to talk about, yet here he was with sex on the brain. Disgraceful.

But, man, she was hot.

And he was juiced from the good news.

And they were alone.

And then Mary did a pirouette and some kind of sashay thing that made his eyes go to her ass and stay there.

Cursing under his breath, he cracked his back and stretched first one arm and then the other.

"Is there something wrong?" God, he hoped not. On a lot of levels. "Mary?"

"Oh, Rhage. Loss is hard, you know?"

The sadness in her voice was like a great eraser, wiping all the erotic right off his mind.

"Is Bitty okay?"

"That's what she wanted to know." Mary smiled in a way that seemed mournful. "That's what Tohr wanted to know, too. Isn't that what everyone does . . . and yes, she's all right. She's just going through a lot."

"She needs a family."

Mary nodded. "On the way here, while I was driving, I talked to one of the social workers, the one Marissa has assigned to our . . . case, or adoption petition, or whatever we're calling it. We're kind of making up the procedure as we go, but she's going to talk to you and me separately and then together. About where we are in our lives. How we came to the decision to want to adopt. What our plans are both with, and without, Bitty."

"What do I need to study to pass that?"

She twirled her way back over to him. "Just be honest. And thoughtful. There are no wrong answers."

"Are you sure about that? 'Cuz I'm pretty frickin' sure she's not going to like my response to 'Do you have a beast living inside of you?'"

"We talked about that with Marissa, remember? We can't hide it, but the beast has never hurt me, and it's never been a threat to anyone in the household—as long as they were not in the field. And I can counter any mortal danger argument with the whole I-can't-die stuff. No problem."

God, what in the world made them think this was going to work, he wondered.

"It will kill me if we can't do this because of my curse."

"We can't think like that." She picked up his hand and kissed it. "We just can't."

"Fine, so assume we pass. Whatever that looks like. What then?"

"After that, if we were to follow human procedure, Rhym would come and do a site visit at the mansion. But it's a little different considering where we live and with who."

"Whatever, if someone has to come here, I'll take care of that."

"Well, let's see what she wants to do, okay?" Mary tucked her hair back. "And listen, while we were talking . . . Bitty's been through so much—and so much so recently. I really think it's better for everyone if we start off in a foster kind of relationship."

"No. I don't want to lose her—"

"Hear me out. Bitty's just lost her mother. It's important that she not feel as though we're trying to eclipse anything. I think when we talk to her, we tell her that she's welcome to stay at Safe Place for however long she wants. Or she could come here with us."

"Can we bribe the kid?"

Mary laughed in a burst. "What? No!"

"Aw, come on, Mary. What do you think she'd like? Ice cream? Unlimited T.V. privileges? A pony, for crissakes. Or can I just buy her off with a handbag. Is she that age yet?"

Mary batted at his chest. "No, you cannot buy her off." Then she dropped her voice. "I think she's an animal lover. When in doubt, we'll play the Boo/George card—with pictures."

Rhage laughed and pulled his female in for a kiss. "Have you thought about where she could stay in the house? I mean . . . if it actually goes down?"

"As a matter of fact, yes, but it's going to mean some reorganization. And a move for us."

"To where? The Pit is full, and Butch and V swear like truckers. They're worse than me."

"Well, I thought maybe we could ask Trez if he'd be willing to switch rooms with us? We could be up on the third floor in those bedrooms he and iAm use? I mean, both suites are their own spaces and have their own bathrooms, but we'd be so close if Bitty needed us."

"That's a great idea."

"Mmm-hmm."

Holding his Mary against him, he became curiously aware of the great space that surrounded them. In the dim lighting, the gym's contours and corners were mostly obscured in shadow, the bald bleachers, the ropes that hung from the ceiling, the basketball markings on the shiny pine floors nothing but footnotes in the cavernous interior.

Rhage frowned, thinking there was a metaphor here.

The world was kind of like this, vast and empty except for who you loved, nothing but a warmer version of space filled with random junk you bumped into. The grounding was your family, your friends, your tribe of like minds. Without that?

He broke away and started to walk around.

No pirouettes for him.

"Rhage?"

He thought about what she'd said, about those meetings with the social worker, him with his beast, her with her . . . unusual situation. And then he remembered lying on the field of that abandoned campus, him on the ground, her over him, his Mary fighting to keep him alive even though they had an out that in a moment like that was a miracle, indeed.

When he stopped, it was on the free-throw line. No basketball in his hands, no hoop to shoot it through, no line-ups of teammates and opponents. There was an urgency, though.

He stared up to where the basket would have been, if the great metal arm with its glass square had been lowered from the ceiling into place.

"Mary, I want you to promise me something."

"Anything."

Looking over at her, he found it difficult to speak, and he had to clear his throat. "If we . . . if you and I end up with Bitty? If we take her in as our own, I want you to promise . . ." The center of his chest began to burn. "If I die, you have to stay here with her. You can't leave her behind, okay? If I go, you stay. I won't have that little girl losing another full set of parents. Not gonna happen."

Mary put her hand to her mouth and closed her eyes, lowering her head.

"I'll wait for you," he said hoarsely. "If I die, I'll wait for you in the Fade just like everyone else does. Hell, I'll watch over the two of you from the clouds. I'll be an angel to you both. But you . . . you have to stay with her."

Bitty, after all, was going to live longer than he would. That was the way you hoped and prayed it worked. Children succeeded their parents, took their places, walked in future paths carrying on the traditions and the lessons so that that which had been passed down could be passed on again.

It was immortality for the mortal.

And that was true whether you birthed your young or opened your arms to them.

"You stay here, Mary."

As the implications of Rhage's request started to sink in, Mary felt her heart pound and her body break out in a cold sweat.

Even though she had confessed a desire to keep him on the planet for exactly the rationale he was laying out, to hear him put it like that? The whole thing made her queasy, returning her to that moment when she'd thought she was going to lose him—even though, at that time, she'd been aware she could go find him in the Fade.

It was as if he were once more lying there gasping for breath he could not quite catch, bleeding inside his chest, slipping away even as his body stayed before her.

Then she thought of Bitty in the back of the GTO, crying, lost, alone.

"Yes," Mary said roughly. "I will stay. For her. For however long she is alive, I'll stay with her."

Rhage exhaled long and slow. "That's good. That's . . ."

They met in the middle, each walking toward the other, and when they embraced, she put her head to the side of his heavy chest, hearing his heartbeat right next to her ear. Staring off across the dimly lit gym, she hated the choice she had just made, the vow she had just taken . . . and at the same time, she was so very grateful for it.

"She can't know," Mary blurted as she pushed back a little and looked up. "Bitty can't know about me—at least not until after she makes her decision. I don't want her fear of being alone coloring the choice she's going to have to make. If she wants to come with us, it has to be because she chooses to freely. All the death in her life can be part of it, but it can't be all of it."

"Agreed."

Mary went back to being close to him. "I love you."

"I love you, too."

They stood there in the gym for the longest time. And then Rhage switched his hold on her, extending one set of their arms out to the side, and snaking his other around her waist.

"Dance with me?" he said.

She laughed a little. "To what kind of music?"

"Anything. Nothing. It doesn't matter. Just dance with me here in the dark."

For some reason, tears pricked her eyes as they started to move, swaying at first, the shuffle of their feet over the smooth floor and the rustle of their clothes the only auditory accompaniment. Soon, they found a rhythm, and then he was leading her in a waltz, an old-fashioned, proper waltz that he was far better at than she was.

Sweeping around the empty space, she discovered that a symphony started to play in her mind, the strings and the flutes, the timpani drums and the trumpets giving majesty and power to their dancing.

Around and around they went until she was smiling up at him even as a tear fell.

She knew what he was doing. She knew exactly why he had asked her to do this.

He was reminding her that the future was unknown and unknowable.

So if you had the chance . . . even if there was no music and no ballgown, no tuxedo or gala . . . when your true love asked you to dance?

It was important to say yes.

SIXTY-THREE

Vishous stood outside of the gym, looking through one of the steel doors that had the glass windows with chicken wire running through them.

Rhage and Mary were dancing in the empty space, twirling around, the female's smaller body held tightly and led by her male's much, much larger one. They were looking at each other, staring into each other's eyes. Shit, you could swear there was a quartet or maybe a full orchestra playing in there, the way they moved so well together.

He wasn't much of a dancer himself.

Besides, you couldn't waltz to Rick Ross or Kendrick Lamar.

Taking out a hand-rolled from the ass pocket of his leathers, he lit up and exhaled as he leaned a shoulder on the jamb and continued to watch.

You had to respect the two of them, he thought. Going after that kid, trying to make a family happen. Then again, Rhage and Mary were always on the same page, nothing ruffling their relationship, everything always perfect.

Which was what happened when you paired a levelheaded therapist with Brad Pitt and Channing Tatum's love child: cosmic harmony.

God, in comparison, his and Jane's relationship seemed kind of . . . clinical.

No dancing in the dark for them, not unless it was the horizontal kind—and when was the last time that had happened? Jane had been flat-out at the clinic, and he'd been dealing with all kinds of shit.

Okay, this was weird. Even though he was not one for envy—it, along with so many emotions, was just a waste of fucking time—he did find himself wishing he was a little closer to normal. Not that he apologized for his kink, or the fact that he was predominantly a head guy, not a heart guy. Still, when he stood like this on the outside looking in at what his brother had, he did feel broken in some un-named way.

It wasn't that he wanted to turn into the male version of Adele or some shit.

Yeah, file that under Good-bye.

But he did wish . . .

Oh, fuck, he didn't know what the hell he was going on about.

Changing gears—before he ended up with a pair of lace panties on—he thought of Qhuinn's daughter, of that tiny little thing that had come back from the dead.

How had Payne known what to do? Shit, if she hadn't . . .

Vishous frowned as a memory of Mary surfaced and refused to sink back down. She had been talking about when she had saved Rhage's life . . . when she had moved the dragon around to the center of his chest so his beast could somehow heal the gunshot wound.

I don't know how I knew what to do, she had said to him. Or something to that effect.

He thought of himself confronting his mother as Rhage had been dying, demanding that she do something before he'd stormed off, all pissed and shit. And then he recalled the demand that he'd sent out as he'd worked on the lifeless body of Qhuinn's daughter.

Shit.

Leaning down, he stamped out his half-smoked cigarette on the sole of his boot and tossed the butt in the trash.

Closing his eyes . . .

. . . he dematerialized up to the courtyard of his mother's private quarters, re-forming in front of the colonnade.

Instantly, he knew there was something off.

Looking over his shoulder, he frowned. The fountain that had always run with crystal-clear water . . . was still. And when he walked over to its basin, he discovered that the thing was bone-dry, its pool empty sure as if it had never been full.

Then he glanced over at the tree that had held the songbirds.

They were gone. All of them.

As warning bells started to ring in his skull, he broke out into a run, crossing over to the entry to his *mahmen*'s private quarters. He pounded on the door, but not for long—once again he braced a shoulder and slammed himself into the panels.

This time, the thing broke free of all its hinges, falling flat as a dead body onto the stone floor beyond.

"Mother . . . *fucker*."

Everything was gone. The bedding platform. The dressing table. The one chair. Even the double-locked cell where Payne had been kept behind drapes was exposed, the white fabric swaths that had hung on runners no longer in place.

Closing his eyes, he let his senses sweep the room, probing for clues. His mother had just been here. He knew it in his blood, some remnant of her energy source remaining in the space as a scent might linger after someone departed. But where had she gone?

He thought of the crowd down below in the training center. Amalya, the directrix, had been among them, standing with Cormia and Phury, and all the other Chosen who had come to pray for, and witness, the births.

The Scribe Virgin had waited until she was all alone before leaving.

She who knew all, saw all, had deliberately picked a moment of crisis down on Earth, when everyone who might have had reason to be up here was otherwise occupied.

Vishous bolted out of the private quarters. "Mother! Where the fuck are you?"

He didn't expect an answer—

A sound rippled to his ears, emanating from somewhere outside of the courtyard. Following it, he went to the door that opened into the Sanctuary and looked across the verdant land.

Birds.

It was the songbirds singing somewhere off in the distance.

Falling into a jog, he tracked the dulcet harmonies, crossing over

the cropped green grass and passing by empty marble temples and dormitories.

"Mother?" he hollered across the barren landscape. "Mother!"

"Hi, *mahmen*, you're awake now."

As Layla heard the male voice above her, she realized that, yes, her eyes were open, and yes, she was alive—

"Young!" she shouted.

A sudden burst of energy had her trying to sit up, but gentle hands eased her back down. And as a flare of pain clawed its way across her lower belly, Qhuinn put his face in front of hers.

He was smiling. From ear to ear.

Yes, his eyes were red rimmed, and he was pale and a little shaky, but the male was smiling so widely, his jaw had to hurt.

"Everybody's okay," he said. "Our daughter gave us a helluva scare, but both of them are okay. Breathing. Moving. Alive."

A tidal wave of emotion swamped her, her chest literally exploding with a combination of relief, joy, and the afterburn of the terror she'd felt before they'd put her under. And as if he knew exactly what she was feeling, Qhuinn started hugging her, wrapping her in his arms— and she tried to hug him back, but she didn't have the strength.

"Blay," she said roughly. "Where's—"

"Right here. I'm right here."

Over Qhuinn's big shoulder, she saw the other male and wished she could reach for him—and as if he were aware of that, he came in, too, all three of them wrapping up in an embrace that left them wobbly, and yet somehow stronger, too.

"Where are they?" she asked. "Where . . ."

The males inched back, and the way Qhuinn looked at Blay made her nervous. "What," she demanded. "What's wrong."

Blay took her hand. "Listen, we want you to be ready, okay? They're very small. They're really . . . very small. But they're strong. Both Doc Jane and Manny checked them over—Ehlena, too. And we video-conferenced with Havers and reviewed everything with him. They're going to be here for a while on the water ventilators, until their lungs mature and they can breathe and eat on their own, but they're doing great."

Layla found herself nodding as she swallowed a load of fear back down into her gut. Looking at Qhuinn, she teared up again. "I tried to keep them in—I tried—"

He shook his head firmly, that blue-and-green stare dead serious. "It was an issue with your placenta, *nalla*. There was nothing you could have done or not done to prevent it from happening. It was exactly the same thing that happened with Beth."

She put her hands on her much-flatter stomach. "Did they take my womb?"

Blay smiled. "No. They got the young out and stopped the bleeding. You can have more young if the Virgin Scribe provides."

Layla looked down her body, feeling a rush of relief. And also sadness for the Queen. "I was lucky."

"Yes, you were," Qhuinn said.

"We were all lucky," she corrected, glancing at them both. "When may I see them?"

Qhuinn stepped back. "They're right over there."

Layla struggled to sit up, taking the fathers' arms. And then she gasped. "Oh . . ."

Before she knew it, she was getting off the mattress, even though it hurt, and in spite of the fact that she was connected to about a hundred and fifty thousand pounds of medical equipment.

"Shit," Qhuinn said. "Are you sure you want to—"

"Okay, we're moving," Blay interjected. "We are up and moving."

With a single-minded focus she had never known before, she didn't pay any attention to anything other than getting over to her young: not the way the males scrambled to organize the rolling monitors, or how much she had to lean on various arms and shoulders, or how much pain her abdomen hollered about.

The incubators were up against the wall, side by side, separated by about three feet. Brilliant blue lights were shining down on the tiny little forms, and oh . . . Fates . . . the wires, the tubes . . .

That was when she got a little light-headed.

"Don't you love the sunglasses," Blay commented.

Suddenly, she laughed. "They look like mini-Wraths." Then she got serious. "Are you sure . . ."

"Positive," Qhuinn said. "They've got a ways to go—but, shit, they are fighters. Especially her."

Layla inched closer to her daughter. "When can I hold them?"

"Doc Jane wants us to give them a little time. Tomorrow?" Blay said. "Maybe the night after?"

"I'll wait." Even though it would be the hardest thing she would ever do. "I'll wait for however long it takes."

She turned the other way and looked at her son. "Dearest Virgin Scribe, does he look like you, no?"

"I know, right?" Qhuinn shook his head. "It's just crazy. I mean . . ."

"What are you going to name them?" Blay asked. "It's time for you two to think of names."

Oh, indeed, Layla thought. In the vampire tradition, youngs' births were not anticipated by any kind of planning. There were no showers as humans did, no lists of boy names and girl names, no stacks of diapers, racks of bottles, or even bassinettes and booties. For vampires, it was considered bad luck to get ahead of oneself and assume a healthy birth.

"Yes," she said, refocusing on her daughter. "We must have a naming."

At that moment, the little tiny infant girl moved her head and seemed to look up, through the sunglasses and the Plexiglas, past the distance between mother and child.

"She's going to grow up to be beautiful," Blay murmured. "Absolutely beautiful."

"Lyric," Layla blurted. "She shall be called Lyric."

Blay recoiled. "Lyric? You know, that's my . . . do you know that's my *mahmen*'s . . ."

As the male stopped speaking, Qhuinn started to smile. And then he bent down and kissed Layla's cheek. "Yes. Absolutely. She'll be called Lyric."

Blay blinked a couple of times. "My *mahmen* will be . . . incredibly honored. As am I."

Layla squeezed the male's hand. "Your parents shall be the only *granhmen* and father these young will e'er know. It is fitting that one of their names be represented. And for our son—mayhap we shall petition the King for a Brother's name? It seems fitting, as their sire is a brave and noble member of the Black Dagger Brotherhood."

"Oh, I don't know about that," Qhuinn hedged.

"Yes." Blay nodded. "That's a good idea."

Qhuinn started shaking his head. "But I don't know if—"

"So it is settled," Layla announced.

When Blay nodded, Qhuinn put his palms up. "I know when I'm beat."

Layla winked at Blay. "He's a smart one, isn't he."

Outside the birthing room, Jane reviewed the chart Ehlena had just handed her, flipping through pages that detailed the blood slave's progress. "Good, good . . . his vitals are really improving. Let's continue to push those fluids. I want to keep him on the IV for a little longer, and then let's see if we can get a Chosen here to feed him."

"I've already asked Phury." Rehv's *shellan* winced. "I honestly don't know how that's going to go, though. That male is in really bad shape. Up here."

As Ehlena indicated her head, Jane nodded. "I talked to Mary about it. She said she's ready to speak with him as soon as he's medically more stable."

"She's awesome."

"Too right."

Jane gave the folder back, trading it for Layla's. Yes, she could have easily transitioned to all-electronic medical records, but she had been trained back in the days before everything was computerized, and she'd always preferred good, old-fashioned paper.

She had to smile as she thought of Vishous's disapproval. He was dying to get a halfway decent computer system going down here, but he respected her prerogative, even as he was frustrated by her. And they did enter summary notes into a database, something that Jane liked to spend Sunday afternoons on when everybody was quiet.

It was a meditation exercise as much as anything else.

"So how're our kids doing?" she murmured as she ran through the notes Ehlena had made during the latest hourly check. "Oh, you go, girl. Look at those oxygen stats. Right where we want them."

"There's something special about that little girl. I'm telling you."

"Absolutely agreed on that." Jane flipped another page. "And, Mom, how you doing—oh, good. Very strong vitals. Urine output is perfect. Blood counts great. I'd like to get her to start feeding as soon as she can."

"I know the Brothers are dying to help. I had to kick them out. I swear, I thought they were going to stay down here for however long it took to get those kids off to school."

Jane laughed and closed the folder. "I'll do a quick check on everyone while you start Luchas's PT."

"Roger that."

"You're the best—"

"Hey, partner."

Jane glanced up. Manny was striding down the corridor, his hair wet, his scrubs clean, his eyes alert. "I thought you were taking off the next six hours?"

"Can't stay away. Might miss something. You going in there?"

"You want to join me on the visit?"

"Always."

Jane was shaking her head at herself as she put her hand on Layla's door and pushed. Medical people were always the same. Just couldn't leave well enough alone—

She stopped in the jambs.

Across the room, the new mom was standing at the incubators, Blay on one side of her, Qhuinn on the other, the three of them staring at the babies and talking softly.

The love was palpable.

And, for the moment, all the medicine that was needed.

"Something wrong?" Manny asked as Jane backed up and re-shut things.

Jane smiled. "It's family time right now. Let's give them a minute, 'kay?"

Manny smiled back. "High five, Doc. You were a helluva surgeon in there."

As she clapped his palm, she nodded. "And you saved her uterus."

"Don't you love good teamwork?"

"Every night and every day," she said as they wandered back down the hall, taking their time for once. "Hey, you want something to eat? I can't remember the last time I ate anything."

"I think I had a Snickers bar last Wednesday," her buddy murmured. "Or was that Monday?"

Jane laughed and bumped him with her ass. "Liar. You had a milk shake. Two nights ago."

"Riiiiiiiiight. Hey, where's your man? He should sit with us."

Jane frowned and looked back and forth down the empty hall. "You know . . . I have no idea. I thought he wandered off for a smoke— but he was supposed to be coming right back?"

Where had Vishous gone?

SIXTY-FOUR

Up in the Sanctuary, Vishous followed the call of the birds past the bathing area and the Reflecting Pool, all the way to the edge of the forest. For a moment, he wondered if the intention wasn't to draw him into the boundary itself, even though it was his understanding that if you tried to go through that stretch of thick trees, the shit just spit you back out where you started.

But then he slowed.

And stopped.

The birds that had been lending their voices to the air fell silent as he looked over at the one place he hadn't even considered ending up.

The cemetery where the Chosen who had passed had been set to rest was ringed on all four sides by a boxwood hedge that was tall enough so he couldn't see over it. An archway broke up the dense, small leaves, and it was on the trellis that the birds sat, staring at him mutely, their job now done.

Walking over, he ducked down as he entered even though there was no need to as the arch was plenty high to accommodate his head. And as he stepped inside, the birds flushed into the air, taking flight and disappearing.

It was impossible not to think of Selena as he stared at the statues of the females, which were not in fact statues at all. They were Chosen who had likewise suffered from the Arrest, perishing, as Trez's mate had, from a disease that was as relentless as it was deadly.

A flapping noise turned his head.

There, on one of the boxwood hedges, waving as if it were a flag, was a block of glowing symbols in the Old Language. The missive was not actually mounted on anything; the text was free-floating, coalesced into an order that presumably would make sense to whomever read it, and yet it moved in folds upon a non-existent wind, like the words had been stitched into cloth and sent up a pole.

With a sense of dread, he approached what he knew his mother had left behind for him.

Reaching up, he grasped the top edge and pulled the message flat, feeling weight, though none existed, and a terminus, though there was none.

The golden symbols fell into a series of straight lines, and he read them through once. And then again. And then a final time.

> There are seasons to all things, and my time has come to its end. I am saddened by much that has transpired between us, and between your sister and myself. Destiny proved to be more powerful than what was in my heart, but such as it shall be.
>
> I shall appoint a successor. The Creator is allowing me that discretion and I shall exercise it when the time comes, which is nigh. This successor shall not be you nor your sister. You must know this is not out of animus, but in recognition for what you both have chosen for your lives.
>
> When I exercised my due to bring the race into existence, this was not the ending I foresaw. It can be difficult, however, even for deities, to differentiate between what they will and what will be.
>
> In another dimension, mayhap we shall meet again.
>
> Tell your sister I send my love unto her.
>
> Know that I bestow it upon you as well.
>
>   Good-bye

When he let the text fall back into place, the symbols scattered into the air much as the finches had, rising up and vacating into the milky-white sky.

Vishous turned around a couple of times, as if the act of pivoting would somehow prove or disprove this reality. Then he just stopped and became one more statue in the cemetery, his eyes fixed, but seeing nothing, his body frozen where he stood.

He couldn't decide whether what he was feeling was relief or grief or . . . hell, he didn't know what the fuck it was. And yes, he had a sudden impulse to go get Butch and have his best friend stretch him out on a rack and whip him until the blood spilled cleaned out the mess inside of his head.

The Bloodletter was dead, V's sire long since having been killed by his sister, the fucker passing on to *Dhund* if there was any justice in the world.

Now, his *mahmen* was gone.

Neither of them had been much in the way of parents, and that had been fine. That had been his normal, such that people who had had a *mahmen* and a father who were functioning properly in those roles had always seemed like the weird ones.

So it seemed utterly fucking bizarre to feel rootless now considering he'd never actually had a family.

He thought back to Rhage's survival on that battlefield. And then considered that tiny little infant pulling through when she really shouldn't have.

"Fuck," he exhaled.

Just like his mother. The last thing she did before she kicked it, if you could call her disappearance by the mortal sobriquet *death*, was grant him his prayer—and save Qhuinn's daughter's life.

A final fuck you, as it were.

Or, shit, maybe that was just his nasty filter twisting everything into a bad light.

Whatever. She was gone. . . and that was that. Except . . .

Jesus Christ, he thought as he rubbed his face. The Scribe Virgin was *gone*.

SIXTY-FIVE

As night fell, Assail was still down in the Brotherhood's training center complex, sitting in the chair opposite Markcus, who had been asleep the entire day.

Given the length of time Assail had been gone, and his plans for the evening, he took his phone out, his fingers flying over the screen as he texted his cousins—

"Whate'er is that?" came a hoarse inquiry.

Whipping his head around, he was surprised to see that Markcus was awake. "An iPhone." He held the device up. "It's . . . a cell phone."

"I am afraid . . ." The male pushed himself up a bit higher on the pillows. "I am afraid that tells me nothing."

For a moment, Assail tried to imagine all that stringy hair being gone, some pounds on that frame, the face filled out so it didn't look so skeletal. Markcus was going to prove to be rather . . . comely, as it were.

Shaking himself, Assail murmured, "It's a phone? You know, you can call people? Or text them?"

"Oh."

"Do you know what a phone is?"

Markcus nodded. "But they were on tables, not in pockets."

Assail sat forward. "How long did she hold you down there?"

The male's entire body reacted to the question, tensing up. But he did not turn away from the inquiry. "What year is it?" When Assail answered, that pale face seemed to crumble. "Oh . . . dearest Virgin Scribe . . ."

"How long."

"Thirty-two years. What . . . what month is this?"

"October. Almost November."

Markcus nodded. "It felt cold. When you carried me out of the house . . . it felt cold, but I was not sure whether that was me or . . ."

"It was not you."

Jesus, Naasha must have abducted him very close to when she'd first mated her *hellren*. She must have known what she was in for with the old male. But why hadn't she taken better care of Markcus? Morality issues aside, blood sources were, after all, only as good as the health of the flesh they inhabited.

Except then Assail thought of the way Naasha had used him, and others. She had clearly found many outlets for feeding.

Neglect had obviously occurred when the necessity decreased.

There was a silence. And then Markcus said, "How did you know I was in there?"

"I was exploring the house in search of . . ." Assail waved the explanation away for its lack of importance. What mattered more was . . . "We have all wondered where your kin are? Who may we call on your behalf?"

"My blood are all back in the Old Country. I left them to come here because I wanted . . ." Markcus's voice trailed off. "I wanted an adventure. I came unto that house to apply for a workmale's position. The mistress passed by my quarters one evening, and then she summoned me unto her presence down in the cellar. She gave me some wine and . . ."

The male's eyes seemed to cloud over, as if his memories were so dark and heavy they were capable of robbing him of consciousness.

"How may we contact your kin?" Assail prompted.

"I know not. I . . ." Markcus focused abruptly. "No, do not contact them. Not now. I cannot see them like this."

As the male lifted his wrists with their tattoos, he seemed as helpless as he had been when chained in that cell. "What shall I e'er tell them? We are naught but commoners—I had to work for my passage on the ship to New York harbor. But all bloodlines have pride. And there is no . . . pride in this."

Assail scrubbed his face so hard that his poor, fucked-up nose hummed. Which reminded him. He had to get more coke before he performed his duties at nightfall.

"You may stay with myself and my cousins," he announced. "You will be safe there."

Markcus shook his head as he ran his fingertips over the band on his left wrist. "Why . . . why would you do that?"

"It is as I told you. You are in need. And I find myself in need of serving someone." Assail put both palms out. "And there is naught that is dodgy. We are but three males who cohabit one among each other."

Naturally, he left out the coke habit, the fact that he had arguably whored out his relations, and also his past as a drug importer and dealer.

Was he starting fresh, then, he wondered.

Hmm. Considering the arms deal he had just made for the Brotherhood? Perhaps the term was more starting *next*, rather than *fresh*.

"Is there work to be done at your home?" Markcus nodded to Assail's clothing. "By your wardrobe and your accent, it is clear you are a male of means. Is there work that I may perform so that I can earn my room and board? Otherwise, I cannot avail myself of your offer. I shall not do that."

Assail shrugged. "It is but menial work."

"No effort is menial if it is done well."

Assail eased back in the chair and regarded the haggard scrap of flesh on the hospital bed. Even barely out of captivity—for over thirty fucking years—and already the male was showing a character of note.

"I shall have to leave you the now," Assail heard himself say. "But I shall return prior to dawn, and when they will release you, you will come home with me. And that is what shall be."

Markcus lowered his head. "I am e'er in your debt."

No, Assail thought to himself. I rather sense 'tis the other way around, my good male.

Rhage and Mary walked arm in arm up the mansion's grand staircase. As they ascended, she smiled as she remembered them waltzing around that empty gym. And then she flushed as she recalled what they'd done as the dancing had slowed to a stop.

That equipment room had never seen so much action.

"When did she say I had to be there?" Rhage asked.

"You've got about thirty minutes to get ready. It's the I've Bean Waitin' coffee shop down on Hemingway Avenue. I think Rhym is going by car, but you certainly don't have to."

"I'm not ordering anything while I'm there. I don't want to have coffee breath."

"Rhage. Seriously." She stopped him as they came up to the second floor. "You're going to do fine."

Taking his beautiful face in her hands, she smoothed his worried eyebrows and stroked the shadow of his beard. "Just treat it like any other conversation."

"I'm being interviewed to be Bitty's dad. How the hell is that supposed to be like any other conversation? And, God, will you tell me what to wear? Should it be a suit? I feel like it should be a suit."

Taking his hand, she led him in the direction of their room. "How about just a regular pair of slacks and one of your black silk shirts. She'll be so distracted by how gorgeous you are, she won't remember her own name, much less whatever she was going to ask you."

He was grumbling as they entered their suite, and his attitude didn't get much better as she shooed him toward the bath.

"No," she said as he tried to pull her along with him. "We'll get seriously distracted. Let me go lay out your clothes."

"You're right. Plus every time I think about where I'm going I want to throw up."

They went their separate ways in the middle of the room, he to a cleanly shaven jaw and freshly shampooed hair, she to the walk-in closet, where—

The scream that emanated from the loo was enough to give her a frickin' heart attack. "Rhage! Rhage—what's wrong!"

She blasted across the carpet and into the—only to slam against his backside.

"Are you fucking kidding me!" he barked.

"What, what are you . . ."

Mary started laughing, and she got on such a roll with it, she had to sit down on the edge of the Jacuzzi.

Someone, or some*ones*, more like it, had *Little Mermaid*ed their bathroom: There were *Little Mermaid* towels hanging on all the hooks and rods, a *Little Mermaid* rug in front of the double sinks . . . *Little*

Mermaid cups and toothbrushes and kids' toothpaste on the counters . . . *Little Mermaid* shampoo and conditioner in the shower . . .
action figures lined up on the lip around the tub and down the sill of
the big window that looked out over the gardens.

But the *pièce de résistance* was undoubtedly the wall stuff. About a
hundred and fifty different stickers, posters, clings, and cut-outs from
coloring books had been stuck, glued, or pinned to every square inch
of vertical surface.

Rhage wheeled around and went to march out—but he didn't
have to go far at all. A gathering of his Brothers filed into their suite,
the males high-fiving one another and smacking Rhage on the ass.

"I'm going to get you back," he growled. "Every single one of
you—especially you, Lassiter, you fuck stick."

"How?" the fallen angel countered. "By flooding my room? You
already tried that with the pantry and Fritz got it fixed in a night."

"No, I'm going to hide every cocksucking remote in this house."

The angel froze. "Okay, those are fighting words."

"Blam!" Rhage yelled as he hit his hips. "Wassup, bitch."

Lassiter started looking to the Brothers for help. "That's not funny.
That shit is *so* not funny—"

"Hey, Hollywood, can I pay you to hide those?" someone said.

"We can still get access to them, though, right?" somebody else
demanded.

"Fuck all y'all, for real," Lassiter muttered. "I'm serious. One of
these days, you are gonna respect me. . . ."

Mary just leaned into her arms and smiled at the bunch of crazies:
In a way, this was exactly what Rhage needed, a little steam-blow-off
on his way to the coffee shop. Heck, on that theory, they all deserved
to release some tension.

It had been a heavy-duty couple of hours.

Fucking *Little Mermaid*, Rhage thought when he left their bedroom
twenty-five minutes later.

Shutting the door, he retucked his already tucked-in shirt and
pulled on the jacket Mary had picked out for him to hide his guns. As
he walked down the hall, he fiddled with his hair, rolled his shoulders,
tugged at his belt.

His palms were sweaty. How the hell was he going to shake the

social worker's hand if he was sweating this bad? She was going to have use a napkin to dry off.

Or a set of drapes.

Coming up to Wrath's study, he saw that the doors were open and he paused, wondering if now would be a good time to tell his brother and his King what the hell they were up to. When he looked around the jamb, though, he got an eyeful of Wrath and V talking together, the King on the throne, the brother right next to him, crouching on the floor. Their heads were together, their voices low, the air so thick there might as well have been *mhis* around them.

What the fuck was going on, Rhage thought as he was tempted to go inside.

But then he checked his gold Rolex, the one that he'd given Mary, but which she'd insisted he wear for good luck. No time to ask, and on that note, no time to go into the whole Bitty thing, either.

Later, he decided.

Hitting the stairwell, he bottomed out on the mosaic floor and beelined for the exit.

"Good luck."

Rhage pulled up short and looked to the right. Lassiter was in the billiards room, bluing up a cue.

"What are you talking about?" Rhage demanded.

As the angel just shrugged, Rhage shook his head. "You're crazy—"

"When she asks about how the father died, don't fudge it. She already knows it was you and your brothers who killed him. It's in the file. She hates the violence, but she knows that the two of them wouldn't have survived otherwise. She wants you to have the kid. You and Mary."

As Rhage felt all the blood leave his head and end up in his shoes, he wished he had something to hold onto.

"How do . . . did Mary talk to you about this?" Even though he found that hard to believe. "Marissa?"

"And the beast. That makes her nervous. Don't try to calm her down about it—you'll dwell too much on the subject and it will rattle her. Mary will handle that. Mary will tell her all she needs to know on that issue."

"How do you know all this?"

Lassiter put the square of chalk down and shifted those oddly

colored eyes over. "I'm an angel, remember? And it's going to work out. Just hang tight—you're going to have to keep the faith. For both you and Mary. But it's going to happen."

"Really?" he found himself asking.

"No lie. I might fuck with your bathroom. But never, ever about this."

Rhage's feet moved of their own volition, crossing the way to the pool table—and the next thing he knew, he was bear-hugging the blond-and-black motherfucker.

"You got this," Lassiter said as they clapped each other's backs. "But just remember. You've got to keep the faith."

Before things got too sappy, Rhage backed off and headed for the front door again. Stepping outside through the vestibule, he took a deep, bracing draw of the cold air . . . and off he went, traveling through the night in a rush of molecules, zeroing in on a very human establishment.

When he arrived at his destination, he was careful to re-form in the back of the shallow parking lot, and yes, he did a re-check on his hair and his shirt before he walked around to the I've Bean Waitin' coffee shop's front door.

Opening things up, he got hit in the nose with a whole lot of coffee aroma, and he had a momentary wobble about the whole not-ordering thing. What was he going to do with his hands while he sat there?

With a curse that he didn't smoke or bring needlepoint, he looked through the human men and women, a lot of whom glanced up at him and kept on staring . . . and then met the stare of the only other vampire in the place—no, wait, there was a pretrans in the crowd he didn't recognize.

He knew who Rhym was, though. He'd seen her in plenty of pictures from Mary's work.

As he took another deep breath, it wasn't quite the cathartic experience the one on the front stoop of the mansion had been, but there was oxygen in here. Right?

God, that coffee smell was making him suffocate. Or maybe that was his adrenal glands.

Rhage tried to pin down his freak out as he began making his way one of the tables in the back.

When he stopped in front of Rhym, he wanted to pass out. Instead, he rubbed his hand on the ass of his pants as discreetly as he could, and then extended his arm.

"Hi, I'm Rhage."

The female was a little wide-eyed as she stared at him—but that was common, and no, he wasn't being arrogant. People did tend to do a little double-take when they first met him, and then yes, they usually ended up looking at him closely, as if trying to figure out whether he was for real.

"I'm sorry," she stammered. "I, ah, I'm Rhym."

As they shook, he nodded at the vacant chair. "You mind if I sit down?"

"Oh, please. I'm sorry. Wait, I already said that. Jeez."

To her credit, she didn't ogle him unnecessarily or come on to him. And the fact that she was also nervous made him feel a little better.

"Are you going to get something?" she asked.

"No. I'm fine. Would you like another . . . what is that?"

"It's a latte. And no, thank you, this is plenty." There was a pause and she opened a little notebook. "So . . . I, um . . . listen, I've got to be honest. I've never been in the presence of a Brother before."

He smiled, being careful to conceal his fangs because they were in mixed company. "I'm just like everyone else."

"Not even close," she muttered under her breath. "So, I, ah, I have some questions for you? If that's okay? I know Mary's talked to you about all this."

Rhage crossed his arms and leaned on the table. "Yes, she has. And listen, if I could just . . ."

He looked down at the wood grain under his elbows and tried to figure out what he was attempting to say. As the chatter around them and the ins and outs of the front door and the seething of the coffee machines droned on, he started to worry that he'd been quiet too long.

Rhage looked at the social worker. "Bottom line is, I'm prepared to lay down my life for that little girl. I'm ready to get up at high noon for her if she has a daymare. I'm ready to feed her and clothe her, and show her how to drive. I'm also prepared to hold her close when she gets her heart broken for the first time, and present her to her mate if she finds someone she wants. I want to help her get a good education, and follow whatever dreams she has, and be there to pick her up when she stumbles. I understand that it's not going to be all puppies and unicorns, and there's going to be conflict, and maybe even anger . . . but none of that will change my commitment. I knew my Mary was the one I was supposed to be with the moment I met her, and I knew the other night, with the same clarity, that Bitty is my kid. If you'll let me have the chance to be her father."

He sat back and held his arms out. "Now, ask me everything."

Rhym smiled a little. And then a lot. "Well, let's start at the beginning, shall we?"

Rhage smiled back. Which yeah, was what happened when you got the very clear sense that you had just hit one out of the park.

"Let's do that," he said with a sense of profound relief.

SIXTY-SIX

Jo Early could not stop staring.

Then again, she wasn't the only one in the coffee shop whose lattes were left unattended and cooling as they tried not to look at the guy. He'd come in alone, sucking up most, if not all, of the oxygen in the building, and then proceeded over to a back table to sit with a nice-looking, if unremarkable, woman.

All things considered, he should have been with a Miss America type: He was huge, just incredibly tall, but also built big, as if he were a professional athlete of the football, not basketball variety. His hair was blond, but it seemed to be actually that shade, no roots showing, no professional streak job growing out, just thick and healthy and . . . blond.

His eyes, though, were the big thing. His eyes were totally a thing. Even from across the crowded coffee shop, they glowed with a color blue that was something you'd see in the Bahamas by the ocean, the color so iridescent, so clear, so resonantly teal that you had to wonder whether it was contacts, because how in the hell could that be found in nature?

And P.S., the clothes weren't bad at all. Nope. He was wearing all black, from a silk shirt and very well-cut and well-tailored slacks, to a

jacket that had lapels like something a suit would have, but a loose body like an overcoat.

The shoes were spectacular, too.

It was as if a movie star had wandered into I've Bean Waitin', and for a moment, Jo wondered if maybe she'd seen him on the big screen . . . ?

As her cell phone went off, she was grateful for the distraction. This hyper-focus of hers kept up and she was going to see that handsome face every time she closed her eyelids. Not that that would have been any great sacrifice.

When she saw who it was, she rolled her eyes, but accepted the call anyway. "Dougie, what's up. No. No, you may not. What—no! Look, I told you, I'm leaving my job, I'm not going to be able to lend you money for a while. . . . Well, then ask one of them. No. No. Okay . . . fine, but only the Fig Newtons. I come back and you've eaten my Milanos and you and I are going to have words. And would you go out and get employed, for godsakes?"

As she hung up, a dry voice said, "I agree with you about the cookies."

Recoiling, she put her hand over her heart. "Jeez, Bill, you scared me."

"What's this about leaving Bryant's?" he said as he sat down with his latte and did that scarf unwindy thing he did. "You quit?"

"It's nothing." Well, other than the fact that her boss was a manipulator and she had allowed herself to be his pawn. "Really."

Oh, but b.t.dub, Bryant thinks we're boning, she tacked on in her head.

"Listen," Bill murmured as he leaned in and pushed those glasses up higher on his nose. "First of all, I'm sorry I'm late. And second of all, I have to ask. With parents like yours, I really can't believe . . . I mean, the money thing . . ."

She opened her mouth to brush things off, but then decided, Screw it. "After I walked out on them and their whole . . . lifestyle . . . they cut me off."

"That must have been a hard thing to do—leave your family, I mean. Well, and the money."

Jo swirled her cappuccino around. "I never really fit in with them. My dad—I'm sorry, my father, as he would insist I call him— engineered my adoption because my mother went through a phase of wanting a kid. I guess she thought babies were like purses or something? After they got me, I was raised by nannies, some of whom were good, some of whom were bad. I was then shipped off to boarding school and college—and by the time I got out, I'd just kind of had it with pretending to be who they wanted me to be when I was around them. Outside of that big house, I was my own person. In the presence of the pair of them, I was a facsimile of myself, just like they were constructed versions of themselves." She batted at the air with her hand. "It's your standard boring poor-little-rich-girl stuff."

"Standard and boring unless you're going through it."

"Be that as it may, I told them I wasn't coming back, and they said fine, and that was it. The monthly checks went poof—and honestly, it's okay. I'm smart, I'm willing to work hard, and I have an education. I'll make it on my own, just like a whole bunch of people before me have."

Bill shrugged out of his coat. "May I ask one more personal question?"

"Absolutely." As she tried her 'cino, she grimaced. Watching that blond man had drained a lot of the warmth out of things. "Anything."

"You say you were adopted—have you ever thought about looking up your birth family?"

She shook her head. "The records of everything are beyond private—or at least that's what they told me. I guess my father paid to keep it that way? And it makes sense—I heard that my mother tried to pass me off as hers in the beginning, saying that she had been hiding the pregnancy under loose clothes and then had spent the last month down in Naples or some place like that. As my hair got redder and redder, though, that lie became more difficult to support—especially as she didn't like the idea of people thinking she'd stepped out on my father."

"So you never hear from them at all?"

"No, and it's all right. At this point, hey, my ivy league education's paid for. If that's the worst thing those two do to me for the rest of my life, I came out on top of the deal."

"Well . . ." Bill cleared his throat. "So segue, here—do you want to apply for something at the paper? I know there are a couple of openings and I could put in a good word. You've shown me that you're a helluva good investigator."

For a minute, Jo just sat there like a lump, blinking. Then she shook herself. "Really? Oh . . . my God, yes. I mean, thank you. I have a résumé I can e-mail you."

"Consider it done. Like, I know they're looking for an online content editor right now. The pay has to be about what you're making as a receptionist, but at least it's a stepping stone."

And better than worrying about Bryant's love life and laundry, she thought to herself.

"Thank you. I mean it." She flashed him the napkin she'd been writing on. "And on that note, I've made a list of the places I've visited. I've got a couple more to go—I want to check out that closed restaurant where Julio Martinez said he got ambushed by a vampire? And I want to go to this alley where . . . have you seen the footage of the shoot out in the alley? Where there's this guy up on a roof who kills someone while this other guy runs out into a spray of bullets? There were no fangs in the clip, but it was put up on YouTube by the same guy who posted a lot of the footage of the massacre at that farm."

Bill took out his phone like he was ready to go 'net surfing. "No, I haven't seen that yet."

"Here, let me get it up for you."

#donteversaythatagain

Assail waited on the periphery of Naasha's *hellren*'s great mansion, tracking the movement of the staff and its mistress in the windows on the first and second floors. One advantage of the female being an exhibitionist was that pulled draperies were an anathema to her, and thus the stages of her dressing were on display for all to see.

At the moment, she was in her bathroom, seated in a make-up chair in front of a window that faced due west. Her maid was rolling her hair in curlers whilst she focused on something in her lap. Perhaps it was e-mail on an iPad. Or a phone.

Taking out his cell, he sent her a text . . . and watched as her head came up and she pointed across the way. The maid put down the roller she'd been about to put to use and scampered out of view. And then she was back, placing a device in her mistress's hand.

Assail's own phone went off a second later. When he read what she had texted, he looked at his cousins.

"You know what to do."

"Aye," Ehric said. "Is the Brother here—"

"Right behind you."

All three of them turned about to find Zsadist exactly where he'd said he'd be at exactly the time he'd told Assail he would arrive. Like the rest of them, the Brother had a large backpack on, and plenty of weapons with him.

"Shall we, gentlemales?" Assail murmured.

At his nod, his cousins dematerialized to the back of the mansion, to the infiltration point that had been established beforehand.

Assail put his backpack down at the base of the tree he had been taking cover behind, and then he strode into view, straightening his suit coat and tugging out his cuffs. When he hit the walkway that led to the front entrance, his loafers made a clipping sound. Zsadist, who tracked in his wake, made no sound as he stuck to the grass, staying just outside of the light thrown by the short lanterns at the edge of the flagstones.

When Assail got to the door, he tried the handle. No such luck this time; it was locked.

Using the bell, he had a smile on his face as the butler answered the summons. "Good evening, I'm afraid I am a good twenty minutes early. I do not wish to inconvenience your mistress, however. May I tarry in her parlor?"

As the *doggen* bowed low, Assail checked to make sure there was no one else in the foyer. And then, as the butler straightened, Assail outed his forty.

Such that the servant looked the muzzle eye-to-eye.

"Do not move a muscle," Assail whispered. "And do not make a sound unless you are answering my questions. Do you wish to live?" Nod. "How many other staff are in the house?"

"S-s-s-seven."

"Is Throe in residence?" Nod. "Where is he?"

"H-h-he is eating upstairs in his bedroom."

Zsadist walked right into the house, and the *doggen* looked like he wanted to faint at the sight of that scarred face and those black eyes.

"Do not worry about him," Assail said softly. "Focus on me."

"I'm s-s-s-sorry."

"Listen to me, and listen to me well. You have seven minutes to get the staff out of the house. That is one minute per person. Do not waste a moment. Do not explain why they have to leave. Tell them to gather at the base of the driveway. Do not alert your mistress. If you tell her of my presence, I will consider you a co-conspirator in the keeping of the blood slave whom I rescued last evening, and I will kill you where you stand. Am I clear?" Nod. "Tell me what I just told you."

"Y-y-you . . . I have s-s-s-seven minutes to get the staff out. Head of the drive—"

"Base. I said the base of the driveway. I'll be able to see you, because there is a streetlight there. And what about your mistress."

A hard look came across the butler's face, one that very probably was going to save his life. "I shall say not a word to her. She and her lover killed my master."

"What is your name?"

"I am Tharem."

"Tharem, I want you to go to the King's Audience House after this. Tell them everything—what was in that basement, what she did to him, what I am doing here. Do you understand?"

"I took pictures," the butler whispered. "On my phone. I didn't know where to go with them."

"Good. Show them. But go now. Seven minutes."

The *doggen* bowed low. "Yes, my Lord. Right away."

The uniformed male took off at a dead run, heading for the kitchen, and before Assail was even halfway to the main stairs, three *doggen* dressed in chef's whites came rushing out through the dining room. One had flour all over his hands, and another had a pot with something in it. Their eyes were wide and afraid, suggesting that the butler had not stayed completely truthful to their bargain.

He clearly had imparted there were deadly forces within the house.

No matter. The motivation had worked, and it was obvious that there was naught to be worried about in terms of allegiances to Naasha. The three chefs took one look at him and his gun—and just ran even faster as opposed to causing a ruckus.

And meanwhile, the sweet smell of gas was already wafting in the air. Soon that would not be the half of it.

Assail walked up the stairs rather than taking them at a run. And as he ascended, two maids came hurrying down, their fastened hair bouncing loose from pins, the pale gray skirts of their uniforms flying. They, too, took a single glance at him and ducked their heads in response, re-doubling their speed without interfering.

Up on the second-floor landing, he took a left and stopped at the first door he came to, just as the butler skidded into view at the far end of the hallway and came down at a run.

"I'll take care of the dressing maid," Assail said. As the male blanched, he rolled his eyes. "Not like that. She shall join you anon."

The butler nodded and scampered off.

Grasping the doorknob, Assail turned the ornate brass knot slowly and then pushed. The panels gave way without a sound, and he instantly scented Naasha's perfume and shampoo. As he let himself in and re-closed things, he had a brief impression of a great deal of pink and cream and silk and taffeta.

The carpet was thick as a male's brush cut, and his loafers were silent as he crossed the distance to the archway. The marble bathroom beyond was larger than some people's living rooms.

And indeed, the set-up could not have been more perfect. Naasha was facing away from him in that professional hairstylist's chair, her long locks falling over its short back, a table with brushes and curling provisions beside her. There were many mirrors all around, but they were trained on her, leaving his presence unreflected.

"—told you I do not care for my hair as such," Naasha snapped. "Do it again! He is going to be here soon—my phone, it is ringing, give it to me first."

As the maid backed off from her ministrations, she happened to turn in Assail's direction—and froze. Pointing the gun right at her head, he put his finger to his lips and mouthed, *Shhhhhh.*

The maid paled.

"Get my phone! What are you doing?"

Assail nodded in the direction of the iPhone, which was vibrating on the marble counter well within Naasha's reach.

The maid went to pick the thing up, fumbled it, and took a verbal lashing as she scrambled to retrieve the cell from the floor.

"Finally—hello? Oh, hello, darling, how kind of you to call. I am devastated, *simply* devastated. . . ."

Assail crooked his finger at the maid, beckoning her over. The poor thing was statued in panic, however—until Assail mouthed *you* and *safe.*

The female came across haltingly. As Naasha continued to play the role of bereft widow, Assail whispered, "Go out the front door.

Keep running until you see the others at the bottom of the driveway. Do not come back into this house for any reason. Am I clear?"

The maid nodded and offered a trembling curtsy—and then she was off like the wind, out of the room.

Assail stalked his way over and waited patiently as Naasha continued to talk whilst she trailed her finger across the screen of her iPad. Looming behind her, he was a Grim Reaper who had fucked her—and was about to fuck her again.

When she finally hung up, she said, "Where are you? Where the hell are—"

Assail clamped a hand on the hair on top of Naasha's head and yanked back. As she dropped the phone, and the tablet scattered to the floor, she started to struggle in earnest—until he put the barrel of the gun into her mouth and stepped off to the side.

Terrified eyes met his.

"This is for Markcus," he growled.

"So how'd he do?" Mary asked as Rhym came into her office at Safe Place.

"Your *hellren* is quite a thing—and he did wonderfully." The female sat down with a smile, arranging her coat over her legs. "He truly did. He's got a huge heart."

"The biggest." There was a pause, and Mary leaned in over her paperwork. "And you can say it . . . I'm not going to be weird about it. I have to live with him, remember?"

"I don't know what you're . . ." Rhym threw her hands up. "Okay, fine. I mean, he's just ridiculous looking. I've never seen anything like it."

Mary had to laugh. "I know, I know. And the good news is that he doesn't particularly care. He's aware of it, sure, but, jeez, if he took that stuff seriously, his head would be so big, you couldn't fit him indoors."

Rhym nodded. "Too right. So, are you ready?"

"Always." Mary got up and went to shut the door. "Anything you want to know."

"I'm sorry, I should have done that."

Mary swiped the air with her hand. "Not to worry."

Back at her desk, she sat down again and acknowledged, at least to herself, that she was nervous.

Rhym shucked that coat. And then stared at the urn by the lamp. "Is that . . ."

"Yes." Mary took a deep breath. "That's Annalye. Originally, Bitty was saying that she wanted to save the ashes for when her uncle came, but now . . ."

"About the uncle. Have you heard anything on him? At all?"

"Not a thing. Rhage even had one of his Brothers search for him. We've come up with absolutely nothing."

Rhym shrugged. "The issue, for me, is how long does the notification period last? Marissa and I agree, this has to be a foster situation while Bitty adjusts and while whatever relations she might have have an opportunity to get in contact with her. But that can't go on forever. Is it a month? Six months? A year? And how do we do the notifications? What's fair?"

Mary's heart jumped off the diving board of her rib cage, somersaulted, and hit her stomach badly, belly-flopping all over the place. Oh, God, a year. Of not knowing for sure. Of wondering every night if they were going to lose her.

Even a month of that seemed like torture.

"Whatever you think is best," she said as she tried to keep her wince to herself. "But I have to tell you, I'm not a good person to weigh in on all that. As much as I try to be objective, the reality is . . . I just want her for our own."

"The Old Laws are not really helpful in this regard, although I did check to see what the humans do. When it comes to terminating parental rights, it's clear that there is a very high standard to be met. But for other relations and next of kin? It depends on state and local law how it's all handled. Accordingly, I'm going to leave it up to the King—it's exactly the sort of thing we need him to weigh in on. Plus, because of Rhage's station, the two of you would have to get his sign-off anyway."

"That sounds very fair. And I really want to make sure we do this right. It's too important to cut any corners on."

"I'm glad you agree—and I'm not surprised." Rhym sat back. "So tell me about your relationship with Bitty. I've seen glimpses of it, but I'd like to get a sense from you not as a professional, but as a person."

Mary picked up a pen and wove it in and out between her fingers, the way she had when she'd been in college. "I've known her ever since she came to the house. I've been her primary caseworker the entire time, as you know, and honestly, she was so reserved and self-protective, I thought I was never going to get through to her. I'm aware that this whole adoption thing seems to have just come up since her mother died, but the truth of it is that Bitty's been on my mind and in my heart for the last two years. I refused to look too close at the opportunity, though. I just . . . as you know, I can't have children, and when that's your reality? You don't want to touch that closed door. All there is, on the other side, are flames that will burn your house down."

"Are you prepared to let the girl go if a relation surfaces? Can you do that?"

This time, there was no keeping the grimace off her face. Then again, when someone got your bare foot even close to an alligator's mouth, you did tend to flinch.

"Whatever is good for Bitty." She shook her head. "And I honestly mean that. If we have to let her go, we will."

"Well, the truth is, I've also looked for that uncle. Looked for anybody tied to her. No one fits any of the information. We lost so many in the raids, it's possible that he died at that time along with others of her kin. Or perhaps in some other way."

"Can I just say . . . I'm really not a big fan of death."

For a moment, she thought back to dancing with Rhage in the gym. They'd had to be close to each other in the wake of their agreement, that future separation they'd had the luxury of not worrying about suddenly looming over them as it did for all other couples.

"Neither am I," Rhym said. And then the female cleared her throat. "And on that note, can we talk about your situation"

"You mean with the Scribe Virgin?"

"Yes, please." There was an awkward pause. "I don't really understand the . . . quasi-immortality, I guess you'd call it—not that it isn't possible. With the Scribe Virgin, anything can happen. And then I need to ask you about the beast. I have to confess, that's the only red flag for me in any of this."

Mary chuckled. "That thing is just a big purple teddy bear. I promise you, it couldn't hurt a fly—or at least not a female one, and certainly never me. But I digress. My story starts back a couple of years ago, when I was diagnosed with . . ."

SIXTY-SEVEN

His mistake had been the unmuffled gunshot.

As Assail proceeded from Naasha's suite to Throe's, and then broke down the male's locked door, he was greeted with an empty bedroom and an open window, the traitor having obviously dematerialized out when he heard the forty go off.

"Goddamn it," Assail muttered as he wheeled around and checked the bathroom. And the closet.

Nothing was particularly out of place, and the true telltale of quick departure was the open wall safe across the way, that landscape that had been ever so slightly cockeyed upon its hook before now sitting on the seat of a chair, the metal belly of the keep-all exposed, the light inside illustrating that its contents had been removed.

But whate'er did it matter? Naasha had been the true target.

Throe could be pursued at leisure on another night.

Assail doubled back to Naasha's, and strode through her bedroom, going to the window that he had seen her in from down below. Willing the lights off in the bath, he peered out of the glass as the sweet chemical stink of gasoline now reached even the second floor.

Down below at the foot of the drive, as prescribed, was a group of eight standing beside the lamppost, the illumination detailing that the seven servants and that butler had arranged themselves in a line and were staring up at the mansion.

"Good male," Assail muttered as he turned away.

He was about to leave when something caught his eye—a gleam over on one of the counters. Reigniting the lighting, he stepped over her dead body and picked up the diamond necklace. The thing was modest, by Naasha's standards, naught but a rivere of two- and three-carat stones.

Below where it sat, there was a series of thin drawers, each with a pair of brass key locks that were engaged.

Mayhap it was nostalgia for his cat burglar, or perhaps a final fuck-you to Naasha, but he extended his gun arm and pumped off a number of rounds into the fucking things, splintering the wood, scattering the locks, ruining the pristine bank of cabinets.

When he had emptied his clip, the top drawer lolled open like a cartoon character's tongue. Inside, in a jumbled mess, were all kinds of things that sparkled, and he grabbed handfuls, stuffing the rings and earrings and necklaces and bracelets into his pockets.

His jacket was near full to bursting when Zsadist came in.

The Brother had ready his flamethrower, the tip of the discharge nozzle spitting blue fire, the wand in those oh, so capable hands like the head of a dragon who was ready to roar.

"Time to go," the fighter said.

One had to admire his disinterest in the thievery. Then again, Assail had just committed murder right over there in that swivel chair, and the Brother seemed unbothered by that as well.

With a last look at Naasha's sprawled, motionless form, Assail walked out with the Brother. In the hall, the fumes were strong enough to water the eye, and that became even more prevalent as they descended.

Ehric and Evale had gathered in the foyer, and, ever thoughtful, they had retrieved his pack from where he had laid it down outside.

After he strapped it on and lit his pilot, so to speak, he pumped off several bursts of orange flame.

"Shall we?" he said.

Splitting up, they went to the four corners of the grand mansion. The gasoline, which his cousins had liberally doused all manner of

textiles and wood in, was perhaps overkill, however, the flamethrowers' kisses would thereby be capable of igniting whole walls of fabric and expanses of pine, oak and mahogany with naught but a burst.

As the arson was initiated with efficiency, Assail moved through the dining room, setting ablaze the antiques and the Zuber wallpaper, the Aubusson rug, the Federal table that was twenty-five feet long and two centuries old. He had a momentary pause before he went on his way into the kitchen, a spark of grief for the Waterford chandelier that was in the midst of the now e'er-expanding bonfire making him wish he had removed it first.

But sacrifices had to be made.

He did not bother with the pantry. It would be consumed soon enough. Instead, he set about lighting afire the fine professional kitchen, starting with the drapes on either side of the banks of windows and continuing on to all the wooden cabinetry that his cousins had so competently covered with accelerant.

The great *whoosh!* as things caught and flames held was a rush every time it happened, and he felt himself get hard, some primal part of him expressing dominance and demanding submission from this static environment of inanimate objects. Indeed, with each explosion of power, it seemed as though he were reclaiming some part of himself that he had lost along the way.

Sure as if he had been the one chained down below.

Soon, the re-doubling heat became unbearable, his hair curling up at the ends, the skin of his face tightening to the point of pain.

As he rounded the circuit back to the foyer, he realized that he was surrounded by the fire he had sought to create, trapped in the inferno. Smoke, billowing and toxic, needled his eyes and stung his nose and sinuses, whilst undulating walls of fire blocked every exit.

Perhaps this was the end, he thought as he lowered the muzzle of his thrower.

All around him, great waves of orange and red flames ebbed and flowed, like mouths chewing on the mansion and its contents, and he was momentarily mesmerized by the deadly beauty of the blaze.

Calming down, he took out his phone.

Summoning up a number, he hit send and turned in a circle slowly as it rang, and rang, and rang—

"Hello?" came her voice.

He closed his eyes. Oh, that voice. Marisol's beautiful voice.

"Hello," she demanded.

There was a silence over the connection, although no silence in the house. No, things were creaking and popping, moaning and cursing as if the studs and plaster had bones that broke and nerve receptors to feel the pain.

"Assail?" she said urgently. "Assail . . . is this you?"

"I love you," he replied.

"Assail! What is—"

He cut off the call. Turned off his phone. And then he removed the pack and placed it at his feet.

As the temperature increased and the chaos rose e'er higher, he straightened his jacket and tugged his cuffs into place.

After all, he might have been a degenerate, self-interested, drug-dealing sociopath, but one should have standards and look good when one passed.

Dhund or the Fade, he wondered.

Probably *Dhund*—

From out of the tsunami of flame, a black figure streaked into the eye of the inferno's hurricane where Assail was standing.

It was the Brother Zsadist. And contrary to the impending death and destruction that was overwhelming things, the gentlemale seemed more annoyed than frantic as he skidded to a halt.

"Not going to die here," the male yelled over the din.

"This is a fitting end for me."

Those black, soulless eyes rolled. "Oh, please."

"Even though this arson is for proper reason," Assail hollered, "your King will have to prosecute me for murder, as there was no due process for the blood slave transgression of that female. So allow me to perish here, on my terms, satisfied that I have—"

"Not on my watch, asshole."

The punch came from the right and plowed into Assail's jaw so hard, it cut off not just his rather poetic speech, if he did say so himself, but his link to consciousness.

The last thing he heard as he went lights-out was, "—carry you out of here like luggage, you goddamn fool."

For Fates' sake, Assail thought as everything went dark and silent. The principles of others were so fucking inconvenient.

Especially when one was trying to kill oneself.

SIXTY-EIGHT

As Rhage went back home after his meeting at I've Bean, he was feeling like a fucking boss.

Rhym had even given him a hug at the end of the interview. And that had to mean something, right?

The first thing he wanted to do, as he headed up the mansion's grand staircase, was call his Mary, but she was in her meeting now, so he'd have to wait. Whatever, he could get changed and maybe go downtown to do some hunting and burn off some—

His phone went off with a *bing!* just as he hit the second floor and saw that the King was sitting on the throne at his desk—as opposed to being at the Audience House, where he should have been.

Ignoring the text, Rhage strode forward and knocked on the open door. "My Lord?"

Wrath's head jerked up as if he'd been surprised by the interruption—which was the first clue that something big had happened: That brother might have been blind, but he had the instincts of the keenest predator.

"You're early," Wrath muttered. "The meeting doesn't start for another twenty minutes."

"I'm sorry?"

"You get V's text?"

Rhage entered the frilly pale blue room with its French furniture and its air of butter-wouldn't-melt-in-my-mouth. The study or parlor or whatever it was the most ludicrous environment to plan fights and wars and strategy in, but now, like so much of Darius's mansion, it was a tradition that no one wanted to change.

Patting his chest where his phone had vibrated, he murmured, "Guess that's what just came through. What's doing?"

Wrath sat back in his father's great ornate chair, and beside him on the floor, George lifted his boxy blond head in inquiry, as if the dog wanted to know whether they were going somewhere or staying put.

The King reached down and stroked the retriever. "You'll find out soon enough with the others. You got something on your mind, my brother? You came by when V was talking to me earlier."

Rhage glanced around the empty room. "Actually, yeah."

"Talk to me."

The story came out in a rush of sound bites: Bitty, her mom, Mary, him, the GTO—yup, for some reason, the fact that the girl liked his car made it in there. He also explained that he'd had his interview with Rhym, that Mary was having hers, that they needed Wrath's approval.

Blah, blah, blah.

When he ran out of nouns and verbs, he discovered that he'd wandered around and ended up sitting in the chair on the far side of the throne, he and his brother separated by the expanse of desk, all those carved figures and sacred symbols marking the divide between their stations.

And yet he felt as though he and Wrath were one and the same as the male smiled. "You got it, my brother. Whatever you need, it's yours. And if they want to do a site visit, or whatever you call it, the social worker is welcome here. We'll have Fritz bring her in."

Rhage was exhaling a fuckload of tension as Butch and Phury walked in. "Thank you," he said hoarsely. "Thank you so much."

"You've come a long way from being that asshole I once knew and tolerated."

When Wrath extended the black diamond ring of the King, Rhage got up and leaned over to kiss it. "Yeah, we all have—"

Just as he was straightening, someone goosed him so hard in the ass, he nearly face planted all over that desk. Wheeling around, he saw Lassiter smiling.

"Sorry," the angel said. "Couldn't help it."

Rhage bared his fangs. "Lass, seriously, could you be anymore annoying."

The fuck-twit put his forefinger to his chin and tapped as he tilted his head. "Hmm, I don't know. But I'm willing to try."

"I swear to God, one of these days . . ."

Except it was a lie. He wasn't going to do shit. The trouble with the current asshole crown holder was that it was impossible to truly hate him. Not when on a regular basis he proved there was a stand-up guy under all that goddamn, fucking irritation.

The rest of the Brotherhood filed in and took their customary places in the room. As Rhage camped out with Butch on one of the spindly sofas, it took him a minute to realize someone was missing.

Nope, here was Vishous. With Payne at his side.

One look into the pair of grim faces, and Rhage cursed under his breath. And he wasn't the only one.

The doors were shut, and then everyone got dead quiet—

Before something could be said, Zsadist burst into the room and everybody recoiled.

"What the *fuck* happened to you?" V demanded.

The brother had steam rising up off of him—and not because he was pissed. There was, like, actual smoke curling from the shoulders of his leather jacket and the bottoms of his shitkickers. And, Jesus Christ, the stench—he smelled like burned rubber, bad chemicals, and a three-day-old campsite.

"Nothing," the guy said as he sauntered over to his twin. "Just roasting marshmallows."

"Is that my flamethrower?" somebody asked indignantly.

"How many square feet was the marshmallow," someone else muttered.

"Hey, was it a Stay Puft?" Lassiter cut in.

The King cursed. "Oh, for fuck's sake, did you burn that bitch's house down?"

Well, hello, everyone clearly thought as they went quiet and stared at Z.

"Technically, it was her old man's," Rhage felt compelled to comment. "Assuming we're talking about the cunt who held that blood slave in her basement."

Wrath shook his finger in Rhage's direction. "Hey, no 'See you next Tuesdays' if you're going to be a father. You need to drop that shit right now and get used to it before you bring that little girl into this fucking house."

Annnnnnnnnnnnnnnnnnd now everyone and their uncle turned around to eyeball him.

Fantastic.

Can we go back and talk about the marshmallow? he thought to himself.

As he hoped for a change of subject, and absolutely nothing like that happened, he shook his head. Wasn't this just like the Brotherhood mansion, where news traveled faster than . . . well, a bonfire, for instance.

"Okay, A," he said to the crowd, "I don't know if we can adopt Bitty yet. Two, that holier-than-thou, no-cussing speech would have been a lot more effective if it didn't have 'shit' and an f-bomb in it. And D, yes, Mary and I are trying to become parents, and no, I don't want to talk about it yet. Can we be done."

Lassiter came over. "High five for the *Home Alone* ref."

"I did it for you, you piece of shit." Rhage clapped palms with the douchebag. "And thanks for your support. Now let's move on to the next crisis. Does anyone want to drop their trousers and admit to having a thong on? Or are we going to get serious and start sharing pedicures."

Wrath spoke up. "Rhage is right. We got problems. V and Payne, take it away."

Instantly, the vibe in the room changed, everybody getting serious as the siblings went over and stood in front of the fire. Man, you could see the family resemblance between them, with that jet-black hair and those diamond eyes. V was a little taller than his sis, broader, too, of course, and then there were those warning tattoos at his temple and the goatee. Payne was no slouch, however, her fighter's body covered in exactly the same leather as her brother's was, her muscled arms and legs making Ronda Rousey look like someone's shrunken grandmother.

"The Scribe Virgin is dead."

As V dropped the bomb, there was a momentary period of silent saaaaaaaaaaaaaaaaaaaaaaay-*whaaaaaaaaaaaaat*. Then a shit-ton of gasps and cursing in the room, all kinds of WTF hitting the airwaves.

Vishous put his palms out. "Before you ask any questions, we don't know more than that. I went up to see her, found all of her shit gone, and a missive in the Chosen cemetery. She said she was going to appoint a successor in due time. That's it."

Rhage glanced back and forth between the pair of them. Payne's face was a mask of not-gonna-go-there, like she had been fed up with the drama about two hundred years ago and was peacing out over her mother. V was much the same.

"How can she die if she's immortal?" somebody asked.

Vishous lit up and shrugged. "Look, I don't mean to blow this off, but I got nothing else to offer you all at this point."

Rhage whistled softly and took a Tootsie Pop out of his pocket. As he saw that he'd outed a grape one, he thought, Well, maybe it was all going to work out somehow.

Fuck. Who was he kidding.

Down in the training center, Layla was going to the bathroom. Again.

Ever since the young had been born, she felt as though she had been peeing, and sure enough, her body was showing the change of not just having jettisoned the infants' weight, slight though it was, but apparently seven hundred thousand gallons of water.

Unbelievable.

Why hadn't anyone told her about this? Then again, there had been a lot more important things to talk about.

And there still were, she thought grimly as she changed the pad in the mesh underwear she'd been given and got back on her feet. As the toilet flushed, she walked across to the sink and washed her hands with the fragrant French soap that Fritz stocked even the clinic rooms with.

As she emerged, she was waddling on account of the size of the pad she needed, but all in all, she was feeling so much stronger.

"How we doing, little ones?"

Even though she was exhausted, every time she was up and around she paid them a visit, and it was so magical: even through the Plexiglas, they seemed to hear her, recognize her, their little heads turning to her voice.

"Lyric, are you breathing better? Yes? I think you are."

The little girl had had some difficulty several hours ago, the ventilation machine increasing its pump automatically in response to a drop in blood oxygen, but now, according to the monitors that Layla found herself reading like a doctor, everything was well.

"And you, Mr. Man? Oh, you're doing very well indeed."

Heading back to the bed, she stretched out and put her hand on her flattening stomach. It was amazing to see the swelling go down by the hour, her body bouncing back thanks to all the feeding she had been doing.

Qhuinn and Blay had been so generous with their veins, to the point that she was convinced she must be bleeding them dry.

There remained a period of recovery ahead for her, however. From what she understood, human women took far longer, even though their pregnancies were shorter—for vampire mothers, it was less in terms of time, but there were still all kinds of things, hormonally speaking and otherwise, that her body needed to do to recalibrate.

Funny, she had wanted her body back. Now? It seemed kind of lonely to just be by herself in her skin.

When a knock sounded, she said, "Come in?"

Visitors were good. Visitors were a respite from the questions buzzing in her head, questions about what she needed to do about Xcor—

Tohrment and Autumn came in with hesitation, and oh, the look on the Brother's face as his deep blue eyes went to the young. Such pain. Such sadness for what he had lost.

And yet he smiled when he glanced at her. "Hello, *mahmen*. You are looking well."

Layla inclined her head, and smiled back. "You are too kind. Autumn, hello."

As Autumn came forward for a hug, Layla studied Tohr's face as she embraced his *shellan*, searching for features that linked him with his half brother.

There were so few. But the color of the eyes . . . exactly the same. Why had she not noticed before now?

For both he and Xcor had sprung forth from the same loins.

"I've come to offer you my vein," Tohr said roughly. "I received permission to approach you from your males? But obviously, if you'd prefer to use only them, I understand."

"Ah, no. No, please, and thank you. I've been concerned that I'm taking too much from them."

Tohr's stare returned to the young.

"You can go introduce yourself," Layla said gently.

Autumn went with her male to the incubators, and the two stood for the longest time, looking at the little ones.

"I always wondered what having a blooded brother or sister would be like," Tohr remarked.

Keeping her voice calm, Layla said, "Have you none?"

He shook his head. "My father undoubtedly spread his seed far and wide, as they used to say, but no one's ever come out of the woodwork."

Until now, she thought.

"Tohrment, I need to—"

"But enough about me." He turned around with resolve. "Let us take care of you. As Autumn says, it's a balm to help others."

While the Brother's female smiled and said something, Layla retreated into her own head.

This was not going to hold much longer, she thought as Tohr began to roll up his sleeve.

SIXTY-NINE

The following evening, Mary couldn't decide who to argue with.

And when she picked the thirteen-year-old in the back of the GTO, that was a heck of a commentary on the two-hundred-year-old behind the wheel.

"All I'm saying is that I think we could wait a little bit. You know . . ." Like, a couple of years? ". . . it's going to be hard for you to reach the pedals."

Bitty looked up into the rearview for help. "But he said we could move the seat up, right?"

"Please, Mary," Rhage whined. "Come on, what's the worst that can happen?"

"Don't get me started on that—"

"Pleeeeeeeeeeeeeeease," Bitty cut in. "I'll drive carefully."

"Oh, look." Rhage put on his directional signal and turned into a strip mall that had a real estate office on the corner and a bunch of high-class-looking shops in it. "If we go behind here, I'll bet there'll be plenty of room."

"Plenty of room!" Bitty echoed. "Plenty!"

Mary put her head in her hands and shook everything she had

back and forth. She knew when she had lost, however, and this was one of those times: The pair of them were not going to let up, and she might as well give in now. It would cut down on greenhouse emissions and global warming from all the hot air.

"You'll go slow," she said into her palms.

"Very!"

"She'll go so slowly, you could walk faster, right, Bits?"

"Absolutely."

All in all, the evening had been a great time, the three of them going to an O'Charley's for dinner before Rhage had to head out and work. Apparently, he had decided it was absolutely crucial to Bitty's development as a living, breathing vampire being to experience every single one of the restaurants in town—and he had set up a schedule for the next fifteen or twenty nights. On it? Places like WW Cousins, the burger joint. Zaxby's. The Cheesecake Factory. Pizza Hut. Texas Roadhouse.

Yes, even McDonald's, Wendy's, and Burger King.

Bitty, not to be outdone, had taken his phone and created a rating system on the darn thing, the pair of them spending a good half hour with their blond and dark heads together, debating the relative merits of various criteria for some kind of point system.

It was going to be a Dickensian march through trans fat and huge portions.

The good news? Bitty did have to gain weight, and this was as good a redress for that as any.

"Here we go," Rhage announced as if he'd found the cure for IBS. "See? Plenty of space."

Okay, at least he had a point. As he hit the brakes, and let the headlights do the talking, the back stretch of asphalt was long and broad, and completely empty but for a couple of Dumpsters: All things considered, there was nothing behind the strip mall but scruffy grass and trees.

"Fine, but I'm getting out of the car." Mary cracked her door. "I've been in two near-misses in the last how long? I'm not risking a third."

As she held the seat up for Bitty, the girl looked grave. "I won't hurt it. I promise."

Mary put her hand on the girl's shoulder and gave it a squeeze. "I don't care about the car—"

"What!" Rhage yelped while he got out of his side. "How can you say that?"

Shooing him, she refocused on Bitty. "Just be careful. Go slowly. You'll do great."

Bitty gave her a quick hug—and what do you know, it was something that stopped Mary's heart every time it happened. And then the girl and Rhage were by the driver's seat, talking in that fast way they did, the rapid-fire chatter making Mary's head spin.

Stepping out of the way, waaaaaaay out of the way, she ended up leaning back against the single-story, long-as-a-football-field building, right next to a sign that read, DELIVERIES ONLY. The night was unseasonably warm, so much so that she let her jacket fall open, and overhead, the sky was cloudy, as if God had pulled a woolen blanket over the Earth against the chill of late October.

"Here we go!" Rhage said as he hightailed it around to the passenger side. "Get ready!"

As he waved like he was on the deck of a cruise ship that was about to depart, she waved back and thought, Please, no *Titanic* here, people.

Fits, starts. Grinding gears. Hopping and skipping—and then Bitty got it. Somehow . . . the girl gathered the reins of that twelve-billion-horsepower whatever-engine under that hood, and she and Rhage were cruising by. At five miles an hour.

Mary found herself jumping up and down and clapping like the kid had graduated medical school with a cure for cancer. "You did it! Go, Bitty!"

God, it felt so good to cheer. To watch a mastery happen. To be a witness as the girl turned the powerful muscle car around at the far end and started back again, waving madly as she passed by once more, her face aglow with happiness as Rhage sat beside her clapping and whistling sure as if Bitty were running a touchdown at the Super Bowl, dunking the final basket at the NCAA championship, and crossing the Boston Marathon finish line all at the same time.

Here they came once more, gathering speed, until Bitty was shifting into third on the straightaway.

It was . . . magic.

It was . . . family.

It was . . . absolutely, positively everything that mattered and was important.

And then it all went into bad territory.

Bitty and Rhage had just made the turn again and were heading away for the long run to the very far end, when the sound of a bottle being thrown against the pavement brought Mary's head up.

Four or five guys came around the corner—and stopped short like they were as surprised to find anyone back there as Mary was to have her white-picket-fence moment interrupted.

"What the fuck," one of them muttered.

"Wassup, bitch."

Mary crossed her arms over her chest and stared right at them, holding her ground without saying a word. They were your typical fifteen-, sixteen-year-old bunch of nitwits, trying to make like they were gangstas with their low-hanging pants and side-tilt baseball hats—when in reality they might as well have been on a mall crawl by Macy's and the Sunglass Hut. The trouble, though? In a pack, they were like coyotes, dangerous even though they were scrawny.

"How you doin'?" a third drawled.

What, like you're Tony Soprano, you little punk, she thought as they closed in on her. Except, when she saw that one of them had a knife down by his side, she stiffened.

What was worse? The boy who was armed was twitching like he was on something.

By this time, Rhage and Bitty had turned around and were making their way back down, and all Mary could think of was, Please just keep going. Get Bitty the hell out of here.

But, no. The GTO stopped a good twenty feet away, its headlights illuminating Mary and the pack of animals.

"Ohhhhhhhhhhhhhh, shit, check that ride out," one of the them said.

"I'm taking that whip home—"

The chorus of whistles and curses toned down as Rhage opened the passenger door and rose to his full height. "Mary. Come over here."

Mary started to walk away, but she didn't get far. Next thing she knew, the one with the knife had grabbed her and dragged her back against him, putting that blade to her throat.

"Whatchu gonna do?" the boy blustered. "Huh? Whatchu gonna do?"

Mary trembled, but not because she was worried about her own life. What the hell could they do to her? Instead, all she could think of was, No, no, not in front of Bitty—

"Keep going!" she called out to Rhage. "Just drive—"

"I'll cut you," came the voice in her ear.

"Fine, do what you want," she muttered. "Not in front of them, though. Let them go and you can cut me up all you want."

"*What?*" the kid sputtered.

"Get out of here, Rhage—"

Yeah, nope.

Not even by half.

All at once, the light shining in her eyes and all over them got brighter by a factor of a hundred and fifty thousand kilowatts. And Mary cursed.

Shit. She knew what that meant.

"It is not much farther."

As Assail spoke, he eased off on the Range Rover's accelerator and made the right-hand turn onto the lane that proceeded down to the peninsula on which he lived. Beside him, riding shotgun, as the humans called it, Markcus was rather quiet, his eyes glued to the windows both in front of him and next to him.

The young male was transfixed by the environs—and also seemingly confused.

"The bridge was different," he said roughly. "The one we just went over. It's different from when I . . ."

"Much has changed indeed, I imagine."

"There are far more tall buildings downtown. More cars. More . . . everything."

"Wait until you encounter the Internet, my friend. Then you shall see a truly dubious improvement."

Soon enough, they came upon the house, and Markcus gasped. "It is so . . . beautiful."

"There is a lot of glass. And much irony in that."

Assail pulled up to the garage doors, triggering the proper one, and then he proceeded inside and under cover. When Markcus went to open his door, Assail stopped him with a hand to the forearm.

"Not until the panels are back down. Precautions must be observed."

"My apologies."

When they were shut in properly, they stepped out on their own

sides, and Assail waited for the other male to come around. Markcus was moving slowly, and using the Range Rover for support, but he had made it amply clear that he would accept no help and would not be availing himself of any canes or walkers, either.

Assail stepped over to the house door and opened the reinforced-steel expanse. The scent that boiled out of the mudroom was heavenly, everything that was good about First Meal. Bacon and eggs, coffee, pancakes . . . no, scones?

Markcus faltered as he entered the house. "Oh . . . that is . . ."

"Indeed. Who knew the bastards could cook."

Assail made his way slowly toward the kitchen, attempting to make it seem as if he always sauntered thus.

In the galley proper, it was obvious that Ehric and Evale had done their utmost to make their guest feel welcome: setting the table—albeit cockeyed and with the forks on the wrong side of the plates; cooking many things—at which they fared far better; brewing coffee—no, wait, that was instant, but still seemed very viable, going by its aroma.

"Sit," Ehric said unto Markcus after introductions were made. "We shall serve you—no, no argument, sit."

Markcus shuffled over, groaning with relief as he took his scant weight off his scrawny legs. As he pushed his long hair back, his face was revealed, the anomaly that had led to him having no beard growth meaning that his cheeks and his jaw, his chin and his throat, were availed to the cousins' curious eyes.

Indeed, Assail thought to himself, the male was rather something to behold.

"I shall prepare you your Last Meal then," Markcus said.

"We'll see about that, mate," Ehric returned as he put a heaping load of food before their guest.

Out of habit, Assail reached into his suit jacket, grasping his vial—but before he retrieved it, he stopped and glanced at the clock on the microwave. Then he confirmed said time on the stove and upon his Piaget watch.

"Join us, then, cousin," Ehric said as he and Evale plated themselves and sat down.

Evale picked up his fork and poked it in the direction of Markcus's plate. "Dug in, yeah?"

"That's 'dig' in," Assail corrected absently.

"Are you not eating, cousin?" Ehric inquired.

Assail turned toward the sink. With steps that were as halting as Markcus's had been, he went over, opened the top of the vial, and poured the cocaine out into the drain.

"Downstairs," he said in a rough voice as he ran a rush of water from the tap. "You know where my blocks are kept."

Of Coke, that was.

"Aye," Ehric whispered. "We do."

"You will get them out of the house." As his cousins went to jump up, he motioned them to return to their seats. "After your meal is fine. I need you to stay and make him eat. Then take him down to the spare suite downstairs with you all."

"I do not require luxury," Markcus said. "Merely a place to lay my head during the day."

"You have more than earned the respite, my dear male."

There was a knocking on the door, and Assail glanced over at the threesome. "You will find that I shall be, how shall I put it, indisposed elsewhere for a number of evenings. I know not how long. Take care of him, will you. I shall be most displeased if Markcus is not fatter and steadier upon my return."

As he lifted his hands, he noted the trembling in them.

This was going to—if he might use a vernacular term—suck ass.

Going to the back door, he opened it wide and felt an absurd urge to bow. Which he promptly followed through on.

In response, Dr. Manello indicated the black Mercedes with the blacked-out windows that was running in the car park. "You ready?"

"Yes."

"How bad is it? You're shaking."

"I fear it shall only get much worse."

The last thing he did before he left his glass house was glance back at Markcus. The male was eating slowly, his bony, skeletal hands holding the sterling silverware he was using awkwardly, as if he had not put utensils to use in a very long time.

It was going to be a long journey back for him.

But if, after all he had been through, he had the courage to grab for the ring of life . . . then Assail could as well.

Assail?

In his mind, he heard Marisol's voice on his cell as he stood within the ring of fire he had created. Detoxing was going to be rather like that blaze, he feared.

"Assail?"

"Indeed," he said to the good doctor. "Let us go."

SEVENTY

As soon as the brilliant light blinded her attacker, causing him to loosen his grip, Mary broke out of the boy's hold and elbowed him in the gut.

And while he bent over and dropped his knife, she ran full-tilt for the GTO.

"Get her out of here!" Rhage said. "Fast!"

Those were the last words he spoke.

The beast was already coming out of him as she raced to get behind the wheel, his huge body falling to his knees, his head bowing as he braced his strength against the pavement as if he were trying to give her time to hit the gas before the dragon emerged.

Skidding to a halt by the driver's door, Mary ripped the thing open just as Bitty scrambled over to the passenger seat.

"Rhage!" the girl screamed. "Rhage . . . ! What's happening, what's wrong!"

Rhage somehow had the presence of mind to reach up and shut his door, and Mary didn't waste a second. "Seat belt! Put your seat belt on!"

"We can't leave him!"

"Seat belt! He's going to be fine, but we have to go!"

Mary hit the clutch and the gas at the same time, slamming the

gearshift into first before releasing her left foot. Tires squealed as all those horses dug for purchase on the asphalt, and she got ready for the momentum to explode them forward.

Meanwhile, back in the asshole zip code, the group of idiots had decided to rush toward the car.

Yeah, like that was going to last.

Cue the slo-mo.

At the very moment the GTO started to scream forward, as Bitty was yelling and Mary was fighting to stay cool, a great roar lit through the night, so close to them that it actually disturbed the traction of the muscle car.

And even though it was just in her peripheral vision, Mary got a totally clear picture of the second Bitty saw the beast emerge from Rhage's body.

The girl froze, a slack-jawed expression overtaking her previous fear. "What . . . is *that*?"

"It won't hurt us, okay?" Mary said.

And WHEEEEEE, they were off like they were shot out of a cannon, careening forward, getting out of Dodge.

Unfortunately, the humans—a.k.a. the bowling pins with the attitudes—were directly in front of the GTO. Which was how Mary's dream of not getting into car accident number three was sorely thwarted. Wrenching the wheel to the right, she avoided killing one or more of them—a courtesy none of them deserved—but the bad news was that she hit a Dumpster, crashing into the thing, all that forward momentum turning into totally-going-nowhere in a split second.

As the steering wheel punched her in the chest and a *Bad News Bears* hissing sound came out of the crumpled hood, she wrenched around in a panic to Bitty.

The girl had managed to put her seat belt on before the impact.

Thank you, God—

Another roar cut through the night, and yup, out the back window she saw that the beast was fully present, not just voicing its opinion. And yup, the humans had changed their minds about their little attack, stumbling over themselves to get headed in the opposite direction.

As if they were very clear that, however improbable it was for a dragon to materialize in the back parking lot of a strip mall, they were not about to argue with what seemed to be happening—

Before she could stop Bitty, the girl was out of the car.

"Damn it! Bitty!"

Mary jumped out, too—and cursed a whole lot more: The beast had curled forward on its powerful legs and was going all *Jurassic Park*, things-are-closer-than-they-appear, crouching into attack position as it blew the cobwebs out of its lungs.

No, no, not lunch. Nope, not going to happen—

"Get back in the car!" Mary barked as she ran into the beast's path, putting herself between the retreating fidiots and her darkling husband.

"What is that!" Bitty yelled out. "What happened to him!"

"Hey! Hi!" Waving her hands, Mary caught the beast's attention. "There you are. Hello, way up there."

The beast chuffed, its jowls lifting off its enormous teeth in a smile. Then it let out a keening sound, part inquiry, part protest.

"No. You may not. You cannot eat the humans."

Yeah, okay, she still couldn't believe it anytime those words came out of her mouth. Oh, the places you will go, indeed.

But the beast dropped its head. Like it was pouting.

"I know. I know, but you have a sweet tooth. You like slayers more—"

Abruptly, the beast's gigantic head snapped to the left. And Mary closed her eyes, thinking, Shit, she knew why.

"Bitty," she muttered without looking away from the dragon. "I told you to get back in the damn car."

The beast's nostrils flared wide. And then it blew out the inhale as it scented the girl.

"Bitty! I mean it! Get back—"

Chuffing sounds abounded as the beast stretched out on the ground, laying its head down on the asphalt toward Bitty.

Mary lowered her hands. Glanced over at the girl.

Bitty stood there, utterly motionless, as if her brain simply couldn't compute it all. And then she came forward, moving slowly, her arms down and her eyebrows way up. Her expression was wary and nervous, but she seemed determined to see for herself what was going on with the dragon.

More chuffing, as if the beast were trying to communicate that it was okay. He wasn't going to be a bad boy. He just wanted to say hi.

Biggest lapdog on the frickin' planet, Mary thought. And let's just hope it stayed that way.

"Be careful," Mary said. "No sudden movements—"

"I think he likes me? I'm not sure . . . but I think he likes me."

A minute later, Bitty stopped right next to the dragon's head, right beside those gnashing jaws, right by those reptilian eyes that blinked vertically, not horizontally.

"Can I pet you?" she asked.

The beast made an inquiring sound, as if it were mimicking her tone.

"Is that a yes?"

When it did the half-purr, half-exhale thing again, Bitty extended a shaking hand and placed it right on the beast's cheek.

"Oh, you're so smooth. You're much smoother than I thought—"

There was a sudden rush of movement, and Mary lunged forward and grabbed the girl, dragging her out of range. But she shouldn't have worried.

The beast had rolled over onto its back, its comparably small arms curling up on its chest, its house-size rear legs stretching out. In order to scratch its belly, Bitty would have needed a six-foot ladder—and Mary two Xanax and a bottle of wine, thank you very much—but the girl made the best of it, going over and reaching up on her tiptoes as the beast angled its head to watch her with soft eyes.

"He's so cute," Bitty said. "Aren't you? Who's a cutie?"

"I really need a drink," Mary muttered to herself. "I need a frickin' drink."

But at least we have this part of it all solved, she thought.

When Rhage came back into his body, it was full-on panic time. "Mary! Bitty! Mary!"

But then he realized that two sets of hands were holding his palms, and there were two beautiful voices that started to reassure him—well, one did the reassuring. The other one was just reassuring to hear.

"It's okay, we're okay—"

"Rhage! You have a dragon! A pet dragon! I got to rub his tummy!"

Say what, he thought in the blindness.

"When can he come back! I want to see him again! Can I play with him!"

His delirium was thankfully not accompanied by stomach pains, so he took that to mean that he hadn't snacked on any of those fucking douches who had aggressed on his Mary. And oh, good, there was a blanket over the lower half of his body, so he wasn't naked.

But he had to start shaking his head even though he wasn't sure where the girl was looking. "That is not a toy, Bits. He's dangerous—"

"He likes me! That was amazing!"

"—and I can't just call him out of me, okay? But when you come to live with us, I'll see what I can do."

Complete. Silence.

And then Bitty said in a small voice, "Come live with you?"

"Oh . . . shit," he muttered. Even though his King had brought up the whole no-cussing thing. "I mean, carp. I mean, *crap*."

"Live with you?" the girl repeated.

As Mary cleared her throat, Rhage tried to sit up, even though he lacked the strength to get very far in the vertical department.

"Bitty," his *shellan* said. "I've tried to find your uncle. Actually, a lot of people have attempted to locate him—and nothing's come of it. I don't know what happened to him or where he is—I can't even begin to guess. But assuming he isn't . . . available . . . Rhage and I have been talking, and you know, we don't want to take the place of your *mahmen*. Not at all. It's just . . . we'd really like it if you'd consider coming to stay with us. It can start out on a trial basis, and if you don't like it, you can always—"

There was a muffled impact and Mary stopped talking.

At which point he smelled tears.

"What's happening?!" He flailed around. "What's wrong? What's she doing—"

All of a sudden, little arms wrapped around his neck, and Bitty's voice was in his ear. "Does this mean you'll be my father?"

Rhage's breath caught in his throat. Then he carefully hugged the girl back, mindful not to crush her. "If you'll have me . . ." Okay, he couldn't talk here. "Yes, yes, I will."

He felt Mary rub his back in circles, and could sense his mate's happiness soaring right beside him—but that wasn't enough. He pulled her in tight so that both females were up against his chest.

So this . . . was his family, he thought with a sudden shot of pride. These . . . were his two girls.

The smile that hit his face stretched his cheeks so much he knew they were never going to be the same.

Especially as he thought back to when he had been holding L.W. down in the kitchen, staring out across a room he did not see, his heart aching for all he would never have.

And yet here he was now, everything he had wanted not just within his grasp, but in his arms.

"Can I move in tonight?" Bitty asked. "And when do I get to meet everybody?"

SEVENTY-ONE

The resilience of children was amazing, Mary thought later as she and Bitty and Rhage drove up to the front of the Brotherhood mansion.

In spite of everything she had been through, the girl was open-eyed and open-hearted at the prospect of a totally different kind of life, ready for anything, excited, happy. Then again, she was with people who loved her, even if it felt too early to speak of it.

Which wasn't to say there hadn't been some sadness. Especially as she and Bitty had been up in that attic room at Safe Place, retrieving the two suitcases. When the girl had asked if she could bring her mother's things too, Mary had teared up. And then there had been the urn.

But overall, this was joyous. And Mary was focusing on that.

As she stopped the GTO right at the foot of the stone steps, it was probably overkill, given that the little girl didn't have more than those two pieces of luggage and the urn.

But somehow, she just wanted to get Bitty in the house—and any distance seemed too far away. After Rhage had called Wrath, and Mary had called Marissa, it was decided that under a foster care situation, there was no reason Bitty couldn't move in. Besides, it would

mean that Doc Jane and Manny could check her out medically more easily, and there was really nothing to hold her at Safe Place.

The fact that there was no paperwork yet made Mary a little uneasy, but Ryhm was taking care of that. What was really worrisome? The six-month waiting period was starting tonight, and until that mutually agreed-upon clock ran out, this wasn't a done deal.

And yes, Mary would continue to look for the hypothetical uncle, even though it gave her a frickin' heart attack anytime she thought of that male coming out of the woodwork.

Still, she had a duty to do right by Bitty.

"Are we here?" Rhage asked. "I think we're here. Bitty, what do you see?"

"Do the Munsters live in this house?" the girl asked. "It looks like the Munsters' house, only . . . how big is it?"

"Hundred rooms or so. It's tight quarters, but we manage to make it work."

Rhage's hand flapped around the door until he hit the handle and opened things up. As he stood up, he tightened the blanket wrapped around his waist and nearly tripped on the curb.

Mary turned the engine off, and pulled the emergency brake. When she glanced back at Bitty, the girl was just staring up at the great stone expanse. Cradled in her arms, right against her chest, were her mother's ashes in that urn.

This was not a restart, Mary reflected.

This was not even a reset, an erase . . . or a replacement of everything that had been hard, brutal, and poor with shiny, sparkly fresh stuff. It wasn't Christmas. It wasn't happy-birthday, surprise-it's-a-puppy, confetti-and-balloon-and-frosting time.

This was another chapter. One that was going to be so much more stable and emotionally supportive, but was still going to have its own ups and downs, its challenges and triumphs, frustrations and happiness.

"Bitty?" she said. "You don't have to do this."

The girl turned and smiled. "Which one is my room?"

Mary laughed and got out. "Rhage, I'll get the suitcases."

"The hell you will." His blind eyes rolled around. "Where are they?"

"Fine, let me just get them and bring them over. And tuck that blanket in again, will you? I don't want you flashing everyone as we make our grand entrance."

Bitty stepped up next to Rhage and held the urn close. "Wow. It's even bigger than it looks."

"Wait'll you get inside."

Popping the trunk, Mary got out Annalye's suitcase first, and she couldn't help herself: She looked at the sky, trying to picture the female staring down from above, watching over all this and hopefully approving.

I'll take good care of her, Mary vowed. I promise.

"Let's go," she said as Rhage shut the car door next to him.

"Suitcases?"

"Right here, big boy." As she turned them over to his very capable hands, they kissed. "How 'bout I take your arm to help you navigate?"

"I can help, too," Bitty said, grabbing onto Rhage's other elbow.

Mary had to blink back tears as Rhage's bare chest expanded to five times its natural size. His pride at having his two females with him as he walked up to the King's residence was the stuff of legend: Even blind and no doubt a little sore, it was plain to see that he was in heaven.

And then they were in the vestibule and Mary was putting her face in the security camera.

"Get ready," Mary murmured to Bitty. "It's a big space—"

The door opened wide and the butler started to smile, only to freeze when he saw Bitty.

"It's Fritz!" the girl exclaimed. "It's Fritz! Hi! I'm Bitty!"

Okay, cue the melting. If that old butler had been any more entranced with the girl, his entire face would have dripped off his skull and landed on the marble floor.

Raiders of the Lost Ark, indeed.

The *doggen* bowed low. "Mistress. And sire. And . . . mistress."

Bitty looked around Rhage's heft. "Am I a mistress?"

Mary nodded and whispered, "You'll get used to it. I did."

The three of them walked into the grand foyer, and the first thing they saw was Lassiter on the couch in the billiards room. He was clicking the remote at the T.V. and swearing.

"I don't care about football! ESPN my ass! Whatever—where the hell's *Who's the Boss?*"

"Lassiter!"

At the sound of his name, the angel looked out over the pool tables to where they all stood. And oh, how he smiled, that gentle, kind expression more associated with angels than the stuff he usually put out

to the world. Rising to his feet, he came over, and, yes, Mary was really glad he was dressed in something normal, just jeans and a black Hanes T-shirt, his blond-and-black hair all over his shoulders.

With him, you never knew.

Getting down on his haunches, he extended his hand. "How did you know who I am, Bitty?"

The girl shook what was offered to her and pointed up at Rhage. "He told me all about you. All about everyone—wait, how did you know my name? Did he tell you about me?"

Lassiter looked up at the three of them and brushed the little girl's cheek. "My little one, I have seen this moment since I first met your new *mahmen* and father—"

"No," Mary cut in. "Don't call me *mahmen*. That's Annalye's title. I'm not *mahmen*, just Mary. I'm not looking to take anyone's place."

"You have the strangest eyes," Bitty whispered. "They're beautiful."

"Thank you." The angel inclined his head. "I'm always here, Bitty. You need something, you come find me, and it's yours. I think you'll find that true about a lot of the folks here."

The girl nodded as Lassiter rose up. And then Rhage put down one of the suitcases and the males clapped each other's shoulders, Lassiter with better coordination because he could see.

"Listen, Bitty," Mary said as the angel went back to the remote, "I have an idea for rooms for all of us, but we didn't know you were coming tonight. So if it's okay, you'll stay in the guest suite right next to ours? If you need us, we'll be—"

Cue the water fight.

Up on the second-floor balcony, behind the gold-leaf balustrade, John Matthew and Qhuinn came racing out of the hall of statues, Qhuinn in the lead, John Matthew pumping off rounds of Poland Spring. Without warning, Qhuinn hopped over the balcony into a free fall of twenty or thirty feet, dematerializing at just the right moment before he went fried-egg all over the mosaic floor.

John was right behind him, sliding down the balustrade on one butt cheek, laughing mutely.

The two stopped as soon as they saw Bitty.

"Qhuinn!" she exclaimed. "With the blue and the green eyes!"

The Brother looked gob-smacked at the little girl, even as he came over and towered above her. "Yeah, that's my name, who—oh, my God! Rhage and Mary! Your little girl! It worked out!"

Mary got a bear hug. A huge bear hug. A gigantic, bone-crushing bear hug from the new father. And then John Matthew was signing.

"You're John Matthew!" Bitty stared at his fingers. "What is he saying—wait, what?" Then she looked up at the humongous fighter and said, "You need to teach me that. If I'm going to live here, you need to teach me that."

Well, that puddled John Matthew. Yup. To the point where his fingers didn't seem to work—the ASL equivalent to someone stuttering.

And jeez, Bitty was amazing, so outgoing and friendly—and courageous considering all she had been through.

Mary rubbed the center of her chest. Yes, she thought, she was getting a real live dose of maternal pride here—and it was better than a million glasses of wine. No hangover, either.

"Are you blind again?" Qhuinn asked his Brother.

"Yeah, I tried to eat some humans."

"Tried? That beast of yours on a diet?"

They were all laughing when someone came out from under the staircase. Instantly, the chatter stopped, as if people were worried about who it was.

Zsadist was dressed in his fighting gear, black leather coating his body in a second skin, weapons strapped on his chest, his thighs, under his arms—

In spite of the way he looked, Bitty broke away and went right over to the scarred male, her well-washed, handmade dress frothing under that ugly black coat of hers.

Z did a stop-short just as everyone else had—kind of like he'd seen a ghost. And then he looked around in what seemed to be confusion.

"You're Zsadist," Bitty piped up. "You have a young—may I meet her? I should like very much to meet her, please."

In response, Zsadist moved extra slowly, lowering himself down to her level. And then he just stared at her for a time, as if she were some wild creature that had unexpectedly proven to be tame.

"Her name is Nalla," he said roughly. "My daughter is much younger than you. She would like to have a big sister, if you'd like to teach her things."

"Oh, yes. I would."

"What's that in your arms, little one?"

Bitty looked down, and Mary held her breath. "This is my *mah-*

men. She passed. That's why Mary and Rhage are fostering me. I hope I get to stay here, though. I like them a lot."

Just like that. The explanation was simple, and heartbreaking . . . and had all the adults blinking back tears.

Zsadist inclined his head low, his yellow eyes glowing. "My condolences for your loss. And welcome to our home—which you should now call yours, too."

Bitty leaned her head to the side and regarded the Brother. "I like you. You're nice."

Hours later, after they got Bitty settled next door, Rhage and Mary headed into their room.

He was still blind as hell, but Rhage didn't care how many times he stubbed his toe or clipped something on a door jamb, Bitty was under the same roof as he and Mary were, so all was hella right in his world. And, man, had she blown everyone away.

Even though she was this little thing in this huge, grand mansion with all these people she'd never met in her life? She had gone up and called everyone by name, introducing herself and smiling and laughing. She had kept her mother's urn with her the entire time, and somehow that had seemed apt, not ghoulish or morbid.

Her *mahmen* was very much a part of her and always would be—and, oh, his Mary was being so respectful of that.

Like his female could make him love her more? Jesus.

"I can't believe we have a kid," he was saying as his *shellan* took him into the bathroom and loaded up his brush with toothpaste. "We are parents. We have . . . a kid."

"And I'm sorry, I may already be biased, but how fantastic is she? Did you see Wrath? He's in love with her. I think he wants L.W. to marry her."

"Well, she's strong. She's smart. Who wouldn't want to—"

From out of nowhere, a snarl twitched his upper lip, and a growl percolated up out of his chest—while at the same time, the beast surged around his back looking for a way out.

And all that got worse as he pictured some male standing next to his Bitty with all kinds of bright fucking ideas in his—

"Rhage. Stop it. She's going to probably want to date someone at some point—"

"Over his fucking dead body anyone is touching my daughter—"

"Rhage, okay, three-part yoga breath." She petted his shoulder like she was soothing a lion. "It's perfectly normal for little girls to grow up and want to get mated to—"

"Nope. She's not dating. *Ever*."

Mary started laughing. "You know, this would truly be funny if I didn't worry that you weren't slightly serious."

"I'm *totally* fucking serious."

"Here we go already." Mary sighed. "I swear, Bella and I are going to have to get you and Zsadist into a support group."

"Yes!" he announced. "My brother will know exactly how this is. Solidarity among fathers—"

Mary cut off his rant by shoving a boatload of Crest toothpaste into his piehole. "Shut up and brush, honey. We'll talk about this after her transition. In, like, twelve to fifteen *years*."

"Bdjgaehu hasdpi knjidhgil."

"What was that?"

"Not gonna change a fucking thing."

But he was a good boy and worked his chompers over. Then he and Mary took a shower . . . where all kinds of other things happened—

ALL OF WHICH REMINDED HIM EXACTLY WHY THERE WAS GOING TO BE NO DATING, LIKE, EVER.

When they were finally lying in their big ornate bed together, he positioned his beloved next to him and let out an exhale that lasted a century and a half.

"Are the lights off?" he asked after a moment.

"Mmm-hmmm."

He kissed her head. "Why do all the best things happen when I'm blind? I met you when I was blind. Now . . . she's here, and I'm blind."

"Must be your version of a lucky horseshoe."

Rhage stared up at the nothingness over their heads as Mary yawned so hard her jaw cracked.

Just before he was about to go to sleep, his lids popped back open. "Mary?"

"Hmm-mmm."

"Thank you," he whispered.

"For what?"

"For making me a father."

Mary lifted her head up out of the crook of his arm. "What are you—I didn't do that."

"You most certainly gave us our family." Damn it, he wished he could see her. Instead, he had to make do with his memory of her beautiful face—good thing he'd spent a lot of time staring at his *shellan*.

"You absolutely made me a father—I was dying on that battlefield, and you saved me. If you hadn't done that, we never would have gotten Bitty, because we would have been up in the Fade, and she would have been down here, alone. You made this happen. And it isn't just about me almost passing. You hung in with Bitty from the moment she lost her birth father, through the death of her brother and then of her mother. You worked with her in the aftermath, helping her come out of her shell. And then when we decided to try to do this, you set up the procedure and made sure it was done right. You coached me with my interview. You focused on Bitty. You . . . you made this happen, my Mary. You birthed my daughter, maybe not out of the womb, but certainly out of circumstance—you *made* me a father. And that is the greatest gift any female can ever give her male. So . . . thank you. For our family."

The sweet scent of his *shellan's* tears wafted, and he found her face in the darkness, bringing her mouth to his. The kiss he gave her was chaste and reverent, an expression of his gratitude.

"You have quite a way of putting things, you know that," she said in a rough voice.

"Just being honest. That's all I'm doing."

When Mary resettled on his chest, Rhage closed his eyes. "I love you, my Mary Madonna."

"And you're always going to be my prince with shining fangs."

"Really?"

"Mmm-hmm. You are the best thing that ever happened to me. You and Bitty."

"That's so sweet." He sighed again. "Jeez, I feel sorry for Bits, though."

Mary lifted her head again. "Why?"

"BECAUSE SHE IS NEVER DATING—"

"Rhage, *seriously*. You *gotta* give that a rest. . . ."

SEVENTY-TWO

Sitting in the back of I've Bean, Jo looked up as Bill came over to the table. "We have to stop meeting like this."

The reporter laughed as he sat down with his latte. "So, good news."

"You found the restaurant Julio was talking about downtown?"

"No, you got the online-editor position. They're going to call you in about an hour and officially offer it. They wouldn't tell me what the salary is, but it has to be in the low thirties."

Jo pumped her fist. "Yes. *Yes.* That is awesome—I can start right after I finish my notice period at Bryant's."

"Do you know he called me?"

"What?"

Bill unwrapped another one of his scarves and draped it over the back of his chair. "Yeah. I think he's obsessed with you. He wanted to know whether or not we were dating."

"You're *married.*"

"I pointed this out to him. P.S., Lydia wants to invite you over for dinner Saturday night. My cousin's coming. Troy, you remember him."

"Tell her I'd love to. What can I bring?"

"Just yourself and not Dougie."

"Done."

There was a slight pause, something she didn't associate with the guy who had somehow become her older brother over the last week or so.

"What is it?" she said.

Bill looked around the crowded coffee shop like he was in search of a familiar face in the crowd. More likely, he was picking out words in his head.

"Employment is good," she prompted. "Dinner is good. Soooooo . . ."

"I don't want you to get pissed at me, but I looked into your adoption."

Jo's heart stopped. Then started thumping. "What did you . . . what did you find? And you had no right to do that, yada, yada, yada."

If he'd asked her, she would have said no. But considering he'd clearly found something?

Bill reached into the pocket of his corduroy coat and took out a sheaf of papers that was folded length-wise. "Your birth mother was a nurse. Up in Boston. She left the hospital there when she found out she was pregnant. Back then, in the seventies, single mothers weren't viewed the same, and she had a son that she gave up for adoption. She stayed, continued to work in various places. Fifteen years later, she gets pregnant again, by the same guy. She never married him, though. Not from what I saw. It was definitely the same man, though, according to diary entries that were copied and put into the file. This time, with you, she moved away, came here, settled in Caldwell. When she had you, she didn't make it, unfortunately. It was a high-risk pregnancy because she was older by that time. She never disclosed who your father was, however, and there were no next of kin who came forward to claim you."

Jo sat back in the chair and felt all the noise and the people around her disappear. Brother? And her mother had died . . .

"I wonder if she would have kept me," she said quietly.

"Your father—your adoptive one, that is—had asked a lawyer to keep his eyes out for possible babies at St. Francis here in town. As soon as your birth mom died, he paid to claim you and it was done."

"And that's that."

"Not exactly." Bill took a deep breath. "I found your brother. Kind of."

The reporter put a black-and-white photograph down on the table. It was of a dark-haired man she didn't recognize. Who was about forty years old.

"His name is Dr. Manuel Manello. He was the chief of surgery at St. Francis. But he went off the grid over a year ago, and no one's really seen him since."

With a shaking hand, Jo picked up the picture, searching the features, finding some that, yes, were like her own. "We both ended up in the same place . . ."

"Caldwell has a way of bringing people together."

"We have the same-shaped eyes."

"Yes, you do."

"They look hazel, don't you think? Or maybe they're brown eyes."

"I can't tell."

"May I keep this?"

"Please. And I'm sorry I stuck my nose in where it arguably didn't belong. But I just started digging and couldn't stop. I wasn't sure what I'd find, so I didn't say anything."

"It's okay," she said without looking up. "And thank you. I . . . I always wondered what my blood looked like."

"We can try to find him, you know?"

Now she lifted her eyes. "You think?"

"Sure. We're investigative reporters, right? Even if he's left Caldwell, there must be some way of locating him. It's extremely hard in modern life to go completely blank. Too many electronic records, you know."

"Bill, are you some kind of fairy godfather?"

He nodded and toasted with his latte. "At your service."

A brother, Jo thought as she resumed staring at the image of an arguably handsome face.

"Just one brother?" she murmured, even though it was greedy, she supposed, to want more.

"Who knows. That's all your mom seems to have given birth to. But maybe through your dad's side? Anyway, maybe there's some way of finding him. The trail might be cold, but we could get lucky."

"You know, this whole vampire search is such a distraction." She smiled ruefully. "I'm well aware that they don't really exist, and certainly not in Caldwell. I think it would be better to start looking for my real family than some fake fantasy, don't you think."

"Maybe that's why you went a little crazy with it all. Although I admit, I've been right there with you."

"Family," she murmured, still staring at the picture. "Real family. That's what I want to find."

SEVENTY-THREE

"Should I wear a suit?"

As Rhage came out of the bathroom, he had a cleanly shaven face, mostly dry hair, and a towel around his waist. "Mary—"

"Coming," he heard from out in the hall. "I'm just helping Bitty."

"No hurries."

He was smiling as he crossed the carpet and headed for the walk-in closet. The ceremony was supposed to start in half an hour, so there was still time to get thought up about which black silk shirt to put on—

"*Motherfucker!*" he screamed at the top of his lungs. "Are you *fucking* kidding me!"

As soon as he let fly with the f-bombs, all twelve kinds of laughter bubbled into the room, his Brothers and his *shellan* and his Bitty girl streaming in, yukking it up like the total defacement of his wardrobe was sooooooooo frickin' hilarious.

It was like *Baywatch* had thrown up all over his shit.

"A surfboard! Fishnets? Is this a . . . a harpoon?" He stuck his head back out of the jambs. "Where do you bunch of lunatics even *find* a harpoon in Caldwell?"

"Internet," someone said.

"Amazon," somebody interjected.

He rolled his eyes and pointed at Bitty. "And you're in on this, too? *Et tu*, Brutus Bits?"

As the girl laughed harder, he went back into the closet and picked up the blow-up great white shark. "How many hours did someone spend putting air into this thing?"

While Rhage threw the nightmare out into the bedroom, Vishous raised his hand. "That was me. But I used a tire pump—and actually, I blew up the first one."

"Good thing we had a back-up," Butch pointed out.

"You guys are insane. Insane!"

"Never gets old," Wrath announced. "Ever. Even without the visual, it's some priceless shi—ah, shitake. Mushroom. That is."

"Ha!" Rhage said to his King. "Having fun with that? Not quite so easy, my Lord, is it."

"Technically, I can have you beheaded for that kind of insubordination."

"Promises, promises."

Rhage rolled his eyes as the crowd began to disperse, and he had to fight to get to his clothes, beating back the—OMG, was that a taxidermied tarpon, for fuck's sake?

"You people have too much time on your hands," he shouted at no one in particular.

Five minutes later, he came out dressed in the same version of black and tailored that he'd put on to get interviewed by Rhym.

His two females were sitting at the end of the bed, his Mary in a black dress and Bitty in a bright blue frock that had been hastily made with pride by the household's *doggen*. Both had silver bows around their waists, and between them on the duvet were two long bindings of satin ribbons in blue, black, and silver.

"Oh, my girls." He just had to stop and look at them. "Oh, my beautiful females."

Both of them blushed, and Mary was the first to cast it off as she got to her feet and put her hand out for Bitty.

"Here're your ribbons," his female said as they came over with the arrangement.

"Our ribbons," he corrected.

As they left the room together, they joined a river of other people, everyone streaming down the grand staircase, making the turn, continuing through the hidden door and into the underground tunnel.

"It's so long," Bitty said as she walked between them. "The tunnel is long."

"This is a big place," Rhage murmured.

"Does anyone get lost ever?"

He thought of Lassiter. "No," he grumbled. "Everyone always finds their way back. Especially fallen angels with bad T.V. viewing habits."

"I resemble that remark," Lassiter cracked from the back of the pack.

Through the supply closet. Out of the office. Into the gym, which had been specially lit with hundreds of candles.

Standing just inside the double doors, Layla, Qhuinn, and Blay were beside the incubators, which had been moved into the gym and skirted with white fabric just for this sacred occasion—and which would be removed back to Layla's room as soon as this was over. Beside them, in a wheelchair and a suit and tie, Luchas was very much a part of the family, even though he remained quiet.

In vampire tradition, this ceremony was critical, and not something that could wait, considering that the medical team felt as though the infants were stable enough.

Still, everything was kept dark, and no one spoke so as not to agitate the young.

After all in the household, including servants, Trez, iAm and iAm's mate, as well as all the Chosen and the directrix, and also Blaylock's parents, had assembled together, Wrath and the Queen entered with George between them, and L.W. in Wrath's arms.

Ordinarily, there would be long speeches in the Old Language, but in deference to the infants, Wrath kept it short.

"We gather here, this night, to welcome into the community the blooded son and the blooded daughter of the Black Dagger Brother Qhuinn, son of Lohstrong, and the Chosen Layla, begotten of the Primale and the Chosen Helhena, and the adopted son and the adopted daughter of Blaylock, blooded son of Rocke and of Lyric. May these young be of health and strength and long life, a testimony to the love of their fathers and their mother. Now, as King, I confer unto this female"—Wrath put

out his hand and Beth guided him over to where the tiny female lay— *"the name of Lyric, in honor of her* grandmahmen *on her father Blaylock's side."*

As Blay's *mahmen* sniffled and Qhuinn and Blay put their arms around her, Wrath laid his hand on the other incubator.

From all around, a burst of energy bubbled through the crowd, and Rhage shook his head, amazed that he got to be a witness to this.

With his royal dagger hand on the little male's bassinette, Wrath pronounced, *"In recognition of this young sire's status as a member of the Black Dagger Brotherhood, it has been petitioned unto me that I confer, as King, a Brotherhood name upon this male. I have considered the request and deem it appropriate. I hereby choose the venerable name Rhampage."*

A growl of approval rose up from the Brothers, and Rhage was right there with the others—because he knew that he was welcoming that male into their midst.

This was done right, he thought. This was the old way. The proper way. The way that preserved the traditions.

Rhampage.

It was a very good, very old name.

With his son in his arms and his *shellan* at his side, Wrath then placed the sacred red and black ribbons of the First Family on the skirting of both incubators.

And then, one by one, everybody did the same, each family unit heading up together, Phury and Cormia and Z, Bella and Nalla going after Wrath and Beth, followed by everyone from V, Jane, Payne and Manny, to Rehv and Ehlena, and John Matthew and Xhex.

When it was their turn, Rhage smiled down at his females and they approached the incubators. It was hard not to be emotional as three hands reached forward with his bloodline's blue, black, and silver lengths, first on Lyric's skirting and then on Rhampage's. And afterward, all three of them went and hugged the family members.

So much love.

All around.

The Chosen went next, and then Trez and iAm and iAm's Queen put a ruby from the Territory on each of the young's bassinettes as a way of participating. After that, the *doggen* went, their ribbons thinner, but no less important.

As Rhage hung back and watched, he had one arm along Mary's shoulders, and one arm on Bitty's.

It was amazing how much things had changed when he thought back to that first night when he'd tried to get Mary to say *luscious* or *whisper* or *strawberry*.

She had countered him back then with *nothing*, said over and over again.

Funny, that she'd chosen that particular word. Because, in fact, she had over these last years given him absolutely, positively . . . *everything*.

SEVENTY-FOUR

It was a great party.

As Mary finally had to take a load off at the foot of the mansion's grand staircase, she was breathing hard, her left heel had a blister on it, and she knew she was going to be stiff later. But the dancing—the *dancing*.

V's version of house music, which was strictly rap and hip-hop, was inspiring all kind of aerobics, and she was proud to note that her hubs was Channing all over his Tatum out here, shaking what his mama gave him with the best of them. Bits was right with him, learning the moves, laughing, eating and drinking soda.

Funny how sometimes the best time could be had just sitting back and watching your kid have a good time.

Through the crowd, Rhage motioned for her to come over, and when she fanned herself and shook her head, he gyrated across with Bitty. "Mary!"

"I just need a minute's rest!" she shouted back. Because that was the only chance of being heard.

"Bitty, can you get your *mahm*—" Rhage caught himself. "Can you get your, ah, Mary, to join us?"

The small bite of pain in the middle of her chest was no big deal, especially when Mary thought about how much the little girl's real *mahmen* would have loved to be a part of all this. And then she didn't think anything more about it as Bitty dived in, grabbed her hand, and pulled her up.

So there was even more dancing.

And more food, and more drink, and more laughter, and more cheering . . . until two in the afternoon, and then three . . .

By four o'clock, even Lassiter had decided it was a wrap, and people started to scatter up and around to various beds.

Naturally, that meant that she and Rhage and Bitty ended up in the kitchen.

"So, Bits, this is my pride and joy," he said as he led the little girl over to a hallway just outside the pantry. "This is my ice cream freezer."

Leaving them to it, Mary made quick work getting out three bowls, three spoons, and three napkins, and she just had to sit back and smile at the setup after she'd put them out on the oak table. Humming to herself, she waited to see what came in from the cold, so to speak, and felt grateful that with Fritz's anal-retentive sense of organization, all the food for the ribbon ceremony had been cleaned up hours ago—

"Okay, wow," she said with a smile. "That is a load."

Four gallons, no, wait, five.

"We have chosen wisely," Rhage said with great gravity. "I present to you this afternoon . . ."

Bit took over from there in the same pseudo-deep voice. "Rocky road, coffee, mint chocolate-chip, raspberry chip, and your favorite, chocolate chocolate-chip."

As the two of them bowed at the waist to her, Mary clapped. "Very well chosen, very, very well chosen."

"And now," Rhage Darth Vadered, "I shall commence the dispensing."

Bitty parked it next to Mary, and the pair of them watched the show, Rhage doing all kinds of tricks, throwing scoops of oh-God-please-catch-that in the air and, in fact, catching them in the bowls. When everybody had what they wanted, they dug in.

Or rather, Rhage and Mary dug in.

As she noticed that Bitty wasn't eating, Mary frowned. "You okay? You have too much of the cakes that were put out?"

It was a while before the girl spoke. "What do humans call their *mahmen*? What is their name for a *mahmen*?"

Mary flicked her eyes over to Rhage's as he froze. Then she cleared her throat. "Ah . . . we call them Mother. Or Mom."

"Mother." Bitty stared into her ice cream. "Mom."

"Mmm-hmm."

After a moment, the little girl looked right into Mary's eyes. "May I please call you Mom?"

Abruptly, Mary found herself not able to breathe, her throat tightening up to an unbearable extent. Leaning in, she cradled that face between her palms and looked over the features that she suddenly knew, without a doubt, that she would watch grow and change into maturity.

"Yes," she whispered roughly. "I would like that. I would like you to call me that."

Bitty smiled. "Okay, Mom."

Andjustlikethat, the girl went in for one of her hugs, wrapping those skinny, but oh, so strong arms around Mary and holding on tight.

Mary blinked hard, but the tears came anyway, especially as she held Bitty's head to her chest and met Rhage's own watery eyes.

Her *hellren* gave her a thumbs-up and mouthed, *Way to go, Mom.*

Laughing and crying, Mary took a deep breath and thought, Yes, indeed, miracles most certainly did happen . . .

And she could just thank God, the Scribe Virgin, whoever you liked, for that.

She . . . was a mom.